D0276993

993469261 9

DEADLINE

JOHN SANDFORD
DEADLINE

**SIMON &
SCHUSTER**

London · New York · Sydney · Toronto · New Delhi

A CBS COMPANY

First published in the US by G. P. Putnam's Sons, 2014
A division of the Penguin Group (USA) Inc.
First published in Great Britain by Simon & Schuster UK Ltd, 2014
A CBS COMPANY

1 3 5 7 9 10 8 6 4 2

Simon & Schuster UK Ltd
1st Floor
222 Gray's Inn Road
London WC1X 8HB

www.simonandschuster.co.uk

Simon & Schuster Australia, Sydney
Simon & Schuster India, New Delhi

A CIP catalogue record for this book
is available from the British Library

Trade Paperback ISBN: 978-1-47113-493-7
Hardback ISBN: 978-1-47113-492-0
eBook ISBN: 978-1-47113-496-8

Printed and bound by CPI Group (UK) Ltd, Croydon, CR0 4YY

DEADLINE

1

Dark, moonless night, in the dog days of early August.

A funky warm drizzle kept the world quiet and wet and close.

D. Wayne Sharf slid across Winky Butterfield's pasture like a greased weasel headed for a chicken house. He carried two heavy nylon leashes with choke-chain collars, two nylon muzzles with Velcro straps, and a center-cut pork chop.

The target was Butterfield's kennel, a chain-link enclosure in the backyard, where Butterfield kept his two black Labs, one young, one older. The pork chop would be used to make friends.

D. Wayne was wearing camo, head to foot, which was no change: he always wore camo, head to foot. So did his children.

His ex-wife, Truly, whom he still occasionally visited, wore various pieces of camo, depending on daily fashion demands—more at Walmart, less at Target. She also had eight pairs of camo underpants, size 4XL and 5XL, which she wore on a rotating basis: two each of Mossy Oak, Realtree, Legend, and God's Country, which prompted D. Wayne to tell her one night, as he peeled them off, "This really is God's country, know what I'm sayin', honeybunch?"

His new, alternative honeybunch wore black cotton, which she called "panties," and which didn't do much for D. Wayne. Just something hot about camo.

A few thousand cells in the back of his brain were sifting through all of that as D. Wayne crossed a split-rail fence into Butterfield's yard, and one of the dogs, the young one, barked twice. There were no lights in the house, and none came on. D. Wayne paused in his approach, watching, then slipped the pork chop out of its plastic bag. He sat for a couple of minutes, giving the dogs a chance to smell the meat; while he waited, his own odor caught up with him, a combination of sweat and whiskey-blend Copenhagen. If Butterfield had the nose of a deer or a wolf, he would have been worried.

But Butterfield didn't, and D. Wayne started moving again. He got to the kennel, where the dogs were waiting, slobbering like hounds . . . because they were hounds. He turned on the hunter's red, low-illumination LED lights mounted in his hat brim, ripped the pork chop in half, held the pieces three feet apart, and pushed them through the chain link. The dogs were all over the meat: and while they were choking it down, he flipped the latch on the kennel gate and duckwalked inside.

"Here you go, boys, good boys," he muttered. The dogs came over to lick his face and look for more pork chop, the young dog prancing around him, and he slipped the choke collars over their heads, one at a time. The young one took the muzzle okay—the muzzle was meant to prevent barking, not biting—but the older one resisted, growled, and then barked, twice, three times. A light came on in the back of the Butterfield house.

D. Wayne said, "Uh-oh," dropped the big dog's muzzle, and dragged the two dogs out of the kennel toward the fence. Again, the younger one came without much resistance at first, but the older one dug in. Another light came on, this one by the Butterfield side door, and D. Wayne said, "Shit," and he picked up the bigger dog, two arms under its belly, and yanking the other one along on the leash, cleared the fence and headed across the pasture at an awkward trot.

The side door opened on Butterfield's house, and D. Wayne, having forgotten about the red LEDs on his hat brim, made the mistake of looking back. Butterfield was standing under the porch light, and saw him. Butterfield shouted, "Hey! Hey!" and "Carol, somebody's took the dogs," and then, improbably, he went back inside the house and D. Wayne thought for seven or eight seconds that he'd caught a break. His truck was only forty yards or so away now, and he was moving as fast as he could while carrying the bigger dog, which must've weighed eighty pounds.

Then Butterfield reappeared and this time he was carrying a gun. He yelled again, "Hey! Hey!" and let off a half-dozen rounds, and D. Wayne said, "My gosh," and threw the big dog through the back door of his truck topper and then hoisted the smaller dog up by his neck and threw him inside after the bigger one.

Another volley of bullets cracked overhead, making a truly unpleasant whip-snap sound, but well off to one side. D. Wayne realized that Butterfield couldn't actually see the truck in the dark of the night, and through the mist. Since D. Wayne was a semi-pro dog snatcher, he had the truck's interior and taillights on a cut-off switch, and when he got in and fired that mother up, none of the lights came on.

There was still the rumble of the truck, though, and Butterfield fired another volley, and then D. Wayne was gone up the nearly, but not quite, invisible road. A half-mile along, he turned on his lights and accelerated away, and at the top of the hill that overlooked the Butterfield place, he looked back and saw headlights.

Butterfield was coming.

D. Wayne dropped the hammer. The chase was short, because D. Wayne had made provisions. At the Paxton place, over the crest of the third low hill in a roller-coaster stretch of seven hills, he swerved off the road, down the drive, and around behind the Paxton kids' bus shack, where the kids waited for the school bus on wintry days.

Butterfield went past at a hundred miles an hour, and fifteen seconds later D. Wayne was going the other way.

A clean getaway, but D. Wayne had about peed himself when Butterfield started working that gun. Had to be a better way to make a living, he thought, as he took a left on a winding road back toward home.

Not that he could easily think of one. There was stealing dogs, cooking meth, and stripping copper wire and pipes out of unoccupied summer cabins.

That was about it, in D. Wayne's world.

2

Virgil Flowers nearly fell off the bed when the phone began to vibrate. The bed was narrow and Frankie Nobles was using up the middle and the other side. Virgil had to crawl over her naked body to get to the phone, not an entirely unpleasant process, and she muttered, "What? Again?"

"Phone," Virgil said. He groaned and added, "Can't be anything good."

He looked at the face of the phone and said, "Johnson Johnson." At that moment the phone stopped ringing.

Frankie was up on her elbows, where she could see the clock, and said, "At three in the morning? The dumbass has been arrested for something."

"He wouldn't call for that," Virgil said. "And he's not dumb."

"There's two kinds of dumb," Frankie said. "Actual and deliberate.

Johnson's the most deliberate dumbass I ever met. That whole live-chicken-toss contest—"

"Yeah, yeah, it was for a good cause." Virgil touched the call-back tab, and Johnson picked up on the first ring.

"Virgil, Jesus, we got big trouble, man. You remember Winky Butterfield?" Johnson sounded wide awake.

"No, I don't believe so."

After a moment of silence Johnson said, "Maybe I didn't introduce you, come to think of it. Maybe it was somebody else."

"Good. Can I go back to sleep?"

"Virgil, this is serious shit. Somebody dognapped Winky's black Labs. You gotta get your ass over here, man, while the trail is fresh."

"Jesus, Johnson . . . dogs? You called me at three in the morning about dogs?"

"They're family, man . . . you gotta do something."

AT TEN O'CLOCK the next morning, Virgil kissed Frankie good-bye and walked out to his truck, which was parked at the curb with the boat already hooked up. Virgil was recently back from New Mexico, where he'd caught and released every tiger musky in what he suspected was the remotest musky lake in North America. Nice fish, too, the biggest a finger-width short of fifty inches. He could still smell them as he walked past the boat and climbed into the cab of his 4Runner.

The day was warm, and promising hot. The sun was doing its job out in front of the truck, but the sky had a sullen gray look about it. There'd been a quarter-inch of rain over the past twenty-four hours, and as he rolled out of Mankato, Minnesota, the coun-tryside looked notably damp. But it was August, the best time of the year, and he was on the road, operating, elbow out the window, pheasants running across the road in front of him . . . nothing to complain about.

As Virgil rode along, he thought about Frankie. He'd known her as Ma Nobles before he'd fallen into bed with her, because she had about a hundred children; or, at least, it felt that way. She was a compelling armful, and Virgil's thoughts had drifted again to marriage, as they had three times before. The first three had been disasters, because, he thought, he had poor taste in women. He reconsidered: no, that wasn't quite right. His three wives had all been pretty decent women, but, he thought, he was simply a poor judge of the prospects for compatibility.

He and Frankie did not have that problem; they just got along.

AND VIRGIL THOUGHT about Lucas Davenport for a while— Davenport was his boss at the Bureau of Criminal Apprehension, and not a bad guy, though a trifle intense. There was a distinct pos-sibility that he would not be pleased with the idea of Virgil working a dognapping case. Especially since the shit had hit the fan up north, where a couple of high school kids had tripped over an abandoned farm cistern full of dead bodies.

But Johnson Johnson was a hard man to turn down. Virgil thought he might be able to sneak in a couple good working days before Davenport even found out what he was doing. A dognap-ping, he thought, shouldn't take too much time, one way or the other. The dogs might already be in Texas, chasing armadillos, or whatever it was they chased in Texas.

Dognapping. He'd had calls on it before, though he'd never investigated one, and they'd always been during hunting season, or shortly before. Didn't usually see one this early in the year.

JOHNSON JOHNSON RAN a lumber mill, specializing in hardwood timber—three varieties of oak, bird's-eye maple, butternut, hickory, and some walnut and cherry—for flooring and cabinetry, with a side business of providing specialty cuts for sculptors. He and Virgil had met at the University of Minnesota, where they were studying women and baseball. Virgil had been a fair third baseman for a couple years, while Johnson was a better-than-fair catcher. He might even have caught onto the bottom edge of the pros, if baseball hadn't bored him so badly. Johnson's mill was a mile outside Trippton, Minnesota, in Buchanan County, in the Driftless Area along the Mississippi River.

The Driftless Area had always interested Virgil, who had taken a degree in ecological science. Basically, the Driftless Area was a chunk of territory in Minnesota, Wisconsin, northern Iowa, and Illinois that had escaped the last glaciation—the glaciers had simply flowed around it, joining up again to the south, leaving the Driftless Area as an island in an ocean of ice. When the glaciers melted, they usually left behind loose dirt and rock, which was called drift. Not in the Driftless Area . . .

Physically, the land was cut by steep valleys, up to six hundred feet deep, running down to the Mississippi River. Compared to the farmlands all around it, the Driftless Area was less fertile, and covered with hardwood forests. Towns were small and far between, set mostly along the river. The whole area was reminiscent of the Appalachians.

Road time from Virgil's home, in Mankato, to Trippton, on the river, was two and a half hours.

FOR MOST OF it Virgil put both the truck and his brain on cruise control. He'd driven the route a few dozen times, and there was not a lot to look at that he hadn't seen before. Trippton was at the bottom of a long hill, on a sandspit that stuck out into the Mississippi; it was a religious town, with almost as many churches as bars. Virgil arrived at lunchtime, got caught in a minor traffic jam between the town's three stoplights, and eventually wedged into a boat-sized double-length parking lane behind Shanker's Bar and Grill.

Johnson Johnson came rambling out the back door as Virgil pulled in. Johnson Johnson's father, Big Johnson, had been an outboard-motor enthusiast who fairly well lived on the Mississippi. He'd named his sons after outboard motors, and while Mercury Johnson had gotten off fairly easy, Johnson Johnson had been stuck with the odd double name. He was a large man, like his father, and well tattooed.

"I can smell them fuckin' muskies from here," he said, as Virgil climbed out of the truck. He leaned into the boat and said, "I hope you brought something besides those fuckin' phone poles," by which he meant musky gear.

"Yeah, yeah, I got some of everything," Virgil said. "What about these dogs? You find them yet?"

"Not yet," Johnson said. He was uncharacteristically grim. "Come on inside. I got a whole bunch of ol' boys and girls for you to talk to."

"We're having a meeting?"

"We're having a lynch mob," Johnson said.

Virgil followed him in. One of the trucks he passed in the parking lot had a bumper sticker that asked, "Got Hollow Points?" Another said: "Heavily Armed . . . and easily pissed." A third one: "Point and Click . . . means you're out of ammo."

"Aw, jeez," Virgil said.

VIRGIL WAS A tall man, made taller by his cowboy boots. He wore his blond hair too long for a cop—but country-long like Waylon Jennings, not sculptural long, like some New Jersey douche bag, so he got along okay.

He dressed in jeans and band T-shirts, in this case, a rare pirated "Dogs Die in Hot Cars" shirt, which he hoped the local 'necks would take for a sign of solidarity. To his usual ensemble, he added a black sport coat when he needed to hide a gun, which wasn't often. Most times, he left the guns in the truck.

He sometimes wore a straw cowboy hat, on hot days out in the sun; at other times, a ball cap, his current favorite a black-on-black Iowa Hawkeyes hat, given to him by a devout Iowegian.

Johnson led the way through the parking lot door, down a beer-smelling corridor past the restrooms, which had signs that said "Pointers" and "Setters," to the back end of the bar, where twenty or so large outdoorsy-looking men and women hunched over rickety plastic tables, drinking beer and eating a variety of fried everything, with link sausages on the side.

When Virgil caught up with him, Johnson said, in a loud voice, without any sign of levity, "Okay, boys and girls. This here's the cop I was talking about, so put away your fuckin' weed and methamphetamine, those that has them, and pay attention. Virgil?"

Virgil said, "For those of you with meth, I'd like to speak to you for a minute out back. . . ."

There were a few chuckles, and Virgil said, "I mostly came to listen. What's going on with these dogs? Somebody stand up so we all can hear you, and tell us."

A heavyset man heaved himself to his feet and said, "Well, I thought Johnson would have told you, but somebody's snatching our dogs."

A drunk at the front of the bar, who'd turned around on his barstool to watch the meeting, called, "Better'n having your snatch dogged."

The heavyset man shouted back, "Shut up, Eddy, or we'll kick your ass out of here."

"Just trying to be human," Eddy said, but he turned back to the bar.

"All right," Virgil said. "Somebody's taking dogs. You know who it is?"

"Yeah, we got our suspicions," the big man said. "There're some hillbillies up at Orly's Crick, all along the valley, and you can hear the dogs howling at night. Dogs, not coyotes. Dozens of them. But when you go up there, there's only one dog per yard. You'd have to sneak up on 'em, to find the ones that are howling. Problem is, there's only one little road going in, and they can see you coming, and they move the dogs before you can get there. I tried to come down from on top, but you can't get down them bluffs without breaking your neck."

"And you could get your ass killed," somebody added. "Fuckin' peckerwoods are all carrying .223s. Pick you off like sittin' ducks."

Another big man stood up, and everybody turned to look; his face was red, and it appeared that he'd been weeping. He took off his camo cap and said, "I'm Winfred Butterfield. Winky. They took my two Labs last night. Right out of the kennel. My dogs're gone, sir. Snatched right out of my yard. Knowed what they was doin', too—left behind some pork chop bone and a cloth muzzle, used to keep them quiet."

He told the story, until he got to the part where he "let off some shots in that direction." He paused and then said, "Maybe I shouldn't have said that."

"You hit anyone?" Virgil asked.

"Naw, I wasn't trying. I mean, I wouldn't mind shooting that miserable motherfucker, if I had a clear shot, but I was afraid I might hit one of the dogs."

Somebody said, "You got that right."

"Okay, just a note here. Let's decide right now that we're not going to shoot anybody over a dog," Virgil said. "Let me handle this the legal way."

The men all looked around, and then one of the women said, "Kinda afraid we can't do that, Virgil." And they all nodded.

"Well, goddamnit, people."

"This is organized crime, Virgil," she said. "If we don't shut these people down, no dog will be safe."

VIRGIL WAS WORRIED. Everyone at the meeting seemed stone-cold sober, and they talked about shooting the dognappers with the cool determination of people who might actually do that, given the chance. They didn't seem anxious to do it, like a bunch of goofy gun nuts—they sounded more like farmers planning to eliminate a varmint that had been killing their geese.

Virgil asked them about the hillbillies on Orly's Creek, and a dozen people gave him bits of information—sightings, rumors, incidents—that made him think they were quite possibly right.

One of the men said, "I saw this old gray truck going by Dan Busch's place, two or three times over a week. Driving slow, looking around . . . Couple days later, Dan's beagles got ripped off."

"Four of them," another man said, who added, "I'm Dan."

The first man said, "Anyway, a couple weeks later I was driving up 26, and I see this old gray truck coming out of the Orly's Crick Road. Same truck. Couldn't prove it, but it was."

Another man said, "There's this guy called Roy, I think his last name is Zorn, he lives up there. Tall red-haired guy, skinny, got about nine million freckles on his face. They got his picture in all the animal shelters and humane societies, telling them NOT to give him any dogs or cats, because he was going around, getting them, and then he'd sell them off to animal bunchers."

Virgil said, "Excuse me? What's a buncher?"

"That's guys who collect animals for the laboratories, for experiments. He'd go around and get these free animals, saying he was looking for a pet, and then he'd sell them off to the bunchers," the big man said. "We know damn well, he'd get kittens that way, too. You know, somebody'd put an ad in the paper, saying, 'Free Kittens,' and he'd take as many as they'd give him, sayin' he needed mousers for his barn. The animal people caught on, and somebody took his picture, and now he can't go into those places."

"I'll go talk to him," Virgil said. He turned to Butterfield and asked, "Winky—how much did you pay for those Labs?"

"These were top dogs, partially trained. I paid fifteen hundred for one, twelve hundred for the other," Butterfield said. "But I don't give a damn about the money—they're my best friends."

"The money makes stealing them a felony," Virgil said. "It always helps to have a felony backing you up, when you talk to people."

"I'll tell you what," said one of the women. "Most everybody here has had dogs stolen, which is why they are here. The rest of us are worried. If you took all the dogs stolen, they'd be worth twenty or thirty thousand dollars, easy. Maybe even more."

Virgil said he'd look into it: "I'll be honest with you, this is not what I usually do. In fact, I've never done it before. I can see you're serious folks, so I'll take it on. No promises. I could get called off . . . but if I do, I'll be back. You all take care, though. Don't go out there with guns, I don't want anybody to get hurt."

WHEN THE MEETING broke up, he and Johnson drove over to the law enforcement center, which housed the Buchanan County Sheriff and the Trippton Police Department, which were one and the same, and a few holding cells. In the parking lot Johnson said, "I'll hang out here. Jeff don't appreciate my good qualities," and Virgil went in alone.

Entry to the sheriff's office was through a locked black-steel door, with a bulletproof window next to it; there was nobody behind the window, so Virgil rang the bell, and a moment later a deputy stuck his head around the window and said, "Virgil Flowers, as I live and die."

"That's me," Virgil agreed. The deputy buzzed him in, and Virgil followed him down the hall to the sheriff's office. The sheriff, Jeff Purdy, was a small, round man who wore fifties-style gray hats, the narrow-brimmed Stetson "Open Road" style; he had his feet up on his desk and was reading a *New Yorker* magazine. When he heard the footsteps in the hallway, he looked over the magazine and saw Virgil coming.

"I hope you're here to fish," he said.

"Not exactly, though it'd be nice to get out for a couple hours," Virgil said. "I just came from a meeting down at Shanker's. . . ."

Virgil told him the story, and the sheriff sighed and said, "You're welcome to it, Virgil. I know those people have a complaint, but what the hell am I supposed to do? We patrol up Orly's Crick, but we never see a thing."

"You know a guy named Roy Zorn?"

"Yeah, yeah, we've been told he cooks some meth up there, but we never caught him at it. Basically, he's a small-time motorcycle hood, rode with the Seed for a while, over in Green Bay, before he came here. And I know all about that thing he used to do with cats and dogs, him getting banned from the Humane Society. But we got nothing on him. Can't get anything, either. If I had ten more men . . ."

"You don't mind if I take a look?"

"Go on ahead. Keep me up on what you're doing," Purdy said. "If you find something specific, I could spring a couple guys to help out on a short-term basis. Very short-term, like a raid, something like that."

"That's all I wanted," Virgil said. "There's a good chance I won't find a thing, but if I do, I might call for backup."

"Deal," Purdy said.

The deputy who'd taken Virgil back to the sheriff's office returned and said, "Sheriff, Sidney Migg's walking around naked in her backyard, again."

The sheriff grunted and boosted himself out of his chair. "I better handle this myself."

BACK OUTSIDE, Virgil took a minute to call Davenport's office. He didn't actually want to talk to him, which was why he called the office: Davenport was out working a multiple murder that everybody was calling the Black Hole case, in which a BCA agent had been murdered.

Virgil hadn't worked the case, and was happy about that, because the killing of Bob Shaffer would have preyed on his mind for weeks, or years, whether or not the killer was caught. He left a message for Davenport, which might possibly cover his ass, if worse came to worst.

Then he and Johnson drove out to Johnson's river cabin and rolled Virgil's boat into the water and tied it to Johnson's dock. Johnson's jon boat had been pulled up on shore, and a long orange extension cord snaked out of the cabin to a power drill that lay in the bottom of the boat.

"You break something?" Virgil asked.

"Changing the oarlocks," Johnson said. "They were getting too wore down."

"You never rowed six feet in your entire sorry life," Virgil said. "How'd they get wore down? I mean, worn down?"

"Pedant," Johnson said. "Anyway, I use them to steer my drifts. Saves gas."

They unhooked the trailer, parked it behind the house, stuck a tongue lock on it, and went inside for coffee and to continue the conversation about dogs and hillbilly dognappers.

Virgil said, "Since the sheriff couldn't handle it, you call the high-priced BCA guy down to figure it out?"

"Actually, I was calling my old fishin' buddy Virgil to figure it out," Johnson said.

"Well, fuck you, Johnson, that puts a kind of unnecessary obligation on it. I mean, would you do that for me?"

"You don't have a dog."

"Well, something like this . . ."

"Suppose you were going away for a couple of weeks," Johnson said, "and you needed somebody to keep Frankie warmed up. I'd jump in my truck—"

"All right, okay." Virgil waved him off. "Where's this Orly's Crick?"

———————

IN SOUTHERN MINNESOTA, the Mississippi flowed through a deep, wide valley. The main channel of the river was rarely down the middle of the valley. Instead, it usually flowed down one side or the other, snaking between steep valley walls. The other side of the valley was often occupied by sloughs or marshes, before they ran into equally steep bluffs.

The bluffs were dissected by free-flowing streams, ranging from seasonal creeks to full-sized rivers. Johnson's place was tucked into the north end of a slough, where the river began to bend away from the Minnesota side, toward Wisconsin; so his cabin was protected from the waves generated by the towboats and their barges, but he still had fast access to the river itself.

When he and Virgil left Johnson's cabin, they drove a few hundred yards west to Highway 26, and then north for fifteen miles. By the time they got to Orly's Creek Road, the river was running right beside the highway. Orly's Creek ran below a fifty-foot-long bridge, into the river, with the road going into the valley on the north side of the bridge.

"Goes back here about a mile, or a little more," Johnson said. "The crick comes out of Orly's Spring, which gathers up a lot of water from west of here, then runs underground to the spring. The good thing about that is, it hardly ever floods at all. Don't believe I've ever seen water over the road."

"Any trout in there?" The creek was maybe twenty feet wide, tumbling over limestone blocks, with an occasional pool.

"Yup. I'd be a little nervous about eating them, down at this end, anyway. Lots of old septic systems, don't work so good, anymore. Up on top, by the spring, the crick would be cleaner than Fiji Water."

"You know about Fiji Water?"

"Fuck you."

THE FIRST HABITATION in the valley was a single-wide trailer, crunched on one end, as though a tree had fallen on it. Two nineties cars were parked in a hard-dirt yard, with a mottled-gray pit bull tied to a stake.

"That's the lookout," Johnson said. "There are more places further in." Johnson tried to scrunch down in his seat, and pulled his hat down over his eyes. "They might kinda recognize me up here."

"Is that bad?"

"I prefer to remain anonymous."

They passed a few more mobile homes, most, like the first one, located fifty or a hundred feet off the road, up the valley wall. "Must be hell to get up there in the winter," Virgil said.

"Doubt they try. They all got cutouts down here on the road," Johnson said. He pointed out over the dashboard to an old yellow clapboard house, with narrow fields on either side of it, running steeply down to the creek. An apple tree stood next to the house, with a Jeep Wrangler parked in front of it, and a half-dozen stripped and abandoned cars off to the right. "That's Zorn's place. His wife's name is Bunny. I think she's probably his sister."

Virgil looked over at him, and Johnson said, "Okay. Maybe not."

Virgil turned off at Zorn's place, past a no-trespassing sign, and pulled up into the yard. All of the doors and windows at Zorn's were open, behind screens; and when they pulled into his yard, they saw Zorn look warily out through the door, disappear for a minute, then come through the door to his porch, where he stood waiting. As advertised, he was a tall, rawboned red-haired man with about a million freckles splashed across his face.

Virgil said, "You wait here."

"Yes, dear," Johnson said.

Virgil got out of the truck, keeping his hands in view, and ambled up to the porch.

"You can't read my sign, or you just not give a shit?" Zorn asked.

"I'm an agent with the Bureau of Criminal Apprehension," Virgil said. "A state cop."

"What you want with me?" Zorn asked. His head twitched to one side. Virgil saw a movement at a window to his left.

"We're looking into some stolen dogs," Virgil said. "We understand you've had some problems in that area."

"Never done a single thing illegal—got them all fair and square, and sold them up to the university for important medical research," Zorn said. "Now, if you're done with me, I'll thank you to get the fuck off my lawn. You come back, bring a warrant."

"Don't want to talk about dogs, then," Virgil said.

"I don't know nothin' about dogs," Zorn said.

"Don't know anybody up or down Orly's Creek who might have come up with a few extra?"

"I don't stick my nose into other people's business," Zorn said. "Now git—or I'll call my attorney."

Virgil considered for a moment, looking into Zorn's narrow

green eyes, and then said, "You keep that attorney close, Mr. Zorn. These recent dog thefts—the dogs are valuable, and the thefts amount to felonies. When I arrest you for them, you'll be going away for quite some time. So keep that attorney close—and you might want to buy a new toothbrush."

"Bullshit—nobody's sending anybody anywhere for some fuckin' mutts."

"You should talk to your attorney about that. He'll set you straight," Virgil said. He backed away, keeping the window in sight. "Be seein' you."

VIRGIL WENT CAREFULLY back to his truck, climbed inside, and found Johnson with a high-capacity Para-Ordnance .45 in his lap.

"Jesus, Johnson, what were you gonna do with that?"

"I saw somebody at the window," Johnson said. "If they shot you, I was gonna hose the place down."

Virgil thought about that for a minute, then said, "All right." He looked up at the porch. Zorn had gone back inside, but Virgil could see him hovering behind the screen. "That's a bad man, right there," Virgil said. "Doesn't even bother to trim his nose hair."

"That is a bad man," Johnson said.

THEY CONTINUED UP the valley, looking at houses and dogs; most of the houses were ramshackle, but a few were neatly kept, with American flags on front-yard poles, and with good-looking gardens and neatly mown lawns. As someone had said at the Shanker's meeting, they hardly ever saw more than one dog per house, usually in a chain-link kennel.

"One thing we ought to do, is get a list of everyone who lives up here," Virgil said. "Looks like there might be some respectable people. If we could get a couple of them to talk to us, we'd be ahead of the game."

Johnson was skeptical: "You think any of these people would talk, knowing their neighbors are assholes with M15s? Respectable is okay, long as it doesn't buy you a bullet in the back."

At the far end of the valley, the road went to a stretch of gravel, then to dirt, which ended at a fence. At the side of the road, the spring appeared, a fifty-foot-long pool, maybe thirty feet wide, and deep, flowing out over six-foot chunks of broken limestone, and on down the valley.

Virgil stopped the truck, and they got out to look at the spring. "That's a piece of water I wouldn't mind owning," Johnson said.

Virgil knelt, put his hand in the water: cool, probably seventy degrees. In a shallow spot, he could see a school of minnows probing through underwater grass.

Johnson muttered, "Uh-oh. Look at this. On your left."

Virgil stood up and saw a kid walking toward them. He looked like he might be twelve; he wore blue-striped bib overalls over a T-shirt, and a Marine Corps utility cap over shoulder-length brown hair. He was thin, and watched them with his head cocked to one side.

He was carrying a scoped .22 rifle.

"What are y'all doing?" he asked. He was standing on the

far side of the fence, which was overgrown with black-raspberry canes.

"Scoutin' out the valley," Virgil said. "You know who owns this spring?"

The kid shrugged. "Nobody, I guess. When it gets really hot, people come up here and fool around in it, after work."

"Pretty cool for swimming," Virgil said.

"That's the truth," the kid said. "I seen women here with goose bumps the size of thumbs."

Johnson asked, "You out huntin'?"

"Just shooting around," the kid said. "What are you scouting for?"

Virgil said, "Dogs, mostly. We heard some folks up here might have some dogs that don't belong to them."

"You cops?"

"I am," Virgil said. "You seen any extra dogs around?"

"Hardly seen nothing like that," the kid said. He lifted the rifle and aimed it at a tree thirty yards away. Johnson and Virgil remained still, and the kid squeezed off a shot. A crab apple exploded off one of the tree's lower branches.

The kid turned and grinned at them, and worked the bolt on the rifle, chambering a new round. Virgil said, "Nice shot. That's a Magnum?"

"Yup. My dad got it to shoot groundhogs. Goddamn things are hard to get at, though."

"They are," Virgil agreed. He sniffed, and looked at Johnson, who nodded. "Well, I guess we'll head on out, if you haven't seen any dogs."

The kid said, "If you're a cop, where's your gun?"

"Don't carry a gun all the time," Virgil said.

The kid shook his head. "You come back in here, looking for dogs, you best carry a gun."

"Thanks for the tip," Virgil said.

THEY MOVED BACK to Virgil's truck. Inside, Johnson said, "That didn't sound so much like a tip, as maybe a threat."

"But nicely put," Virgil said. He was watching the kid in the rear-view mirror. The kid was standing with the rifle across his chest, in the port arms position. "The kid's no dummy."

"And a really good shot. That apple couldn't have been much bigger than a quarter," Johnson said. "You think he knows about the dogs?"

"You noticed how he went sort of shifty, there. 'Hardly seen nothin' like that.' He doesn't lie well."

After another moment, Johnson asked, "You smell that shit?"

"The acetone, yeah," Virgil said. "Not right away—I couldn't tell where it was coming from. Wasn't close."

"Well, it's cool down here and hotter up above. Cold air flows down . . . so probably up on the valley wall, somewhere."

"The sheriff heard that Zorn might be cooking some meth. We're quite a way from Zorn's."

"Nothing to keep him from hiding his cooker up the hill, like an old-timey still," Johnson said. He looked around at the overgrown valley walls hanging over them. "Virgie? Let's get the fuck out of here."

They got the fuck out of there.

"Now what do we do?" Johnson asked, when they bounced back on Highway 26.

"I want to look at some aerial photography of the place. See if there's any other way in or out."

Johnson nodded and said, "You know who's got the best pictures? The ag service." He looked at his watch. "Gonna be too late today, though. I'd recommend a run up the river, instead. We can look at the pictures first thing tomorrow."

On the way back to Johnson's cabin, Davenport returned Virgil's call from that morning. Virgil saw his name flash on the phone screen, and said to Johnson, "Keep your mouth shut. This is the boss. I'll put him on the speaker."

"What's up?" Davenport asked, when Virgil answered.

"Man, I hate to ask this, with Shaffer dead and you working the Black Hole. But you know my friend Johnson Johnson?"

"Yeah, I know him," Davenport said. "There's a goddamn accident waiting to happen."

"Actually, it's happened several times already. Anyway, Johnson needs some help on, mmm . . . a non-priority mission," Flowers said. "I'm not doing anything heavy, and nobody's called me for the Black Hole group, so I'd like to run over to Trippton. It's down south of La Crescent."

"You're not telling me what it's about," Davenport said.

"No, but if Johnson is telling the truth, and I make a couple of busts, it'll bring great credit upon the BCA."

Johnson nodded sagely, from the passenger seat.

"We don't need credit," Davenport said. "The legislature's already adjourned. But, go ahead, on your best judgment. From the way you're talking, I don't want to know what it is. If it blows up in your face, it's your problem."

"Got it. I just wanted you to know where I was," Virgil said.

"You taking your boat?" Lucas asked.

Long pause, while Virgil sorted out the possibilities. He decided to go with the semi-truth. "Maybe."

"Let me know if you get in trouble," Davenport said. "But otherwise . . ."

"You don't want to know."

"That's right."

"YOU'RE GOOD," Johnson said, when Virgil had rung off. "Got the backing of the big guy himself. Let's get out on the river."

"I'm not going catfishing," Virgil said.

"Nah. Get your fly rod out. I know where there's a whole bunch of smallmouth, and they do like their Wooly Buggers."

So they did that.

On his first night in Buchanan County, Virgil went to sleep in Johnson's cabin with the feeling he hadn't gotten much done.

But he'd gotten some heavy vibes—and the vibes were bad.

3

ABOUT THE TIME that night that Virgil hooked into a two-pound smally, the Buchanan County Consolidated School Board finished the public portion of the monthly meeting. The last speaker had demanded to know what the board was going to do about buying better helmets for the football team.

"I been reading about how blows to the head turn the boys into a bunch of dummies when they grow up. Murph Roetting's kid's still not right after he got took out last season. . . . I don't want to think we're paying a million and a half dollars for a sports complex so we can raise a bunch of brain-damaged dummies."

The board talked about that in an orderly fashion, each in his or her turn: the five board members, the superintendent, the financial officer. Because school was not in session, they were all dressed in Minnesota informal: button-up short-sleeved shirts and blouses,

Dockers slacks for both men and women, loafers and low heels. All their haircuts, ranging from maple-blond to butternut-brown, were gender-appropriately short. They were neat, ironed, and certainly not assertive.

When everybody had his or her turn on the football issue, the board voted to ask community doctors to look into it and prepare a report.

That done, the board ran everybody off, except one fat man, with the excuse that they had to deal with personnel matters, which was almost true.

When the last of the public had gone, they sent Randolph Kerns, the school security officer, to flush out the hallways, including the bathrooms, to make sure everybody had really gone away. He found the school janitor polishing brass, and told him to knock it off and go home. The janitor went.

"We're clean," he said, when he came back, locking the meeting room door behind himself.

Jennifer Barns, the big-haired chairwoman and one of three Jennifers on the five-person board, said, "I guess you all know what's going on. The fact is, if something's not done, we're all headed for disgrace and prison. Anybody disagree?"

Jennifer Houser said, "Clancy came around to see me this afternoon. He was threatening me. He said if I didn't talk to him, he'd put me right down with the rest of you. He seems to think that . . . I'm a little more honest than the rest of you."

The other four board members, the school superintendent, the financial officer, the security chief, and the fat man all chuckled; Houser was crooked as a sidewinder rattlesnake.

"So what are we going to do?" Bob Owens asked. He was the senior board member, and one of the founders of the retirement-now scheme.

"We all know what's got to be done. The question is, can we sustain it?" the third Jennifer (Gedney) said. "I'd rather go to prison for embezzlement than first-degree murder."

They all went hum and hah, and wished she hadn't put it quite so starkly. She persisted: "We know what we're talking about here. Randy?"

"Yeah, we know," Kerns said. "We could do it right now. Tonight. But you're right: once we do it, we can't go back."

"How would you do it?" Barns asked.

"Been scouting him. He runs right after dark, when it starts to get cool. I'll come up behind him, shoot him in the back. He won't suffer."

"What about his trailer?" Owens asked. "We never did develop a consensus on that."

"I been thinking about it," Kerns said. "I know some of you think we should burn it, but that worries me. If they find his body in a ditch, it might have been some crazy kid with a gun. A random killing. If we kill him, and burn his trailer . . . then it's obviously covering up something."

"What if he's told somebody about us?" Houser asked.

"He hasn't," said the ninth man in the room, the fat man, the only one who wasn't directly involved with the schools. "I told him to hold the whole thing close to his chest. Not to tell a soul—and he doesn't have any close friends. No: the biggest problem would be if he's written a lot of it down. What I'd suggest is, Randy takes care of him, in the dark. He won't be found right away, and I could say I got worried and went up to his trailer looking for him. Give me a chance to go through the place, and clean it out."

"But what if he is found right away?" asked Larry Parsons, the fifth board member.

"Tell you what," the fat man said. "I'll get up on top of the hill about first light, and watch. And at eight o'clock, I'll go on into his trailer. I got a key."

Kerns said, "That'll work. If there's nobody around, I'll get him right at the bottom of that last hill before he goes back up to his place. The ditch is deep and all full of cattails. Nobody'll see him down there."

Barns, the chairman, looked around the room and said, "Okay. We can do this. Let's see a show of hands. It's unanimous, or it's prison. Do we kill Clancy Conley?"

They all looked around at each other, each of them reluctant to go first. Then the fat man raised his hand, and then Kerns, and then the rest of them.

"It's unanimous," Barns said. She unconsciously picked up her gavel and rapped it once against her desk.

CLANCY CONLEY WAS a human train wreck. He hadn't started out that way, but he'd discovered speed halfway through journalism school, and that started his slow slide to hell, if hell can be defined as being a reporter/photographer/paste-up man on a small-town weekly newspaper.

In his twenties, he'd moved around, going from the *Cape Girardeau*

Southeast Missourian to the *Cedar Rapids Gazette*, peaking at the *Omaha World-Herald*, where, after a three-day run on the really fine pharmaceutical Dexedrine, he got in a violent one-sided argument with the city editor. One-sided because the city editor didn't understand a word he was saying.

"He sounds like a chicken. He thinks he's using words, but he's just going puck-puck-puck-puck puck," he told the executive editor, as they both peered through the blinds on the executive editor's office. Conley was flapping his wings around the city desk.

From there it was Sioux Falls, South Dakota, then Worthington, Minnesota, then through a run of smaller and smaller rural towns, finally landing, at forty-five, at the *Trippton Republican-River*, which was mostly supermarket advertisements, with a smattering of school board news, sheriff's news, county commission news, city council news, and paid obituaries.

Then, in Trippton, Conley had inadvertently discovered that the school board was stealing the school system blind, taking out nearly a million dollars a year from a budget of thirty-nine million. It was all hard to see—for example, who really knew if the school buses got ten miles per gallon or eight, or exactly where they got the stuff that went into school lunches?—but it added up.

Conley got the first tip from a school bus driver who knew how much diesel her Blue Bird used, and how much the school said she used. The same driver suggested that he talk to a lady who worked in the high school cafeteria, about food costs. The anecdotal information had been confusing, but suggestive. Then Conley stole a confidential school budget document that made it all perfectly clear.

He was thinking about the document as he puffed along

Highway A, going west out of Trippton, the night after the school board meeting. He'd started running every night, because it was one thing he'd once done well. He was now twenty pounds overweight, but had been forty pounds overweight at his forty-fifth birthday. The discovery of the school board embezzlement had stirred some of the original journalistic vinegar in Conley's veins. He'd stopped drinking, mostly, and didn't do speed more than twice a week. His weight was down, his brain was clearer.

He was even thinking that after he broke the school story, and moved to a bigger paper, he might actually start looking for something with tits. So his life was changing for the better. His biggest current problem would be explaining how he got the detailed budgetary information.

He didn't cover the school board himself; the paper's editor, Viking Laughton, did that. And the bare fact was, he'd broken into the school finance office on several weekend nights, cracked the finance officer's computer, and had taken photographs of the computer screens over fifteen nerve-racking hours.

It had taken him the best part of six months, and two more break-ins, to winkle out all the details. He'd then confided the findings to Viking "Vike" Laughton, the fat man who owned the newspaper.

Vike had been astonished: "I never saw it in them. They must be taking out a hundred thousand dollars a year, each of them."

"Something like that," Conley agreed.

Vike told him to keep it all top secret. "This here's a Pulitzer Prize, boy, if we play it just right," he said, slapping his hands on printouts of the budget documents.

Vike suggested Jennifer Houser as the one likeliest to turn on the others—he'd been covering the school board himself, for years, and was familiar with all the members.

Conley had finally gotten to Houser just that afternoon.

"This is going in the paper next week, Jen," he'd told her. "Everybody's going down, but when the police arrive, I'll tell them that you were the person who cracked the case. I'm sure, if you cooperate, they'll take it easy on you. You might have to do a little jail time, but you ask anybody who's been to jail, and they'll tell you—a little is way, way better than a lot. Way better."

She'd started crying, and asked for a couple of days to think it over. Conley had just put the paper to bed for that week, and had time, so he'd agreed: "Two days is fine, Jen. Take three, if you need it. But . . . it's going in the paper one way or another, next week. I've already cleared it with Vike."

She'd crack, Conley thought. He was coming to the bottom of the hill, by the cattail swamp, just before the last hard climb back up to his trailer, his running shoes flapping on the warm blacktop. A truck came up in front of him, slowing as it went by, and Conley moved over to the shoulder. Wasn't sure, but it looked like Randy Kerns behind the wheel.

He turned his head to look back, but the next thing he knew, he was lying in the cattails, the cold water soaking through his shirt and shorts.

Before he died, which was only a few seconds later, it occurred to him that he wasn't too surprised. . . .

Vike was really, really close to the school board.

4

THE ALARM ON Virgil's cell phone went off at eight o'clock. He rolled out, remade the bed, more or less, got cleaned up, and took a call from Johnson Johnson.

"You up?" Johnson asked.

"Yes."

"I'm in my truck. I'll meet you at the Gourd."

"Ten minutes," Virgil said.

Johnson and his girlfriend lived west of town, in a sprawling ranch-style house with a barn out back, for the horses, which his girlfriend trained and endurance-raced. Johnson's sawmill was a mile back behind the house, on the other edge of his twelve hundred and eighty acres of hardwood forest.

Johnson was hunched over a cup of coffee, reading the *Wall*

Street Journal, when Virgil walked into the Golden Gourd. "Don't know what I'm going to do about insurance," he said. "Gotta have it—I got six employees, and it's rough work, but Jesus, it costs an arm and a leg."

"You need to work for the government," Virgil said. "Insurance is free."

"Free for you, not for the rest of us," Johnson said. He put the paper down and waved at a waitress. They got breakfast, argued about insurance, and talked about what they'd be doing that day.

"We need to find a way to come down from the top," Virgil said. "There's gotta be one—there's probably a whole bunch of ways. If you have to go in on that road, everybody in the valley knows you're coming."

"The south side of the valley is steeper, and not so many houses over there," Johnson said. "If they're hiding dogs, they're probably on the north side."

"Ought to look at a plat map, see who owns what," Virgil said.

"Do that at the courthouse," Johnson said.

"Might be handy to have a rope to come down off that bluff line," Virgil said.

"Get that over at Fleet Farm," Johnson said.

When they finished eating, Johnson looked at his watch and said, "Ag office oughta be open."

They left their cars in the street and walked two blocks over to the Buchanan County Soil and Water Conservation District, where they talked to a clerk who pulled out large-scale, high-resolution aerial photos of the land around Orly's Creek.

The clerk left them, and they bent over the photos, tracing Orly's Creek Road up to the spring. The cleft of the valley was clear on the photos: the land up on top was the dark green of heavy forest, cut by the lighter green of the valleys, from which most of the trees had been cleared.

Virgil tapped County Road NN, which ran west a half-mile north of Orly's Creek. "If we leave my truck at this bridge"—he looked at the scale—"which is about three-quarters of a mile from 26, we could walk along the edge of this field and into woods, up the hill and down the other side. No houses close by . . . and it looks like there's a gap in the bluff line . . . here . . . and here."

"Still gonna be pretty goddamned steep," Johnson said.

"That's why we take some rope."

"We could probably get down, but we won't be able to get out in a hurry," Johnson said. "If we have to run for it, we might best go all the way down to the road. Tell you something else—might be tough calling for help. In those deep valleys, the cell phone service is kinda iffy."

Virgil said, "We'll take it slow." He tapped the map, a line that ran near the top of the valley, just below the bluffs. "See this line? It looks too heavy to be a game trail, and it comes up to this flat patch. It looks like something built is in there."

"Kennels?"

"Looks like something. If we can come over the bluff line . . . here . . . we could move right along the trail, and it's not more than a couple hundred yards."

"Worth a look," Johnson said.

VIRGIL GOT THE CLERK to make a Xerox copy of the photo, paid for it, and they continued down the street to the county courthouse, where they looked at plat maps. The man Virgil had talked to the day before, Zorn, owned the land from the road up to his house, and perhaps fifty yards on either side of it, and behind it—not more than two acres or so, a relatively small patch compared to some of the other holdings. The largest plot was at the end of the valley, on the north side. A hundred and twenty acres of woods, and what looked like a small house, showing no mowed fields or outbuildings, under the name of Deland.

"Don't know any Delands," Johnson said. A quick check with the tax records showed a mailing address in the Twin Cities suburb of Eagan.

"Could be a hunting cabin," Virgil said. "That kid must have come down from here." He touched the image of a house on the south side, on twenty acres, showing a large garden to one side, and what appeared to be a small orchard, judging from the way the trees were spaced. The tax records said the bill went to a Julius Ruff. After a last review, he said, "Let's get some rope and go on out there."

THEY BOUGHT a hundred feet of three-quarter-inch nylon rope at Fleet Farm, stopped at Johnson's cabin on the way north, so they both could change into running shoes, and took Highway 26 past Orly's Creek Road for half a mile, took a left on NN, and drove to the small bridge where they'd leave the truck. The creek below it was barely damp.

Virgil had weapons in the back, and after debating with himself about the options, put a "Bureau of Criminal Apprehension" sign on the dashboard, activated the car alarm, and locked everything up.

He did take his pistol with him, a standard-issue Glock 9mm, and though he didn't ask, was sure that Johnson had his .45 in his military-style rucksack, along with a couple of cans of Budweiser and a GPS receiver that he'd bought for his boat. Before leaving the ag service, Johnson had found the GPS references for what looked like the easiest breaks in the bluff line above Orly's Creek valley.

In his own pack, Virgil carried two bottles of water, the rope, a multi-tool and two extra magazines for the Glock, a Sony RX100 compact camera, and a homemade first aid kit.

They left the truck and crossed the roadside ditch, climbed one fence into an alfalfa field, and walked along another that stretched up to the woods at the top of the hill they were climbing. The woods would extend over the crest, down into the Orly's Creek valley.

The day was hot, and they took it easy climbing the hill, breaking a light sweat that attracted mosquitoes when they crossed from the alfalfa field into the woods. The climb got steeper as they got deeper into the woods, and eventually they moved from one sapling to the next, hanging on to the brush to stay upright. Fifteen minutes after they left the truck, they reached the crest of the hill, which was punctuated with outcrops of soft yellow rock.

A game trail ran along the crest. Johnson shucked off his pack and said, "We should replace some fluids while we have the time. Stay quiet, see what we can hear."

Virgil took a few sips of water, while Johnson popped open a beer, and they listened: and heard the woods, but nothing out of place. When Johnson had finished the beer, they walked to their right along the game trail until Johnson, who was watching the GPS, said, "We're about there. We need to go off this way. . . ."

He led the way downslope, into the Orly's Creek valley. A few dozen yards into the trees, they found themselves paralleling a shallow dry gully, and Virgil said, "This probably goes down to the break in the bluff."

Johnson nodded, and they followed it down; a minute later the gully got deeper, and the way was blocked by a shoulder of the yellow rock. They moved into the gully, which got steeper, but took them through the lip of the bluffs. At that point, the slope became even steeper, and they paused to assess. The ground beneath their feet was a combination of damp black earth and crumbled bits of the yellow rock.

"It's doable, if we use the rope," Johnson said. "But we couldn't get back up unless we left the rope here."

"Don't want to do that," Virgil said. "If we had to get out some other way, they'd know where we're getting in."

They decided to take a chance—they'd use the rope, doubled around a tree trunk, then they'd pull it down, and find another way out of the valley. Doing that, after the decision, took only a couple of minutes, with Virgil leading the way down. They pulled the rope down after them, repacked it, and walked down the valley wall to the trail they'd seen in the ag service photos.

It turned out to be six feet wide, and well packed, marked with ATV tracks. A few incipient gullies across the trail, caused by water draining from above, had been filled with broken rock.

"Some good work here," Johnson said. He looked up and down the track. "But why would they build it?"

"Cooking meth," Virgil said. "But it'd have to be an industrial operation to build a road like this."

Johnson was looking up at the overhanging trees. "You know what? Half the trees here are sugar and black maple. They could be cooking syrup."

"Thought that was all up north."

"No, they got sugar bushes all the way down into Iowa," Johnson said. "The wood makes damn good flooring, I can tell you."

"I know about flooring, now. Frankie salvages it from old farmhouses."

"Yeah, that's a fashion," Johnson said. They were both looking up and down the trail.

Virgil asked, "Which way?"

"Right. I think."

They moved off down the trail, listening and watching. Virgil asked, "What is it with these trees?" He pointed to a young maple that had been girdled with an ax or hatchet, but left standing.

"They're killing the tree, but leaving it standing to dry out. Making firewood," Johnson said. A hundred yards farther on they came to the built spot that Virgil had seen on the photos, and it turned out to be a woodlot, with a few face cords of stacked wood set off to one side.

"Could be the answer to the trail," Johnson said. "Somebody's harvesting firewood. You'd need an ATV to tow it out of here."

"But this isn't the end of it . . ."

Virgil led the way out of the woodlot. The trail had narrowed to a single-wide track, blocked by a pile of brush—the leftover ends of trees cut up for firewood. An ATV could get around it, but nothing wider. The trail eventually led to three metal sheds of the kind sold at lumberyards. They'd been painted with a green-on-black camouflage pattern, and all had tightly sealed doors, with padlocks. A half-dozen propane cylinders sat on the ground beside one of them.

"Smell it?" Virgil asked.

"Yeah."

They could smell the acetone.

"Cooking meth," Virgil said. "And not long ago."

"They could use the same setup to cook syrup, the same setup I have," Johnson said. "I wonder why that never occurred to me."

"Because, despite your many enormous personal flaws, character weaknesses, and innate criminality, you're too much of a gutless coward to cook meth," Virgil said.

"I wondered about that," Johnson said. "Thanks for the explanation."

Virgil tested all the locks and found them solid. He took out his camera, made a few photos, and then saw, farther down the slope, a hump of raw dirt, like the fill from a double-long grave. When Virgil went to look, he found a dump: trashed containers that once contained the raw materials for methamphetamine. He took some more photos, then put the camera away and walked back up the slope to Johnson. "Can you get a GPS reading here?"

"Maybe," Johnson said, looking up at the canopy of maple leaves. He had one a minute later, and saved it to the receiver's memory.

"Let's go upslope and see if we can find a way out," Virgil said.

"What about the dogs?"

"This operation is more important than the dogs," Virgil said. "They could be taking a ton of meth out of here. Johnson: this is sort of a big deal."

"I'll give you that," Johnson said. "I still want the dogs."

"We'll be back," Virgil promised. The trail had ended at the shed, and following the points on the GPS, Johnson led them to another of the openings in the bluff line. When they got there, the slope was still too steep, and they moved along to the last one, two hundred yards farther along the valley. This one was steep, but had saplings growing all the way up, and by using the trees to pull themselves along, they managed to climb to the crest.

Twenty minutes later, they were back at the truck.

"Now what?" Johnson asked. He cracked his second Bud as they did a U-turn and headed back toward the river.

"Got to think about that," Virgil said. "To tell the truth, I don't entirely trust your trusty sheriff."

"You're more perceptive than you look," Johnson said. "Not to say that he's an outright criminal. He may accept a little help now and then."

"Okay. I'm thinking DEA. I've got a good connection there."

"It's your call," Johnson said. "I'm just in it for the dogs."

———

Virgil's man with the DEA was named Harry Gomez, and he was now working out of Chicago. He'd directed the biggest shoot-out Virgil had ever seen, and one of the biggest he'd ever heard of.

Back at the cabin, Virgil called Gomez, who was a modest-sized big shot, and had to talk his way through a protective secretary. "Just tell him who's calling," Virgil said. "He'll take it. I've saved his life on many occasions."

She didn't believe him, but Gomez took the call. "Hey, Virg. Please, please don't tell me you found another meth lab."

"I was calling to shoot the shit for a while," Virgil said. "I'm not doing much, and I was wondering, what's Harry Gomez doing? I mean, other than blowing some higher-up—"

"Really?" Gomez sounded almost hopeful.

"No. I found another meth lab. A big one."

"Ah, shit. Why do you keep doing this, Virgil? It causes a lot of trouble for everyone. Couldn't you just shoot the cook and call it a day?"

"That would be unethical," Virgil said. He explained how they'd found the sheds, and about the dogs. "Anyway, they've got three fifteen-foot metal sheds hid out in the woods, along with an ATV trail to haul the stuff out. It's nothing like the first one we hit, but it's substantial."

"All right. They cooking right now?"

"Not at this very minute, but they were at it not long ago. I could smell it yesterday. . . ."

Virgil told him about the layout, and Gomez said that he'd move in a six-man team to do surveillance, and then fire off the raid when the cooking began again.

"When do you want to start?" Virgil asked.

"The team can be there tomorrow morning. They'll go in like you did, from the top. We can stash them up in Winona, so nobody'll know. You stay out of there until we do this: don't go chasing the dogs through there."

"All right. Tell your guys to call, and we'll hook up."

"We'll bring maps . . . and, Virgil? Thank you. Really. We could use a good one. The budget's being parceled out and most of it's going down south."

"Thank me after no one gets killed," Virgil said.

When he'd rung off, Johnson asked, "What about the dogs?"

"They're gonna have to wait," Virgil said. "The DEA is going to swat that place in the next few days, and they don't want a lot of cops running through there beforehand."

"Well, Jesus, Virgil, the dogs could be gone before that happens."

"Johnson—"

"Yeah, yeah, I know. It's a big operation. But you know what, Virgil? You're never going to stop it. Meth's too easy to make, and there's too much money involved. But the dogs . . . we could get the dogs back, and change some lives."

"You know what we're gonna do?" Virgil asked. "We're gonna organize a posse."

Johnson was confused: "What?"

"You got all those hunters with their dogs, let's stick a few of them in the trees on the other side of the highway, watching everything that comes out of Orly's Creek—twenty-four hours a day, until the DEA raids the place. I'll be on standby, right here in the cabin, and if anybody sees more than two dogs in a car coming out of there, I'll pull them over. That good enough?"

"Oh, a posse." Johnson thought about it for a minute, rubbed a lip and said, "Yeah . . . I guess. I'm sure I can get a few of the boys to be the watchers. Need to scout out a place for them to watch from."

"We can do that," Virgil said. "You start calling the best guys, and we'll go find a lookout, and a way to get in there."

"Come in by water," Johnson said.

"See? You're already thinking," Virgil said. "This'll be a snap."

As IT TURNED OUT, not quite a snap. People were willing, but had to work, too, and they had more volunteers for overnight watches than for daytime. Because the watcher would be close to the river, and the mosquitoes would be bad, they found a volunteer who had a deer blind with shoot-through mesh that would be inconspicuous. Another of the volunteers had an expensive pair of second-generation night-vision hunting binoculars that he could lend to the effort.

Virgil: "Why would anyone have a pair of night-vision hunting binoculars?"

Johnson: "Let's not ask that question."

Virgil: "By the time it was dark enough to use them, it'd be too dark to shoot anything."

Johnson: "Let's not ask that question."

Virgil: "Oh."

It wouldn't be too dark to shoot, say, a trophy buck—not if you were wearing night-vision glasses.

THEY SPENT THE REST of the afternoon setting it up: hauling the blind up the Mississippi River bank, hiding it in the brush, then cutting a trail up from the river; and organizing the watches.

Gomez called at seven o'clock and said his team was on the way.

"Two guys'll meet you by that bridge tomorrow, right at first light. You can show them the site, and we'll be five by five."

Virgil said, "Good. Okay. I'll be there," though he didn't know what five by five meant. He looked it up later, in Wikipedia: "Five by five is the best of twenty-five subjective responses used to describe the quality of communications, specifically the signal-to-noise ratio."

Five by five—he'd have to use it next time he talked to Davenport.

That evening, just before sundown, they ferried the first shift of watchers up to the blind, with binoculars, sandwiches, bottles of water, and a few beers to cut the taste of all the water. On the way back down the river, Johnson said, "We'll be running right over a nice little walleye hole, behind that wing dam."

"Be a crime not to take advantage of that," Virgil said.

So they did; and sat, anchored, off the wing dam, and watched the towboats going to and fro, and the night fishermen going out, and the pleasure cruisers running for home, the white, red, and green lights winking across the river, the tip-tops of the Wisconsin trees going pink as the sun disappeared below the Minnesota horizon.

"Don't get much better than this," Johnson said, his voice low in the quiet of the night.

"No, it doesn't," Virgil said. "I could do this for a thousand years."

They were still sitting there, in the growing darkness, when Clancy Conley got shot in the back.

5

OVERNIGHT, THEY HEARD NOTHING from the lookouts by the river. At first light, Johnson ran two more guys up the river, and retrieved the ones who'd spent the night in the blind. They were surprisingly pleased with themselves, though they'd seen nothing relevant. Like back in National Guard days, they said.

While Johnson was managing the watch, Virgil was heading north. The morning was cool, but promising more hotness. He turned off 26 onto NN. A black Suburban, the kind that members of the Ruffed Grouse Society tended to drive, was parked near the bridge; Virgil pulled up behind it, got out, and met two cowboy-looking guys with guns.

"Virgil," said Gomez, touching the brim of his ball cap.

"I thought you were too high up to do this yourself," Virgil said.

"I am, but I like to spend some time with my underlings, to

demonstrate that I'm just like one of them, the salt of the earth, though far more important," Gomez said. He bent a thumb at his underling. "George Blume."

Blume said, "His salt-in-the-wound thing don't always work," as they shook hands. He looked up at the ridge: "We'd be heading for that notch up there? About . . ." He read a bunch of numbers off a piece of paper.

"I can show you, but I'm no damn good with a GPS," Virgil said.

"Anybody see you going in yesterday?" Gomez asked.

"No, but I'm sure quite a few people saw my truck," Virgil said.

"I don't think this'll work, but we paid money for them, might as well use them," Gomez said. He popped the back of the Suburban and took out two magnetic door signs that said: "U.S. Geological Survey." He stuck them to the doors of the Suburban.

"Probably cause more trouble than if you just had a sign that said 'Feds,'" Virgil said. "Anyway, I got a rope and some water. . . . You gonna stay up there awhile, or just look?"

"Today, just look," Gomez said. "Be back in an hour, if we don't get shot."

THEY DIDN'T GET SHOT. They went in the same way that Virgil and Johnson had, taking care not to leave tracks or disturb foliage. When they got to the sheds, Gomez put his nose in the air and sniffed and said, "Yeah . . . this is the real thing."

Blume put his pack down, took out a set of lock picks, and picked the lock on the first shed in about nine seconds. They went in and looked around, found three two-head gas burners and a lot of glassware, along with five large polypropylene carboys full of purified water. The second shed held raw materials, mostly in gallon jugs, while the third shed held some basic tools—a chain saw, axes, a couple of cans of gasoline—along with a table, a radio, two decks of cards (one pornographic), and three plastic chairs.

When they'd locked the sheds back up, they looked at the rubbish dump, and Gomez took some more photographs.

"All right," he said. "A nice little commercial lab. And you could manufacture other shit in here, if you wanted, and knew how. They got all the glass they'd need to make acid."

They left the same way that Johnson and Virgil had, after making a long detour along the game trail at the crest of the hill toward the mouth of the valley, checking out whatever houses were visible. Virgil pointed out Zorn's place, which they marked with their GPS.

They continued down the trail, to the mouth of the valley. "Looks like that ATV track goes right down the hill to the highway," Blume said, looking down the hill through a pair of compact binoculars.

As they were making their way back, a dog started to bark, and then several more. Virgil couldn't make out exactly where they were, but they seemed to be across the valley from the hill they were on.

"Sound mournful, more than excited," Gomez said.

"If they're gonna be taken out to medical laboratories, they've got good reason," Virgil said.

They were back at the cars an hour and a half after they left. Gomez said that the watchers would be dropped off after dark in the evening, and before dawn in the morning. And, he said, they had another asset.

"It's considered kinda top secret, but I'd appreciate it if you wouldn't go shooting any shotguns up in the sky."

"You gotta drone?"

"Shhhh . . ."

THEN, AS OFTEN HAPPENED on sophisticated, hot-running, high-energy investigations, nothing happened for four days.

Rather, something happened, but only after Virgil did a lot of fishing, talked on the phone to Frankie, went to a 3-D archery range with Johnson, and tried to avoid phone calls from Davenport, in which he was not always successful—but nothing related to his two separate cases.

During the first three days, he kept trying to spot a drone, but never did; Gomez reported that the barking dogs were definitely on the south hill, that the dogs sounded large, and that there were quite a few of them. So Johnson had been wrong about the location.

On the fourth day, two skaters who took their boards out to County A to challenge the big downhill east of Clancy Conley's cabin spotted his body in the ditch on the side of the road.

The sheriff called Virgil, and Virgil took off for the crime scene. On the way, Davenport called. "I'm on the way," Virgil said, before Davenport could say anything.

And after he'd rung off, it occurred to Virgil that life was becoming complicated. He was juggling a dognapping ring, a meth lab investigation, and a murder. Trippton, it seemed, had a little darker underbelly than he'd been prepared for. He'd better have a serious talk with Davenport about it, sooner rather than later.

SHERIFF PURDY and four deputies were waiting at the ditch where Conley had landed. Conley's body was already inside a black body bag, although the bag had not yet been zipped up. Virgil spent no time looking at Conley's face, because a face that had spent four days in a wet ditch in the middle of August was not an attractive sight; he did spend a few seconds contemplating the exit wounds on Conley's chest.

One of the deputies, whose name was Paul Alewort, and who did crime-scene processing, said, "Shot three times in the back. We hauled him out of there because there wasn't a single damn thing we'd get out of that ditch that would mean anything. Only thing that was really unexpected when we pulled him out was a 'clunk' sound when we put him on the bag. I looked, and he was packing a revolver, an old .38, six rounds. We bagged it."

"Maybe he was worried about something," Virgil said, looking at the ditch. "Find any brass from the shooter?"

"Haven't really started looking yet," Alewort said.

Virgil said, "If he was running up the hill, and was shot by one guy in a car or truck, coming up from behind him, the shells would have ejected into the truck. So you won't find any brass. If he was running down the hill, and was shot in the back by a guy who was coming toward him, and stopped to shoot him in the back, then the shells will be on the road up ahead a ways. Unless he was shot by a P6 or P38 or a mirror-image .45, which would be wonderful, because they'd probably be the only ones for a hundred miles around, and somebody would know about them. Those are the two choices, unless you believe there were two men in the vehicle, and the passenger did the shooting."

"What if it was somebody in the woods who ambushed him?" Purdy asked.

"Probably not," Virgil said. "Looks to me like the bullets came straight through. If somebody was shooting from the side, the bullets would have come out on the far side of his chest."

"That sounds right," Alewort said. "I don't believe he was shot with a pistol. I'll leave it to the ME to say for sure, but it looks to me that he was shot with a rifle and hollow points. Lot of damage on his chest. Maybe by somebody who fired a burst. The bullet wounds are in a perfect spaced stripe right across the middle of his back, two inches apart."

"You think .223?" Virgil asked.

"That's what I'm thinking," Alewort said. "It's unlikely we'll ever recover any of the slugs, but there's small entries and big exits—a rifle-class weapon, and .223s are a dime a dozen around here."

"Anybody selling three-shot-burst conversion kits?"

Purdy shook his head. "Not that I know. There was a guy in Trippton making silencers a couple of years ago, but the BATF shut him down."

"He still around?" Virgil asked.

"Yeah. He's selling turkey fryers now."

"You can make a living selling turkey fryers?"

"Never thought about it," Purdy said. "But off the top of my head, I'd say no. His wife works, though."

"I'll talk to him," Virgil said. "Who else should I talk to?"

––––––––

VIRGIL GOT an exceptionally short list: Buster Gedney, the turkey-fryer salesman; Viking Laughton, Conley's employer at the *Republican-River*; Gary Kochinowski, owner of the bar where Conley drank; and Bill Don Fuller, who rented Conley the trailer where he lived.

"Fact is," Purdy said, "Conley was not well liked, because he was a drunk and an addict of some kind. A pill head, would be my guess. That made him cranky and aggressive. Every time we busted somebody for anything more than disturbing the peace, he'd be looking around for police misbehavior."

"He thought of himself as an investigator?"

"He did. Nobody else did. He couldn't investigate his way out of a convenience store. I mean, the guy could fall in a barrel of titties and come out suckin' his thumb."

"Girlfriends?"

"I heard he'd pay the town prostitute on occasion, but that's all I know."

"Who's the town prostitute?" Virgil asked.

Purdy's eyes shifted away, and he rubbed the side of his nose, as though trying to decide how far he could trust Virgil. Finally he said, "Wendy McComb, but don't you dare tell her I called her a prostitute, 'cause she's a nice girl," Purdy said. "Say you understand that she and Conley were friends." He thought about it for another moment, then added, "Least he wasn't queer."

Virgil added her to the list in his notebook, along with a description of where she lived, which Purdy said would be better than an address.

"I'll tell you what," Purdy said, scratching his ass and looking around the quiet valley, "I think it's about seventy-five percent what we got here is somebody who shot him because . . . he wanted to try out his gun on a human being. You know what I'm saying?"

"Unfortunately, I do," Virgil said. "But you better pray that's not the case, because if it is that kind of guy, he'll be really hard to catch, and he'll do it again."

He didn't say it, but at the back of his head he clicked back to the earlier thought about Trippton's underbelly. Given even the little that he knew—newspaper reporter, pill head, what looked like a pretty efficient murder of a man not well liked, who patronized prostitutes, even if they were nice girls—he had a feeling that the killing wasn't random.

THEY WALKED up the road and spent fifteen minutes looking for brass, but didn't find any: the conclusion was, the shells had been ejected into the killer's vehicle. Alewort said he'd walk a few deputies back into the woods, to look around obvious sniping stations, but he didn't think they'd find anything.

They were walking back to the cars when a deputy called, "Hey." They turned, and he was pointing into the gravel in the middle of the road. "Here's one. A shell."

They went to look, and found a crushed .223 shell. They scuffed around in the gravel for a few minutes and found another one. Virgil said, "The car came up in front of him, and the guy stopped, stepped out of his car, and shot him in the back," Virgil said. "Treat those shells carefully—we might still get a print or DNA off them."

————

THEIR NEXT STOP was Conley's trailer, which sat in a rough patch of dirt at the edge of a hill, with oak trees on three sides and a cornfield on the other; a pretty site, with an opening through the trees down into the valley below. An old tire swing hung from one of the oaks, but looked as though it hadn't been swung in for years.

A car sat in the circle of dirt, a ten-year-old Subaru Legacy station wagon. They opened it with a key from a key ring found in Conley's pants pocket, looked inside, and found an extensive collection of road maps, a few unpaid bills, four crumpled white bakery bags with no bakery inside, two ice scrapers, one broken, and an empty, dusty Old Thompson American Whiskey bottle in the one-pint size.

Alewort examined the bottle and said, "I didn't know he'd fallen that low."

Nothing in the car suggested a reason for an assassination. They were closing it up when a sheriff's car rolled into the yard, and a deputy got out: "Talked to Vike," he said. "He thought Conley was off on a toot—hadn't heard from him for a few days, and was going to come up and look around for him, but hadn't gotten around to it."

"All right," Purdy said. "Though it's a long time not to be more curious."

"He said Conley was gone for more than a week on a couple occasions, and always came back," the deputy said. "And he'd started drinking again, after being off booze for a good while."

"Loose way to run a business," Virgil said.

The deputy said, "Vike told me that they were running ahead on copy, and he really didn't need more until next week."

WHEN THEY FINISHED with the deputy, Virgil, Purdy, and Alewort walked over to the trailer and as Alewort opened the door, he said, "Now, I want y'all to keep your hands off the stuff inside: I need to process it, unless it's something that just can't wait."

The interior was not well kept, but wasn't a complete shambles, either. They went through it, with Alewort opening a few cabinets at Virgil's request—he used a screwdriver with a tip that had been bent ninety degrees, and filed as thin as a razor blade. The tool allowed him to open the cabinets without touching or disturbing anything, and Virgil decided he needed a tool just like it.

One of the cabinets was lockable, but unlocked. Inside, one of the cheaper Canon DSLR cameras sat on a book, with a couple of lens cases stacked behind it. Virgil noticed the book title—an explanation of the latest Macintosh operating system. "Do the camera right away—I want to look at the memory card," he told Alewort.

"Hell, just take it—we're not gonna get anything off it," Alewort said.

Virgil thought that himself, so he took the camera and slung it over his shoulder. On the way out, he noticed another thing that he hadn't seen on the way in—sitting on a kitchen chair, half under the table, was a plastic computer stand, of the kind used to lift a laptop to eye level, while the user typed on a keyboard at hip level. Virgil wouldn't even have known what it was, if he hadn't once had one himself. He reached under the edge of the kitchen table and felt an under-desk keyboard tray. He pulled it out and found a Logitech wireless keyboard and wireless mouse; the keyboard was a Mac version.

"What?" Purdy asked.

"He was home from work, and went for a run, but didn't bring his laptop home. At the same time, he has a pretty complete workstation here. That's . . . odd."

"Probably left it at work," Purdy said. "Ask Vike about it."

"Mmmm." Virgil thought, *Vike.*

"Wouldn't have an Internet connection out here—no cable, and the only satellite dish is for TV," Alewort said.

They moved back outside, not to mess up the place any more than they already had, and Virgil told Purdy, "I'll get in touch with the people on the list. You should send a couple deputies around to talk to neighbors, see if any of them heard gunfire in the last few days."

"I'll do that," Purdy said. "Call me when you get done with the interviews, and we'll trade information."

Before he left, Virgil gave Purdy and Alewort a lecture on tires and tire swings.

"You see this?" he asked. "You know what this is?"

"A tire swing?" Alewort guessed.

"Good guess, but wrong," Virgil said. "It's a mosquito hatchery. If you were to hire a really expensive engineer to design a mosquito hatchery, he'd spend a couple million bucks and come up with a used tire. They are sturdy, they are protective—no mosquito fish, no purple martins getting in, no bats—they collect water, and because they're black, they absorb the sun's rays and keep the water warmer than it might otherwise be. Unless you're in the middle of a drought, you cannot find a tire laying out on a riverbank or hanging from a tree that doesn't have water inside it, and mosquitoes."

"Well . . . thank you for that," Purdy said. "I'll keep it in mind."

BACK IN HIS TRUCK, Virgil hauled his laptop out of the back, plugged in the memory card, called up the Lightroom program. Lightroom began loading the contents of the card, and a moment later Virgil was looking at eighty photographs of a computer screen with a different bunch of numbers on each of them, but nothing that identified where it was from, or what the numbers meant. Johnson's office sawmill was only about a mile away, and he had a decent-quality printer, so Virgil drove over and walked into the office.

Johnson was out in the woods, but his girlfriend, Clarice, was there, and she made prints of the photos: "That's an Excel spreadsheet, but I can't tell you what's on it. It's about expendables. The codes will go out to the various products. The last part might be diesel fuel."

Virgil looked down at the meaningless lists and asked, "How'd you figure that out?"

"Because there's a category called DF, and then there's some numbers on the right which is about what we pay for wholesale diesel fuel for the trucks," she said. "Maybe a little higher, but close."

Virgil underlined the DF category and Clarice, leaning over the counter, tapped one of the photos—"He was being sneaky about it. You never did say who took these."

"No, I didn't," Virgil said. "But it was Clancy Conley, who was found shot to death in a ditch over on Highway A. Been dead a few days."

"Really," she said.

"You don't seem shocked."

"Didn't really know him," she said. "But maybe I am a little shocked."

"You said he was being sneaky. Why do you think he was being sneaky?"

"Well, if you look around the edges of these pictures, you see it was dark. He was taking pictures in the dark," she said.

"Maybe you should have been a cop," Virgil said.

"Nah. I couldn't put up with the bullshit," Clarice said.

"You're living with Johnson Johnson, and you can't put up with bullshit?"

"Got me there," she said. "He is a bullshit machine. But he gets things done."

VIKE LAUGHTON WAS a short, fat man with a pale, jiggly face who should have gone to Hollywood to get acting roles as corrupt Southern politicians. He sat in a wooden office chair with worn arms, in front of a rolltop desk with a laptop sitting on an under-desk shelf, and hooked into a big Canon printer. Framed photos hung on the wall behind the desk, all with a light patina of dust. Some of them were news shots, others were pictures of Vike as a younger man, getting plaques for one thing or another—Jaycees Young Businessman of 1984, Kiwanis Distinguished Service Award. None of them were recent; things must have slowed down since the turn of the century.

Possibly, Virgil thought, he was being unfair, but he doubted it.

"I was sorry to hear that he was killed," Laughton said. "The sheriff called and told me, and I can't say I was completely surprised. The only reason I kept him around was because he did good work when he was clean, and I paid him shit—but he was an addict, and he was buying drugs, and I suspected he'd come to a bad end. I thought he'd die of an overdose, or in a car accident. Getting shot, that's something else. . . . I don't know where he was buying his dope, but I knew he was doing it. If you hang around with those kinds of people . . ."

"You know any of the local dope dealers?"

"No, I don't pay attention to that," Laughton said. "There's some around—marijuana, anyway. We had a kid suspended from the high school when they found a bag of weed in his locker. We're a river port, so there's always a few lowlifes going through. Those guys who work on tows, they're a different breed entirely."

Conley's job, Laughton said, was to write about a hundred and fifty inches of copy a week, on any subject, and provide a half-dozen photos of anything. They didn't do online. "We've had more mist-on-the-river shots than you could shake a stick at," he said. "When he'd go off on a toot, I'd have to do his job, along with mine. I've put everything in the paper except the dictionary."

Laughton's main job, he said, was collecting the advertisements from local stores. "We're one of those papers where, if the IGA goes out of business, I'll be working as a Walmart greeter the next week. So Clancy wrote two-thirds of the copy and took all the pictures, and I wrote the other third and collected the ads."

"I wondered about the possibility that he might have been working on a story that got him in trouble," Virgil said. "Would you know anything about that?"

"Virgil, Conley didn't do anything serious. He was incapable of it. He was a lost soul, trying to get through life as easy as he could. And I have to tell you, there are not many stories in the *Republican-River*. That's not what we do here. We have obits, and the occasional drowning, sometimes a house burns down, and boys go off to the army and navy, and we do the county commission and the town council and the school board . . . election night is always big. But we're not up there investigating the president."

"You're sure he wasn't wandering off the reservation? Trying to redeem himself, or something?"

Laughton looked perplexed for a moment, then said, "No, no, no. Something else, Virgil, that you should know about, from the wider world of journalism. Journalists get killed in wars, and by accident, but they don't get hunted down by people they're investigating. Not in the USA, anyway. That's movie stuff."

"All right." Virgil looked around the office and asked where Conley worked—there wasn't much room and only one desk—and Laughton heaved himself to his feet and led the way through a curtained doorway into a wide dim room at the back, filled with piles of undistributed papers. A metal military-style desk sat in a corner, with a table next to it. Plugs for another Canon printer and a couple small speakers lay on the desk. Vike nodded at it. "Feel free."

Virgil went through the desk, found a checkbook with a couple of unpaid utility bills tucked under the cover, a book of stamps, a few pieces of computer equipment—a dusty USB hub, some cables, a CD disk containing an obsolete copy of Photoshop—and other desk litter. No laptop.

"Couldn't find a laptop up at his trailer," Virgil said. "You know where it might be?"

"He carried it around in a black nylon backpack. He did half his writing down at Stone's Coffee Shop. Should have been at his house, or in his car, anyway."

"Wasn't there," Virgil said. "A Macintosh, right?"

"Yeah, one of those white ones. Older. You think that means something?"

"Yes, I do," Virgil said. "He was out jogging when he was killed. Could have been some crazy guy, looking for somebody to kill—but not if Conley's laptop is missing. They would have had to stop at his house, and risk breaking in to get it. Though, there was no sign of a break-in. Might want to look for somebody with a key . . ."

"Well . . . I don't know," Laughton said.

LAUGHTON HAD ONLY ONE suggestion for the direction of the investigation: "Like I said, I paid him shit, and when he wasn't working, I didn't pay him anything. Still, he managed to hang on, buy gas, pay the rent, and drink. I don't know exactly how he did that. I don't think he got enough money from me. I'm wondering if he might have been your dope dealer? He knew everybody in town, so he'd know who the local buyers would be."

"I'll check into that," Virgil said. "Thank you. That's a possibility."

VIRGIL DIDN'T LIKE two things about the interview. The first was his sense that Laughton had processed Conley's murder too thoroughly, in too short a time—didn't ask enough questions about it, didn't ask about the investigation, didn't speculate about alternate explanations of what might have happened. At the same time, he seemed exactly like the kind of McDonald's-coffee-drinking hangout guy who'd do all of that.

The second thing was, Laughton had spent a good part of the interview poor-mouthing, and judging from the paper itself, and Laughton's shabby office, he might have had reason to do that. Which didn't explain why there was a very new Nissan Pathfinder parked outside his office.

Virgil had been shopping for a replacement for his five-year-old 4Runner, and knew that the Pathfinder—which looked pretty optioned-out, including a navigation system—cost something north of $40,000.

But who knew? Maybe Laughton had inherited money or something. And the possession of money, or the ability to get a truck loan, didn't seem to have much to do with a guy getting shot in the back.

VIRGIL HAD INTENDED to drop in on the other people on his list, but before he could get started, Johnson called and said, "We got a mutiny going on. We need to meet with some of our guys."

"What do you mean, exactly?"

"They know about the dogs on the south hill. They're getting their guns together, they're going in."

"Aw, Jesus, where are they?"

"At Tom Jones's place."

Virgil got the location and drove over in a hurry. At Jones's house, he found Johnson arguing with four men in camo, including Winky Butterfield.

All of them turned to look when Virgil drove in, and when he got out of his truck, Butterfield said to Johnson, "Goddamnit, you weren't supposed to tell him."

"I got no choice. Virgil's my guy and I can't turn my back on him," Johnson said. "He's got his reasons for working the way he is."

"What reasons?" one of the men asked. Virgil found out later he was Jones.

Instead of answering, Virgil asked Johnson, "Can you trust these guys? They got any relations up Orly's Creek?"

The men all looked at each other, then Butterfield said, "No, none of us do," and Johnson said, "Yeah, you could trust them. Are you going to tell them?"

Virgil said, "Listen, men. This is supposed to be top secret, but I'm telling you anyway. You tell anybody else, you could go to prison for a long time. Anybody not want to hear what I'm going to say, you better walk away. If you listen, and you tell anyone, including your wives, and the word gets out, we will track it down, and you will go to prison."

The men all looked at each other again, then Butterfield said, "What the hell are you talking about, Virgil?"

"Anybody walking away?" Virgil asked.

They all shook their heads, and Virgil said, "Okay. Johnson and I went up there and scouted the valley."

"Didn't know that," Jones said.

"'Cause we didn't tell you. We didn't find the dogs, but we did find a commercial-sized meth lab. The place is under surveillance by the federal government right now. As soon as we nail the people running the lab, we'll go looking for the dogs."

One of the men smiled and said, "My goodness. That is a reason."

"But what about the dogs?" Butterfield asked. "Goddamn meth labs are all over the place—the goddamned dogs are like my god-damn children."

"Look: that's the reason we have you guys sitting out by the river, watching people coming and going—we don't want to let the dogs out of there," Virgil said. "We think they're up on the south hill, which is hard to get at, but we can hear them barking at night. So as soon as the feds move, which has to be any day now—I'm kind of surprised that they haven't gone already—we'll be up there after the dogs. And if somebody tries to move them before then, we should see them."

"They could be torturing them," Butterfield said.

"Probably not, if they're gathering them up to sell them," Virgil said. "Look, guys, give me a couple more days, and we'll be all over the dogs."

Once again, they all looked around, then Jones said, "Two days, Virgil. Then we're gonna have to do something."

JOHNSON CAME and sat in Virgil's truck while he made a call to Gomez: "Anything happening up there at all?"

"Yeah, we saw a guy go up there yesterday in one of those Gator utility vehicles," Gomez said. "He was dropping stuff off, it looked like. I think they're getting ready to roll some smoke. You getting antsy?"

Virgil explained about the dog owners, and Gomez said, "Oh boy. All we need is a bunch of rednecks running through there with rifles. If it looks like you can't hold them off, call me—I'll come down and preach a sermon to them."

"I'll do that," Virgil said. "You heard about my murder?"

"Yeah—does that have anything to do with the Orly's Creek boys?"

"Don't know. I hadn't really thought about that possibility. But the victim was a pill head, according to the sheriff. His boss thought that he might have another source of income. I'll keep it in mind."

"Well, if you've got a local source, and you have a pill head who might be dealing . . . that's a pretty interesting coincidence, if it is a coincidence."

"I'll stay in touch," Virgil said.

He rang off, told Johnson about Gomez's end of the conversation, then called up Alewort, who was still at Conley's trailer. "I'd be interested in any trace of any street drug. Deeply interested," Virgil said.

"We'll look," Alewort said.

When Virgil was done with Alewort, Johnson asked what he was most thinking about—the murder, or the dogs.

"I gotta juggle them," Virgil said. "The murder's the main thing, but I won't forget the dogs."

6

Virgil needed to talk to Bill Don Fuller, who owned the trailer where Conley had lived, and to the other people suggested by Purdy. He recited the list to Johnson, who said that Fuller ran a welding service down by the river port, and that he'd be driving right past Wendy McComb's house on the way to Fuller's place.

"Is she gonna be a problem?" Virgil asked.

"Not if she's sober," Johnson said. "She tends to drink a little."

"By 'a little,' you mean 'a lot,'" Virgil said.

"Well, yeah. She had a pretty hard life before she started screwing for money."

"I suspect this isn't news to you, Johnson, but screwing for money is a hard life," Virgil said.

"Tell you what," Johnson said, "she used to work as an aide down at the River View nursing home, changing old folks' diapers and colostomy bags for the minimum wage, drinking every night, and screwing for free. Now she just drinks and screws, for ten times as much money, and that's about a thousand percent improvement. So don't get your feminist panties in a knot about what she does for a living."

"You got a colorful town here, Johnson."

"Could get more colorful in two days," Johnson said. "Two days and there'll be a bunch of boys going up to Orly's Creek with guns."

VIRGIL LEFT JOHNSON at Jones's place and drove back toward town. Just short of the city limits, Thunderbolt Road veered off toward the river. A dirt track with a scattering of gravel snaked through a swampy swale and across a short concrete-slab bridge to the levee, then along the land side of the levee toward town, eventually winding past a weathered white cottage with green shutters and a floodwater stain just below the first-floor windows.

Virgil pulled into a dirt parking area and walked around to the front porch. He could hear a TV inside as he knocked on the screen door.

A woman called, "Who is that?"

"Police, state Bureau of Criminal Apprehension," Virgil said.

McComb was a completely ordinary-looking woman, a bit heavy, wearing a white blouse buttoned to the neckline, and black Capri pants and flip-flops. She had dishwater-blond hair, pale green eyes, and a few freckles. She had a white plastic bowl of cornflakes in her hand, and a spoon in the other.

"What have I done?" she asked through the screen door.

"Nothing, as far as I know," Virgil said. "But I understand you're a friend of Clancy Conley."

"Who? I'm not sure I know that name—"

"Conley was found dead today. He was shot to death."

"Oh, Jesus!" she said, taking a step back. She sputtered a few soggy cornflakes onto the screen. "What happened? Where was this? Are you sure it's Clancy?"

She asked all the questions that Laughton should have, Virgil noticed; and she'd popped the hook on the door, almost unconsciously, to let him in. She backed across the living room and dropped into a chair, pointing him at a couch. The house was furnished like any middle-class suburban home, except the television was smaller.

"What happened?" She seemed to notice the bowl in her hand and set it on an end table.

Virgil told her about Conley, and as he did, the blood drained out of her face and she put both hands on her cheeks; no tears. When he finished, she asked, "How can I help?"

"Do you know . . . Everybody who knows him says he didn't have much going for himself. Drank too much, probably did some dope. Maybe dealt a little? Sound right?"

"No. He quit drinking. Quite a while ago, and he said he wasn't going back. He was working out, he was running, he was getting in shape. He was working on a story, he was all excited about it. In fact . . . Okay, he might have known he was in trouble. He once told me, we were in bed, and he said if a cop comes asking about me, tell him to look up the songs of some singer."

"Some singer?"

"Yeah, but this was like a month ago. I can't remember her name, but . . . Wait, I think she was the chick singer for the Mouldy Figs."

"The Mouldy Figs?" The Figs were a local jazz band in the Twin Cities. "The Mouldy Figs don't have a chick singer—they're a jazz band."

"Well, that's what he said. And he said, their chick singer," McComb said.

"Huh. Do you know what his story was about?" Virgil asked.

"No, I don't—but he said he had a great story, he was working on it, but then he shut up and said he didn't want to talk about it, really."

"Did he say when he was going to publish it?"

"No, nothing like that, but I feel like it was pretty soon," McComb said. She got up, took two or three quick steps around the living room, and sat down again. "He was as happy as I'd ever known him to be."

"How about the drugs?" Virgil asked.

"He used some. He had one of those orange pill bottles, and it never changed. It said Prozac on it, but it wasn't Prozac. But it wasn't powder, it was pills, and I believe it was some kind of speed. I don't think he was dealing, though—never tried to sell me anything, anyway. I never heard from anybody else that he was a dealer. We do have a few dealers around town. I don't use myself, except a little pot on Saturday night."

"Vike Laughton kinda hinted to me—"

"There's a snake in the grass. I wouldn't trust him any further than I could spit a brick," she said.

Virgil said, "Hmm."

"What did he hint to you?" she asked.

"That Conley was dealing. He said he'd started drinking again."

"I bet Vike did it. Killed him," McComb said. "He was trying to direct you away, to make you think Clancy got killed in a dope deal."

"That's not a very charitable thing to say about a neighbor," Virgil said. "Why would he kill his only employee?"

"That's for you to figure out, right?"

"I could use a little help . . ."

"Well, I don't have any, about that," McComb said. "But it only makes sense. Nobody else in town really had much to do with Clancy. He was not a big socializer, especially since he quit drinking. Didn't have any real friends, that I know of."

"You're sure he quit drinking?"

"I'm sure. I last saw him, mmm, maybe a week ago. He was dry. He wasn't even worried about it—about going back. Didn't even talk about it anymore."

They chatted for a while, but she didn't have much that was relevant, other than her belief that Vike Laughton had something to do with the killing. Virgil finally closed his notebook and stood up, fished a business card out of his pocket and handed it to her. "Think about everything that Conley ever talked about—if you could point me at that story he was working on, or somebody who might know about it . . . just keep thinking about it, and call me if anything occurs to you. Especially if you can think of the singer."

"I will," she said. As they walked to the door, she asked, "Did anybody tell you what I do for a living?"

"They shared some rumors," Virgil said.

"You don't care?"

"I don't like it, because I think it messes people up, but I'm not interested in doing anything legal about it," Virgil said. "It's a situation I don't have a good answer for."

"Yeah, well, if you ever start feeling lonely, you could inquire about the law officer introductory discount," she said.

Virgil stopped. Dark underbelly. "Does that coupon get used much?"

"Everybody has his needs," she said, sounding like a therapist. "Even cops."

BACK IN THE CAR, Virgil thought: Laughton and Purdy both had ridiculed the idea that Conley might have been involved in a serious story—but he apparently had been, if he'd been telling the truth to McComb. And if he'd been telling the truth to McComb about drinking, then Laughton had been lying to him. On the other hand, he might have been a hapless loser, bragging to the only woman he could get in bed, to give himself a little shine.

He got on the phone and called a BCA researcher. "Sandy, I've got a murder down in Buchanan County—"

"I heard."

"I'd like you to take a look at the victim's state tax returns, see how much money he had coming in. Dig around, see where else he worked, you know, as far back as you can go. Maybe check his Social Security records. His name was Clancy Conley. . . ."

He also asked her to peek at the tax returns from Vike Laughton: "He says most of his income flows from a paper he runs down here, the *Republican-River*. I'm mostly interested in what other sources of income he has, investments and so on. And take a look at his deductions for property taxes, see if he owns other property."

"You think he might be trying to hide some income?"

"He's doing something, but I don't know what it is," Virgil said. "When you check his tax records . . . I'd like you to keep that between the two of us."

"You mean, instead of going to the Department of Revenue and asking nice, I should hack into them," she said.

"I don't really want an explanation of how you do it," Virgil said. "I just want them quick, and I don't want to have to play ring-around-the-bureaucrat."

"You don't want an explanation of how I'd do it, because that might be a criminal conspiracy."

"Sandy . . ."

Every day in every way, he thought, it seemed harder and harder to get anything done.

VIRGIL CONTINUED DOWN Thunderbolt Road, which eventually crossed the levee and rolled down into the port. The port didn't look like anybody's picture of a port, because it wasn't much—just a half-mile-long line of wharfs that ran parallel to the riverbank, with tie-up posts every hundred feet or so, and a dozen corrugated buildings in various stages of disrepair. A small marina had been built into an indentation in the shoreline; twenty small boats rose and fell with the waves coming in from passing towboats.

Virgil crossed the levee and rolled along until he saw a Fuller's

Barge Service sign on two big steel Quonset huts, one enclosed and one open. Both were surrounded by an eight-foot chain-link fence, with three strands of barbed wire on top.

He could see flickering welding torches in the open hut, but couldn't see what was being done. The closed hut had a white sign on it that said: "Office." Somebody had written "Wipe your feet" below the "Office" with a Sharpie, which was apparently a joke, Virgil thought, because most of the area outside the door was a mud hole.

Avoiding as much of the mud as possible, he stepped inside and found himself in an open space, partly filled with welding equipment and a couple of Bobcats. A balding man was working in a cubicle off to the left; he'd turned to look when Virgil walked in.

Virgil said, "I'm looking for a Mr. Fuller."

"That's me," the man said cheerfully. "What can I do you for?"

Virgil identified himself and said that he was investigating the murder of Clancy Conley.

"Oh, boy, that's just a disaster," Fuller said. "First murder we had down here in quite a while, and it had to be my tenant."

Fuller said that Conley had been living in the trailer for two years. "Never had a bit of trouble with him. I heard that he was a slacker, but he stayed employed, and never caused anyone any trouble. He was handy with a wrench, and that helped."

Fuller cleared up some of the mystery of how Conley survived on a minimal salary: "I didn't charge him rent. Our deal was, he'd keep the place clean, make sure it didn't get broken into, and maintain it, and pay the utility bills. During deer season, he'd move out, and my buddies and I would move in. I own that woodland around there, two hundred and forty acres, and there are three of us hunt over it. We stay in the trailer. Last year, while we were up there, Clancy came down here and bunked out in one of our sheds that the tow crews use from time to time. Got a toilet, sink, and a couple cots, but that was good enough for him."

"So the trailer's actually a hunting shack."

"Yeah, exactly."

He repeated Wendy McComb's statement that Conley had quit drinking, and hadn't gone back. "He told me once that he didn't really like booze all that much—and he didn't like beer at all. He liked to get cranked up, not pulled down. He told me his dream was to get some fast hot car, like a Porsche, and see if he could drive across Nebraska from Omaha to the Wyoming line in four hours. He had it all planned out, he had the highway patrol radio frequencies, so he'd know where they were at, where he'd make his gas stop . . . he even figured out how to make a trucker bomb, you know, so he could pee in a bottle and wouldn't have to stop."

"Did he ever say anything to you about a big story he was working on?" Virgil asked.

"No. Nothing like that."

"Nothing at all unusual, then? Just Clancy Conley, as everybody knows and loves him."

Fuller opened his mouth and then his eyes clicked away, as if he were thinking over what he'd been about to blurt out. Virgil said, "As you were about to say . . ."

Fuller leaned back in his chair, put his hands behind his head.

"My daughter was having a kid a while ago, back in early July. July eighth, to be exact. She was going over to La Crosse to have it, and so, sure enough, she starts into labor at three o'clock in the morning. My wife and I drive over to her house in our Suburban, and we pick up her and her husband, and haul ass for the bridge. I'm going through town at about a hundred miles an hour, and all of a sudden we catch Clancy in our headlights getting into his car with his camera. He had his camera in his hand. I didn't pay much attention to it, just kept going for La Crosse, but it stuck in my mind, because he looked kinda scared. Or guilty."

"Guilty?"

"Yeah. Guilty. So I see him about a week later and ask him what he's doing wandering around the streets with his camera at three o'clock in the morning. I asked him if somebody was out there with their bedroom window shades up. He started to deny that it was him, and then he pretended to remember and said he'd been shooting the shit with some friends and it got late and he just had the camera with him. . . . I don't know. I didn't think about it, but he seemed kinda flustered. That's probably nothing, but like I said, it stuck in my head. He was acting . . . furtive. Like he'd been caught doing something."

"Where was this? That you saw him?"

"Right in the middle of town, across the street from the QuikTrip. Right where the high school lawn comes down to Main Street."

"You didn't really think he might have been peeping in somebody's window?"

"Oh, no. No. He wasn't that kind of guy. But when I think about it now, it seems like something was going on."

WHEN VIRGIL LEFT FULLER, he drove up Main Street to look at the QuikTrip and the high school. Trippton was built on a series of river terraces that rose step-like from the water. The high school was built on the fourth terrace up, above Main Street, which was on the second terrace. The school had a wide sloping front lawn, with a big concrete walk and concrete steps leading up to the early twentieth-century brick building. A four-by-eight red, white, and blue sign on the front lawn said: "Vote 'Yes' on the new High School Sports Arena bonds."

The QuikTrip was on a corner, on a street that dead-ended at Main Street. If Clancy had parked across from the QuikTrip, he'd either been down in the residential neighborhood behind the Quik-Trip or at the high school. Virgil made a mental note: find out if Clancy really did have some friends that he hung out with at night, and if so, where they lived.

Next stop was at G&Ts, a bar on Main Street, three blocks up from the high school. The owner, Gary Kochinowski, had gone to La Crosse to watch the Loggers play baseball, but his wife, Tammy, was working the bar.

"What an awful thing—everybody's talking about it," she said. She hadn't seen Clancy in several weeks, she said, and then only on the street. "He don't come in anymore, since he quit. It's a shame, because this was his whole social life, right here."

"When he was drinking, how bad was he?"

"Oh, he got drunk from time to time, but he wasn't like a full-blown alcoholic," she said. "I mean, he was an alcoholic, but it wasn't like he was a stumbling drunk. We never found him in the gutter. Gary would drive him home every once in a while, but most of the time he could drive himself. He used to say he'd like to drink more, but he couldn't afford it."

"Be a lot cheaper to buy his own bottle."

"Well, that's the thing that kept him from being a stone-cold alkie—he didn't do that. He didn't get a bottle and sit home and drink it. If he was going to drink, he wanted to talk to people."

"Did he talk to anyone in particular?" Virgil asked. "Were some people better friends than others?"

"No, I wouldn't say that. There were just a bunch of regulars who'd come in every night, and he'd come in and shoot the breeze and sip through four or five rounds . . . and go home."

"Did he ever mention anything about a big story he was working on?"

"Not to me, but you might check with Gary when he gets back. Gary talked to him more than I did, but like I said, we haven't seen him for a while."

"Huh."

"Not helping you much, am I?"

"Everything helps a little," Virgil said. "It's putting it all together that's hard. A couple people told me he'd gone back to drinking, but now a couple more have said that he didn't."

"I think we would have heard about it if he had," Tammy said.

"That kind of thing gets around, and pretty quick, in a small town. If he was drinking again, I think he would have done it here."

HIS LAST STOP was at Buster Gedney's house, a small two-bedroom place crowded close to the river, right on the leading edge of the second step of the floodplain. In a bad flood year, the property might take on some water. A sign in the front yard advertised a blockbuster sale on turkey fryers, with another sign stuck on the bottom of the first that said: "We Beat All Internet Prices."

Buster was around at the side, in a garage full of power lawn mowers, a short, pale man with thinning hair. He was wearing a long-sleeved shirt with three pens in the chest pocket, and jeans. When Virgil called out to him, he stood and wiped his hands on an oily rag and asked, "Looking for a fryer?"

"No, I'm a cop, I came to talk for a couple of minutes. . . ."

Virgil introduced himself, and asked about the silencers.

Gedney shook his head. "Man, I quit that."

"I heard."

"I don't do silencers. Honest to God, those government guys scared the hell out of me. I do lawn mowers. That's all I do now— lawn mowers."

"You can make as much money on lawn mowers as on silencers?"

"Damn right you can. These idiots can't get their mowers to start, so they take them out to the landfill and go to Home Depot and buy another one. Ninety-nine percent of the time, all they need is a new gas filter and clean the gas line, maybe put a new air filter in, sharpen up the blade. Takes me fifteen minutes, and they're good as gold. Ten dollars in parts and a little knowledge, and you've got a fifty-to-hundred-dollar lawn mower. Of course, some of them, it's a different story. This one . . ." He touched a newer-looking blue mower with his toe. "This one, guy changes the oil, forgets to put the plug back in, the oil drains out, he fires it up, and three minutes later the engine blows. All it's good for now is parts."

"I didn't know about the lawn mowers. I was told you were a machinist," Virgil said. He waved his hand at the back of the garage. Virgil didn't know much about machine shops, although he'd once investigated a case where a machine shop had been cleaned out on a weekend by machinery thieves. He knew enough to recognize the CNC lathe and a nice mill in the back of the garage.

Gedney looked at him sideways and said, "I didn't know all the legal stuff about silencers. Really, I'm telling the truth. I had a friend—didn't turn out to be much of a friend—comes over and gives me a burned-out silencer, and asks if I could build one like it. Well, it was a challenge, and I got a little machine shop, you know, so I built one for him. I guess the word got around."

"You ever build a silencer for an M15?"

He shook his head. "Don't know. I don't know much about guns. I'd mostly duplicate the things, right down to a thousandth of an inch. They call them suppressors, the gun guys do. They'd already have one, but it'd be shot out, or something, and I'd duplicate it. Never really saw the guns. That's why I thought it was okay—see, these guys already had permits. At least, that's what they told me. I told all this to the agents at the BATF."

"Any of the gun guys ask you to work on the trigger assembly? Say they needed something fixed, or . . ."

A woman came out the side door of the house and called, "Buster? Who's there?"

"Oh . . . this is an agent with the state police. Virgil Flowers, right?"

She came up, a tall, thin woman, who was nervously rolling her hands together. Buster said to Virgil, "This is my wife, Jennifer."

"Buster's all done with that silencer business," she said. "He sells turkey fryers now—"

"I'm investigating the murder of Clancy Conley," Virgil said. "Have you heard about it?"

"About ten minutes ago," Jennifer said. To her husband, "Jennifer One just called and told me. It's awful. They found his body in a ditch." To Virgil: "What does this have to do with Buster?"

"I'm checking out something about the gun that was used," Virgil said. "Excuse me for a minute, I'll be right back."

He walked out to his truck, got an iPad out of the seat pocket, brought it back, went out to the 'net, Googled "What does a three-shot burst kit look like?" and showed the pictures to Buster.

Buster's Adam's apple bobbed a couple of times and he muttered, "No, no, never seen anything like that. Not that I recall." He was so bad at it that Virgil expected a flag to pop out of his ear, on a stick, saying, "I'm lying."

"You're sure?"

"I don't want to mess with guns anymore," Buster said. "The BATF guys said the next time I do it, I could go to jail."

"Do you have one yourself?" Virgil asked. "An M15. An AR15?"

"We don't have any guns," Jennifer said. "We don't even have a BB gun."

"That's a pretty nice machine shop," Virgil said. "That come from making the silencers?"

"No, no. Not at all. My business is mostly with farmers and car dealers, looking to get parts duplicated. Like, a farm busts a part on a combine . . ."

His wife waved him silent and asked, "What about Clancy Conley? You getting anywhere with that?"

"Yeah, as a matter of fact," Virgil said. "The killer wasn't very sophisticated, we already got a bunch of leads. I figure to close it out by the end of the week."

"What kind of leads?" she persisted.

"Can't really talk about that," Virgil said. "But with the crime-scene stuff we have now . . . Well, I better leave it at that."

He turned back to Buster. "Go online and take a long look at the three-shot burst kit. If you remember seeing one of them, or even an individual piece of one, give me a call. And, Buster . . . if you remember something, you can't just let it go and hope for the best. You'd be implicated. This is a first-degree murder. Somebody's going to jail for thirty years, no parole. By the end of the week."

7

THE SCHOOL BOARD MET that night at Jennifer Barns's house, after Jennifer Gedney called and asked for an emergency meeting. She recounted Virgil's sudden appearance at her house and said, "I spent an hour after supper looking this man up on the Internet. I am telling you, he is dangerous. He is the man who caught those Vietnamese spies a few years ago, and remember those three teen-agers who were driving around killing people? He had that case, too, and those people who were trying to buy that sacred stone from Israel? That was him. He says he has several leads, and I be-lieve him, else how did he get to our door? He is a killer, and I'm scared to death."

Vike Laughton told them about Virgil's visit to his office. He was less impressed: "Here's the thing, folks. From what I could tell, he's got almost nothing. What he'll do is run around town and tell everybody that he's breaking the case, when what he's trying to do is play us off each other."

"You think he knows that there's more than one person involved?" asked Jennifer Barns.

"There's no way he could know that, and nothing he said to me suggested that he did," Laughton said.

Randy Kerns, the shooter, said, "I'll tell you up front, I made a mistake with the gun. I used one of Buster's burst kits, and I'll bet that's how he got to Buster—they figured out the shot pattern, and asked themselves, 'Where could you get a burst kit?' and they remembered about him making those suppressors. But if everybody keeps their mouths shut, we'll be okay."

They all looked at each other, and Larry Parsons asked, "What's a burst kit?"

"Mechanical gizmo that lets you fire off three shots with one pull of the trigger," Kerns said.

Jennifer Barns: "So everybody just stay calm. Don't talk about it, don't ask about it."

Jennifer Gedney said, "Buster's worried. He thinks Flowers might send him to prison for making the burst kits. If Flowers digs around enough, he'll find out that Buster made some of them. I don't know what Buster would do, then."

Again, a quick, silent exchange of faces, then Kerns said, "You've got to keep track of Buster, then. If he gets too weird about it . . ."

Jennifer Gedney said, "What? You're going to kill him, too? That's absurd."

Delbert Cray, the financial officer, said, "It's not logically absurd, though I have to admit that it would probably cause this Flowers to focus on Buster's various links."

"None of the links would point to us—they'd point to people who bought the burst kits," Jennifer Barns said. "Randy bought one, but nobody knows that, except Buster, and if something happened to Buster before he could give Flowers a list . . . the threat is sealed off."

"Could figure out a way to make it look like an accident, or a suicide," Kerns said. "Buster's kinda old, and not in that good a shape. Two of us guys could get him out in his workshop, grab him and hang him without bruising him up. . . . I'd want to do some reading about it, and about DNA, before we did it. But it could be done."

Jennifer Barns said, "You want to put that in the form of a motion?"

"So moved," Kerns said.

Bob Owens, the senior board member, said, "Two murders are way worse than one. It makes it clear that something is going on. Right now, as far as Flowers knows, Conley was shot by some crazy, out looking to kill somebody."

"That's true," said Jennifer Houser. "I think we should hold in reserve the whole idea of killing Buster. It's too drastic a measure, for what we know right now."

Jennifer Gedney asked, "What if something happened to Flowers?"

"Another possibility," Kerns said. "The rumor around town is that he came here to investigate some dognappings, and the victims are telling him that the dognappers live up Orly's Creek. If he was to get shot, the BCA would send somebody else down, and maybe a whole bunch of people, but if there was something that pointed at the dognappers . . ."

"Like what?" Owens asked. "I can't think of what it would be."

"Maybe because you only had one second to think about it," Kerns suggested. "With a little more time, we could come up with something. He hangs out with Johnson Johnson. Maybe Johnson could get an anonymous tip about the dogs that takes them out somewhere, looking for dogs, and Flowers gets killed. That links it to the dogs, and not to Conley."

"So moved," said Jennifer Gedney.

"I'm sorry, but that sounds way, way too complicated. We have to have something better than that," said Jennifer Houser. "But I've got a question for Jen Three. If we voted to kill Buster . . . would that be a problem?"

"Well, yes," Jennifer Gedney said. "Not an emotional problem, or anything like that, it's just that I think it would only focus attention. I'd vote against killing him because it seems too extreme right now. Later? Maybe not."

Laughton grinned and said, "The marriage is maybe not as solid as it could be?"

"Just looking at him makes me tired," Jennifer Gedney said. "All those wrenches. And he's covered with oil most of the time."

"All right," said Henry Hetfield, the superintendent of schools, looking down over his steel-rimmed glasses. "We've got a lot on our plates right now. Here is what I'd suggest: we table the motions to kill Buster and Flowers, with the understanding that they could be brought back before the board if Buster gets too shaky— Jen Three, you'll have to monitor that—or Flowers gets too close. But we also instruct Randy to do what he can to monitor Flowers, and to make plans to remove one or both of them if the situation worsens."

Jennifer Barns said, "So moved."

"I think we have two motions already on the floor," Owens said.

"Oh, fuck that," Jennifer Barns said. "Let's have a show of hands on Henry's proposal. All in favor, raise your hands."

All nine hands went up.

"So that's settled," she said. "We watch and wait, but Randy is ready to move if we need to. My personal view is, we don't have much to fear at the moment."

"As long as Flowers doesn't find out about the story that Clancy was working on," Jennifer Gedney said.

"If we even get a sniff of that . . ." She looked at Kerns, who nodded.

Vike Laughton spoke up: "Flowers originally came here to investigate dogs, and he thinks they might be up Orly's Creek. I have heard, and I'd suspect a couple more of you have, that those people are cooking some meth up there. Anybody else hear that?"

Jennifer Barns said, "Where'd you hear that?"

"Well, from Conley, actually. He was a pill-popper, as you all know," Laughton said.

Jennifer Houser said, "I heard that. Just a rumor, but I heard it."

Jennifer Barns asked, "What does that have to do with anything?"

"I was just wondering if there is any way we might tie Conley's death to the Orly's Creek people. Drug users. A drug shooting. Something going on there . . ."

"How'd we do that?" Owens asked.

"I don't know. We could think of something," Laughton said. "I don't think it's healthy, though, to have Flowers focused on Conley and his job, or what he might have been looking into."

"Well, if you think of something, let us know," Owens said.

"I will do that," Laughton said.

Barns said, "All right. Let's go on home, folks. And Jen Three— keep an eye on Buster."

As THEY WERE going out the door, Laughton asked Kerns, "How difficult would it be to, mmm, take a look at one of those Orly's Creek hillbillies?"

"You mean, shoot one? It's pretty dark there, houses are up from the road. Lots of pullouts along the creek. It'd be ideal for an ambush, except for one thing—there's only one way out. That could be handled . . ."

"One of the people up there, he's a gangster who used to ride with the Bad Seed. Roy Zorn. You see him around town. If something should happen to him that was . . . consonant . . . with what happened to Clancy, Flowers would have to take that connection pretty seriously, I would think."

"You don't want to talk to the board about it?" Kerns asked.

"No. They're too shook up right now. Making motions, calling for votes," Laughton said. "Like Jen Three. She swings from 'No killing' to 'Let's kill Flowers.' Killing Flowers would be insane, except for the most desperate circumstances. No—what we need is Flowers alive and well, and pointed in totally the wrong direction."

"Let me do some research," Kerns said.

"Things are moving fast . . ."

"Won't take long."

8

Virgil was sitting on the screened porch at Johnson's cabin just before dark when Johnson stopped by: "Me'n Clarice are going down to Friday's, you wanna come along?"

"Thanks anyway, Johnson. I need to do some reading."

"Clarice said you stopped by the office to look down her cleavage, and had some photographs of a spreadsheet. You want me to take a look?"

Johnson bore a slight resemblance to a bear, but had made a lot of money in a variety of businesses, and despite the jean jackets, tattoos, and boating, automobile, truck, airplane, and motorcycle accidents, was occasionally referred to as a "prominent businessman."

"Might as well," Virgil said. "It's all a bunch of gobbledygook to me."

He dug the pack of paper out of his briefcase and handed it over.

Johnson carried it inside, to the dining table, put on his reading glasses, and started paging through it.

Virgil's phone rang, and he looked at the screen: Sandy, his hacker.

"Why are you still at work?" he asked.

"I took the afternoon off to do some apartment shopping, if you must know. Anyway, I have some information on this Clancy Conley person, and also on Laughton."

Virgil put a legal pad on his knee, took out a pen, and said, "Give it to me."

"Conley was a drug addict, has five arrests, all as a user, never as a seller, always for amphetamine. The arrests were in Missouri, Iowa, two in Nebraska, and one in Minnesota. I'll put the details in an e-mail. As far as income goes, he shows a little over eighteen thousand last year, most of it from a newspaper called the *Republican-River*, and three thousand dollars from Minnia Marketing, which is an Internet phone-sales operation. He worked there for four months."

"Selling what?"

"As far as I can tell, almost everything. It appears that Minnia Marketing—the name comes from 'Minn,' as in Minnesota, and 'Ia,' as in Iowa—basically owns nothing except some telephones. What it does is advertise on the Internet for all kinds of things, from manufacturers where they've qualified for wholesale prices, and then when somebody orders from them, they contact the manufacturer and have the product drop-shipped to the buyer."

"They're a boiler room."

"Yup. Not a very good one," Sandy said. "They reported earnings last year of twenty-six thousand and change, after expenses and taxes."

"What else?"

"Okay, this is kind of interesting. I talked to the executive editor at the *Omaha World-Herald*, who said that when Conley wasn't high, he was a terrific police reporter, and showed signs of becoming a good investigator. Had very good instincts and big balls. But he couldn't stay away from the drugs, and finally they had to fire him. I found it interesting that he was supposedly really good . . . which could bear on your case."

"Yes, it could," Virgil said, thinking of the photos. Through the porch window, he could see Johnson bent over the spreadsheets. "Send everything you've got by e-mail. This is all good. Now, what about Laughton?"

"Another interesting case," she said. "Last year he reported income of thirty-one thousand and change. So maybe he got a sweetheart deal on the truck? I wouldn't know. I do know his income tax returns don't show either gains or losses from investments, which should mean that he doesn't have any. What's more interesting is this guy, who doesn't make any money, showed a real-estate tax deduction for four thousand dollars for a house in Tucson, Arizona. I checked on a real-estate site, and he apparently bought it two years ago, and probably for cash, for three hundred and ninety-eight thousand dollars—I can't find a mortgage document anywhere."

"Send me all that. And, Sandy—you're a genius."

"I know. Unfortunately, a low-ranking, outstate investigator whose most often used first name is Fuckin' is the only one who recognizes that."

THAT FUCKIN' FLOWERS took his notes back inside, where Johnson looked up and said, "Well, this is boring. Lots of these whatchama-callits. Numbers."

"You see anything?"

"A few things," Johnson said. "It looks like a purchase list from some big nonprofit organization, though I can't tell you which. County government, maybe, although it seems too big for that."

"How do you get nonprofit?"

"Because there's an entry column for taxes, but whoever it is doesn't allot money for taxes, which means it's either public or nonprofit."

"Could be the schools—schools are big."

"Huh. You're right. I never think of schools as being much . . . but they are, aren't they? Not from here, though, not from Bu-chanan County. Maybe across the river, in Wisconsin or something. Can't tell from this."

"Where do you get that?"

"Clarice said she thought some of it might be diesel fuel, and I think she's right—but the costs are too high. They're paying close to retail. With an operation this big, and with no gas taxes, I mean, they should be paying fifty cents a gallon less than this shows."

"Really."

"Really."

Virgil rubbed his nose. "If it was the local school district, and they were paying too much for gas, how would anybody know?"

Johnson said, "Well, they could be doing it two ways. They could be buying fuel from a dealer, paying too much, and getting a kickback. Fifty cents a gallon . . . I mean, holy buckets, Batman! Give me your pen."

He scribbled on some paper for a moment, adding up numbers, and when he was done, said, "I had to make some guesses, here. We got six elementary schools in the county system, a middle school, and a high school, and they all use buses. I'd guess . . . maybe fifty buses. I'd guess maybe fifteen gallons a day per bus, for two trips, one morning, one afternoon . . . say two hundred days a year . . ."

"I don't think it's that many days—"

"Not too much less, though, plus they use the buses for extracurricular activities. Virgil, if they were somehow clipping money off the fuel, that'd be . . . maybe seventy thousand dollars a year."

"If they were taking kickbacks, that means I'd have to find out who was selling diesel to them, and put that guy's ass in a crack."

"Who wouldn't want to talk about it, 'cause he'd go to jail," Johnson said.

"I could fix it so he wouldn't go to jail, but everybody else would," Virgil said. And after a few seconds, "You said there were two ways they could be doing it."

"Sure. They just cook the books. They take a bid from the diesel dealer straight up, for, say, $2.80 a gallon, then they write down in the books that they paid $3.30. That way, there's no kickback, and no outsider to know about it. You'd have to see their books to figure it out. You'd have to have an audit and so on—somebody to talk to the diesel dealer, get his records, and match them against the district's."

"Okay. Listen, Johnson, we could be on to something here," Virgil said. "This could be Conley's big story. I want you to put on your thinking pants and figure out other ways you could clip the district."

"Don't know it's the district, for sure. Not yet, anyway," Johnson said. "I'll tell you what you could do, though . . . you got all these numbers. Get somebody to look at the school budget—it's public, it's probably online—and see if you can make any of the expenditures line up. They can't be clipping everything."

"I got somebody who can do that," Virgil said.

And Johnson said, "I'll think about it: but I'll tell you, just from reading the newspaper, the big money wouldn't be in clipping the diesel. It'd be figuring out a way to clip the teachers' salaries and maybe the state's pupil payments. Both of those gotta be in the millions of dollars a year. Suppose they had five ghost employees . . ."

"Bless me," Virgil said. "If that's the case, there'd have to be several people in on it."

"Yes, there would. You know ol' Buster Gedney? His wife's on the school board."

"Do tell. I talked to her, and she didn't mention it," Virgil said. He waved at his laptop. "According to my research, he has a fifty-thousand-dollar machine shop in his garage, which he apparently paid for by selling turkey fryers out the back door."

"That's a lot of turkey fryers," Johnson said. "But these spreadsheets . . . I wonder why there's no identification on them? They just start, on page 128, and they go on for a while, and then they end. But the end is not the end of the spreadsheet."

"I suspect it's because he had several batches of photos, and I only found the last batch," Virgil said. "Maybe he could only spend a certain amount of time shooting. If that's what happened, he'd go back home and unload the photos into his laptop. Which nobody can find."

"I'd semi-buy that," Johnson said. He added, "If this story was really that important to the guy, a kind of redemption, you'd think he'd make a backup of all his computer files. The story so far. You know, in case his hard drive croaked, or his laptop got stolen."

"If he backed it up on a flash drive or a Time Capsule, it probably went with the computer," Virgil said.

"Flash drives are so last year," Johnson said. "I wonder what the chances are that he stuck them up in the Cloud?"

"Hmm. Maybe Sandy could find out for me," Virgil said. "I knew there was some reason I hung out with you."

"You mean, besides attracting women that you can make a run at?"

"Yeah. Besides that."

A TRUCK ROLLED into the yard, and they both looked out the window. "It's Clarice," Johnson said. "I called her and told her to meet me here."

Clarice came in a moment later and said, "Goddamnit, Johnson, you been reading again, without your Chapstick." She looked at Virgil, who was looking down her cleavage again. Clarice was on her way to Friday's, and looked, Virgil thought . . . nice. "His lips get chapped when he reads too much."

"Yeah, I got that," Virgil said. "You look . . . nice."

"Especially with her tits out to here," Johnson said.

Clarice's eyes narrowed. "I don't have tits, if you'll just excuse the shit out of me, Johnson. I have breasts."

Johnson agreed that she did, indeed, and Virgil nodded in agreement, and she and Johnson went out the door. "Don't let those pictures get out of sight," Johnson said. "They are something."

WHEN THEY WERE GONE, Virgil called Sandy back and asked her to start working on the Cloud concept. "Gonna need subpoenas and all that," she said.

"I'll leave that to all you large brains back at HQ," Virgil said. "Let me know what happens."

VIRGIL WENT BACK to his computer and read the e-mails that Sandy had sent earlier, the details on Conley and Laughton. When he was done, he got a Leinenkugel's from the refrigerator, kicked back on the glider, and thought about it. Was it really possible that Conley had discovered a case of public corruption, and had been killed to cover it up? If so, how big would the conspiracy have to be? How many people would have had to know about the planned killing? Had it been one guy, panicked, who decided to solve the problem? Or had it been several people?

As soon as Johnson mentioned the possibility of a big public organization, Virgil had thought of Bill Don Fuller, who'd seen Conley getting into his car in the predawn darkness, right there by the high school. . . .

He was still thinking about it when Frankie called and spent a half hour keeping him up on the happenings around the farm, and her architectural salvage business. Her second-oldest boy had taken his girlfriend up the Minnesota River to an island where he knew there were lots of raspberries, and he and his girlfriend had picked four quarts, and in the process, had gotten two of the worst cases of poison ivy in the history of poison ivy.

"They had to go into the clinic to get special stuff. Tall Bear is bad enough, but poor old Tricia went back in the bushes to pee. . . ."

"Ah, God . . ."

"Yup. Won't have to worry about Tall Bear knockin' her up for a month or so. Anyway, the Bronsons are over cutting hay, be nice if you could be home when we're doing this sometime. You missed all of last year and the first cut this year when you had to go out to Windom."

"We weren't seeing each other last year," Virgil said. "And you know how much I love baling hay. I'd give anything to be there with you."

"I'm beginning to suspect you're not telling the whole truth about that."

"Aw, Frankie . . ."

If Virgil were given a choice between following a hay wagon around a field, throwing bales, on a hot summer day, or dropping his testicles into a bear trap, he'd have to think about it. They were still talking when another call chirped in. Gomez.

"Gotta go, Frankie. Gomez is on the line. We could be moving on the meth—"

"You be careful! Take your gun!"

"Yep. Call you back." He clicked off and answered Gomez's call. "What's up?"

"They're cooking," Gomez said. "We're moving in on them. If you want to come along, get down by that bridge in the next fifteen minutes."

"I'm coming. Wait for me."

VIRGIL RAN OUT to his truck, missing a porch step and nearly falling on his face. Night had settled in since he'd started talking with Johnson. On his way north, he called Frankie back and said, "Yeah, the feds are going in. I won't be on the front line, though."

"Call me back and tell me what happened. I won't sleep until you call."

"Could be late."

"Call me."

Kind of an odd feeling, he thought, having a woman who wanted to know where you were, and what you were doing, and wanted daily updates. Virgil had been married, very briefly, three times, and he couldn't actually remember any of the other three worrying about where he was; he could remember wondering where the hell they were.

Another interesting thing about Frankie, Virgil thought, was that she had no problem with him going face-to-face with people who carried guns. Unlike some cops' wives and girlfriends, she didn't pay much attention to possible negative consequences. She her-self liked excitement, and she liked guys who liked excitement, and she thought his job was exciting.

Which it was, at times. Knowing that his job wasn't a burden on her lifted a burden off him; left him free to feel the rush.

WHEN HE GOT to the bridge on Highway NN, he was last in the line of five SUVs. He got a vest, gun, and camo jacket out of the back and hustled down to the bridge, where he found three DEA agents waiting for him. Gomez was not one of them. The three were dressed in black-and-tan night camo and were wearing vests and helmets with night-vision glasses, and had M16s dangling from their hands. They also had headsets with earbuds and microphones.

"Where's Gomez?"

"He's already up the hill," said the shortest of the three. "We've got four guys spaced around the place already, in case we get run-ners. Four more are going in now, with Gomez and Jackson behind them. We're the backstop. You got night-vision gear?"

"No, I don't."

"Gomez thought you might not. We don't have a spare set, but I've got some glow tape. I'll stick a couple inches on the back of my helmet—stay close and you shouldn't bump into any trees. If there's trouble, I'll pull the tape off, and you get behind something solid, and wait. We've got an audio link for you, so you can hear what's happening, and talk to us if you have to. There shouldn't be too much trouble. We expect to be right on top of them before they can move. After we leave here, try not to talk unless you have to. Voices carry in the night."

"I've got a Godzilla-rated flashlight in the truck," Virgil said.

"You might want to get it. Just make sure you don't accidentally turn it on."

Virgil went back and got a 2800-lumen flashlight, of the kind that poachers used to jacklight deer; in fact, he'd gotten it from a game warden. He slung the carry bag over his shoulder and went back to the DEA guys. One of them gave Virgil an earbud and a microphone that attached around his neck, with a microphone that looked like a stick and pointed at his mouth. It was hand-activated by a button set at the base of his throat. When he'd figured it out, which took about eighteen seconds, they set off across the first field, and Virgil wondered, *What if the assholes have a lookout up on that ridge?* Of course, if they did, they'd have already started running.

STAYING WITH THE GUY with the glow tape wasn't a problem, and while there wasn't much moon, there was enough to light up the overall landscape. The biggest problem was stepping into holes or onto bumps, and he stumbled a few times as they crossed the field.

The leader stopped at the far fence, held the top strands of barbed wire as Virgil climbed over it, and then they were in the trees and climbing. The climbing was actually easier than walking through the field, because it was slower, and he was only a couple feet behind the guy in front of him, and could sense what the other man was doing. The biggest sensory input was olfactory: he could smell the damp earth beneath the matted oak leaves, and the brush they were passing through, and thought of Tricia and the poison ivy. . . .

At the crest of the hill they turned down the game path to the notch in the bluff. A voice in his ear said, "I'm going to give you the rope. You've been down here once before, so you know—just use the rope to keep your balance. Don't try to hang from it, or anything. Stick your hand out."

Virgil did, and a nearly invisible shape put a rope in his hand. He turned and backed down through the notch in the bluff, feeling his way. At the bottom, a man's hand clapped him on the back and whispered, "You're good."

TWO MINUTES LATER a new voice, which might have been Gomez, spoke through the earbud. "We're cocked. Everybody set? We go in five. Four. Three . . ."

At "Go!" a half-dozen lights exploded through the forest and the screaming started and then a calm Gomez said, "We've got two runners. Danny, one of them's coming right at you. The other one's coming right at Raleigh."

Another new voice: "Raleigh here. He's gone up the hill. You guys in the notch, spread out, I'm looking for him."

A brilliant light down to their right swiveled toward them and burst through the trees like a flight of arrows. Virgil put a hand up to protect his eyes. Gomez said, "Mike, watch the guy by the door, he's got his hand low, watch his hand, watch his hand . . ."

Somebody started screaming about hands, and Virgil, able to see again, began drifting down the hillside. The three DEA agents with him were moving forward, to his right, and a voice in his ear said, "Virgil, the trail's right below you, twenty feet. Stay back and if I tell you, use that flash of yours to illuminate it. You got all that?"

"Five by five," Virgil said. He pulled the flash out of its bag. It was made of plastic, but was heavy, with an oversized rechargeable battery down in the handle.

Somebody else said, quietly, "Here he comes," and then somebody else said, "Shit, he's turned down, I think he saw us—"

"No, no, no . . . He's on the trail. He's on the trail—"

"No, no, there are two of them, two of them, goddamnit . . ."

Virgil felt the trail underfoot, and now could see well down to his right; to his left he could make out the opening in the overhead above the path, a lighter streak in the dark woods, and somebody said, "Virgil, one of them's coming at you. The other one's going sideways down the hill. Stay low. If anybody uses a gun, I'm going to light him up."

He didn't mean with a flashlight; he meant with a machine gun.

Virgil crouched by the trail, making himself into a stump, and heard footfalls coming fast. Virgil said into the microphone, "Virgil here. Anybody running up the trail?"

"No, just the one guy. I'm trying to get in front of him, but I don't think I'm gonna make it, I'm— Ah, shit!" The voice in his ear stopped but the same voice, shouting in the clear, "I fell, I'm down, I fell . . ."

The man running up the trail was close now. Virgil waited until he thought he could see motion against the background, then hit the runner in the face with all 2800 lumens. The man shouted something unintelligible, and he was right there, right on top of Virgil, about to go by, and Virgil stuck out a leg and the man tripped over it and went down, hard, grunted, tried to get back to his feet just as Virgil was trying to stand up, and their legs got tangled and they went down again, and the man hit Virgil in the shoulder with what felt like a gun—fuck that, it was a gun—and Virgil smashed him in the face with the end of the flashlight.

The man dropped and stopped moving, and Virgil pointed the flash at him. He was on his back with a wicked cut across his forehead, his eyes full of blood; but he was breathing, and Virgil didn't see any brains leaking out.

A gun lay by his side, and Virgil used the toe of his boot to edge it off the trail. Somebody was screaming in the clear about somebody running down the hill, and Virgil turned the thermonuclear flash that way, the light smashing between the tree trunks. He picked up a thin figure, moving fast, and what might have been a hint of red hair, and then the man was gone.

Virgil pressed the button at his throat and said, "I got one down here, he was armed, another's heading out toward the mouth of the valley. I think it might be Zorn. Watch for guns . . ."

One of the DEA agents ran into the lighted area of the trail and called, "Where?" and Virgil pointed with the flash, and the agent went crashing off through the brush, and a few seconds later, was followed by a second man.

The man with Virgil groaned and tried to sit up, but Virgil pushed him back down. Virgil said, "Lay back. You're hurt. We need to get you to a doctor."

"What happened?" the man asked. "Did I wreck the truck?"

"More like assault with battery," Virgil said.

One of the DEA agents came up, looked at the man, and asked, "How bad?"

"Might have a concussion. I hit him with the flashlight. Gun's right there by the side of the trail."

"Okay. Let's get some cuffs on him. We got an ambulance one minute out."

"That was quick," Virgil said.

"No, we had it waiting, just in case. It's on its way up the valley now."

WHEN VIRGIL GOT DOWN to the sheds, five men were sitting on the ground, hands cuffed behind them, looking like prisoners of war. "We lost one of them," Gomez said. "We saw two runners, but there were three. Bricks and Mortar are down at Zorn's place, his old lady says he's up in the Cities. We said, 'So what's his cell phone number, we need to call him.' She said he doesn't have one. We said, 'Everybody has a cell phone.' She pulls out a wooden kitchen match, scratches it on the screen door, fires up a Camel, and says, 'Fuck you.'"

"That's a high-class hillbilly, right there," Virgil said.

"Yes, it is. Anyway, we got the crew, we got the sheds, we got the makings. We'll make a movie of it all, and package it up for the U.S. Attorney. He'll find the weak sister, and get him to talk about Zorn. Good job all the way around."

"What about the drone?"

"Ah, it broke."

"It broke?"

"Yeah, it broke. Don't mention it, okay? I mean, if anybody asks. We've got some bugs to work out."

VIRGIL LOOKED at the group of sitting men and asked, "You mind if I talk to the POWs?"

"They've all asked for attorneys, so you won't get anything usable."

"I don't need it for a court. I just need some information."

Gomez shrugged: "Go ahead."

Virgil walked over to the prisoners, who were sitting in a shallow semicircle, all dressed in jeans and boots and work shirts, looking more like lumberjacks than dope manufacturers. He squatted down and said, "You all get attorneys, and you don't have to answer any questions at all, but I've got one that doesn't have anything to do with this."

They all glanced at each other, then one of them said, "We're not talking."

Virgil: "You all look like country people to me, and some of you probably got dogs, and like dogs. Some asshole up this valley has been stealing dogs, including some pretty good hunting dogs. We know what they're going to do with them—they're going to sell them off to medical laboratories for experiments. Now, I know you wouldn't want that to happen to your dogs. . . . So, you know anything at all about these stolen dogs? Where they might be? We know you don't have them, but somebody up this valley does."

After a few seconds one of the men said, "We didn't have nothing to do with no dogs."

"I'm not claiming that anybody did," Virgil said. "You had other business up here. But I'm not DEA, I'm not a fed—I'm just trying to get these dogs back to their owners."

"There's some dogs on the other side of the valley, I don't know where at," one of the men said.

"Shut up, Eddy," said another one of them. "You know we're not supposed to say anything."

"Fuck you, Dick," Eddy said. "The man's asking about dogs. Nothing to do with us." He turned back to Virgil and said, "They sound like they're close to the front end of the valley, high up on the other side."

A third man volunteered, "Something weird about it, though. You won't hear nothin' at all, then you'll hear a lot of dogs, all of a sudden, but the volume is down low, like they're a long ways off. Then the volume gets turned up, and that goes on for a while, and then it gets turned down. The barking keeps going, but the volume gets turned down, until you can't hear them at all. It's like they're on an amp."

"That is a strange fuckin' thing," Eddy said. "I heard that myself. The barking just fades away, like when you're listening to an AM radio out on the prairie, in your car, and the radio signal starts to fade out."

"Huh. Lots of dogs?"

"Lot of them," said the man called Dick, who'd told Eddy to shut up. "I wondered what the hell was going on over there."

"Anybody know what a beagle sounds like?"

"They got beagles, I think," Eddy said. "That's a sorrowful sound, when an unhappy beagle gets going. Could be bassets, though."

"Thanks, guys," Virgil said. He patted Eddy on the shoulder as he stood up.

He walked back to Gomez, who said, "You got a very strange job, Virgil."

THE AMBULANCE HAD SHOWN UP on the road below them, and the paramedics had carried a stretcher up the hill. They loaded up the man Virgil had hit, and then a van showed up down below and a couple of feds got out and looked up at them.

"Crime scene," Gomez said. "The bureaucracy begins."

Virgil hung around for a while, as the bureaucracy got going. Gomez asked, "You remember Matt Travers, the regional guy out of Washington?"

"I met him."

"He said to tell you we've still got a job, if you want it."

"Man, I appreciate it, but I like it here," Virgil said.

"You could get a whole fuckin' state if you came with us. Get some guys working for you . . . It's kinda fun, if you like that kind of fun."

"I'll think about it . . . but I'm just being polite. You guys are the most interesting feds, no doubt about it, but like I said . . ."

"You like it here."

"Yes, I do."

9

VIRGIL CAUGHT A RIDE to his truck with one of the DEA agents, and on the way back to Johnson's cabin, called Frankie and told her about the raid.

"Goddamnit, I wish I'd been there."

"Maybe you ought to be a cop," Virgil suggested.

After a moment of silence she said, "Nah. I'd feel too sorry for most of the people I arrested. But I would like to run around screaming and yelling and chasing through the woods."

"Well, shoot, we could do that at your place," Virgil said. "Naked."

"Aw, Virgie . . ."

VIRGIL CALLED JOHNSON: it was well past midnight, but Johnson had called him at three o'clock in the morning about rescuing some dogs. Johnson answered the phone: he didn't sound sleepy, he sounded interrupted.

"What?"

"We cleaned out the meth labs. We need to get the posse together tomorrow. We're going after the dogs."

"You called me at one o'clock in the morning about some dogs?"

Virgil could hear Clarice laughing in the background. Satisfied, Virgil hung up, and when he got to the cabin, fell into bed.

THE POSSE MET the next day at high noon, at Shanker's: nine guys and a woman in various pieces of camo, plus a sheriff's deputy named Boyce, but who everyone called "Bongo," which caused Virgil to worry. Only he and Bongo would be armed, he told everybody, and he caught a quick flash of eyes between some of the men, which meant that a few of them probably had sidearms tucked into their belts.

"Listen, I'm serious now, if anybody other than myself and Bongo is carrying a gun, I'm telling you, leave it in your truck," Virgil said. "If I see one up on that hill, I'll send you home."

Communications would be through a whole bunch of hunter's walkie-talkies, since phones didn't always work up in the deep valleys. One guy suggested that the slower climbers—"You know who you are"—stay behind to look after the vehicles. "These hillbillies, if they thought they were gonna lose the dogs, they'd come down and slash our tires, or worse."

"Whatever happens to the vehicles, don't go shooting anybody," he said. "If you're watching the trucks, and anybody gives you trouble, you yell for help and we'll come running."

Virgil explained how the process would work: "This is basically just a search of public property. Before last night's meth lab raid, the federal agents did quite a bit of research, in an effort to find out who would be legally responsible for the meth lab—who the landowner would be. As it turns out, the privately owned land involves fairly compact tracts bordering on the road, and going no more than a couple hundred yards back. The forest land along most of the top and sides of the valley is state forest. So we'll be on public land. We'll spread out across from it, with me in the center and Bongo at the top near the bluffs, and Johnson Johnson at the bottom, along the edge of the privately owned land. We'll climb up from the shoulder of the highway, so we never cross private land. And, by doing it that way, we might surprise somebody. That's gonna be a tough climb though, so if any of you people have heart problems . . ."

WHEN ALL WAS said and done, two of the guys opted to stay with the cars. The rest were prepared to climb. With that all settled, they loaded into their pickups and SUVs and trucked on up Highway 26 in a caravan.

Virgil led them to the shoulder of the road, and after the car-watchers were subtracted, nine of them began climbing the steep hill just south of the entrance to the valley. The hill was roughly as high as the Washington Monument, climbing through weeds and sumac and, higher up, scrubby oaks and then full-sized oaks. When they got into the tree line, Virgil called for a rest, and they sat on the hill and looked out over the Mississippi, and didn't talk much. Virgil gave them ten full minutes, and then they resumed the climb. They stopped once more, for another ten minutes, talking via the walkie-talkies to the trucks below.

Another ten minutes saw them to the top of the hill at the end of the valley; there would be more hill to climb later, but at the moment they walked single file, bunched too close for a combat patrol, over the edge to the downhill slope of the south valley wall.

Virgil spread them out down the hill, with Johnson on the bottom and Bongo at the top. Virgil was in the middle, and they began walking west. They'd walked perhaps a quarter-mile when Bongo called and said, "Hey, we got something up here. Looks like a pen. Another twenty-five yards, right under that yellow bluff."

Virgil got on his radio and said, "Okay, guys, let's climb up to the bluff."

They all began clumping up the hill, and could smell the cage before they got to it. When they got to the bluff, they found Bongo and the four guys who'd been above Virgil looking at a chain-link fence, a semicircle with the bluff forming the back side. Inside the wire was a lot of raw dirt, a lot of dog shit, and three beaten-up dogs who wobbled to their feet when they saw the men walking up to the fence. Scattered inside the fence were a bunch of plastic tubs; most were empty, the others contained some water.

Bongo said, "Looks like they moved them."

One of the men said, "Those dogs . . . don't know those dogs, but they look like they're starving."

The fence had a gate, but no lock. Virgil flipped the latch and they all filed inside. Two of the dogs tried to get away from them, backing away to the far edge of the fence, tails between their legs. The third one sidled toward them, licking his muzzle nervously, head down, tail between his legs. They were dogs of no identifiable breed: mutts. All three of them were about knee-high.

"We waited too long, we moved too slow," somebody said.

"How'd they get them out? Looks like there were a lot of dogs here, and nobody's gone out of here in the last week, with a truck big enough for a lot of dogs."

"Took them out one or two at a time . . . people coming and going all the time. Somebody must've tipped them off that we were watching," Bongo said.

"That doesn't sound right," Virgil said. "They knew somebody was watching, but a whole crew of professional meth dealers goes in anyway, and has no clue?"

"I want to know where they went, the dogs," one of the men said. "What we need to do, is figure out who had them up here, and then beat the information out of him."

Johnson said, "We know they were here. I say we send one guy back to the trucks with the three dogs we got, and then the rest of us walk back to the end of the valley. Maybe there's more than one place."

They decided to do that. The three dogs they found were leashed up and taken back down the hill, while the rest of them spread out over the hillside again and began walking. An hour later, tired, hot, and mosquito-bit, they walked down the hill to the spring.

Virgil said, "I'll tell you what, boys. The feds heard the dogs up there yesterday afternoon, so I don't know exactly how we missed them. But I'll be working the road down here, starting today. I'll find out what happened. I promise you. Pisses me off."

"We'll ask some questions around," one of the posse members said. "See what we can find out. Maybe they took them over the top, and out some other way. Maybe the meth raid scared them."

"We'll find out," Virgil said.

THE PEOPLE at the trucks brought two trucks up to haul the posse back to the parked caravan. There wasn't quite enough room for everybody, so Johnson went to get the truck, and Virgil sat on a rock at the edge of the pool and watched the water, and after a couple of moments saw a dimple of the kind made by trout. He pulled a long stem of grass out of a clump next to the rock and chewed on it for a moment, thinking about the dogs, and then a boy's voice said, "Find them?"

Virgil turned and saw the kid they'd met the first day they'd come up the valley. He was standing on the other side of the fence, with his rifle slung across his shoulder, holding it in place with one hand. "No, no, we didn't," Virgil said. "Well, we found three dogs in a big pen up next to the bluff, looking pretty beat up, but not the big bunch of them we were looking for. You know where the rest of them went?"

"No, I don't. I watched those federal agents pull off that raid last night, and I heard the dogs early this morning, but . . . if you couldn't find them, I don't know where they might've gone."

"You've seen that pen up there?"

"No, my dad told me to stay away from there. Plenty of places to walk out west, and more interesting," the kid said. "Funny thing was, I heard them this morning, and now you say, no dogs."

"Huh," Virgil said. "When you say you watched the feds pull off that raid . . . you were up there?"

"Oh, yeah. I saw the feds sneaking in there, every day, and then last night I saw the drug guys going in, so I figured the raid would be coming, and I went over to watch. Were you up there?"

"Yeah. Sort of out on the end of things, down the road. Saw a guy running away, and we never did catch him."

"Yeah, that was probably Roy Zorn. I saw him take off as soon as the lights came on and you-all started yelling at them."

"You know for sure it was Zorn?"

"Well, yeah. I mean, I couldn't see his face, but he moved through the woods like Roy does."

"Okay."

Virgil stood up and dusted off his pants and asked, "Your folks up at the house?"

"My dad is. My mom died."

"Sorry about that. Mind if I talk to your dad?"

"He was asleep when I left." He looked up at the sky and said, "Probably awake now, though." Virgil thought, *Holy shit, he looked up at the sky to see what time it is.*

The kid pointed out a driveway that came off the road down fifty yards or so. "You walk right up the drive, it's a way, but it's easy. Or you can drive up, when your buddy gets back."

"He oughta be here in a couple of minutes," Virgil said. "We can wait."

"I'll see you up there," the kid said.

"What's your name?" Virgil called after him.

"McKinley," the kid called back, as he faded into the brush. "McKinley Ruff."

JOHNSON JOHNSON SHOWED UP three or four minutes later, driving Virgil's truck. Virgil took the wheel, and told Johnson about the kid as they bounced up the gravel driveway, past a mailbox that said "Ruff." The driveway came off at right angles to the street, but then took a left turn and led straight west, past the pound, and four hundred yards deeper into the valley.

At the end of the track was a rambling house with a brown-stained rough board siding, a wide covered front porch, and a low-pitched roof covered with cedar shingles. A garden spread off to one side, heavy with the vine plants—squash, cucumbers, watermelon—and a half-dozen fruit trees were spotted around the side yard. A metal shed, which would probably take four cars, was set well back from the house and partly obscured by trees.

"Not bad," Johnson said. "I could live here."

McKinley Ruff was waiting for them on the porch, his rifle still cradled in his arm. "Reminds me of myself, when I was his age," Johnson said. "If it wasn't a gun, it was a fishing rod. Three whole summers like that, and then I discovered women. Which was a lot more dangerous than any gun. As you would know."

"Not a bad-looking place, but speaking of peckerwoods, I have a feeling that the Ruffs could qualify."

"We'll see," Johnson said.

They got out of the truck and walked up to the house and Virgil noticed that Johnson's shirt was hanging loose, which meant that he was probably packing. Not a good time to object, Virgil thought.

McKinley Ruff said, "Dad's inside, transposing. He said you should come on in."

Virgil and Johnson glanced at each other: transposing?

They followed McKinley through the screen door and the heavy front door behind it, where they found the elder Ruff sitting at a plank table with a pile of paper in front of him. Standing in ranks along one wall were eight or nine guitars on guitar stands, two keyboards, and an older upright piano, a bunch of amps and other electronic music equipment, including a drum machine.

Ruff was a scruffy-looking man, a little overweight, wearing silver glasses. His hair fell almost to his shoulders, and he wore a short but poorly trimmed gray beard. When they came in, he looked up and said, "Hey, there. I understand Muddy's been talking to you. You're the cops, right?"

"Right," Virgil said. "You're a musician?"

Ruff's eyebrows went up. He looked around the room for a few seconds and then said, "Jeez, I hope so, since I got thirty thousand dollars' worth of guitars and fifty grand worth of other shit."

Virgil said, "McKinley, uh, Muddy, uh, didn't mention . . . You call him Muddy?"

"Sure. We named him after Muddy Waters. Muddy's real name was McKinley Morganfield," Ruff said. "Anyway, what can we do for you? You're looking for those dogs?"

"Yeah, you know about them?"

"Just what Muddy told me. And we can hear them howling in the mornings. That's about it."

"But they're gone now," Johnson said.

"They were howling this morning. They usually start around seven o'clock or so, at least on the mornings when I'm up then."

"Always about then," McKinley said. "Lasts about ten or fifteen minutes, then they shut up again."

"Where are they at?" Johnson asked.

"South side, I'd say down toward the far end. Pretty high up," Ruff said.

McKinley said, "That's about right."

Ruff said, "I told Muddy to stay away from there. There's a bad element out here, moved in over the past five or six years. Real white trash. I understand you busted some of them last night."

"A meth lab—nothing to do with dogs," Virgil said.

"Good riddance. But I saw Zorn down the road a while ago, so you didn't get him."

"You think he's involved?"

"Of course he is," Ruff said. "Although I wouldn't be surprised if his old lady was the real brains behind the business. There's a god-damned snake if you ever met one."

Ruff had no proof of anything, just rumors and gossip picked up from the neighbors. "Lotsa these places down here were cabins, there's sort of a communal landing down under the bridge. Then the economy went to hell, and a lot of them got sold off cheap, and the trash moved in."

To pinpoint the dogs, Ruff suggested that they contact a neighbor called Ralph Huntington. "He's a good ol' boy, and he lives right down there. I wouldn't go there in a car, though. That might cause him some trouble. Give him a call."

He had Huntington's phone number, and Virgil wrote it down. "What's your name?"

"Julius. Ruff. R-U-F-F."

Johnson asked, "You play in a band, or something?"

"I play in three or four of them, mostly over in La Crosse," Ruff said. "Polka, country, big band jazz, and sometimes with the chamber orchestra up in St. Paul, when they need a competent guitar." He looked closely at Johnson for a minute, then said, "The one you'd probably be familiar with is Dog Butt."

Johnson brightened. "Really? You play with Dog Butt?"

"I am the man behind the sound," Ruff said.

"I like that song 'Goose Gone Truckin',' " Johnson said.

Muddy said, "Dad wrote that."

"Are you kiddin' me? Man alive, you got some serious talent. . . ."

BACK IN THE TRUCK Virgil said, "Jesus, I thought I'd stepped into old home week."

"Hey, Dog Butt is a good band," Johnson said. "Tight. They got two lead singers, a man and a woman, taking turns, and honest to God, you can boogey your ass off. You take your woman to hear Dog Butt, and you don't get laid that night, you got a problem."

"I will look into that," Virgil said.

"Fine. But what we really got to look into is the dogs," Johnson said. "This morning's hike did not go down smooth with the guys.

I'm a little worried, really. I don't know what would happen if Zorn stopped in at Shanker's at the wrong time. I even started wondering if we have a spy in the group—I mean, everybody said that nothing came out of this valley big enough to carry a lot of dogs, and we know people have heard a lot of dogs up there, but when we look— there aren't any."

"Only in the mornings, and then they shut up," Virgil said, look- ing up at the hillside as they rolled out toward the end of the valley. "There's something in that. It's been mentioned a couple times: they bark, and then they shut up."

"Not up there now. We didn't miss much, this morning."

"Not much, but maybe some small thing," Virgil said.

10

Virgil dropped Johnson in town, back at his truck. "What are you gonna do next?" Johnson asked. "You gonna work on the dogs, or waste more time on that Conley thing?"

"Gotta waste some time on Conley, to keep up appearances," Virgil said. "He was shot to death on a public highway."

After dropping Johnson, Virgil drove back to the cabin to take a shower and change clothes. He hadn't wanted to stop at the house of Ralph Huntington, the name given to him by Ruff, to ask about the dogs, because Huntington lived almost across the road from Zorn.

Instead, he called the number he'd gotten from Ruff, and when nobody answered, went to take his shower.

Out of the shower, he ate a bowl of cereal and tried to figure out who might have a copy of the school district's budget, other than the district itself. He called the Department of Education and got a runaround of such massive proportions that he finally gave up: his feeling was, they had one, but nobody knew where it was, and nobody was inclined to look for it.

He talked to Sandy again. "I don't want you to do anything illegal, but if you could take just the quickest peek inside the DOE's computers, it'd be nice to find a digital copy of the Buchanan County Consolidated School's annual budget. It ought to be in there somewhere."

"You try the public library down there in Trippton? They'd probably have one."

"I was just on my way there," Virgil lied. "I wanted to get you started, in case they don't have one."

"Liar," she said.

THE PUBLIC LIBRARY had a librarian who caused Virgil, at first look, to think, *Now, that's a librarian.* She was tall, her dark hair pulled back in a bun, and she had what Virgil's mom called "a good figure." She also wore rectangular gold-rimmed glasses. If she'd had an overbite, Virgil thought, the world would have been complete, but she didn't.

He came in, waited at the vacant librarian's desk for a moment; the good-looking librarian glanced at him, then went back to filing something. Another librarian, a cheery short woman with a round face, started toward him from the magazine racks when the tall one finished filing and stepped back to the desk. "Looking for a quick read?"

"Hmm, well, I'm actually looking for a copy of the, uh . . ." He couldn't remember for a moment, then quickly filled in, "The, uh, budget for the school district."

"I don't know if we'd have that," she said.

The round-faced woman, who'd arrived only a step behind the tall one, said, "Sure we do. But I think it's checked out."

Virgil: "Checked out? Somebody checked out the school budget?"

"I think so. Let me check the system." She went over to the desktop computer and typed for a while, and then said, "Yup. It's checked out."

"Could you tell me who's got it?"

"No, we're not allowed to do that," the tall one said.

"I'm an agent with the Bureau of Criminal Apprehension," Virgil said. "I'm investigating the Clancy Conley murder. I really would like to see that budget."

"I'm sorry. Still can't. We would probably submit to a subpoena, but we'd have to have a board meeting to decide that," the tall one said.

"What?"

"A board meeting," she said. "We have a board made up of—"

"I know what a board is. All I want to do is look at the godforsaken school budget for a couple of minutes."

The short one said, "If you leave your phone number, we could call the person who's checked it out and see if she—"

"Or he . . ." the tall one interjected.

"Or he would be willing to return it. Then we could call you and you could come in and look at it."

"We just can't give out our readers' names to any police official who comes waltzing through here," the tall one said.

Virgil said, "Man . . . all I wanted . . ." The tall one gave him the bureaucrat's death stare, and he folded. "All right, I'll give you the number."

He gave the number to the tall one, and stalked out of the place, fuming. Thirty feet down the street, his phone rang, an unknown number. He answered: "Virgil Flowers."

"Hey, this is the chubby one, back at the library. Don't ever let Virginia know I told you, because she can be an enormous pain in the ass, but it was borrowed by Janice Anderson. You want her address?"

He did.

The short one gave it to him, and added, "Janice is a little nuts, so go easy with her."

"How nuts? Does she carry a gun?"

"No, no gun. A gun isn't nuts, that's just Monday in Trippton. Anyway, Janice thinks the school spends too much money on math, science, and sports, and not enough on the arts."

"That's outrageous," Virgil said.

"Like I said, take it easy with her."

JANICE ANDERSON was an elderly white-haired woman who came to the porch door leaning on a cane, and asked through the glass of a screen door in which the screen hadn't been installed, "Who are you?"

Virgil showed her his ID. He was wearing his cowboy boots, well polished, and a black sport coat over a vintage Guy Clark "Old Pair of Boots" T-shirt. He was carrying his briefcase. She looked at him, and the credentials, with some skepticism, but said politely, "Give me a moment."

She went away, and came back ninety seconds later and unlatched the door and said, "Come in."

"You found somebody to vouch for me?"

"The sheriff. He said you looked like a hippie who's lost the faith, or a cowboy who's lost his horse. That fits."

"Remind me to shoot the sheriff," Virgil said, as he stepped inside.

"Say, isn't that an old Eric Clapton song?"

"I think it is," Virgil said.

"Bob Marley, too. Probably before your time," she said. She took him into what once would have been called a parlor, and pointed at a couch with her cane, said, "Sit there," and took a high-backed chair.

Virgil sat down, his elbow falling on a couple of poetry collections edited by Garrison Keillor, which sat on a side table, atop a yellowed lace doily.

"What can I do for you?" Anderson asked. "I didn't know Clancy Conley, other than by sight."

"I need to look at the school budget," Virgil said. He patted his briefcase. "I understand you checked it out of the library."

Her eyebrows went up. "The school budget? The state finally figured out what's going on with all this science and math bullshit?"

"No, no. I'm strictly working on the Conley case. Well, and a couple other things. But I need to look at the budget."

She used the cane to push herself up out of the chair, winced, and said, "Let me get it."

"Are you okay?"

"No, I'm not. I cracked my hip a few months ago and it hasn't quite healed," she said.

"Sorry to hear that," Virgil said, as she limped toward the kitchen. "How'd you do it?"

"I was skateboarding on the levee and lost my edges," she said.

"You were skateboarding?"

She turned and looked at him and shook her head in exasperation: "No, you dummy, I fell. On the ice. On the sidewalk. Like old people do."

Virgil: "Oh."

She shook her head again. "Jesus wept."

SHE BROUGHT BACK the school budget document, which was thinner than Virgil expected, thinner even than the sheaf of papers he was carrying—and since the papers were only part of somebody's budget, it seemed unlikely that it was the school's.

Anderson watched him thumbing through the school document for a moment, then asked, "Exactly what are you looking for?"

He thought about not answering, but couldn't think of any good reason to do that. So he told her: "I found a bunch of photos of a spreadsheet in Conley's camera, and I thought it was possible that it was the school district's budget. But the budget just isn't big enough."

"I know all about this stuff," she said. "Let me look at the spreadsheets."

Virgil hesitated again, and said, "It's gotta be just between you and me."

"I can keep a secret," Anderson said.

"Good, because one guy has already been murdered," Virgil said. "I'd hate to find out that your hip was better, but your neck was broken."

"Give me the spreadsheets."

She took them, thumbed through the stack of prints, and said, "Yes, this is the school. What you're looking at here is the specific line-item list of everything they buy. The budget itself is not so specific—but the title headings are the same for each section. Look here . . ."

She pointed out that the names for the various sections were identical, and in the same order. "Of course, it's possible that this is a standard form, so every school in the state would use the same section names . . . but I don't think so. I think this is the Buchanan County budget."

"You know who the auditor is?" Virgil asked.

"Fred Masilla. He's with Masilla, Oder, Decker and Somebody Else up in Winona."

"You know how long he's been working for the schools?"

"Nope. But a pretty long time," Anderson said. "You think he's a crook?"

"Do you?"

"I wouldn't rule it out," she said. "If there's something funny going on with the school money, he'd pretty much have to know about it."

"Then he sounds like the guy to talk to," Virgil said.

"Shouldn't you have something to hold over his head before you do that?"

"I already do. It's called selective immunity—he pleads guilty and turns state's evidence, and we give him a break on the sentence."

"What if he tells you to take a hike?"

"They don't usually do that," Virgil said, "because by the time we ask them, we've already got enough to hang them with. We don't negotiate, and we don't give them a second chance if they turn us down the first time."

"Sounds like a nasty business, but not uninteresting," she said.

"Thank you for the uninteresting," Virgil said. "Too many people would have said disinteresting."

"Do I look like a fuckin' moron?"

WHEN VIRGIL LEFT ANDERSON'S, he was confident that he'd found at least a piece of the story that Conley had been working on. Thinking about Conley got him thinking about the crime-scene work at Conley's trailer, and he called Paul Alewort, the sheriff department's crime-scene specialist, and asked if he was done processing the trailer.

"Yeah, we finished late last night. Got nothing for you. The only thing that's not quite right is that missing laptop—didn't find anything that might suggest where it is. Was he killed for it? Beats me."

"Could I get in to take another look at the place?"

"Sure. Are you in town?"

"Yes."

"I'm at the office. Stop by and I'll give you a key."

VIRGIL PICKED UP the key and drove up to Conley's trailer, let himself in. The place was a mess: Alewort had warned him that they'd torn it apart. Everything had been taken from every drawer and closet, and piled on every flat surface: tables, countertops, bed, and floor. Virgil poked through the detritus of Conley's life: dozens of movies, including a half-dozen girl-on-girl pornos, a hundred music CDs, mostly grunge and punk, stacks of paid bills and newspaper clippings of stories he'd written, a two-foot-high stack of printouts of stories, a shelf of science fiction novels, all in paperback. A tangled mass of computer cables and accessories had all been stuffed in a plastic box. A jar of pennies sat on the floor next to the bed.

Virgil poured the pennies on the floor and found nothing but lots of pennies. He scooped them back into the jar. On one of the tables he found a half box of .38 shells; both the box and the shells looked new.

That was interesting, because it suggested that Conley had bought the shells for a new threat, but what Virgil really needed was a more substantial account of the story that Conley was working. There was nothing at all in the printouts—and he couldn't find any reporter's notebooks. He'd seen some at Laughton's place, with spiral binding at the top, like narrow steno notebooks.

After an hour he gave up, but left with the feeling that the place had been cleaned out by somebody. Who might have access to Conley's keys? The landlord, for sure, but . . .

He liked Vike Laughton for it. If Conley had ever left his keys on his desk, Laughton could have walked down to the hardware store and duplicated the key. If he ever came up with more evidence, Virgil would talk to the people who ran the store.

Outside, he looked down into the valley for a minute or two, looking for deer. Saw squirrels, but no deer. He gave a push to the tire swing as he went by, got in the truck, and headed back to town.

ON THE WAY, he called a friend at the state attorney general's office and asked about the possibility of a surprise audit of the Buchanan County school system, based on a limited amount of evidence of embezzlement.

His friend said, "We could do that, but it'll be a while."

"How long is a while?"

"A few months. The department that does that kind of a thing is always jammed up. Not a lot of money for investigating politicians. If you know what I mean."

"It could be tied to a murder," Virgil said.

"How strong is the tie?"

"Somewhat strong."

"Give me a call back when it's really strong, and I'll go talk to the AG."

HE CALLED JOHNSON, who said, "I'm in the office. Come on by."

He went on by, and found Johnson sitting on a battered leather couch, feet up, watching a Moonshine Bandits video called "Dive Bar Beauty Queen." Johnson pointed a longneck Leinie's at the TV screen and said, "This is the future of American music, right here."

"Certainly explains your attachment to a band called Dog Butt."

"So you're telling me that this isn't the future of American music?"

Virgil watched the rest of the video and then said, "No, I wouldn't tell you that. You may be right. You ought to go out and buy some Moonshine Bandit stock."

"Would if I could," Johnson said. Then, "What about the dogs?"

"I was gonna ask you—what about the dog guys? I hope they're not pushing my luck."

"Something's gonna happen there, Virgil. I'll keep you up on it, best I can, but they know we're friends. They might stop talking to me."

"Do what you can. I'm gonna go jack up the sheriff, see if he'll put another guy on it."

PURDY WAS RELUCTANT. "What's one guy going to do? You went up there this morning and didn't find anything."

"I'm just hoping to keep the posse from going freelance."

"Well, if you hear anything like that going on, give me a call and we'll get on it. I'll have Bongo keep an ear to the ground, too. He knows all those guys."

BY THE TIME he left the sheriff's office, it was getting late. He decided to swing past Buster Gedney's house, to put a little more squeeze on him. When he got there, the house was dark: nobody home. The squeeze was going to have to wait.

The town was closing down for the evening, and there wasn't much more he could do. He went to Ma & Pa's Kettle for a light dinner, and then Johnson called and said that he and Clarice were going to an art film at the Masonic Lodge; Virgil went and it turned out to be *Mulholland Drive*.

At nine o'clock he felt his phone vibrating against his leg. Purdy was calling. Virgil left as quietly as he could, and had just gotten to the vestibule when the message chime went off. He looked at it, and it was from Purdy and said: "Call me. Urgent."

He called.

"Virgil. Goddamnit, you and those dog guys. You know that guy Zorn that you say was cookin' that meth? And probably had something to do with the dogs?"

"Yeah?"

"He just got ambushed and shot to death on his driveway up on Orly's Crick. Get your ass up there. I'm on the way."

11

VIRGIL WAS AT the crime scene fifteen minutes after he went running out of the Masonic Lodge. Zorn's body was lying at the bottom of his driveway, head aimed up the hill, feet down toward the street. An oval pool of blood on the pale cracked concrete extended down past his feet. The blood was black in the headlights of the cop cars. Zorn's arms were folded beneath his body: it appeared that he may have been attempting to crawl up the driveway, and then collapsed on his arms.

Alewort, the crime-scene guy, was taking pictures with a big black camera and a flash, the flash flickering up the valley like heat lightning.

A half-dozen rubberneckers stood out at the rim of the circle of light from the cars, neighbors, and a stout woman stood in the driveway itself, ten feet above the body. She was wearing a dark sweatshirt and jeans, and had her arms crossed. As Virgil got out of his car, he picked up a flicker of gray outside the lit area, a watcher who didn't want to be seen. Muddy Ruff, he thought.

The sheriff came over and said, "He was dead by the time he hit the ground. I have two theories: he was shut up by one of his meth customers, or we have a nutcase who's going around shooting people."

"Not the dog guys?"

"Definitely not. Come look."

Virgil walked over and looked at the body, which showed a hand-sized bloody patch in the center of the back. Purdy shone a light on the wound, and Virgil picked out three holes in a circular pattern not more than four inches across. "Uh-oh. Same shooter as the one who hit Conley," Virgil said.

"That's what I thought. And Conley was a pill head, with a preference for amphetamines."

"You find brass?"

"Yup. A .223 shell, and I bet your tool-marks guy will tell you it's the same firing pin as in the Conley killing. We got us either a nutcase, or a drug link."

"Who found him?"

Purdy tipped his head toward the woman up the driveway: "His wife. She heard the shots, and came running out to see what it was. Found him, and called for help. We had a car here in four or five minutes, and the ambulance a minute after that, but there was never a question of transporting him. He was gone."

Virgil looked up at Zorn's wife: she looked like a chunk of stone. "What's she say? She got any ideas?"

"She says not. She says she has no idea of what happened."

"You ask her about the meth?"

"Virgil, I got here about three minutes before you did."

"Let's go talk to her."

THEY WALKED UP the driveway and Purdy said, "Miz Zorn, I know this is a bad time, we need to get you up to the house and talk a bit."

"I knew it was gonna happen sooner or later," she said, without moving. She had a nearly rectangular face, black hair and eyebrows, a small nose and a small tight mouth that made a natural down-turned new-moon shape. "I told him to quit fuckin' around with that meth, he was way out of his league. Did he listen?"

"We oughta go up to the house," Purdy repeated.

This time she turned and led the way up the driveway. The house was a simple single-story square. The small living room was just inside the front door, with no entry, the kitchen off to the right. A battered couch, with a matching easy chair, backed against one wall, with a glass-topped coffee table in front of it. The table was stacked with hunting and women's magazines. The couch faced a wide-screen TV, with a pair of red leatherette beanbag chairs on the carpet to the right of the couch. The place smelled of bacon and cooked cabbage.

The woman flopped on the couch and Purdy took the chair; Virgil leaned against the wall next to the television.

Purdy asked, "What did you see?"

"Nothing. I heard the shots, then I heard the car or the truck, sounded like it was laying some rubber, and it was all pretty close, so I went out to see what Roy was doing, and there he was, just like you see him. I went running down, but . . . I could see he was dead. I ran up here anyway, and called you cops, and here we are."

"You knew he was cooking meth?" Virgil asked.

"I'm not talking about meth," she said.

Virgil said, "Look, Miz Zorn, if somebody killed him to keep him from talking about his meth business, then they could come after you, too. They'd think that you knew everything that he knew."

She considered that for a moment and then said, "That's what a cop would say."

"Yeah, it is, and the cop would be right."

She said, "I need a cigarette." She pushed herself off the couch, went into the kitchen, and came back with a pack of Camels and a book of matches. She lit one, blew smoke, and said, "That ain't it. Nobody killed him because of the meth."

"You can't—" Purdy began.

She interrupted. "He cooked that shit for the Seed. He's done time, twice, in Wisconsin, and he never said a single fuckin' thing to the cops. He knew if he ever did, the Seed would kill him."

The Seed was a neo-Nazi motorcycle gang based in Milwaukee, with alliances in the Twin Cities.

"You know, another guy was killed the same way Roy was," Purdy said. "We know Clancy Conley was a pill head, so it seemed like there might be a natural connection there."

"No," she said. "Roy had one hard rule: no retail. Never sell to locals, because this is a small town, and the word would get out. All the retail was done out of Milwaukee. We were going to sell out this winter and move on, because we were already worried that somebody might start thinking about us up here."

Virgil looked at Purdy, who shrugged.

They talked to her for another fifteen minutes, but she asked for a lawyer and said she wouldn't answer any more questions. Back outside, Virgil called Gomez, the DEA guy. Gomez said, "Friendly chats don't usually start this late at night."

"Roy Zorn just got shot to death, and it looks like it's the same shooter in the other murder I'm looking at."

After a moment of silence, Gomez asked, "What the hell does that mean?"

"I don't know—are you getting anything out of the guys you busted?"

"They don't know anything. They know how to cook, and that's about it—they weren't in the business end of things. Now they're lawyered up. We'll get them, of course, and we're talking to the lawyers about cooperation. But if Zorn's dead, we don't have anything to talk about. He was the guy we were trying to get."

"Maybe talk to them about who might be crosswise with Zorn? Ask them about the first guy who got killed, Clancy Conley?"

"We can do that. Send me an e-mail, and we'll push them on it tomorrow morning."

"You'll be talking to the Buchanan County sheriff's investigator. I'll have him get in touch."

———

PURDY CAME OUT of the house and said, "She was terribly upset by her husband being killed. Not."

"I noticed," Virgil said. "A guy down the valley told me that she was the brains behind the operation. Doubt that you could prove it, but keep it in mind."

"Our investigator will be here in ten minutes: I'll tell him," Purdy said.

Virgil told him about Gomez: "You need to get in touch with him, interview the guys who worked for Zorn. See if you can get something on Zorn's old lady, and squeeze her. But I'll tell you—I think the link between Zorn and Conley is pretty funky."

"But, Virgil, you saw—"

"I know. It's the same shooter," Virgil said. "But I don't think it's drugs, I think there's gotta be some other connection."

"What are you going to do?"

"Right now? Gonna shout and yell."

"What?"

Virgil walked down into the road, looking into the darkness on the other side, and shouted, "Muddy! I'm going to your place! See you there!"

WHEN VIRGIL ARRIVED at the Ruffs', a porch light was on, and a couple of interior lights, but there was no movement. There were two chairs on the front porch, looking down the valley, and he took one of them and waited. Muddy Ruff materialized out of the dark five minutes later; he didn't have his gun.

"What do you want?"

"You see who did the shooting?"

"No. I was here, eating dinner. Dad was already gone, he's got a gig over in La Crosse tonight. I heard the shots and went running out of here. I knew it wasn't hunters, the shots just ripped out. Bap-bap-bap. Nothing I heard before. I saw the taillights of the truck, going out, but I didn't see who was driving it."

"That's all you got?"

Muddy hesitated, and Virgil saw it, and Muddy saw Virgil seeing it, so he went on. "I think it might be a red Ford F150. Pretty new."

"License tags?"

"Never looked. But I think they're from here, or maybe from Iowa. If they were from someplace else, I would have noticed that. And I didn't. Some of the Minnesota and Iowa plates look alike, and I see them all the time . . . so I didn't notice."

"Why do you think it was a red Ford?" Virgil asked.

"Because I saw a red Ford sitting behind that line of bushes in the Carlsons' turnout. But the Carlsons aren't home, they're up north at their cabin. And if you were a friend of theirs, checking on the house, why wouldn't you go up the drive?" Muddy said. "The thing is, if you were going to ambush Zorn from a truck, right after he got home, that's where you'd wait for him. At the Carlsons' turnout."

"How long was it there?"

"I don't know, I didn't see it come in. I was down at the river on my bike and rode up after it got dark. I've got a light on my bike, and pedaled past the turnout, and that's how I know it was a red Ford. Got here, stuck a potpie in the microwave, and it was still cooking when I heard the shot and went running out."

Virgil: "How long does it take to cook a potpie?"

"Fourteen minutes in our microwave, seven minutes on fifty percent power, seven more at a hundred percent," Muddy said. "It was in the second seven minutes that I heard the shots. I went running out, the red Ford was gone, but I saw taillights down at the end of the valley."

"And you didn't see anybody. No faces."

"Nope. Some of the neighbors went down there, to look—I think they were calling each other on the phone. I stayed back in the woods."

Muddy had one more thing—"We heard the dogs this morning. I'm going to sneak up there tomorrow and see what's what."

"Not a good idea," Virgil said.

"I'll take my rifle."

"Even worse idea," Virgil said. "Leave it to us. Your old man told you to stay away from there, and that's very good advice."

They sat without talking for a moment, then Muddy said, "I got lucky."

"Yeah?"

"The guy in the truck—he must've been slouched down in the truck, or sitting in the weeds off to the side. If I'd pulled in there and looked in the window, if I'd seen him, he might've killed me."

Virgil nodded. "Yeah. I'll tell you what, Muddy. I don't want to scare you unnecessarily, but we've got a nutcake on our hands. That's why you've got to stay clear. If this guy came back, it wouldn't make any difference if you had your rifle. He's a back-shooter. He'd kill you like he was stepping on a bug."

"Okay," Muddy said.

Virgil looked at him for a moment, then said, "Okay." He added, "I need to talk to your father. You got a cell phone for him?"

VIRGIL DROVE BACK down the valley to a mailbox that said "Carlson," got a flashlight out of his toolbox, and walked around the turnout. He found nothing useful: it was all loose gravel, nothing that would hold tire tracks. Neither did he find any fresh cigarette butts, matchbooks from Spike's Biker Bar and Grill, or discarded receipts with a credit card number. He did see a Northern Walkingstick, Diapheromera femorata, making its ponderous way across the gravel.

He went up the driveway, and a motion-sensor light came on, and there were lights in the house, but nobody answered the door. As he was standing there, one of the lights in the back winked out, but a lamp turned on, and he could see it, and nobody was standing by it: timer switches.

He drove back to the crime scene, where somebody had put a plastic sheet over Zorn's body, and checked with Purdy: "Are you okay with Alewort working this, or you want me to bring down a BCA crime-scene team?"

Purdy said, "I think we're good, Virgil. There just isn't much to the scene."

Virgil told him to have his investigator check with Muddy Ruff: "He saw a red Ford pickup parked up the valley. He thinks it could have been the shooter's truck. He might be right, but he doesn't have much on it. Tell your investigator that I might stop back here tomorrow and have another run at Miz Zorn."

On the way out of the valley, he called Muddy's father, but the call clicked through to the answering service, and he left a message asking for a callback. He called Johnson Johnson: "You gotta call around to your friends. I need to know if any of them might have gone after Roy Zorn tonight."

"What happened?"

"Somebody shot Zorn in his driveway."

"Better than shootin' him in his heart," Johnson said.

"Johnson . . ."

"All right, all right. Is he dead?"

"Yeah, and it looks like the same guy who took out Conley. There's something going on, Mr. Johnson, and we don't know what it is."

"If one of the boys shot Zorn, they wouldn't tell me, but I might find out if somebody's nervous," Johnson said.

"You be careful when you ask, I don't need to teach somebody else how to fish."

"I beg your pardon?"

"And listen, I'm going back up there early tomorrow—same place we went the other day, but at five o'clock in the morning. I want to be hidden by five-thirty. You up for that?"

"Can I bring my gun?"

"Would it make any difference if I said no?"

"Not really, but I'm a polite guy, so I thought I'd ask. There's a carp fisherman's turnoff four or five hundred yards south of where we parked the other day. Let's go back in there, we can leave our cars by the ramp. Shouldn't nobody from the valley see them back there."

VIRGIL WAS BACK to town when Julius Ruff called him back: "Something happen?" he asked, sounding scared.

Virgil told him about it, and said, "You gotta nail down Muddy—he can't go wandering around up there, not until we're done with this. He said he was going up tomorrow, and I told him not to, but he might anyway. Keep him out of it."

"I will. I'll keep him out of it, I swear to God," Ruff said.

BACK AT THE CABIN, Virgil got in bed and read one of Johnson's Randy Wayne White novels for a while, then spent some time thinking about God and why he would allow dogs to be mistreated. Before he fell asleep, he thought that it was time that he catch Buster Gedney by himself, away from his wife, and squeeze hard. He was the source of the three-burst .223 kits, Virgil knew it in his heart. He set his clock for five in the morning, and killed the light.

Turned it back on five minutes later, read one more chapter in the Randy Wayne White novel, then turned it off again and went to sleep.

12

THE NIGHT WAS losing its grip, and the early morning steam was hanging off the river's surface, when they pulled into the parking area near the dirt ramp. A pickup followed them in, towing a trailer that carried a twenty-foot-long jon boat.

The truck driver swung in a wide circle, backed up—fast—toward the waterline at the ramp, hit his brakes, and the boat slid off the trailer into the water. The fisherman jumped out of the truck, walked around to the trailer, untied the line that kept the boat from floating away, tied it to a pole stuck in the ground next to the ramp, got in the truck, and pulled it up beside Virgil's SUV.

He hopped out, nodded at Virgil, and said, "Johnson, morning," and Johnson said, "Syz, how they hangin'," and they all went their separate ways. By the time Virgil and Johnson got to the highway, Syz was roaring out into the river.

"He's a Polack from Chicago, a carp fisherman," Johnson told Virgil. "They like their smoked carp, the Polacks do. Smoke it almost till it's brown. Kinda nicotine-colored."

They walked up the highway, dodged across when they got a break in the high-speed traffic, and began climbing the hill. They were both carrying their packs; Virgil's pistol was in his, with a couple bottles of water and the large-sized Payday peanut candy bar. At five-twenty they were at the top of the ridge at the far eastern end of the valley. They found a grassy mound inside a clump of sumac, made sure it wasn't an anthill, and sat down.

Johnson took a beer out of the pack and popped the top.

They were waiting, and didn't have much to talk about, so Virgil said, "I'm starting to worry about your drinking."

Johnson said, "Me, too."

"Then why don't you quit?"

"I don't know. I've thought about it, but never got around to it," Johnson said. "I talked to Clarice about getting married, you know, but she said she won't do it, if I keep drinking."

"How many beers are you up to?"

"Don't really count, but I pretty much do a six-pack a day, I guess. Give or take. Mostly give."

"Jesus, Johnson, you gotta quit," Virgil said. "You're hanging around a lumber mill, for Christ's sakes. Circular saws. Chain saws."

"Yeah, I guess. All right."

"All right, what?"

"All right, I'll quit. I'll drink these two, and that'll be the end of it," Johnson said.

Virgil told him about the murder of Zorn, and the scene the

night before, and his encounter with Muddy Ruff. "That kid knows more than he lets on," Johnson said. "You ought to get close to him. If he thinks you're a friend, he'd talk."

"You mean, exploit him."

"Well, yeah."

They didn't talk for a while. Johnson popped the top on the second beer, took a long swig, then tossed the nearly full can over his shoulder and down the hill. "Good-bye, old friend," he said.

"I'll believe it a year from now," Virgil said.

Johnson: "Say, this whole stop-drinking thing . . . it doesn't include margaritas, does it?"

VIRGIL WAS CHECKING the time on his cell phone—6:50—when they first heard the dogs, like a distant pack of foxhounds off in the English hills, somewhere. The barking got louder, over the next couple of minutes, and faster than a dog could run, Virgil thought. He took his weapon out of his pack, with its holster, tucked it into the back of his pants, and said, "Let's go. I don't want to see your gun unless I'm shot."

They came down off the hump and walked through the neck-high sumac, into the oak forest, following a thin game trail that led them below the emerging bluff line, toward the sound of the dogs. They'd gone three hundred yards when the sound of the dogs grew sharper, with some canine shrieks, and suddenly the barking began to diminish. "They're moving them," Johnson said. "We've got to run."

They began to jog toward the sound of the dogs, which suddenly stopped altogether, cut off as cleanly as the flick of a switch on an amplifier. Virgil said, "Faster," and they broke into a full run. A minute later, they could see the pen they'd found during the first search. The pen was empty. Johnson was running behind Virgil, but he suddenly sped up, reached out and caught Virgil's shirt, yanked him to a stop. He said, "Shhh!"

Virgil went quiet, and then he heard it: other people running, at least one downslope, and far away, the other closer, and upslope. Virgil said, "They spotted us coming. You watch the pen. Don't shoot anyone. I'm going."

Johnson jogged on toward the pen, as Virgil cut uphill, running hard, now. He couldn't hear the other runner when he was actually running, so he had to stop, and listen, and then follow on. He'd run four or five hundred yards, tough going all the way, when he came out at the edge of a bean field that stretched away to the west, on the narrow valley crest.

He stopped to listen, and a moment later saw a man break out of the trees, run along the fence for a few yards, then dodge back into the trees, probably three or four hundred yards ahead. Virgil doubted that he could catch him, but ran on as hard as he could, trying to follow game trails as best he was able, but much of the time, busting through the underbrush. When he reached the corner of the bean field, where he'd seen the other man, he understood why the man had broken into the open: there was a notch in the valley wall right there, and the man had run around it.

And had vanished.

Virgil listened, but didn't hear anything. He went on another hundred feet, and then saw a more-used path, leading toward the edge of the bluffs. There, he saw a pathway down, with recently scuffed yellow dirt.

Good place for an ambush. He took his pistol out and slid cautiously down the trail, through the bluff line, down probably fifty feet, where he found another trail that followed the line of the bottom of the bluffs. That trail went in both directions; he was thinking about which one to take when he heard the other man again, running down to his right, then the sound of a truck, and as he ran that way, a truck door slamming, and then the sound of the truck accelerating away on the road below.

He thought about continuing down the hill, but there was no hope: the truck would be long gone before he got there, and then he'd have to re-climb the valley wall to get back to Johnson.

He thought about the choices, then jogged back along the bluffs to the pen. Johnson was waiting there, inside the pen.

"Nothing here," Johnson said, scuffing around inside the wire. "The feeding tubs, that's all. But I can smell dogs."

Virgil sniffed: "So can I. They must have them hooked together, somehow, and must've taken them off somewhere."

"Why did they stop barking?"

"I don't have a dog, so I couldn't tell you . . . maybe they're all hooked into choke chains or something? Would that do it?"

"Maybe," Johnson said.

Virgil walked around the pen, and it looked as though a lot of dogs had been in residence for a long time. The bluff had some overhanging places, with hollows beneath the ledges, where it looked like dogs had lain when the sun got hot. One little dirt run followed the fence line then actually went up the bluff a few feet, but then hit a dead-end wall.

"All right," Virgil said finally. "Let's go. Tonight you can drop me, and I'm going to sneak all the way back up here to the pen."

"They might be planning to do the same thing," Johnson said. "Sneak up here early, before you do."

"I'll think of something," Virgil said.

"The boys have already thought of something," Johnson said. "They thought about catching Zorn out somewhere, and beating it out of him."

"But not shooting him."

"No—I mean, what good would that do? You couldn't find your dogs if you killed him."

"Good point," Virgil said.

"So maybe they'll catch Mrs. Zorn, and beat it out of her," Johnson said. And, "Mrs. Zorn. Wonder what her first name is."

"Bunny," Virgil said.

THOUGH HE WAS FEELING SLEEPY, Virgil drove back through town to Buster Gedney's house. Gedney wasn't home, but there was a coffee shop a couple blocks back toward the downtown area, and he stopped, thinking he might get a bagel or a scone. He took his laptop with him, and when he got his scone and a Diet Coke, saw some umbrellas on a back deck and went that way. Where he found Gedney sitting at a café table.

Gedney looked shocked when Virgil came over with a bag and bottle: "You're following me?"

"Not exactly, but we are . . . mmm . . . aware of where you're at," Virgil said. He glanced quickly up at the sky, then brought his gaze back down.

Gedney caught it and asked, "You've got a drone?"

"Oh . . . of course not," Virgil said. He dragged a chair from a nearby table to where Gedney was sitting, and made himself comfortable. "Why would you be important enough for us to . . . to task a drone with keeping track of you?"

"I'm not," Gedney said. "I'm not."

Virgil said to the air, "You hear that, Spike? He says he's not important enough."

Gedney: "You're making fun of me—that's not right."

Virgil unscrewed the cap on the Diet Coke, keeping his eyes on Gedney as he did it, took a sip, and said, "Tell you something, Buster. You heard what happened to Roy Zorn?"

"Everybody's heard," Gedney said. "He got shot."

"He got shot by the same guy who shot Conley, and he did it with your burst kit." Gedney opened his mouth to object, but Virgil cut him off: "I know you made those kits. You're a terrible liar, Buster, and I could see it in your face. Sooner or later, I'll prove it, and then you'll go to Stillwater prison for thirty years, no parole. That's the penalty in Minnesota for murder-one."

He took a bite of the scone.

"I didn't—"

"Yes, you did," Virgil said. "Buster, maybe you need to talk to a criminal lawyer about this. Or maybe you should just take my word:

you are part and parcel of a vicious pair of crimes. In most other states, you'd qualify for the needle. Here, we just pack you away forever. You're what, in your forties? You'd be in your middle seventies before you get out. At the earliest. You've got exactly one chance: Turn. Talk to me."

"But I . . . but I . . ."

"We think the shooter is killing people to cover up another set of crimes. I even kind of think you might know what those crimes are, which gets you even deeper in the shit. It also gives this guy a solid reason to kill you. In fact, that's why we're keeping track of you—in case you get shot. Sooner or later, he'll know that we'll be looking for those burst kits, and where they came from, and when that happens, Buster . . . he's gonna kill you, man."

"I . . . I gotta think," Buster said, running his hands through his sparse brown hair.

Virgil leaned forward: "See, Buster, right there you told me that you've got something to think about. We need to talk to the county attorney, and right quick—so I can close this case out and lock up the killer. Right now, if you help us, you might even qualify for a free ride. Can't promise you anything, but I think there's a good chance, unless you're the one who actually pulled the trigger."

"No! I'd never do that!" he said. "But . . . I gotta think. Give me your phone number."

Virgil said, "I'll give you the number, Buster, but this coupon has an expiration date. If you talk to me five minutes too late, you're going to the joint. The pen. The big house. The Minnesota Correctional Facility at Stillwater. You get up there, a nice-looking guy like you . . . Well, you know that old country saying, 'Butter my butt and call me a biscuit'? Well, they'll be buttering your butt, but not because they think you're a biscuit."

"That's disgusting," Buster said.

"Sure wouldn't want it in my future," Virgil agreed.

Virgil scrawled his phone number on a napkin and pushed it across the table. Buster snatched it up, stood, and said, "You're a . . ." He groped for a word. ". . . a jerk."

VIRGIL WATCHED HIM trot out of the place and, suspecting he might look back, squinted up into the sky; when Buster was gone for good, he sat for a while, wondering what he should do next, and finally opened his laptop and looked up the Mouldy Figs.

He didn't find much that seemed to apply to the case, but then he thought, *Why would Conley drop that hint about the Mouldy Figs if it was meaningless, or hard to figure out?* He went back to the Figs' main site and saw that they'd made a number of CDs. Virgil had a Mac laptop, like Conley, and he also had a SuperDrive. What if Conley had dumped his story on a CD and put it in a Mouldy Figs CD case?

He had nothing better to do, and still had the key to Conley's trailer, and it was only five minutes away . . . And if what he'd said about the Figs was actually a tip . . .

HE FINISHED THE SCONE, threw his bag in the trash can, and took the Diet Coke and laptop with him. Ten minutes later, he was looking through Conley's CD collection. There were no Mouldy Figs albums. . . .

There were two by Moldy Peaches.

"What?"

He got on the phone to Wendy McComb, who picked up on the fourth ring but couldn't hear what he was saying because, she said, she was in a supermarket and the music was too loud. He shouted at her to go to a quieter place, and when she had, he said, "Mouldy Figs? Or Moldy Peaches?"

"Oh, Jesus! Moldy Peaches! That's what it was. I knew about the Mouldy Figs, and I just . . . just . . . said the wrong thing. He said the chick singer for the Moldy Peaches."

"Thank you," Virgil said, and clicked off.

Chick singer for the Moldy Peaches. He had no computer link for his laptop, but he did for his phone, and quickly figured out that Kimya Dawson was the singer he needed to find. When he punched her name into Google, he instantly came up with a song called "Tire Swing."

His eyes snapped to the window that led out to the side yard, and the swing that hung over the valley. He turned off the phone and, hardly daring to hope, went out to his truck, got a flashlight from the door pocket, and carried it over to the tire swing.

The flash drive was duct-taped into the top part of the swing, just to the left of the rope tie, where nothing could get at it, where it would be nice and dry and safe. Like a mosquito, it was going to sting somebody.

Virgil held it in the curl of his hand and smiled.

———

Back at Johnson's cabin, Virgil got a Diet Coke, plugged in his laptop, and brought up the flash drive, where he found a half-dozen Pages files and a couple hundred photographs.

He started by checking the files. All but one had cryptic titles, meaningless to Virgil but presumably not to Conley. The non-cryptic one was entitled "To Whom IMC," which to Virgil meant "To whom it may concern," which certainly included him.

He opened it and found a rambling note:

If this is me reading this, I told you that you were a dumb shit. They're a bunch of small-town school board members, for God's sake. They aren't killers.

If this is not me reading this, and especially if it's a cop, then, uh-oh, I was right, and I'm probably dead. If I disappeared and you can't find me, I'm probably dead, too. Probably shot. The guy who probably shot me is named Randolph (Randy) Kerns, the school security officer and a gun nut. If you're a cop, be careful, because Randy has more guns than any other single human being.

If this is Randy reading this, fuck you.

Anyway, assuming that this is a cop, and you're reading this because of one of the hints I scattered around, good for you. (And for me.) Here's the situation, and you might not believe it, but it's true.

The school board—all of it—with the help of the superintendent of schools, Henry Hetfield, the financial officer, Delbert Cray, the security *officer (Randy Kerns, who I mentioned above), and Vike Laughton, the editor of the* Republican-River, *have been systematically ripping off the school district for years—as of this writing, seven years, ever since Evelyn Hughes was defeated in her effort to be reelected to the board. If you look at my file entitled "Hughesrun" you'll find the paper's coverage of that campaign, and you should interview Hughes, who lives in Elixir Springs. Vike drove her off the board so they could start stealing.*

What's the take? At least a half million, and maybe as much as a million dollars a year. As I said, hard to believe, but they rip off some of every single transaction that the board is involved in, and they legitimately spend just under forty million dollars a year on the school system.

The theft is done in a variety of ways: in the transportation area, they over-budget and overspend on fuel and maintenance. The overspending part mostly involves fuel, on which they overstate costs and mileage. They also have a maintenance contract with Lanny Brooks at Brooks and Mann Automotive, on which I believe Brooks kicks back about twenty percent. I can't prove the Brooks part, but if you look in my file "MainCom" you will find comparative maintenance records for several nearby districts, and for buses of equivalent age and mileage. Maintenance costs in Buchanan are running about twenty percent ahead of where they should be.

I think Viking Laughton gets much of his money from printing what the district lists as "educational materials," which supposedly are custom lesson sets for social studies, English, and mathematics classes. I have spoken privately to two teachers, whose names I won't include here, because this might be Randy Kerns (fuck you) reading this, but who will tell you they have never seen these lesson sets. You will need to investigate this on your own. The Minnesota Department of Education issues some of these

lesson sets, which supposedly were reprinted here, and you can find the ti-
tles purchased by Buchanan County and copies of the reprints filed with
the MDE. (Viking actually made reprints with materials from the MDE,
but I believe he only made enough copies to file with the school archives and
with the MDE, and pocketed the money from the rest of them.)

There are several ghost workers with the school system—they simply
don't exist. This is much harder to see than you would think, because none
of the school district's salary numbers are broken out by job or by salary
amounts—they are always aggregated. I can't tell how much is missing,
but I think they could be taking out a quarter of a million dollars with this
skim alone. To find these workers you would have to go check by check
through the entire system, which I have been unable to do. The system sup-
posedly holds these records for three years and then destroys them, so there
might be some way to dig out the amounts for the last three years. One
problem: Fred Masilla, the auditor, is in on the deal, and he certifies the
payroll as accurate, but only in aggregate amounts. If the district should
have a fire, and if the mini-computer in the accounting office should be
destroyed, I'm not sure there would be any way to tell what happened.

The whole board has been fighting for the new sports complex, which
will be paid for with a bond issue; the vote is in September. I have to believe
that they plan a major rip-off on that thing. . . .

CONLEY'S NOTE WENT ON for a while, outlining a scheme, which, if
it was actually occurring, would be one of the biggest public em-
bezzlements in Minnesota history, Virgil thought. The photographs,
Conley wrote, were taken from the system's computer system,
which he said he had hacked into. Virgil suspected he was lying

about that, because the computer screens in the photographs looked nothing like Conley's laptop screens. What he had done, Virgil thought, was find a way to break into the school system offices at three o'clock in the morning.

VIRGIL SPENT THREE HOURS going over all the material on the flash drive—skimming some, because there was just so much, and some of it would take an accountant to untangle.

One thing: he found no mention of Buster Gedney, although Buster's wife, Jennifer, was mentioned frequently. Conley seemed to think she was one of the ringleaders in the scheme.

Virgil checked the time: he'd read into the late afternoon. He had to do several things—one was to get some backup. If not real-time, in-person backup, he at least needed to tell Davenport what was going on, and where he was headed. And he had to copy the flash drive and send the copy to Davenport for safekeeping.

Davenport was in California, delivering his adoptive daughter to Stanford University. Pacific time was two hours ahead of Central time, so Davenport should be up and moving around.

Virgil called, and Davenport answered: "I'm on vacation."

"I know. I just want to tell you, I'm going to the post office and I'm mailing a flash drive to you. This is in case I'm shot to death or I disappear."

After a moment's hesitation, Davenport said, "You're serious now."

"Yeah. Tell you what, Lucas, I've come up with the damnedest thing. . . ."

Virgil described the contents of the flash drive, and when he finished, Davenport said, "First, send me the drive. Then, you're going
to need to harden up the information. Nail down what is what. Interview the people you can, without getting back-shot. Then find
the weak sister—"

"I think I've already done that," Virgil said, thinking of Buster
Gedney.

"Good. I'll ship Jenkins and Shrake down there, they'll be there
tomorrow morning. The three of you can squeeze him. Or her. Or
whatever. In the meantime, this is going to be a big enough stink
that the AG—"

"I've already talked to one of his guys."

"Okay. I'll talk to him about providing a lawyer and a forensic
accountant. We'll keep them on tap, until you need them."

"That sounds right," Virgil said.

"And hey," Davenport asked, "what about the dogs?"

"That's a whole 'nother problem," Virgil said.

VIRGIL WENT OUT to Blackbeard's Steak & Brew for dinner. BS&B
was a roadhouse a mile south of town, and probably the best place
around, if you liked meat and beer. He was thinking about a second
beer, and was picking at the remnants of a New York Strip, when
Johnson called and said, "Darrell and Bill called, they were in the
tent tonight and said that a truck pulling a horse van just busted out
of Orly's Creek and headed north on 26 at about a hundred miles an
hour. The thing is, there's no horses up Orly's Creek. They called

Ben and Winky—Ben lives up north of Orly's Creek, and Winky's down south—and they both hauled ass up and down the highway and they met up and didn't see a horse trailer. Whoever it was, cut up through the hills."

"Goddamnit. Maybe they spotted the tent."

"That's what we're thinking," Johnson said.

"What are they doing now? Your dog guys?"

"They got a couple more of the boys and they're running all over the place looking for the trailer."

"What if it was a decoy?"

"Well, Darrell and Bill moved out to the road," Johnson said. "They, uh, they've maybe got some guns with them. They're not gonna let anybody out Orly's Creek without checking them out."

"Aw, for Christ's sakes. Johnson, somebody's gonna get killed," Virgil said.

"It's got me worried."

"I don't want to go up there and bust your friends. You gotta get them to back off."

"I already told them. They think the truck is owned by a guy named D. Wayne Sharf, who was pals with Zorn. Sharf wasn't there when you guys hit that cookery. But we know he's sold off dogs in the past."

Virgil: "What do you want me to do?"

"Well, you're not going to keep the guys from looking for Sharf and his truck, but if you could talk down Darrell and Bill, that would be good. I'd meet you up there."

"I'll see you there in twenty minutes."

———

JOHNSON GOT THERE faster than Virgil, because Virgil had to get out of the restaurant and then head north through the entire town. When he arrived, the three men were standing behind Johnson's truck. They didn't show any weapons.

Virgil got out of his truck and said, "Guys, I know you love your dogs, and I really don't want to drop you in the county jail, but if you go shooting at somebody, that's probably what's going to happen. The county attorneys around here don't want to hear about dogs, if somebody gets shot. They got no patience for guns."

"Not gonna shoot anybody," Darrell said.

"Yeah? You're standing here with your dicks in your hands, looking to stop cars coming out of Orly's Creek. What are you gonna do if somebody does come out with a load of dogs? Throw rocks at him? Wave good-bye? What?"

"Talk to him . . ."

"Yeah? Want me to give you the dialog? 'Get out of the truck, you motherfucker.' 'Fuck you.' 'Yeah? Fuck me? I'll pull your ass out of that fuckin' truck . . .'"

Bill started to laugh, and when Virgil stopped talking, said, "That's pretty much how it'd go."

Darrell nodded.

Johnson said, "Tell you what, guys. Virgil's got an idea for tomorrow morning. If you want, we'll just sit here in my truck, right on the road. I don't think they'd try to run past us with a load of dogs. So, that'd probably keep them up the valley, at least until Virgil can get something going again."

Darrell said, "I guess that sounds okay."

Virgil slapped Johnson on the shoulder and said, "You oughta be secretary of state."

Bill: "Maybe not."

Virgil took Johnson aside and said, "Keep talking to them. Keep them calm. Don't go jumping into anything yourself."

"What are you going to do?"

"I'm going to bed. I gotta be out here before first light."

"Probably still be here," Johnson said.

"Call me if there's trouble."

13

At five o'clock in the morning, Virgil crept up to Johnson's truck and pulled in behind it. Johnson was asleep, but Bill got out, shoulders hunched against the early morning damp and cool. He scuffed dirt off the shoulder onto the empty road and said, "Nothing much. Empty pickups and a couple cars. No dogs. Didn't see Sharf, either coming or going. God knows where he is by this time."

"See any movement up on the hill?"

"Not a thing. Darrell's up there now, listening. Johnson was up there for a couple hours, before he came down to catch some rack time."

Virgil said, "Okay. Call Darrell down, and you guys can take off anytime. Get the boat back, so the day shift can take over."

"If they know we're there . . ."

"Yeah. We'll talk this afternoon," Virgil said. "Might be time to call off the watch. At least for now."

"Need those goddamn dogs, Virgil. This is as mad as anyone's been—if they beat us this time, they'll just keep coming back."

"We'll get them, Bill. Swear to God."

VIRGIL GOT BACK in his truck and drove up Orly's Creek Road, all the way to the end, and then up the Ruffs' driveway. He parked in front of the house, and as he turned off the engine, saw a light come on in what he thought was probably a bedroom. As he walked up to the porch, the motion-sensing porch light snapped on, and Julius Ruff looked out the window at him, then met him at the door.

"What happened?" He was wearing a white knit Henley bed shirt and blue boxer shorts.

"Nothing, so far. I'd like to talk to Muddy for a minute if I could."

"He's—"

"I'm up," Muddy said from the darkened back of the house. He came to the door, barefoot, wearing a T-shirt and jeans.

Julius pushed open the door, and Virgil and Julius and Muddy gathered around the kitchen table, and Muddy sketched out the best route up the hill and down the bluffs to the dog pen, where Virgil planned to wait.

"You can't leave from here, in our driveway," Julius Ruff said. "You gotta start down the road. I don't want the assholes to know we're talking to you."

"Neither do I," Virgil said.

Muddy said, "Okay. If you go down the road, maybe a two-minute walk, you'll see this mailbox with a big wooden rooster cutout on top."

"I've seen that," Virgil said.

"Then a little ways further, there's a turnout where you can park, and there's a trail along the creek there. Follow down the creek about, mmm, a little ways, and there's a place where the creek breaks between some rocks. You can walk dry across the rocks, and there's a little trail that goes up the hill from there, and hooks up with the trail under the bluffs."

"Thank you," Virgil said. "If I use a flash for part of that, is somebody going to see me?"

"Probably not, if you don't use it too much. And that turnout is where some trout fishermen park. So . . . you could be a fisherman."

Virgil said to Julius, "Don't let Muddy out of the house until eight o'clock or so. I don't want somebody up there that I don't know about. I'll be carrying a shotgun."

"He'll be here," Julius said. To Muddy: "We'll work on your theory for an hour, and then do some licks from *Guitar Techniques*."

"I'd just like to get some more sleep," Muddy said.

"That's because you think I don't know about you sneaking out the window. I want you where I can see you," Julius said. To Virgil, he said, "Good luck."

VIRGIL FOUND the turnout two hundred yards back down the road, fifty yards past the rooster mailbox. His watch said that it was 5:30, and though sunrise was more than a half hour away, there was enough light to see the hole in the brush that led to Orly's Creek. He wouldn't need the flash.

He got the shotgun out of the back, loaded it with buckshot, put some extra shells in his jacket pocket, along with a squeeze bottle of DEET. Stopped and listened, and heard nothing but birds announcing with the dawn.

The transition from darkness to full light comes suddenly in the woods. Virgil walked down the creek, where the rocks were barely visible, poking up through the black water. He crossed carefully and began climbing the hill, and by the time he got to the trail along the bluff, he could see a hundred yards through the heavy brush and trees. He moved slowly, no hurry, stopping to look and listen.

With his slow movement, he took more than a half hour to make it to the dog pen. No dogs. He found a downed tree, back in the brush, and sat down behind it. Listened.

The sun showed up on schedule—which, when he thought about it, was a relief, given the alternative. If the dog feeders showed up at 7:30, as they usually did, he'd have another hour to wait. A mosquito buzzed past his ear. . . .

At eight o'clock, he was still waiting. He could see squirrels running up and down the oak trees, all the way down to the road, which meant nobody was creeping up on him. He waited a while longer, but was about to give up when he noticed a growing silence behind his position. He settled back, and ten minutes later, saw Muddy Ruff easing from one tree to the next, his rifle under his arm.

He got downhill from Virgil, twenty yards away, following the trail toward the dog pen. Then he stopped, looked around and finally up the hill where Virgil was hidden. Virgil said, "I asked you to stay away from here."

"Got to be eight o'clock, I was done with my lessons. We figured you'd be gone."

"How'd you spot me?" Virgil asked, as he stood up.

"I could smell that insect stuff," Muddy said.

"Okay."

They walked over to the dog pen, and Muddy said, "I can smell the dogs. They were here, not long ago. I don't know how long, maybe a couple of days, maybe a couple of hours."

"Not a couple hours," Virgil said. "Nobody was moving in the woods."

A dog barked. Faintly, but not clearly. Muddy looked at Virgil: "You hear that?"

"Yeah. Where is it?"

"Didn't sound like it was far away," Muddy said. "Sounded like it was close, but the dog was gagged or something."

They both looked at the pen, which looked the same as it did when Virgil was there the first time. Virgil said, "Weird place for a pen. Got to walk all the way up the hill every day, got to carry bags of dog food."

The hurricane fencing was eight feet high, a semicircle stapled to 4×4 posts, with both ends of the fence pinned to the bluff. Part of the bluff was undercut, with a shallow cavity perhaps two feet high and two feet deep, where the dogs probably went to get out of the sun. They both walked over to the gate, and into the pen, and they both bent to look at the undercut: just an undercut. They could see both ends, and it was empty.

They'd backed off and were looking up at the bluff when they heard another bark.

They looked at each other, then Muddy handed Virgil his rifle and said, "Hold on to this." He went over to the bluff, lay down, and looked up at the roof of the undercut.

"There's a board here. Must be a cave."

"What?"

Virgil stacked their guns against the bluff, took a look around, then got down on his back and looked up at what should have been the sandstone ceiling of the undercut. Instead he saw an eight-foot length of board, fourteen inches wide, two inches thick. The board had toggle bolts at one end, and hinges at the other.

"Keep an eye out," Virgil said to the kid.

Muddy rolled out of the cavity, and Virgil humped over to the end of the board and twisted the toggle bolts. The board dropped down at one end, and a minute later a beagle hound ran down the board.

"Holy crap," Muddy said.

More than a dozen dogs, including four beagles, a half-dozen Labrador retrievers—four black and two chocolate—a golden retriever, two Brittany spaniels, and two black-and-white dogs and one speckled brown one that Virgil couldn't name, but looked like serious gun dogs, followed down the board and milled around, sniffing for food. They looked like they needed it. One of the beagles started baying at them—where's the food?

Virgil picked up the shotgun, waved Muddy out of the pen, closed the gate, and said, as a couple other dogs joined in the howl, "Keep an eye out down the hill, in case the noise pulls somebody in."

"Right."

Virgil got on the phone to Johnson.

"You hear them?"

"We all can. Where the hell are you?"

"At the pen. Get up here. Don't have to be subtle about it, park on the road and come on up."

When he was off the phone, he said to Muddy, "I owe you one. I don't think I would have seen that plank."

Muddy nodded.

"You got any idea of who might've done this?"

"Roy Zorn is the one everybody thought did it. His best pal, his assistant, is D. Wayne Sharf—not Duane, but D, the initial, and Wayne, everybody calls him Dee-Wayne. He lives almost straight down the hill, and I've seen him up here in the spring, looking for mushrooms. He might've been the one who found the cave."

"Okay. D. Wayne Sharf, we're already looking for him," Virgil said. "You go on home. I don't want anyone to see you up here with me. You've got to live here."

Muddy nodded again and said, "You should get some different insect stuff. I could smell you a mile away."

And he was gone down the trail.

JOHNSON PARKED straight down the hill from the pen and started climbing. He was alone, and when he got to Virgil, gasping for breath, Virgil asked, "Where are the rest of the guys?"

"I called them, they're coming. I told them to look for my truck and climb straight up from there." He looked at the dogs. "Where were they?"

Virgil showed him the undercut. Johnson took Virgil's flashlight and stuck his head into the hole above the undercut, then stood up. Virgil was the tiniest bit claustrophobic, and said, "Careful, think about a cave-in."

Johnson dropped back to his knees and crawled out of the undercut, handed the flashlight to Virgil. "Stinks like hell. Looks like a regular sandstone cave—they're all over the place around here. Should have thought of it before. Could have hid a hundred dogs in there. Smells like dog shit and dead animals . . . probably ought to send somebody up there to look around."

"Not me," Virgil said.

"What if they killed somebody and stashed the body up there?" Johnson asked.

"Goddamnit, Johnson, why'd you go and ask that?"

"Because I'd rather have you up there, than me—and you're skinnier, anyway, so you could walk right up that board, if you did it sideways."

Virgil thought about it for a while, and Johnson saw him thinking about it, and said, to encourage him, "Try not to be too big a pussy, pussy."

EVENTUALLY, Virgil agreed that he should at least do what Johnson did, which was get his feet on the bottom of the plank and stand up. Sweating a little, he did that. Using his flashlight, he could see the roof of a fairly roomy cave, maybe ten feet high and fifty across, with a floor that showed shovel marks. A pile of fallen rubble sat at one end. The cave got shallower as it went deeper into the bluff, and finally, twenty-five or thirty feet back, twisted out of sight. He couldn't see much on the floor of the cave, because of the angle he was at.

He called, "How solid you think this plank is?"

"Felt pretty solid to me."

Virgil edged up the plank until he could see into the cave in some detail. The doggy odor was so strong he could hardly breathe, but he could feel a thin draft of air from the back of the cave. There's another hole going out, he thought, and maybe another room farther back. With the plank closed from below, the dogs must have been held in total darkness. He didn't see any bodies.

Enough. He backed down the plank and crawled out of the undercut and Johnson asked, "Why didn't you go up inside?"

"'Cause I'm not a stupid asshole," Virgil said.

"You see anything?"

"Not much to see, except dog poop."

"Bet you could find some old Indian stuff in there, if you dug it out," Johnson said.

"Good luck with that," Virgil said. And, "Here are some of the guys."

A red Chevy pickup had pulled to the side of the road below, and two men got out and looked up the hill. Johnson shouted, "Manny. Winky. Right straight up."

MORE TRUCKS STARTED ARRIVING, and a line of climbers stretched down the hill. When the first two came up, one of them said, "I believe those are Dan's beagles. That one was a rescue, and had fly-bitten ears, and there he is. Are there any more?"

"This is it," Virgil said. "They had them up in a hidden cave, which is how they could hide them so fast."

"Six Labs, but not mine," Butterfield said. "Where'n the fuck are my Labs?"

"Goddamn Sharf took them out in that horse trailer," the second man said. "Find him, we find the rest of them."

Butterfield said, "These are all high-grade dogs. They supposedly were snatching some mutts, too. Where are those? Sharf take them, too?"

Johnson said, "I bet they were stealing the high-enders for resale, and the mutts were going to the dog bunchers."

Butterfield said, "Dan is coming up the hill." He turned and shouted, "Hey, Dan, might have some of your dogs up here."

"Hope to Christ nobody has a heart attack climbing that hill," Johnson said.

"Good thought," said Virgil. He looked at the roiling swell of dogs. "Let's see if we can get these dogs wired up or roped up and get them down the hill."

After some more yelling down the hill, one of the younger men got a roll of twine from a truck and started up the hill.

In the meantime, Dan arrived, a big man in jeans and a cotton work shirt. He looked at the beagles and started to cry, and the beagles gathered around his knees, whimpering, trying to climb on him, and he gave Johnson a big hug, which made Johnson look seriously uncomfortable, and then Dan sat on the ground and the beagles gathered around and tried to lick him to death.

He was followed by the woman who'd been at the Shanker's meeting, and had spoken about rescue dogs and ordinary mutts being stolen. She looked at the dogs still in the pen and said, "None of my dogs. My God, they could already be in the laboratories."

The guy with the twine arrived, and while Dan took his dogs down the hill as a pack, they hooked the other dogs together with makeshift collars and the twine, and led them down the hill.

They'd recovered sixteen dogs altogether, and eight of them were immediately identified by owners, either present or known. Johnson called the Humane Society, which sent a truck to collect the rest of them, where they'd be held until they were identified.

It was eleven o'clock before it was all settled, and Virgil went down the hill and called Davenport, and told him about the dogs.

"Are you pulling my leg?"

"No, no, I'm not," Virgil said.

"Well, Christ, I hope nobody else finds out about it."

"I'd like to put out a BOLO on Sharf's truck and horse trailer. Can we at least do that?"

"You're in the same place as that guy who was killed, right? That Corn guy?"

"Zorn. Yeah."

"All right. Put your BOLO out, but say it's in connection with the investigation into the murder of Corn."

"Zorn."

"Zorn. Whatever. That could almost be true."

"When I think about it, it is true," Virgil said. "That's what I will do."

A number of the dog owners were still hanging around, some with dogs, newly recovered, and some without—tears in a few eyes—and Virgil gathered them around and said, "One of the big shots in the BCA just okayed a be-on-the-lookout alert for Sharf's truck and trailer. We'll spread it all over southern Minnesota, northern Iowa, and western Wisconsin."

"'Bout time," somebody said.

Another guy said, "I got Bobby back, but I'll go out after the rest of them, if you call me. We all oughta hang together, not just guys still looking for their mutts."

They all agreed they'd do that.

And he said, "Virgil, you're okay."

They started breaking up, and Virgil got a ride with Johnson back to his truck.

"I'll tell you something, Virgie. No matter what you do, you're never gonna get people more grateful to you than these guys," Johnson said. "You ever need to get somebody killed, all you gotta do is ask."

"You got me all choked up, Johnson," Virgil said. "I'll make a note about it, you know, needing to kill somebody."

"You never know," Johnson said. He shook his head. "Never know."

VIRGIL WENT BACK to the cabin to change clothes, shower, and shave. Standing in the shower, scrubbing off the DEET, he decided that the time had come to give Buster Gedney a deadline. Gedney, he was convinced, was a linchpin. If he could turn him, he could crack the whole case. Gedney could give him Kerns, the security guy who may have done the shooting—he could almost certainly get a search warrant based on Gedney's testimony and Conley's notes—and that would likely get him Kerns's rifle.

From there, using the legal levers he'd have, involving plea bargains and reduced sentences, he could get the rest of them.

He was out of the cabin a little after noon, stopped at a McDonald's for a Quarter Pounder with Cheese, fries, and a strawberry shake, and drove over to Gedney's place while he ate.

He'd finished the burger and almost with the fries when he arrived, and found Jennifer Gedney standing in the driveway, the fingers of one hand pinching at her chin, while she looked into the open garage.

So preoccupied that she didn't see him coming, she turned when Virgil called, "Mrs. Gedney," and dropped her hand and asked, "Where is he?"

"Where's who?"

"Buster. I know you've got him."

"I don't have him. I came over to talk to him." She stared at him, as if working through the possibilities, then nodded and turned back to the garage. Virgil asked, "You haven't seen him today?"

"I saw him this morning, before I went to work. But when I came home for lunch, he wasn't here, and he always is, and when I came out to look in the garage . . . I was kind of worried . . . I found this."

Virgil peered into the garage: "What?"

"His lathe is gone. And a bunch of his tools. All the welding equipment is gone. And his truck."

Virgil noticed the hole in the line of equipment. The milling machine was still there, but that would have been too big to move, anyway, without a truck and a serious hoist. "Goddamnit."

She turned to him again: "You know where he went?"

"No, but I know why he went," Virgil said. "He knew the net's about to drop on the whole bunch of you, and he wanted out."

"The net?"

"The police net." Virgil turned back to his truck, took a few steps, then looked back at her. "If you kept your cut in cash or other valuables, you better check your safe-deposit box, or wherever you keep it. If Buster's running, he'd need all the cash he could get."

She was still standing in the driveway when Virgil pulled away from the house. He drove down the street, over a low rise, down in the dip that followed, up the next rise, then executed a technical law enforcement maneuver called a "U-turn." Rolling back up the hill until he was just high enough to see the end of the Gedney driveway, but the bulk of his truck was still below the crest, he got a pair of binoculars out of the back and sat and waited.

Jennifer Gedney pulled into the street three minutes later. She stopped at the end of the driveway and took a long look in both directions, then turned toward town. Virgil followed her in, watched her park at the Piggly Wiggly. He parked again, and waited, and five minutes later she came back out, hands empty, looked in both directions, got in her car, drove two blocks, and took a left. Virgil hurried after her and made the turn in time to see her turn into the Second National Bank parking lot.

Ten minutes later, she came back out, hands still empty. She got in her car, but the car didn't move for five minutes. Virgil edged closer and looked at her with the binoculars. She had her head down on the steering wheel.

Weeping?

Hard to tell. He waited, and after a couple more minutes she started the car, and Virgil drove on past the bank and watched as she turned away from him and disappeared back around the corner toward her home.

When she was out of sight, Virgil turned around and followed her. Five minutes later she pulled back into her driveway, got out of the car, and went into the house. Virgil drove back to the bank, went inside, identified himself, and asked to see the manager.

The manager was a heavyset, blue-eyed man with white hair, named Marvin Hiners, who emerged from a small office carrying a sheaf of papers, and asked, "Mr. Flowers?"

Virgil followed him back into the office and said, "I'm investigating the two murders we've had here, Mr. Conley and Mr. Zorn. I need some information from you. I'm not asking for documents, I'm only interviewing you as a witness. I'm telling you this so that you know I don't need a search warrant. If you wish, I'll wait for you to get legal advice about answering my questions."

Hiners leaned back in his chair, concern on his pale German face. "What . . . uh, I'll reserve the right to talk to the bank's legal counsel . . . but ask the questions, and I'll figure out if I want to answer. I can tell you, I've had no part in any crime."

"I doubt that you have. Here's the first question. Did Mrs. Jennifer Gedney, who was just here, get access to a safe-deposit box?"

Hiners had taken a yellow pencil out of a pencil jar on his desk, and he twiddled it for a few seconds, then said, "Yes. Well, she went into the safe area, where Carol David may have given her access, although I didn't see it. But that's the only reason for going back there. To access your safe-deposit box."

Virgil nodded. "Do you know if Buster Gedney came in here earlier today and accessed the same box?"

More twiddling, then, "Yes. I will also tell you that I approved a withdrawal of nine thousand dollars from their joint savings account, which was almost everything in it. There's less than a thousand left. Buster said he needed the cash to buy some kind of machine for his machine shop, and the man who had it wanted cash. I warned him that such deals can involve stolen equipment, but he took the money."

Virgil: "I want you to isolate and preserve all the documents that show this, both the entry into the safe-deposit boxes, and the withdrawal. I'll be back with a subpoena."

Hiners asked, "Did Buster kill those people?"

"I don't believe so," Virgil said. "But I do need to talk with him."

Virgil went out to his truck, called the BCA duty officer, and said that he wanted to issue two BOLOs, one for Buster Gedney and the other for D. Wayne Sharf, in connection with the murder of Conley and Zorn. He gave the duty officer what details he had on their vehicles, then rang off and scratched his head.

Now what? He couldn't just sit around and see if somebody caught Buster Gedney, but admitted to himself that he'd been leaning pretty hard on the idea that Gedney would talk.

HE WOUND UP driving over to Janice Anderson's house, the woman who'd given him the copy of the school budget.

She was outside nipping the heads off expired coneflowers with a pair of side-cutters, and when she saw him coming, dropped the pliers in the pocket of a gardener's apron, picked up her cane, and walked over toward him.

"Good day for gardening," Virgil said.

"I don't do small talk," Anderson said. She pushed her glasses up her nose. "You want something?"

"Need to talk to you. Confidentially."

"Good. I'm bored," she said. "You want an iced tea?"

"Thank you anyway—"

"Lemonade?"

"I could take a lemonade," Virgil said.

"Sit there," she said, pointing him at a garden table. She hung her cane on the back of one of the garden chairs, went in the house, and came back carrying two glasses and a pitcher of lemonade. She poured the glasses two-thirds full and pushed one toward Virgil.

He picked it up, took a drink. "Good," he said. "Homemade?"

"Yes, inasmuch as I made it in my home, with a can of Birds Eye frozen lemonade."

"Okay," Virgil said. "I got a trustworthy vibration from you the other day, and I need to ask a somewhat, mmm, sensitive question."

"Stop beating around the bush and ask the question."

Virgil nodded. "A brief preface. I had a guy who I was going to squeeze like a ball of Silly Putty. Buster Gedney. But early this morning Buster ran for it. Loaded a good part of his machine shop into his truck, apparently, and headed out. I've got people looking for him in four states, but he could be damn near to Missouri or Nebraska or Ohio by now, and if he drives all night, he could be anywhere between the Appalachians and the Rockies by tomorrow morning."

"You might not find him, then."

"Having spoken to Buster, I think we've got a chance," Virgil said. "But you can't tell, and I've got two dead people on my hands. I've got an idea of who might've done it, but no proof. Here's my question: If you assume that a good part of the school board and school administration is in on this, who'd be most likely to crack under pressure?"

"Hmm." She took a sip of the lemonade, grimaced, stared at the sky over the roof of the neighbor's house, and finally said, "Wouldn't be Jennifer Gedney, she's a pretty tough nut. I guess I'd go after Henry Hetfield, he's the school superintendent. He'd almost have to be in on it. He's a fussy old woman, and the idea of prison would terrify him. In fact, you'd have to be careful. He could wind up jumping off his workbench with a rope around his neck, or choking down a bottle of sleeping pills."

"Can't have that," Virgil said.

"Okay. Well, there's the auditor, Fred Masilla. He'd have to be in on it, too, but he's pretty soft-looking. Soft-talking."

"Okay."

"You know who could really answer this question, is Vike Laughton. He covers the school board."

"That would not be a good idea," Virgil said.

Her eyebrows went up. "Really. Vike?"

"I have no proof, but Conley thought so."

She took another sip of lemonade, then said, "You want to know the thing about this part of Minnesota?"

"Sure."

"We're isolated. We're out in the sticks. There's no other big town anywhere near here. I mean, La Crosse, but that's on the other side of the river, and it's a good long drive over there. Caledonia's a bit closer, but it's still a long way. We're down here by ourselves, and we get to thinking that we really are by ourselves. The people who are stealing this money from the schools, it probably never occurred to them that an outsider might take an interest in what they're doing. And insiders, people who live here, can be managed—they can be ignored, like me, with my silly campaign for art and music classes, or they can be bought off. The schools spend a lot of money, millions of dollars, and most of it they spend right here. Nobody but an outsider would want to get crosswise with them. We'd never say that out loud, not even to each other, but that's the fact."

"Can't have people getting shot in the back," Virgil said.

"Of course not—but keep in mind that they were both outsiders. They don't really count for so much." They sat without speaking for a while, then she added, "You know how much a house costs here?"

"No idea."

"You could get a very nice dry lot on the river, with a dock, three or four acres, big modern house, excellent condition . . . for maybe four hundred thousand. I saw one like that last spring. You could get a house in town, an ordinary house, for a hundred."

"Yeah?"

"Yes. The point is, whatever these people have been stealing has probably been making them rich in Trippton terms. In this town, two schoolteachers married to each other are rich . . . so the money won't have to be big. Not in New York terms, or Minneapolis terms, anyway."

"Henry Hetfield."

"He's the one I'd go after." She looked at a small gold watch that she wore as a locket. "You're a little late in the day—he'll be gone. He only works until three o'clock, and sometimes not even that, in the summer."

"Does he live here?"

"Yes, he does. I'll get a pencil and paper and draw you a map of where he lives."

WHEN VIRGIL GOT BACK to his truck, he sat and thought about it for a minute, but in the end decided that Hetfield would have to wait until morning. He needed to do some research on him, talk to Johnson Johnson, look again at Conley's notes, see where Hetfield fit in. He'd seen Hetfield's name in the notes, now he wanted to nail down what Conley thought about him.

He put the car in gear and drove back to the cabin; on the way he called Johnson and told him they needed to hook up again, at least for a few minutes.

"I think I might have been an alcoholic," Johnson told him, on the phone. "Two days without a drink and I feel like somebody put a vise on my neck. The thing is, when I was drinking, I was a hell of a nice guy—ask anyone. Now I'm not sure I'm so nice anymore."

Virgil didn't want to say it, because he really wanted Johnson to stop, but the opening was too tempting. "Don't worry, Johnson. Everybody thought you were an asshole. The change is all in your mind."

14

WHILE VIRGIL WAS at Janice Anderson's house, Jennifer Gedney was using the only remaining pay phone in Trippton, the one at the back of the drugstore, to call Jennifer Barns, the chairwoman of the school board. "We need a meeting and it's urgent. We need to talk about personnel matters and budgetary questions."

Barns asked, "How urgent?"

"Very." Gedney looked around, half-expecting to see Virgil lurking behind the greeting-card rack.

"Is this a DefCon One?"

"No, but it's a two," Gedney said. "Maybe going to one."

"Oh, shit. Are you sure?"

"Yes."

"At my house tonight at nine o'clock," Jennifer 1 said.

"You'll have to call everybody—I'm afraid to use my cell," Gedney said.

"That bad?"

"Yes."

AT TEN AFTER NINE, Gedney parked her car on a side street, a block
away and around the corner from Jennifer Barns's house. She collected her purse and got out under a starlit sky, stood for a minute,
decided it might get chilly, got her sweater from the passenger seat,
and slipped it over her shoulders.

She was deliberately late, waiting to see if the arrival of the others
stirred any interest from . . . anybody. Other than familiar cars being
parked on the street by Jennifer 1's, she'd seen nothing unusual.

She'd started to walk to Jennifer 1's when her cell phone chimed,
and she looked at it: a text message. WRU?

She texted back: 1 min.

WHEN SHE ARRIVED, they were all waiting, some looking skeptical,
some scared, a couple just curious. Jennifer 1 had provided a couple
bottles of white wine, and everyone but Jennifer 2, a recovering alcoholic, had a glass. She could smell the fear rolling off them.

"So what happened?" Vike Laughton asked.

They'd left an empty chair for her, but Gedney spoke on her feet:
"The state agent, Virgil Flowers, was pushing Buster around. Buster
was intimidated. Flowers came back yesterday and told Buster that
if he didn't identify the person he sold the . . . I can't remember

what he called it, but it's the parts that make Randy's gun shoot three bullets—"

"Burst kit," Kerns said.

"Yes. He knew that Buster made them. Buster denied it, but he knew anyway, because Buster couldn't get a lie past a two-year-old. So yesterday he told Buster that if Buster didn't tell him who he sold the burst kit to, he'd be charged with first-degree murder. He said he'd go to prison for thirty years, and when he was there, he'd be . . . sodomized. Buster was so scared—"

"He told you all this, Buster did," Barns said.

"Yes. Last night. He said he wouldn't tell Flowers about the burst boxes, but he sounded really shaky."

"Time to do something about Buster," Laughton said. A couple of people nodded.

Gedney waved them down: "Too late. When I came home for lunch, I found out that Buster had loaded up most of his equipment, everything movable, and he'd run for it. He also cleaned out our savings account, and the safe-deposit box."

"Oh my God," Jennifer Houser said. "Did he get it all?"

"No, I'm not dumb enough to put it all in one place. I've got another one, but he took everything at Second National. More than a hundred thousand, plus nine thousand from our savings. Anyway, I'd just found out about it when Flowers showed up looking for Buster. Buster had left the garage doors open, and Flowers saw that his lathe was gone. He knew that Buster had gone, and he took off: I suspect they've put out some kind of watch for him."

"Buster's too damn dumb to get away clean," Henry Hetfield said. "I believe when they catch him . . . I believe he'll talk."

"That's correct," Gedney said about her husband.

Laughton said, "I don't have a philosophical problem with killing Buster, but there's a practical one. Randy shot Zorn to steer Flowers away from us. That makes total sense. If we kill Buster, that steers him back. If you'll excuse me for saying so, a string of three murders does tend to catch the eye. If that happened, we'd have more than one cop down here. We'd probably attract the FBI."

"You should have called a meeting on Zorn," Barns said. "I would have voted against it. If I had seen—"

"Water under the bridge," Laughton said. "It's done—and to tell you the truth, I think it still has some value, should this all get to court. It's an alternative theory on the murders, and a good defense attorney will make it into something."

"What do we do about Buster?" Gedney asked.

"We hope you can reach him before Flowers does, or that he calls home," Laughton said. "If Randy can get to him, then Buster, bless his heart, could disappear. Instead of leaving the body out there for all and sundry, Randy could put him down someplace deep, out in a forest or a swamp, and it'd just seem like he ran away and was never found."

Kerns said, "I could do that."

Laughton held up a finger. "I'm officially scared shitless. But—all Buster knows is that he sold a burst kit to Randy. I suggest that Randy get rid of that gun, soak the burst kit in some gasoline to get rid of any powder residue, then wash it with soap and water and put it in a plastic bag. If Flowers gets to him, he could claim he never used the kit. Then he gets another gun—hell, I'll give him mine, I got it at a gun show, there are no numbers on it—and if the cops ever get that far, he denies everything. They check the gun, it wasn't used to kill anyone. They got nothing."

"Buster knows we've gotten a lot of money we shouldn't have, and he knows where it came from," Gedney said.

"Did you put the money somewhere they could find it?" Laughton asked.

Gedney said, "Well . . . not exactly. They could find out about my safe-deposit boxes. I've got one here and one in La Crosse. I could clean out the La Crosse one, leave a couple thousand dollars there, tell them I was hiding it for a divorce."

"That should work," Houser said.

Larry Parsons, the fifth board member, who hadn't spoken, said, "Here's what I think. I think it's time to shut down, at least for a while. I think we need that really bad fire at the school board offices, something that takes out the whole computer system, all the records. We've talked about it—I think it's time."

"That'll attract a lot of attention," Hetfield said.

"We've worked all through that," Parsons said. "Leave behind something that makes it look like kids did it. Vandals. The thing is, Flowers can believe anything he wants. He can know anything he wants. But to charge us with anything, he's going to need proof. Burn the office, where's the proof?"

They all considered that for a while. There were a few places here and there where they might be vulnerable—places where they'd had to take kickbacks, rather than simply cook the books—but if those people kept their mouths shut . . .

Jennifer Barns said, "Larry's right. It's time. How many people vote for a fire?"

"Who'll do it?" Hetfield asked.

They all looked at Kerns, who said, "I've done some reading up on it. The office is in the middle of the building, so nobody'll actually see the fire until it breaks through the roof. I'll pull the battery in the smoke alarm. . . ."

He walked them through the details. Five gallons of gas for flames and heat, a quart of motor oil to give it some substance; evidence of an amateurish break-in . . .

"When do we do it?" Hetfield asked. He was nervous, polishing his glasses with the tail of his shirt.

"Soon as possible."

"I got a couple things I'd like to get out of there."

Kerns shook his head. "No. Leave them. The cops and fire people will want to talk to you. We want you kinda messed up about the fire. Talking about what you lost. When I was doing my research, the one thing arson investigators always look at is whether anything was taken out in the days before a fire. If something was, that's the guy they always look at."

Owens, the senior board member, shook his head. "My God, where have we gotten?"

Gedney said, "Buster is still the loose cannon. I'm really worried about him."

Laughton said, "If we can find him . . ."

Barns said, "Everybody—if Flowers manages to dig something up, to turn somebody on us, we shut up and we lawyer up. Instantly. Nobody talks. If anybody turns, we'll all go down, and frankly, with two killings, the state's not going to let anybody go free. The best you could probably hope for is twenty years, instead of thirty. We're all old enough that we wouldn't see daylight until it hardly mattered anymore. So: if push comes to shove . . . don't give it up."

Gedney looked around the room: "Everybody understand that?"

"I think we all do," Laughton said. "And what Jen One said is exactly right. We won't be able to buy our way out of this. The only way out is straight ahead."

Barns said, "The fire. We were talking about a fire. We all know the plan, and Randy suggests we go ahead with it. Let's see a show of hands, all in favor . . ."

They were unanimous: burn it.

15

JOHNSON AND VIRGIL sat drinking on the cabin porch, Johnson a bottle of lemonade—he'd brought three quarts with him—Virgil a beer. Johnson said, "You're a cruel man, Flowers. Taunting an ex-alkie like me."

"It's a test, which I fervently hope that you pass," Virgil said. "Besides, everybody you know will be doing this. You gotta get used to it. Anyway, if I squeeze this Henry Hetfield's nuts, will he talk?"

"Don't know him that well, but from what I've seen, I'd say, probably," Johnson said. "He's one of those bureaucrats who thinks about everything in terms of deals and arrangements. With a couple murders in the mix, though, you'd have to be pretty convincing. He'd have to know that even if he makes a deal, he's gonna spend a few years in jail, at best."

"I can be convincing, if I have just a piece of evidence," Virgil said. "I've got a little bit, but it's all sort of hearsay—a dead reporter's notes. I've got the name of a school bus driver who might talk. I'm afraid if I go to her too soon, she'll let the cat out of the bag. And she might be worried about keeping her job. If I can get a piece of something to stick up Hetfield's ass, and he points me at the right computer files, I can get a state auditor down here and hang all of them at once."

"Gonna have to do something. Time to fish or cut bait," Johnson said.

VIRGIL DREAMED OF Frankie and sex, and dogs in caves, and late at night, of a fire in Frankie's barn. He tried to keep the barn from burning down, but when he ran for the hose, the hose was all tangled in knots; it took forever to undo the knots, and when he did, no water was running, and Frankie was screaming something about the circuit breakers for the pump, and he ran down to the basement but couldn't find the breaker box in twenty minutes of running from one basement room to another; the rooms were endless. Virgil had a certain ability to edit his dreams, and he finally forced himself to find the circuit-breaker box, but when he did, there were about a thousand breakers, none of them marked. And all the time, the barn was burning, and Frankie was running buckets from a stock tank and screaming to him to start the pump, and he was failing . . . failing.

He woke then, and sleepily wondered for a few seconds exactly what tangled psychological meanings the dream could possibly have. Then he heard the sirens.

For a moment he thought he'd somehow slipped back into the dream, then realized that the sirens were real, but far away, and had probably caused the dream. At the last moment before tipping back over into a deep sleep, he thought that if it were another killing, that Johnson would be calling, because Johnson never in his life could resist a siren.

What seemed like a quarter-second later, but was probably a couple of hours, Johnson called.

Virgil fumbled the phone off the nightstand and asked, "What?"

"You know that idea about getting the state auditor down here to seize the school books?"

"Johnson . . ."

"Yeah, well, you can forget it," Johnson said. "They had an untimely fire at the school district offices that apparently took out every computer in the place."

"What!"

"I'm told the first firemen in the place backed right out, because the gasoline fumes were so thick. The fire was so hot the desks melted like a bunch of marshmallows."

"The desks melted? You've seen them?" Virgil dropped his feet to the cool floorboards.

"I talked to Henry Hetfield. He knows me because I'm rounding up votes for the sports arena bond issue. Anyway, he said he suspected arson, kids who want to delay the beginning of the school year. He said the firemen say that it looks like a door was pried open."

"I'm coming," Virgil said.

———————

NOTHING LIKE A FIRE to get you out of bed. Virgil had been to more than one of them, when he was a cop in St. Paul, and once when investigating a series of murders in western Minnesota. In the early morning, the stink of burning insulation and burned wet boards hangs all around the fire site, and people talk in hushed voices and firemen hustle around and red emergency lights flick off all the surrounding windows and car chrome.

Johnson was standing by himself with his hands in his jean-jacket pockets when Virgil arrived, and he walked over and said, "They wouldn't let me in, but I talked to Greg Jones, he's the assistant chief, he says there's nothing left in the office except a big hole. Henry Hetfield said he had a scrapbook with pictures of his late wife, most of what he had of her, and it apparently burned up."

"Let's go look," Virgil said. "Point me at the chief."

Virgil talked to the assistant chief, and showed him his ID, and explained that the fire might be entangled with an investigation he was conducting. Jones led him into the building—he allowed Johnson to come along, when Virgil said Johnson was working as a consultant for him.

"The fire itself was mostly restricted to the district offices. There's quite a bit of smoke damage down the second floor, into the high school. There'll have to be a lot of cleanup."

Johnson said, "Henry Hetfield said you suspect arson."

"Yeah, unfortunately. The door down at the end of the first-floor hallway, at the back of the school, was forced with a crowbar, and so was the door into the offices. The inside of the door is badly burned, but the outside still shows splinters around the lock. Henry thinks it was some kids trying to delay the school year."

"Then why did they set fire to the district office, instead of the school?" Virgil asked.

The chief shrugged: "Because they're kids?"

"Some of the guys said they could smell gasoline," Johnson said.

"The first guys in said so. Not so much anymore, everything's wrapped in foam. But it was a fast-burning fire. The wall clock there is stopped at three fifty-two, and we were here a couple minutes after four—there's an automatic alarm system—and we knocked it down in a hurry, but . . . it was fully engaged. It was a flash fire, and it was hot."

The offices were a mess. Everything was charred, and sound-proofing tiles were either burned or hung from the ceiling like dead black bats. Virgil could see fire-blacked wires and pipes in the ceiling, and water and foam had wrecked anything the fire hadn't gotten to. A half-dozen computers were literally melted on the burned desks, as though somebody had poured acid on a bunch of over-sized mushrooms.

"Nothing to do about this," Virgil said. "I'm going to get the sheriff's crime-scene guy up here, see if there are any prints on that door downstairs. See if you can tape it off or something, keep people away."

"You think it might not be kids?"

"I don't know," Virgil said. "What do you think?"

The chief said, "We've had vandalism here a few times, and a small fire once, you know, over the years. Usually they come during the school year—a kid freaks out because he's going to fail, or get kicked out of school, or whatever. Never had one in August."

IT WAS TOO EARLY in the morning to start ringing doorbells, so Virgil said good-bye to Johnson, who said, "I hope they had good insurance. I hope they don't try to take some of the stadium money to fix up the offices," and went back to the cabin and fell into bed.

No dreams this time, and when Virgil woke up again, it was after nine o'clock. He cleaned up, ate a couple pieces of peanut butter toast, and dug out Conley's notes. The school bus driver was named Jamie Nelson, but the notes didn't say whether that was a man or a woman, because, Virgil thought, Conley would know that, and wouldn't have to write it down.

Jamie Nelson was a woman. He found her at her tiny house, set well up the hill past the school; Virgil lived in a small house himself, but Nelson's house couldn't have enclosed more than a few hundred square feet: a living-room-sitting-room-kitchen, a small bedroom, a bath. Maybe some storage up under a pitched roof.

She came to the door carrying a cup of herbal tea. She was in her fifties, Virgil thought, and had once had red hair, now mostly gray, with a few vagrant strands of red threaded through it. She had blue eyes, a long straight nose, a million freckles, and lips as thin as a No. 2 pencil, straight and grim. When she opened the door, she said, "What now?"

Virgil held up his ID and said, "You talked to Clancy Conley about some ideas you had about the price of the school's diesel. I'd like to talk to you about that."

She said, "Nope. I'm not talking anymore to nobody."

"I'm investigating a couple of murders, Miz Nelson, or I wouldn't be bothering you."

"Think about that, and you'll know why I'm not talking to nobody," she said. She began to ease the door shut. Through the diminishing crack, she said, "If you come back, you better bring a judge or court papers or something."

"Miz . . ." But the door was shut.

VIRGIL CALLED JOHNSON: "You know I don't entirely trust Sheriff Purdy, and I don't know the local county attorney at all. If I go to see him about compelling Nelson to talk, is there any chance I'll get that done, without everybody in town knowing about it?"

"No, not really," Johnson said. "But tell you what. Let me see what I can do."

VIRGIL SAT IN his truck and ran over the possibilities. Eventually, he turned around and headed back downtown, to Viking Laughton's storefront newspaper. Laughton was in, banging on a computer.

When Virgil came through the door, he turned and said, "Shit. I was hoping it was an advertiser."

"Doing a story on the fire?"

Laughton frowned: "What fire?"

"The school's district offices burned at the high school. I thought you'd be all over it."

Laughton looked at his watch: "Too late for this week's newspaper, anyway. I'll catch it next week. How bad was it?"

"Not much left in the office," Virgil said. "Somebody poured a lot of gasoline in it, and touched it off."

"Goddamn kids," Laughton said.

"Don't think it was kids," Virgil said. "I think it was somebody trying to cover up two murders. Which is why I'm here to talk to you. I need to talk to you confidentially, not as a reporter or editor or whatever. Can you keep your mouth shut?"

"For a while, anyway," Laughton said, twisting around in his office chair. He pointed Virgil at another chair. "Murder? You mean Clancy? What's going on?"

"You cover the school board, right? What I need to find is, the weakest person on the board," Virgil said. "I suspect the whole bunch of them are running a huge embezzlement scheme. I've got some details, but I need somebody to talk to me. I thought you might have some ideas about who the weak sister might be. I need to squeeze him, or her. I've already talked to the attorney general's office about an immunity deal, but I have to find somebody who'd cave."

Laughton rubbed his chin. "I've known a lot of the school people most of my life. . . . I can't really see the whole bunch of them being involved in a big embezzlement. Most of them aren't smart enough, for one thing. For another thing, they're mostly pretty honest folks. I mean, I could see some of the professionals, the hired people, dipping into the cash if they saw the chance, but even then, it wouldn't be huge."

"Well, it is huge, take my word for it," Virgil said. "I think Conley was killed to cover it up, and then Zorn was killed to pull us away from the real reason Conley was shot."

Laughton shook his head. "Jeez, Virgil, I hope you've got something substantial to back that up. It just doesn't sound like us. Not in Trippton."

Virgil, who'd taken the chair, now stood up. "I do have something substantial. My problem is, I don't understand all of it. A bunch of numbers. But I'll figure it out."

"Let me know when you do," Laughton said. "Sounds like a hell of a story . . . if there's any truth to it."

"You'll be the first to know," Virgil said.

HE LEFT, satisfied that the cat was now among the pigeons, if it hadn't been earlier, and drove north to La Crescent, across the bridge to La Crosse, Wisconsin, and pulled into the Holiday Inn in time for lunch.

Inside, he found two large men eating pizza. Virgil nudged the marginally smaller one and said, "Move over, Shrake."

Shrake's partner, Jenkins, said, "This is really inconvenient. We're shutting down one of the biggest cases in recent history, involving two thousand elderly people who were swindled of their life savings, and we get shifted down the river to fix that fuckin' Flowers's problems with a bunch of rednecks."

"Got some nice golf courses in La Crosse," Virgil said. Jenkins's eyes shifted away, and Virgil asked, "You didn't bring your clubs, by any chance?"

Shrake said, "Maybe."

"Probably never get a chance to use them," Jenkins said.

They both brightened up when Virgil told them what he wanted. "So basically, a body-guarding job," Jenkins said. "Early in the morning, late in the afternoon."

"Right."

"Which, by pure mathematics," Jenkins said, "would leave the midday wide open for other pursuits."

"It would."

"We can do that," Jenkins said. "Probably have to buy some specialty clothing on the government dime, but we can do that, too. Have some wood-fired pizza."

VIRGIL TOLD THEM about the situation, and they agreed to meet him at Johnson's cabin at five o'clock. When they finished the pizza, Virgil headed back down the highway to Trippton, and on the way, took a call from Johnson.

"Where you at?"

"Up north, probably twenty minutes out, heading that way," Virgil said.

"Okay, twenty minutes from now, stop back and talk to Jamie Nelson again. I asked around, and one of the dog guys knows her. He called her up and vouched for you, and she says she'll talk to you. But she's scared. I got her phone number—call her and tell her when you get there. She wants to get you out of sight real quick."

"I understand her being scared. Thank you, Johnson. I'll be there in twenty."

———

VIRGIL WENT INTO TOWN on the backstreets, circling around to come up to Nelson's house from the side. When he'd parked, he called, and she said, "I'll be waiting at the door. Get in here quick. I can't talk long, I got to get to work."

Virgil did as he was told, crossing her side lawn, up the steps and inside, in less than half a minute. She shook her head and said, "I oughta have my goddamned head examined, after what happened to Clancy. I knew that had something to do with the schools. Probably that goddamned Kerns."

"A couple of people have mentioned his name," Virgil said, "He must be . . . out there."

"He is. He's gun crazy. He'd like shooting somebody. He likes roughing up the kids. Be surprised if he hadn't already shot somebody somewhere, just to see what it felt like."

She sat at her kitchen table, and Virgil took the second chair and crossed his legs, facing her across the checked oilcloth. "How're they stealing the diesel money?"

"Ah, jeez. Listen, I'm not a hundred percent on this. But I'm ninety-five percent. What I do is, I take my bus out in the morning, and the fuel tank is good for three days, and I refill it. So I know exactly how much fuel I'm using, which is about twenty-eight gallons, give or take. What I did was—"

"Hold on," Virgil said. "Where'd you get filled up?"

"At the school's motor pool. They have two pumps there, and buy in bulk. What I did was, last winter I was in the office out there while Dick, he's the supervisor, Dick Brown, was out. I Ic was filling out the usage reports, and I saw that my bus was down for thirty-three gallons. Well, we have a bunch of drivers, you know, and there isn't a lot to talk about, and we see each other filling up, and we know about how much diesel we use. So I looked at some more slips, and every one was over. My friend Cory uses about thirty gallons every three days, and his slip was down for thirty-five. He was bumping it up five gallons per bus. You take forty-four buses, that's a good chunk of change."

"You told Clancy about all of this."

"What I did was, I waited until Dick was out again, and I xeroxed a bunch of the usage slips, and then I watched people filling up, and wrote the actual amount on the slips and gave them to him."

"Wouldn't the amounts change from day to day?"

"No. Oh, they might change a little from season to season, but not from day to day. That's because it's the same people, driving the same bus, exactly the same routes, every day. Never goes more than a gallon, one way or the other. Every one of the slips jacks up the usage."

"How do you know Dick isn't just taking the money?"

"Oh, I don't doubt old Dicky gets paid to do it, but I don't know by who. Because, see, he just runs the garage and makes out the slips. He never touches the money. There are only two ways Dick could get paid. The wholesaler delivers us short, and Dick overstates the use, and the wholesaler pays him. Or Dick overstates the use, but only orders from the wholesaler when the tank gets empty, and Dick collects from the school. Either way would work, but I think it's from the school."

"Did anybody ever ask about it?"

"Davey Page did—and that's why I think it came out of the school, because Kerns—"

"The school's hired gun . . ."

"Because Kerns came around and whispered in Davey's ear, and Davey came to me that night and said, 'We don't talk about this anymore.' He was scared. He said, 'You want to keep your job, you stop snooping, and keep your mouth shut.' I need the job. I don't have this job, I don't eat."

"Your job is okay," Virgil said. "Your job isn't going anywhere."

"That's fine, but I just as soon you don't tell anybody about me until they're all in jail. Especially Kerns."

"I'll see to it," Virgil said. "Now, tell me about these usage slips. What do they look like? Where does Dick keep them? And tell me about Dick. . . ."

SHE TOLD HIM about Dick, and then she added, "Something else. I really, really shouldn't tell you about this . . . but you seem like a good guy. I mean, for a policeman." She put a twist on the word "seem," a little extra skepticism.

"I try to be a good guy," Virgil said, as earnestly as he could manage.

"The dog boys said you seemed okay. I'll tell you this last thing, and you can see where it gets you. The school janitor's name is Will Bacon. I suspect he lives at the school. I suspect he was probably there last night when the fire started."

"What do you mean, he lives at the school? You mean, he lives at the school? Secretly?"

"That's what I think. He's supposed to come to work around two in the afternoon, and leave around ten o'clock at night," she said. "But I've seen him there before the school opens—and I once thought I saw him there at midnight, when I got back from a basketball trip. I know where he used to live, but he doesn't live there anymore. Usually, in a town this size, you know where everybody lives, everybody that you know. I don't know anybody who knows where Will lives."

"How would I find him, if he never goes out?"

"You're the cop. Shouldn't you be able to figure that out?"

VIRGIL DROVE TO the high school, parked in the student lot, next to a fire-engine-red Toyota van. The van was fire-engine red because it belonged to the Trippton fire department, and the parking lot entrance to the school was standing open.

Virgil went inside, heard people talking, and followed the noise to the burned-out district offices. Henry Hetfield was there, talking to three people in civilian clothes, and two uniformed firemen, and a deputy sheriff that Virgil didn't recognize. They all turned when Virgil walked in, and Hetfield said, "Agent Flowers . . ."

Virgil said, "Hello," and, "Wanted to check to see if there's any new information."

"Pretty much what we thought this morning," Hetfield said. He added, "People, this is Agent Virgil Flowers from the BCA. He's investigating the murders of Clancy Conley and that Mr. Zorn, apparently because of some drug tie-in. . . . Agent Flowers, this is Bob Owens and Jennifer Barns and Jennifer Houser, three of our school board members."

Virgil said, "Actually, I think Zorn was killed to create an apparent tie between him and Conley that didn't really exist. After we busted those meth cookers up there, everybody in town knew we were looking at Zorn."

"If Clancy wasn't killed because of drugs, why . . . what happened to him?" one of the Jennifers asked.

"Don't know yet, but I'm beginning to assemble some pieces," Virgil said. "When I get enough, I'll stick them together and call the attorney general's office. I think this fire could be part of the puzzle."

"This fire?" Hetfield's hand went to his throat. "How could this fire be involved?"

"Part of what I'm working on," Virgil said. "I see the school's mostly empty—I'd like to walk around it for a while, get a sense of it."

"I could show you around . . ." Hetfield began.

"No, that's okay. I'll just walk around on my own. You've got more important business here, I'm sure."

He left them looking at each other, and wandered away, hands in his pockets, peering into classrooms and checking open lockers.

THE HIGH SCHOOL WAS three stories high, built around an open square. Originally the square must have been designed as a park-like area for sitting or eating lunch. Now it was filled in with a one-story later addition that housed the district offices. The offices had a series of pyramid-shaped skylights of hazy glass. The fire had broken all of the skylights at the back of the addition.

Starting from the first floor, Virgil walked most of the way around the square, to get a sense of the building, then took a set of wide steps to the second floor and walked around that, and looked out some windows into the square, and down to the district offices. He could see a guy in yellow fireman's gear through one of the broken skylights, but couldn't tell what he was doing.

The second floor showed a lot of soot and smelled of smoke: somebody was going to make a lot of money on the cleanup.

At the next set of stairways, he could hear a hammer working on the third floor, so he went up, and found Will Bacon working in a smoke-stained hallway. He was using a hammer and chisel to knock broken glass and old hard putty out of a big window, one of a line of windows that looked out over the roof of the district offices. A half dozen of them were broken or cracked, apparently from the heat of the fire. Bacon was tall and too thin, but with the hard thinness of a man who worked with heavy tools, and had spent his life lifting and carrying. Virgil thought he was probably in his fifties, his close-cropped hair going gray.

He saw Virgil coming and asked, "You lost?"

"Not if you're Will Bacon."

"That's me. Who are you?"

Virgil identified himself, and asked, "Were you here last night when the fire started?"

Bacon answered with a question, frowning as he did so. The frown was supposed to look bewildered or surprised, but it came out looking guilty. "Here? Why would I be here?"

"Because you live here?"

"You think I live here?"

"Mr. Bacon, I don't care if you live here," Virgil said. "And I won't tell anyone, unless I absolutely have to. Did you see anybody here? Do you know anything about the fire?"

Bacon looked up and down the hall. "Where is everybody?"

"They're all down in the offices."

Bacon looked at Virgil for a moment, then said, "You better come along."

Virgil nodded, and Bacon led the way halfway around the top square to a maintenance room stocked with custodial supplies. At the back of the room, half concealed behind a row of metal HVAC pipes, was a narrow door. Bacon kept his keys on a belt-mounted ring, and used one of them to open the door. Behind the door was a set of stairs.

"Careful. They're steep."

Virgil followed him up, his nose almost at the level of Bacon's heels. At the top he found himself in a low attic-like storage room probably fifty yards long and thirty feet wide, with a low ceiling, of maybe six and a half feet. A few dozen cardboard cartons were stacked along the outside walls, some with notations: World History Texts, Hyram Algebra, and so on. The floor, walls, and boxes were covered with dust. A narrow strip of cheap carpet ran to the end of the room.

Bacon said, "Don't step on the wooden part of the floor—it's almost impossible to get that dust right. Stay on the rug."

The rug ended at another pile of cardboard cartons that had "Band Uniforms, 1985" scribbled on them. In the same line, against the end wall, were boxes that said: "Football equipment, 1988," and at the far end of the interior wall, five large moving boxes that said:

"Algebra, 1962, 1968, 1974." One of the boxes was broken, and old algebra books were spilling out.

Bacon picked up three of the band-uniform boxes, one at a time, set them aside to reveal another narrow door. He pushed it open, flicked on a light switch, and said, "Come on in."

Behind the door was a small, tidy one-room apartment—an easy chair with a reading lamp, a television with a cable connection, and a line of bookcases that separated the sitting area from a tiny kitchen. The kitchen had a dining table that might serve two in a pinch, with a wooden chair. A compact refrigerator sat under a food-prep bench, which held a microwave oven and a toaster. A six-drawer bureau divided the kitchen from the sleeping area, which held a single bed, another lamp, a nightstand, and another wooden chair. A variety of jackets and overalls hung from hooks along the inside wall, along with a mop, broom, and dustpan.

One round decorative window looked out over the town.

"No plumbing. If you don't rat me out, I think I can get some in next year," Bacon said. He picked up the dining chair and offered it to Virgil, and took a seat himself in the easy chair. "So—the fire."

Virgil sat down. "Yeah. The fire."

Bacon sat, gathering his thoughts, and then said, "Okay. See, what happened is that in 2007, I had this little house, wasn't worth much, but it was okay. I started this business, a side business, doing handyman work. I needed a truck, and I spent too much on it, and tools, and I spent too much on them. I got loans for it all, secured by the house. Then the economy went in the ditch, and nobody was hiring handymen, and I couldn't make the payments. They said I could keep the house or the truck, and I needed the truck, so they took the house. Sonsofbitches."

"Doesn't sound right," Virgil said.

"Wasn't right. Did get some good tools out of it, though. Anyway, the school pay is . . . bad. They pay me twenty-two thousand, eight hundred and eighty dollars a year, but there just aren't any other jobs around. Jobs I could do, anyway. Walmart pays even less, I'm too old to work the tows. I tried renting a room for a while, but that was a crappy way to live. Then I thought about this place. Put down the carpet, so I could walk back here without disturbing the dust, snuck in lumber for the walls, built the room, brought the pieces of furniture in one at a time, in the truck . . . and here I am."

"Not a bad place," Virgil said. "I could live here . . . if I had to."

"Just fine, for me," Bacon said, looking around the room. "Anyway, here's what I do. I do my job, and more than my job. If something in the school needs fixing, I fix it. In return, I eat out of the cafeteria. Plenty of food, nobody notices one more mouth. There's a janitor's room in the basement with a shower, so I can shower and shave down there. Plus, I can put away money for my retirement— out of the twenty-two thousand, last year I put away more than nineteen, 'cause I really don't make enough to pay any taxes. And I've been living here so long, I know every creak in the building, especially at night. I heard a creak last night. Four in the morning. I knew somebody was inside, but I was a little scared, you know? If it was somebody with a gun . . . I don't have a gun."

"Gotcha," Virgil said.

"I snuck down there, being real careful. When I figured out that somebody was in the district offices, and the lights were still out, I let myself in a room down there, Mrs. Duncan's social studies room, so I could duck out of sight if I had to. I was in there when I started to smell the gasoline—I don't have a cell phone, but there's a wired phone down in the basement, in my room down there, and I was going to sneak down there and call nine-one-one, when . . . This is strange . . ."

"What?"

"Somebody was already inside the offices, you know? Before I could leave Mrs. Duncan's room, they came out in the hallway and broke into the offices. They were already in, but then they broke in. Then they went to the side door, down the hall, the outside door, and they broke in there, too. Then they came back, and whoosh, the fire goes up, and they ran. I heard them running, and I peeked out, and I don't know who it was, but it was a full-sized man. Wasn't a high school kid."

Virgil said, "Huh." Then, "Somebody had a key, and then they faked a break-in."

"I believe so," Bacon said. "The fire was burning for a couple of minutes—the alarm in the district offices should have gone off right away, but it didn't, and I was headed for the basement to call the fire department, but then another alarm went off—I think one out in the hallway. So I didn't have to call anyone. The firemen showed up in five or six minutes and put the fire out in one more."

"If I say a name, could you keep it under your hat?" Virgil asked.

"Nobody but you knows about this room—I've kept it under my hat for all these years."

Virgil said, "Randy Kerns."

Bacon said nothing for a minute, then cupped his chin in his hand and rubbed for a couple seconds, and said, "I didn't want to say that."

"You think it was him?"

"Never saw his face, and it was dark in the hallway, except that the fire was going—but when I saw him running, something made me think of Randy."

"Is Kerns a big enough asshole to do this?"

"Randy's a big enough asshole to do anything," Bacon said.

VIRGIL GOT UP and took a turn around the apartment; he felt like he had to keep his head down because of the low ceiling. Then, "Mr. Bacon, I believe that Clancy Conley was killed because he discovered some serious corruption here in the school system. I think another man was killed in an attempt to throw us off the scent. Would you know anything about that? About people stealing from the school?"

He shook his head. "I don't. I can tell you that sometimes when the school board meetings end, the board runs everybody off, and then continues the meeting. Sometimes for an hour or more. A couple times when I was working around there, Randy came out and run me off. Didn't want me to hear what was going on. That's all I know about that."

"All the school board?" Virgil asked. "Or did some of the board members leave, too?"

"They all stayed: the board members, the superintendent, the accountant . . . uh, Viking Laughton, he's the newspaper editor, and Randy. They all stayed in there. Just about every meeting."

Virgil looked at Bacon's bookshelves: mostly young adult fiction and textbooks, probably from the school library. "I'll tell you something, Mr. Bacon. I believe those people are stealing a lot of money from the schools. A lot. Hundreds of thousands of dollars a year. I think they're taking enough to pay every one of them four or five times what you get, and they're not doing a thing, except stealing taxpayers' money."

"That ain't right, either," Bacon said. "Lots of bad people in this world, that's for sure."

"Yes, there are," Virgil said. He returned to the chair and sat down. "With this fire down in the offices, how long you think it'll take before they can meet here again?"

"Oh, the meeting room didn't get burned," Bacon said. "They meet in the little auditorium, where the choir practices and they have the student council. I think they were talking about meeting tomorrow night, about the fire."

Virgil nodded. "Good. If I brought you a court order, and some video equipment and a microphone, do you think you could fit that in there where nobody could see it? Close enough to record everything?"

Bacon scratched the back of his head, then said, "I could probably fit it up among the stage lights. I don't know how you'd turn it off and on."

"Remote control. You'd have to step inside the room just for a moment, like, when the regular meeting ended," Virgil said. "I can't do it, because it might spook them if I showed up."

"I could do that," he said. "I usually go in right when the meeting ends and pull out a trash basket. Then Randy runs me off, and I bring the basket back later at night."

"Let me see if I can get the equipment and the court order before tomorrow," Virgil said.

"You could bring it in tomorrow afternoon, late, when everybody's eating dinner," Bacon said. "Shouldn't take more than a few minutes to stick it up there. Black duct tape, make sure the remote works. Might need some help getting the ladder up there."

Virgil said, "Okay. I'll call you—but you don't have a cell?"

"No, but there's a message machine on the custodial phone down the basement. Just say that you either have, or don't have, the plumbing equipment I ordered. If you got it, show up about five o'clock at the back door. I'll let you in."

"That's a deal," Virgil said, and he stood up.

Bacon asked, "How'd you find out about me?"

"A certain person has noticed that you sometimes seem to be at the school when you shouldn't be. Late at night, early in the morning. This person said that normally, everybody in town that they know, knows where the other person lives. Not you. Nobody knows where you live."

"Since you said it was a 'person,' I guess it was a woman?"

"Could be," Virgil said. "But then again, maybe not."

"I'll have to think on that," Bacon said. "Makes me nervous, somebody knowing."

"I don't think the person will tell," Virgil said.

Bacon showed just the hint of a smile. "You almost said 'she.'"

"Did I?"

16

VIRGIL CALLED HIS FRIEND in the attorney general's office about getting a court order for the surveillance equipment. "You don't need a court order for a public meeting," the lawyer said.

"I'm told they kick everybody out, saying that that meeting concerns personnel action," Virgil said. "I was told that was an exception."

"Hmm. Yeah, it probably is. You got anything on which we could base a court order?"

"Got two witnesses," Virgil said. He explained, and possibly polished the potential testimony. "The fact is, if we don't get anything with the camera, we'll never mention it. If we do, then people won't care what prior testimony we had—anything will work."

"Okay, let me talk to the big guy, see if he's up for a court order. Is this gonna come back to us anywhere?"

"Only if you prosecute some people for stealing a few million bucks from the state, taking full credit for cleaning up public corruption and stopping the theft of taxpayer funds, on your way to the governor's office."

"You do know how to present a concept, I'll give you that," the lawyer said. "Okay. I'll push it, call you back tonight. You got the gear?"

"I can get it."

"Stay by the phone."

VIRGIL WOUND UP the day by backtracking to the Gedneys' house. Jennifer Gedney wasn't home, so he knocked on a neighbor's door and asked the woman who answered where Gedney worked, and was told that she was the manager at the Woolen Mill, on Main Street. "Can't miss it: looks like a windmill."

Virgil drove out to the edge of the business district and found a two-story replica of a Dutch windmill, with two cars in the parking lot. One, he remembered, was Gedney's; the other belonged to the customer with whom Gedney was talking when Virgil went inside.

Gedney did a double take when Virgil walked in; Virgil busied himself with some balls of yarn in a bushel basket, and Gedney hurried her customer along and when she'd gone, asked, "What do you want?"

"Heard anything from Buster?"

"Not a word. He's run away, and it's your fault, with your threats. I'm talking to a lawyer."

"Good luck with that," Virgil said. "I'll tell you what, Mrs. Gedney. Buster was about to give me the whole bunch of you. I guess he couldn't stand the stress. But we'll find him. One of the two of you is going to prison—if you want to talk to me first, it'll be Buster. If not, well, like I said, we'll find him. It's only a matter of time."

"Get out of here."

"You know who the last guy was, who told me to get out of here? Roy Zorn. Two days later, he was shot in the back. So, take care of your back. People see me coming around to your place, they might think you're making a deal."

She pointed at the door: "Get out."

MODERATELY PLEASED with himself—adding another log to the fire—Virgil called Shrake.

"We're on it. We looked over the whole place, and set up on the bank right behind the cabin. Nobody's coming through there without us picking them up, especially if we leave the yard light and that back wall light on. We'll take four-hour shifts, starting at seven-thirty. Probably be best if you took the first shift."

"Lots of mosquitoes," Virgil said.

"Got that covered, too."

"See you at seven-thirty."

VIRGIL WENT TO DINNER, and halfway through, got a call from the lawyer at the attorney general's office. "You got your warrant. You can put up a camera only for tomorrow's meeting, and we'll have to file a return on it within ten days, although we can probably get an extension on that, if you need it."

Virgil called Davenport and asked about a camera and recording equipment. "No problem about the gear, but there might be a hitch getting it down to you. Could you meet somebody halfway?"

"I could check and see if Johnson could meet somebody in Rochester."

"Do that," Davenport said. "Then I can just have a guy run down with it, won't have to worry about overtime."

"You know, I'm working a double murder down here, why are we sweating the overtime?"

"Come work here sometime," Davenport said. "The Black Hole case ran our overtime budget into the middle of next year. I can pretty much fuckin' guarantee that if you put in for one minute of overtime for chasing dogs, Rose Marie will personally come down there and shove the overtime chit up your ass."

Rose Marie was the commissioner of public safety.

So JOHNSON AGREED to go to Rochester—"Clarice can hit the Macy's"—and Virgil finished dinner, and as he was walking out to the parking lot, Gomez, the DEA agent, called.

"One of the guys we arrested was more scared of going to jail than he was of talking, so he's talking to us. He says Zorn once got drunk and told him that the Seed would never fuck with him, because he had the goods on them. We've got a search warrant for his house, and we're going to hit it early tomorrow morning. Also, there's another guy, D. Wayne—"

"Sharf."

"Ah. You know him. We're going to hit him, too," Gomez said.

"We're looking for him all over four states, on the Zorn shooting. We don't think he did it, we want him for a different reason, but . . ."

"The dogs?"

"Well, basically, yeah. Anyway, he's not home," Virgil said.

"Okay by me. We'll take the house apart, and leave him a note. Anyway, you're invited. Be there, or be square."

After a moment Virgil said, "I last heard that, 'Be there or be square,' when I was in high school. Seventeen years without it, and you ruined the run."

"We're going in at six."

"I'll be there," Virgil said. "And I won't be square."

AT SEVEN, Virgil rolled down the dirt track to Johnson's cabin and found Shrake and Jenkins on the deck, though there was no sign of their vehicle. "We parked at a neighbor's, up the road," Jenkins said. "We got a deer blind up on the bank behind the house."

Virgil told them about the raids planned for the morning, and asked if he could cut an hour and a half off his share of the ambush. "Got to be up by five-thirty. If I can get to bed by ten . . ."

"Not a problem," Shrake said. "I'll take it until two, Jenkins will take it until six, and by then you'll be gone."

"What do you think the chances are?" Jenkins asked.

"Maybe twenty-five percent," Virgil said. "The shooter's nuts, and I've dropped enough hints that I'm on to them."

"They might think it's more dangerous to kill a cop than to let it go," Shrake said.

"They might," Virgil admitted. "But they've already murdered two people. If they go down for that, they're all looking at life sentences anyway. Killing a cop won't make any difference on that."

"Still, they'd have to be panicked . . ."

"I'm doing my best to get them there," Virgil said.

AT SEVEN-THIRTY, with the Wisconsin trees going pink across the water, Virgil took a flashlight, a 12-gauge shotgun, two bottles of water, and a peanut butter sandwich back to the deer blind and zipped himself in. Jenkins and Shrake had pulled all the blinds on the back and sides of the cabin, and would take care to move around one at a time. The foliage around the cabin was thick enough that the shooter would have to get in close for a shot.

The night was still and warm, and Virgil sat cross-legged for a half hour, then in a series of increasingly twisted forms for another hour, and then lay down and looked out over the edge of the screen, as the hands on his watch crept around the dial.

At ten, Jenkins whispered, "Go on down."

"Nothing moving," Virgil whispered back, as they traded places.

Nothing moved that night, until Virgil twitched at five-thirty, when his cell phone's alarm began to vibrate.

HE GOT CLEANED UP, waved toward Shrake's hideout on the way past, and turned north toward Orly's Creek.

Virgil had served a few dozen search warrants in his life. His favorite had been a raid on a set of burglars who'd been working the Highland Park neighborhood of St. Paul, during his first year as a St. Paul detective. For a bunch of dumbasses, they'd been remarkably hard to catch.

The burglars were two couples, involved in a sexually ambiguous foursome, working out of a rented home. They always hit in broad daylight, as far as Virgil had been able to tell. They were hard to catch because they didn't dress like burglars. They dressed like tennis players, or like joggers, while they were scouting targets, and they scouted all the time.

When they picked out a target, they'd break a garage door or a back door, pull up in the alley—they always worked homes with alleys behind them—in a Toyota van with soccer-ball stickers in the back window.

That didn't make them dumbasses; that actually made them smart. What made them dumbasses was what they stole.

When Virgil finally identified them, he tracked them, watched them break into a house, then followed them back to their hideout. When he and the SWAT team kicked the door two hours later, they found the entire house packed from floor to ceiling with the kind of plastic kids' crap that you get at Walmart and Target—Big Wheels, play kitchens, wetting dolls, inflatable swimming pools, used croquet sets, ancient lawn darts—along with small TVs, DVD players, CD players, video games, stuff that would sell for ten dollars on the street. Literally, floor to ceiling—they'd had to walk sideways down narrow aisles cut in the piles of junk, just to get to the bong room, where they all slept, and the kitchen and bathroom.

It turned out that the women drove, and the men stole, but they couldn't steal anything big, because they both had bad backs and couldn't lift anything heavy.

When Virgil asked them, "Why'd you steal all this shit?" one of the men had answered, "I dunno. I guess 'cause it's what they had."

At SIX-TWENTY THAT MORNING, ten federals from the DEA, all armored up, led by Gomez, simultaneously hit Roy Zorn's and D. Wayne Sharf's homes, both off Orly's Creek Road. Bunny Zorn was arrested, cuffed, read her rights, and put on a couch. Sharf's place was unoccupied, but it appeared that Sharf was planning to come back, because all of his stuff was still in place, including four one-gallon Ziploc Double-Zipper freezer bags full of methamphetamine. The meth was cleverly hidden behind a loose board under the basement stairs, the second place the feds looked.

Virgil was more interested in Zorn's computer than anything else, and so was Gomez. The five-year-old PC was password-protected, but one of the feds cut through the password in a few minutes and popped open the e-mail file. Zorn didn't do much with e-mail, and none of the e-mails mentioned any names that Virgil recognized. When Virgil did a search for "Kerns," "Randy," "dog," and "dogs," he came up empty. A check of website history showed that Zorn mostly visited hunting, gun, and porn sites.

Sharf's place was a long step down from Zorn's in just about all ways, including odor and neatness. He hadn't taken the garbage out before he left, and the non-air-conditioned one-bedroom shack smelled of old tomatoes and rotting meat. Like Zorn, he had a computer, and when Virgil looked for "dogs," he found an e-mail from somebody named Con that said that he'd be bunching up dogs starting at eight o'clock sharp. The date was only three days away.

"Find something good?" Gomez asked, when Virgil began taking notes.

"Maybe. If D. Wayne Sharf doesn't come back before then, he's got a date to sell some dogs. I've been dealing with a lot of angry dog people—they might know where this sale's gonna be."

"We can keep that date," Gomez said. He patted the case that contained the bags of meth.

"Let me take it," Virgil said. "I really do need to see the man about a dog."

A SEARCH WAS always interesting, especially when dealing with assholes like Zorn and Sharf, and it was nearly noon before Virgil got out of the house. Jenkins and Shrake were playing golf at Trippton National, so Virgil called Johnson, who'd picked up the video surveillance equipment in Rochester the night before, and arranged to meet him for lunch at Ma & Pa's Kettle.

Johnson was more than pleased by the discovery of the dog note. "I'll get the posse together, see if anybody knows where this thing is."

"It's gonna be more complicated than that, Johnson," Virgil said around his cheeseburger. "For one thing, the dog sale itself isn't illegal, and the ownership of the dogs will probably be contentious. And—"

"Hey, no need to harelip the Pope. We'll just get the boys to-gether and hammer the place flat. You cops can pick up the pieces."

THEY LINGERED OVER LUNCH, because Virgil had nothing to do until it was time to meet Bacon, the school janitor. When they left the Kettle, it was almost two o'clock. Johnson gave him the bag with the video camera, an integral telescopic mike, a remote con-trol, a battery charger, a set of earphones, and a roll of dull black gaffer's tape. Virgil went back to the cabin, checked the approach road for unknown parked cars, and found none. At the cabin he made sure he knew how to operate the camera and that the batter-ies were charged, then took a nap.

AT FIVE O'CLOCK he hurried across the school's parking lot to the back door, where Will Bacon was waiting. "There are still a few people around, but we can go in through the stage entrance to the little auditorium, and that comes off the gym, and there's nobody in there, because I checked," Bacon said. "You got the camera?"

Virgil: "Here," and he patted the bag.

"Let's go. Stay close, listen for voices."

They were at the back of the school, walking past metal- and wood-shop classrooms and then hesitated outside the gym while Bacon poked his head in. "Let's go," he said, waving Virgil through the door.

They crossed the gym, went through a double door into a long narrow hallway with closed, knobless doors all along the way. "These are the emergency exits from the shops and the little auditorium," Bacon said. He used a key on his key ring to open the door at the end of the hall, and peeked inside. "All clear."

The auditorium was small—no more than a hundred or so seats arranged in eight curved rows, each row eight inches or so higher than the one in front of it.

Bacon had left a ladder in the auditorium earlier in the day. Together, they extended it up to a light rack along the ceiling. "Got tape?"

"Yeah." Virgil threw the bag over his shoulder and climbed to the rack. There were lots of crossbars—the rack was made to hold lights and other equipment—and he turned the camera on, adjusted the volume to "8," placed it on a crossbar, aimed it toward the stage, and checked the monitor. When he had it aimed right, he started taping, and when he was satisfied, turned the camera off and on with the remote. Everything worked.

"Go on down to the stage and say something," Virgil said to Bacon.

Bacon went down to the stage, looked up, and said, "Mama always said life was like a box of chocolates. You never know what you're going to get."

"*Forrest Gump,*" Virgil said.

"My favorite movie," Bacon said. "Is that enough?"

Virgil plugged in the earphones, listened to the recording. Good and clear. He turned the camera off and backed down the ladder.

"We're good," he said. "Let me show you how the remote works. When you turn it on, you'll see just a tiny green LED come on. . . ."

Virgil gave him a demonstration, and Bacon was sure he could handle it.

"Just be careful you don't re-push it. Just push it once, and look for the light," Virgil said. "We've got four hours of recording time, which should be plenty."

Bacon nodded: "I'll call you when everybody's cleared out."

"Do not take any chances," Virgil said. "We've got a killer on our hands."

VIRGIL HELPED HIM get the ladder down. He'd put it in a storage area behind the stage, he said. Then he frowned, and cocked his head, and Virgil asked, "What?"

"There's somebody else in the school. . . . Can you feel that?"

Virgil couldn't feel anything. "What?"

"It's like a vibration . . . people make it when they walk . . ."

"I don't feel anything."

"Shhh . . ."

They listened for another minute, then Bacon said, "Gone now. Listen, there's somebody around. I'm going to stash the ladder, make a little noise doing it. You go on out that hallway, and at the main hall, turn left instead of right. That'll take you to the door that goes out to the baseball diamond. You'll have to walk around the school to your right to get back to your car. You won't be in the school so much that way."

"You be careful," Virgil said.

"You, too," Bacon said.

Virgil was out of the school in a minute, stayed close to the outer wall as he walked around the building, beneath the windows that looked out over the playing fields. He saw nobody as he crossed the parking lot to his car, and drove away. He'd turned off his phone to go into the school, and when he turned it back on, he found a message from Johnson: "I got your dog posse. We're ready to roll."

Was that good? Virgil wasn't sure.

17

THE SCHOOL BOARD meeting didn't start until seven o'clock, so Virgil had a few hours to kill, and not much to do. He didn't want to put further pressure on anyone, because they might call off the board meeting—and the after-meeting.

He went back to Johnson's cabin and found Jenkins's Crown Vic parked at the most visible spot in the driveway. Jenkins and Shrake were sitting on the glider drinking gin and tonics.

"The key thing," Shrake said, "is to keep Kerns away from here when we're not ready for him. Hence, we park in the driveway, and if he's watching, he'll see us driving away."

"Leaving you alone, ripe for the picking," Jenkins said.

Shrake added, "It wouldn't work, except we found a back way in. Fortunately, I'm driving a Crown Vic, which can handle it. If it'd been a Prius, we'd of had to let him shoot you."

They sat around and talked about Davenport's Black Hole case, in which a BCA agent had been killed; and about Del Capslock, another agent, who'd been seriously wounded by old people, gunrunners, in Texas.

"Not been a good month for the BCA," Jenkins said. "I recommend that we all keep our asses down."

At seven o'clock, while it was still light, Jenkins and Shrake left, and Virgil bumped out after them. Virgil would call them before he came back, and give the two of them time to set up behind the cabin again.

VIRGIL WANDERED AROUND town for a while, parked by the turnout over the river, and called Frankie, who told him how lonely she was, and he said he was lonely himself; went to the only store in town that had magazines and bought one on the upcoming deer season; went to a diner and got a grilled cheese sandwich and read the magazine, and kept looking at his watch.

Bacon called at nine o'clock, talking in a hushed voice. "They're all gone. They had the extra meeting, too. The whole bunch of them. Kerns kicked everybody else out and went sneaking around the hallways making sure everything was clear."

"And the camera was rolling?"

"The green light was on. Had to look to see it, but it was," Bacon said.

"You take it down yet?" Virgil asked.

"Nope. I was afraid I'd push the wrong button and erase everything."

"Won't happen. Anyway, doesn't make any difference. I can be there in five minutes."

"Might want to bring a flashlight, so we don't have to turn the hall lights on. Come in the same door as yesterday—I'll go down right now and stick a newspaper in the door so it won't lock. And I'll go ahead and take the camera down."

"Five minutes," Virgil said.

It took him ten. When he got to the school parking lot, he went to the side door and found it locked. Thinking that he might have misunderstood, he walked around the school to the back entrance by the baseball field and found that was locked as well.

There were no visible lights in the school. Now worried, he called the phone Bacon had used, and after four rings was switched to the answering machine. He hung up, then banged on the door with a fist, then seeing no light and getting no answer, began kicking the door.

Still no answer.

Now VERY WORRIED, he thought about calling the sheriff's office, but if Bacon were really in trouble, there'd be no time—and not knowing what officer would respond, or his level of competence . . . he didn't want to go into a dark school with a scared guy with a weapon.

He jogged back around to his truck, unlocked it, got his pistol and a heavy, fourteen-inch-long nut wrench that he used to tighten the trailer ball on the truck. He hustled back to the door, pounded a few more times. There was a small window in the door, maybe six-by-eight inches, with chicken wire embedded in the glass.

Between the window and the wrench, it was no contest. Having carefully knocked out all the glass, Virgil reached inside and pushed down on the door's lock bar, and it popped open. Just inside, he found a rolled-up newspaper, like an old-time newspaper delivery boy might have done it. It was pinched in the middle, as though it had been used to jam the door open, and then had been pulled out. He dropped the wrench by the newspaper—clang—and hurried down the hall to the back entrance to the little auditorium, but he had to go through the gym to get there, and the gym door was locked. No window here: the doors were solid, thick yellow oak.

He turned back, trying to figure out where the main entrance to the auditorium might be, following the light from his flash. He took another two minutes to find it, and again, the doors were closed, but there were windows. He no longer had the wrench, but the butt of the small flashlight worked nearly as well, and he knocked the window out, went through the door.

There was a light switch right at the door, and he flicked it on. The ladder was standing in the middle of the auditorium, up to the spot where the camera had been.

Bacon was nowhere around—and the camera was gone. Virgil could see a few bands of tape hanging down, as though Bacon had cut the camera free, but hadn't bothered to peel the gaffer's tape off the light rack.

That didn't seem like him.

He went back to the hall and shouted, "Bacon! Will Bacon! Where are you?"

No answer.

AFTER A FAST RUN through the auditorium, just to be sure Bacon hadn't fallen, and crawled someplace, he went back to the main hall looking for stairs that would take him up to the third floor.

He jogged past the scorched front hall outside the district offices, and just past the offices, found a flight of stairs going up. At the third floor, not knowing quite where to find the janitor's room that would lead him to the attic, he dashed along the halls in the light of the flash, turned a corner, then another one, felt like he might have missed it, and found it on the third side of the square.

The door was metal, and was locked, but the lock was fitted into an oak frame. He'd never done anything like it before, but Virgil pulled his pistol and fired three careful shots into the wood next to the lock. The sound was thunderous down the hard empty hallways: the third shot did it, breaking enough of the wood frame that Virgil was able to pry the door open.

He found the lights, went up the stairs into the attic. There was a lock on Bacon's apartment door, but Virgil simply kicked it. Nobody home.

He was about to head back out when he felt the vibration: somebody was in the attic.

"Bacon?"

No answer. But somebody, he thought, was out there, and he was trapped. He moved to the far back wall, not because it was any more protective than any of the other thin walls of the makeshift apartment, but because he'd remembered that at the end of the wall there was a stack of boxes full of algebra texts. Boxes of books would be tough to shoot through, even with a rifle.

"Bacon? Bacon, is that you?"

No answer, but he did hear a shuffling from out in the attic. Rats? Sounded too heavy. He touched his jeans pocket, where he usually carried his cell phone, and got the instant mental feedback of the phone plugged into the charger in the truck.

He squatted, hoping that he was behind the algebra texts, and said, quietly but loud enough to be heard in the silent attic, "This is Virgil Flowers. I'm at the high school, and there's somebody here with a gun. I need a couple cars in a big hurry."

He had no chance to elaborate, because a burst of three gunshots broke the silence from the attic, the cracking explosion of a .223, unlike the boom of a shotgun, or the deeper report of a .30-06. Splinters smashed across the room. The shooter had made one mistake—he was shooting at what he could see, rather than where Virgil might be. Then another three cracks, and more splinters like shrapnel, and Virgil, scared to death, had the feeling that the shooter might be about to rush the room. If he did, he'd probably come in low. . . .

Virgil was a good shot with a rifle, an excellent shot with a 12-gauge, but couldn't hit a barn with a pistol, even if he was inside it. He didn't like pistols, and thought of them as generally useless. If you're going to shoot somebody, he thought, take the proper equipment. Like a 12-gauge. And he had one . . . out in the truck.

Another three rounds from the .223, sending splinters of dry wood whipping across the room. Virgil did a quick calculation: if the shooter had a standard military magazine, that would mean . . . only twenty-one more rounds? Great.

With the last sequence of three shots, Virgil could see that the shots were coming through at an angle, hitting the far wall of the room closer to him than the shots coming through the inner wall. He decided that the shooter was near the door, but probably still a few feet back from it, getting his guts up for a rush. He got to his knees and fired three quick shots at the wall four feet from the door, at an angle, and was rewarded with a "Goddamnit . . ." and then the other twenty-one rounds, hosing down the room. Virgil was flat on the floor, as close as he could get to the wall with the protective book boxes on the far side, his hands stretched toward the door, his gun ready for anyone coming through.

Then he heard a magazine clatter to the floor of the attic, and the metallic ratcheting of another magazine going in, nine or twelve more rounds flaying the room, in fast bursts of three, and a vicious burning pain in his scalp. He looked sideways, figuring the angle of the incoming rounds, and fired three more shots at the wall.

The other man ran away—Virgil was certain it was the killer, because of the three-bursts, and was equally convinced it was Randall Kerns. Virgil heard him pounding down the attic, then heard him on the stairs. He waited for just a second, realized that his scalp was on fire, put his hand to his head and came away with blood. He felt again, and found the splinter under the skin, and let it alone.

He'd need a doc to pull it out and make the necessary repairs, he thought. He didn't seem to have any bigger holes, but scalp wounds bleed like crazy. He got to his knees, then into a crouch, and moved to the door, then slowly, carefully followed his pistol to the stairs . . . and saw blood that wasn't his.

A smear, then several drops farther down. He feared that Kerns might be on the other side of the door, waiting for him to come down. Framed in the narrow doorway, Virgil would be almost impossible to miss.

On the other hand, he was sure that the shooter had heard the phony call to the sheriff's office, and didn't everybody carry a cell phone at all times? The sheriff's cars should be arriving any minute. . . .

HE LISTENED, and listened, and imagined things, and finally, with his heart in his mouth, eased down the last few steps to the door and peeked around the doorjamb. The outer door stood open. He listened for another minute, his patience reinforced by the fact that his life depended on it.

Then moving slowly, he again peeked at the outer door. As far as he could tell, the hallway was empty.

He was wearing boots. He stepped back, listening, sat down, his gun right by his hand, and pulled the boots off. On his feet again, he peeked: nobody. He took a chance and ran, nearly soundless in his stocking feet, boots in one hand, gun in the other, around to the front of the building and down the same stairs he'd come up. At the bottom he listened again, heard nothing—but the shooter could be planning an ambush—and took the chance and dashed to the side door where he'd come in.

He forgot about the glass on the floor until the last second. He hadn't been shot at, so he skidded to a stop, walked carefully around it, looked out at the parking lot. His was the only truck.

One final break: he ran across the lot to the truck, a distance of perhaps twenty yards, then dropped to the ground next to a tire, aiming his pistol at the side door. Nothing.

He gave it a full thirty seconds, then popped the door on his truck, climbed inside.

JENKINS ANSWERED on the first ring: "We can be there in ten minutes."

"Forget it, man, there's been a shoot-out at the school, I'm bleeding like a water hose, I need you guys down here now."

Jenkins's voice went calm and cold, as it tended to when he was tense and angry: "That's on the main drag, right? Two minutes. We're in town, you'll hear us coming."

And he did. Virgil had a good first aid kit in the back of the truck, got it open, pulled out the thickest bandage he had, pressed it to the wound, not too hard, because with the splinter in his scalp, the harder he pressed, the more it hurt.

Then he called the sheriff. The duty officer answered. Virgil filled him in, and the duty officer said he'd call the sheriff himself and send the patrol car around as fast as it could get there.

Jenkins and Shrake arrived in the next moment, in a dazzling display of LED emergency lights from the front of the Crown Vic, and they both hopped out as the car rolled to a stop and jogged over to the truck.

Shrake took one look and snapped at Jenkins, "Roll an ambu-lance."

Virgil: "Nah, nah, nah. It's all blood, I got a cut in my scalp. I'm afraid there's a dead man inside, but maybe he's not dead. We need to get inside—"

"You need to get to the hospital," Shrake said, adding to Jenkins, "Fuck him. Roll an ambulance." And to Virgil, "Sit right there or I'll coldcock you, I swear to God. Then you will need the bus."

THE SHERIFF'S PATROL CAR rolled in a few seconds later, as Jenkins was shouting on his phone at the EMS service. A deputy got out, and Virgil, still holding the now-blood-soaked pad to his head, and with blood running down his face, pushed his way past Shrake, and when Jenkins got off the phone, told the two agents and the deputy what had happened.

"The big thing is this: it was our killer, he's firing bursts of three, I'm afraid he might have done something to the janitor who was helping me, so we've got to go through the school and look at every possible hiding spot. I don't think the shooter is in there, but I'm sure, one way or another, that Bacon is. I just hope he's locked up. . . ."

He told them about the attic room, but added that there was nobody up there. "Stay out of there. There's blood there that's not mine—it's the killer's. I don't think I hit him bad, because there's not much, but there's enough to get DNA. Wait till I get back to identify it."

They said they would, and they'd start pulling the school apart. The deputy said he'd roust the rest of the force and have them all there in twenty minutes or so, and that the sheriff was on the way.

"We need to find Randall Kerns—it's ninety percent that he's the killer," Virgil said. "That he's the shooter. But you gotta be careful. . . ."

Virgil was still talking when an EMT pushed him to the ambulance, and they started down the main drag.

THERE WAS ONLY ONE doc on duty at the clinic, and he was trying to remove a fishbone from the throat of a young girl. He stopped doing that for a moment to look at Virgil's wound, and said, "It's either not bad at all, or it's terrible, but either way, it won't make any difference if I take the bone out of this kid's throat first."

Virgil said, "Yeah, go ahead," and the doc spent two minutes extracting the bone. The girl's worried father walked back and forth in front of the bay where the work was going on, and every time he passed Virgil, he said, "I'm sorry about this, I'm sorry about this."

When the bone was out, the doc gave it to the kid as a trophy, and a nurse took them away to get the insurance information, and the doc put Virgil in another bay, said, "Shoot, I thought I might get to do some brain surgery. I guess not."

"I love medical humor," Virgil said.

The doc got a needle and some anesthetic, killed the nerves around the wound, made a couple minor skin snips with a pair of surgical scissors, and picked the splinter out, all the time questioning Virgil about the shoot-out. When the wound was clean, the doc killed three bleeders with a cautery, which smelled like wet burning chicken feathers, and sewed him up. "Fourteen stitches, and very skillfully done for a small-town hospital," he said. "Who's gonna pay?"

Virgil called Shrake for a ride back to the school, and was told Bacon hadn't shown up, either dead or alive, but the school was a nightmare of nooks and crannies. "This could take all night."

"Then we take all night," Virgil said.

"Uh, by the way, somebody might have mentioned this to Frankie."

"Goddamnit, Shrake—"

"Hey, it wasn't me who called her, but if Jenkins hadn't, I would have—a guy gets shot, the old lady gets to know about it. I told her it didn't look too bad, but I wouldn't be surprised if she showed up—"

"Goddamnit, Shrake—"

"He told her you'd been hit in the head. She said, 'Thank God, if it'd been in his dick, it would have killed both of us.'"

Virgil: "She did not."

"No, but it's a good story and I plan to tell people she did," Shrake said. "I'll see you in five minutes, if I actually know where the clinic is. I think I do."

"Yeah, it has a big brightly lit sign on the front, and it says 'Clinic.' You can't miss it."

18

THE CRIMINAL CONSPIRACY—the school board—called an emergency rump session at Jennifer 1's house, attended by Randy Kerns,
the three Jennifers, Vike Laughton, and Henry Hetfield, the school
superintendent.

They immediately fell into a screaming brawl.

Kerns started it: ". . . so I know that fucking Bacon was up to
something. He came into the meeting, which he never does, and he
did something with his hand, which I didn't know what it was, but I
thought he might have took a picture or a remote control or something, I couldn't tell what. Anyway, I hung around afterward, when
everybody was gone, and he brings this ladder over and he climbs
up into the lights and takes down a movie camera—I think he filmed
the whole thing, the whole meeting after the meeting."

He was carrying a gym bag. He put it by his feet, dipped inside and came up with the camera. "I don't know how to work it, but it's got a tag that says, 'Bureau of Criminal Apprehension' on the side of it. That goddamned Flowers must have gotten Bacon to put it up there in the rafters. To do that, he had to get a warrant. To get a warrant, he had to have some evidence, and pretty good evidence, too."

"Well, what'd you do?" Jennifer Gedney asked. "If Will wants money, we could all chip in . . ."

Kerns shook his head. "Couldn't take the chance."

They all looked at him aghast. Jennifer 2 said, "You didn't . . ."

"I had to," he said. "But that's not the worst of it."

Vike had launched himself from his chair and shouted, "Well, Jesus Christ, what could be worse?"

Kerns said, "The BCA guy, Virgil Flowers, showed up. I thought our only chance—"

Henry Hetfield said, "Oh, no, no, no no . . . you didn't kill a police officer."

Kerns said, "I tried, but the problem is, I didn't. And if he doesn't know who I am tonight, he will in a week."

He told them about following Flowers up into the school attic, to some kind of hideout. "I don't know what's up there, but there's a room, and there are lights. I think Bacon built himself some kind of hidey-hole, or maybe even a whole private room up there, because Flowers went straight up there. We got in a gunfight. I couldn't get at him, he was barricaded in, he'd called nine-one-one so I had to run for it. He never saw me, but . . ."

He rolled up the sleeve of his long-sleeved shirt and showed a large bandage. "He shot through the walls and I got hit by a big splinter. The thing is, I was bleeding pretty hard, and I think I probably left some blood behind. If I did . . . they'll get the DNA, and I'm cooked."

Vike had stumbled back into his chair, where he said, "Oh, Jesus. Oh, Jesus, Oh, Jesus . . ."

Jennifer Barns recovered first: "What do you want from us?"

Kerns said, "It takes time to do DNA—a few days, anyway. I've got cash stuck away in a safe-deposit box in the Cities, and I can get to that. I've got a few thousand in my truck. You all know I used most of the money to buy a place up on Lake of the Woods. I can make it across the border, all right, I've got a new name up there. But I gotta leave everything behind, even my truck. So what I want from you all is money. I know you all got cash, we talked about it. What I want is, I want fifty grand from every one of you. One of you can get it all together, next month, and I'll meet you someplace up north and come get it."

Gedney asked, "You're gonna leave tonight?"

"I got to," Kerns said. He rolled his sleeve down, fumbling with the cuff button. "I'm afraid they're all looking for me right now. I can sneak up to the Cities, I think, back roads, get to the bank to-morrow morning, get the money, unless they already got me on TV. I'm going to have to leave the truck there, and go north in a fuckin' bus. My problem is, they might have my blood, and they sure as hell know I've been cut up—and that would be enough to hold me until the DNA comes back. I gotta go. I gotta run."

They argued about the necessity for flight, and Kerns convinced them: no other way out. He had a Canadian ID and passport with a different name, he said, so crossing the border wouldn't be a problem.

"I can ditch myself up in Kenora, grow a beard, stay close to the cabin, and in a year or so, sell out and go far away. But I need the money. I need the cash, until I can establish myself up there."

Henry Hetfield said, "Leaves the rest of us in the lurch."

"That depends," Kerns said. "We burned all the records. You can afford good attorneys—and you can blame the killings all on me. I'm done anyway, if they've got that blood. And they will find Bacon's body, sooner or later—if not right away, when he starts to . . . smell."

Jennifer Houser: "I can't believe this. I can't."

Kerns: "Where'd you put your money?"

She shook her head: "I'd never tell you that. But it's safe. And I'll chip in fifty thousand, that's not a problem."

"If any of you run, they'll know for sure you're guilty," Kerns said.

Another argument flared: Jennifer Houser and Kerns and they thought Del Cray, the finance officer, who wasn't there, might be able to run. The others, for one reason or another, were anchored by their money. Couldn't run with it, if it was all in stocks and bonds or real estate, but couldn't run without it, either.

"All they've got now is Randy," Houser said. "The fire took out most of the other evidence. And Randy did most of the talking to outsiders, like that bus driver. We can still blame this all on him . . . that he set up a ring. But if I were you, I'd start cashing in stocks and bonds. If Flowers gets any closer, we might have to run ourselves."

To Kerns, she said, "I'm willing to pay you the money—but you've got to swear, right here, that you'll take the blame for all these crazy killings if you do get caught. And the money, too. You won't try to spread the blame around. You'll get a half million dollars from us, and you'll get a chance . . . but you can't turn on us, if you get caught."

"If I get caught, there's no profit in trying to spread the blame," Kerns said. "You get me the cash, I'll keep my mouth shut."

They argued about that some more, and Vike said he had twenty thousand stashed at his house, but he couldn't get more for quite a while—"I put all the money in Tucson real estate after the bust."

Jennifer Houser said, "From what Randy says, this roof isn't likely to fall in for at least a few days. That gives us some time. Let's just stay calm, but prepare."

Kerns said that he would be in touch with all of them, in a week, to set up a meeting. "Your lives are hanging by my thread," Kerns said. "If you get me that money, I've got a real good chance of getting away. If not, that cuts my chances way down. You don't get it to me, and I get caught, I'll drag every one of you motherfuckers into the shit with me."

They all swore they would.

JENNIFER HOUSER LOOKED UP at the sky as she walked out to her car, a clear night, lots of stars, a good night for driving. A thrill ran through her, raising goose bumps down her arms. The whole scheme was coming down around their ears. It had worked well, for a long time—longer than she had originally expected it to. But she had always known this day would come, and she was ready for it.

Like Kerns, she had an alternative identity, one that had once belonged to her late sister-in-law. She could be in Chicago by early morning, in Belize City by midday.

Belize was a good place for an American to hang out, because English was the official language, and for people with money, Belize was extremely slow to extradite. A logical place for her to go, if anyone managed to trace her that far.

But the best thing was, it was a great red herring. Getting across the Mexican border from Belize was not a huge problem. She knew that, because she'd done it, on a practice run.

After several tiring bus rides, Jennifer 2, in less than a week, would be settling into her apartment in Gringo Gulch in Puerto Vallarta, where everybody knew her as that nice middle-aged Lucy lady, from Virginia, who wore wide-brimmed straw hats and liked to sail and bicycle and get giddy on daiquiris and fuck younger Mexican men.

Houser had some other ideas. Uneaten toast in a toaster, uneaten egg in a skillet, undrunk milk in a glass, a smear of her blood on the kitchen floor . . .

Kerns wouldn't see a dime from her. She was gone.

KERNS LEFT. He looked up at the sky and the stars as he walked down the driveway and got in his truck. He had to take it slow going up to the Cities, he thought. Hide the truck in a parking ramp in St. Paul, get some sleep, get up in the morning, go to the bank, never look back. He had a bag in the back of the truck with everything he needed to travel: he was leaving behind a house with a mortgage and some decent equity that he'd never see, but he wouldn't see it in Stillwater Prison, either.

Vike walked out behind him, shook his hand. "You got enough cash?"

"I got some, as long as I can get to the bank box tomorrow. Most of it's up in Canada. If I can just get up there, get out to my island, I'm okay."

"I could give you a few thousand right now, if that would help."

"That would help. If they put me on TV tonight, I'll just have to keep going north."

The others followed them out, at intervals of a half-minute or so. Nobody said good-bye to anyone else.

Jennifer Barns and Henry Hetfield walked out separately and separately looked at the sky and asked themselves,

"Is this the end?"

19

EVERY LIGHT IN the school was on when they got back. Shrake called ahead to say that Virgil had survived, and the sheriff was waiting in the school doorway where Virgil had broken in.

"You sure Bacon's in here?" he asked.

"I talked to him on the phone. He said he'd jam the door open for me, and go pull a surveillance camera out of the little auditorium. That was maybe eight, ten minutes before I got here. When I got here, the door was locked, the paper he was gonna jam it with was by the door, and he and the camera were gone."

"Surveillance camera?"

"Yeah. The school board here has been stealing the school system blind—that's just between you and me and Shrake and Jenkins, for the time being."

The sheriff looked as though somebody had hit him between the eyes with a plank. "I know the board, I mean . . . How sure . . . ?"

"I think their security guy is the one who shot Conley and Zorn—Zorn for no other reason than to pull me away from the schools. Conley had cracked the whole thing, and he was planning to publish it. I think he made the mistake of telling Vike Laughton about it."

"Vike . . ." The sheriff turned away and stared sightlessly across the parking lot. "Hate to say it, but I can believe Kerns and Vike. I'm having trouble with all the Jennifers. You think the fire . . . ?"

"The fire was set to destroy the district's financial records. I can guarantee they're not up in a Cloud, somewhere. They were melted. But Conley got copies of enough of them to hang them all. Now, Sheriff, you're an okay guy, but this ring has feelers all over town. You'd do best not to mention this to anyone, not until I figure out how to pull them in. Kerns is out there with a rifle, and he did his best to kill me tonight, and we can't find Bacon. He won't hesitate to shoot a deputy, or a sheriff."

"We gotta find that sucker."

"Yes, we do. But first we've got to find Bacon. I keep hoping that he's locked up somewhere."

"We're tearing the place apart."

"Let me look."

THERE WERE EIGHT COPS walking the school. A sergeant who seemed to know what he was doing had them run all the obvious places in a hurry, which had taken twenty minutes or so, he told Virgil.

Then they'd backtracked, and were doing the whole place inch by inch.

"The shooter knows the building," Virgil said. "He could have stuck him someplace weird."

With the deputies doing the search better than he could, Virgil took Jenkins, Shrake, and Alewort, the sheriff's crime-scene guy, up to the attic. Jenkins and Shrake had to bend their necks to walk down to Bacon's apartment. Virgil spotted the shooter's blood for Alewort, who began doing his crime-scene routine, and Virgil led Shrake and Jenkins into the apartment.

"Holy shit," Jenkins said. He was looking at the splintered walls. "You were in here? You're living right, Virgil—brick walls on the outside, you should have been killed three times by ricochets."

"Or splintered to death," Jenkins said. He tipped his finger at the side of one of Bacon's bookcases, which had three six-inch splinters embedded in the wood, like straws in a telephone pole after a tornado.

Virgil explained how he'd huddled down at the far end of the room, stretched on the floor with the book boxes on the other side. "He couldn't get the angle on me," Virgil said. "I got lucky."

THEY LEFT ALEWORT to do his work and went back to the auditorium, where Virgil climbed the ladder to make sure the camera was really gone, although he was sure that it was. When he got to the top, he saw that it was, indeed, gone; and then turned and looked down at the stage, where he saw five bumps arrayed across it, four small and one a bit taller and longer.

A phrase popped into his head: prompter box.

And he thought something he should have thought of sooner: in the small space of ten minutes, Kerns wouldn't have had time to kill Bacon and carry him all over the school. He would have hidden him quickly, if, in fact, he'd killed him.

And if he knew every nook and cranny . . .

With a growing dread, he backed down the ladder in a hurry, and then hustled over to the stage, hopped up on it, walked over to the prompter box, and looked down into it. The opening in the box was only a foot high and three feet wide, big enough for perhaps two people. He looked down into it, but couldn't see anything.

Shrake: "What you got?"

"How do you get down into this?"

Jenkins looked at the outside of the box, down below the stage level, facing the audience, and said, "Nothing on this side. Must go under the stage."

They found a trapdoor on the left side of the stage, half-covered with a pile of ropes and canvas. "It's been moved," Virgil said. "Let's pull it off."

"Could be prints and DNA," Shrake said.

"So don't touch the pile, push it off with your shoes."

They did that, and Shrake pulled up the handle set into the trapdoor, and then lifted the trapdoor on its hinges. A set of narrow stairs went to the area under the stage, a space perhaps five feet deep.

Will Bacon's body was crumpled at the bottom of the stairs.

"Ah, shit!" Virgil went down the stairs, clumsily stepping over the body. "We need a light, get a light."

Jenkins shouted at a deputy, and a minute later Jenkins dropped down the stairs with a Maglite.

Bacon was dead. His head looked like he'd been beaten with a baseball bat, or a fat pipe of some kind, his shiny broken teeth grinning up at them through a mass of pulped flesh, bone, and blood.

Virgil looked down at him, locked his hands on top of his head, and started rocking back and forth, unbelieving, and Jenkins was saying, Virgil-Virgil-Virgil, and then Jenkins said, "Shrake, get him out of here, he's fucked up."

VIRGIL WAS LOCKED UP for a while, sitting in a chair in the auditorium, remembering and replaying his meeting with Bacon, thinking that Bacon was a good guy making a tough way in the world, and that he'd been killed because Virgil hadn't taken enough care. Because Virgil worked alone, he tended sometimes to lean on civilians; other cops had thought that was weird, but that was because they fundamentally didn't trust civilians, it wasn't because they'd get the civilians killed.

Virgil was somewhat aware of the arrival of a doctor, who went down the stairs and said what everybody already knew, that Bacon was dead. Alewort then kicked everybody out of the space around the trapdoor.

But Virgil didn't pay much attention for a while, just sat and rocked back and forth, and then Jenkins came over and slapped him on the back and asked, "How you doin', buddy?"

Virgil nodded, more of a body-humping than a real nod, and

said, "I am kinda fucked up. I killed that guy, and he was a good guy. Jesus. I just—"

"We got shit to do, so pucker up," Jenkins said. "The sheriff's department has a deal with the medical examiner over in Rochester. We're thinking that might be the way to go—"

"Whatever. We gotta find Kerns."

"The whole sheriff's department is looking for him. We've got the highway patrol looking for his truck. They been over to his house, but it's dark. Don't know if we have enough to get a warrant, since you never saw him."

"I gotta think," Virgil said. "I gotta go somewhere and think."

"The cabin," Jenkins said. "Shrake went over there with a couple of deputies. We thought that crazy as he is, he might have been making a last run at you, but there's nobody there. We're going to keep a couple of cops there overnight, just to make sure. And we're putting a couple cars on Kerns's place until we get a warrant figured out, and I've called back to St. Paul for a crime-scene crew. They can be here in three hours, but that's about as good as they can do."

WHEN THEY WERE SURE that the sheriff had everything handled, Virgil and Jenkins drove over to the cabin in Virgil's truck. A cop car was sitting on the entrance road, Jenkins's Crown Vic was parked beside the house, blocking the driveway, and Johnson's travel vehicle, an enormous GMC Tahoe XL, was parked on the front lawn, between the water and the porch. Virgil parked behind the Crown Vic, and he and Jenkins walked around the collection of vehicles and up on the porch, where Shrake and Johnson were waiting.

"You're better protected than the fuckin' president," Johnson said. He gestured at his truck and said, "We thought he might come up by boat and take a potshot from the water, so we're blocking out the door with the truck."

Virgil nodded and said, "Thanks," and they all went inside and sat on a long couch and a couple of chairs and Shrake asked, "You okay?"

"Pretty unhappy," Virgil said. "But I'm not gonna start chewing on the rug."

"Good thing, too, when you think about what's been on that rug," Johnson said. "We'd like to know that you're functioning again."

"Yeah, I'm good."

The side window lit up, with headlights bouncing down the rough road, and Johnson asked, "Who're we expecting?"

"Don't know," Jenkins said.

The approaching car stopped, and a second later the door slammed, and Virgil said, "That sounds like Frankie's truck door."

Shrake and Jenkins both had weapons in their hands when Frankie came through the front door carrying a backpack and a well-used Remington pump shotgun. She looked at them and said, "I give up."

Everybody had something to say, but Frankie ignored them and came to Virgil and said, "Sit down and let me look at your head."

"Ah, my head's okay," Virgil said.

"Sit the fuck down, and let me look at your head. What'd they do, take a bullet out?"

"Splinter," Virgil said. "Not too bad. Besides, I got a lot bigger problem."

VIRGIL HADN'T HAD a chance since the shooting to tell everything that had happened in one coherent story. He did it now, starting with his talk with the bus driver, the connection with Will Bacon and the secret apartment, the delivery of the camera and microphone, and finally, the call from Bacon before he was killed.

They all thought about the story for a few minutes, then Frankie said, "I'm not a cop, but I'm probably the smartest person in the room, and I've got some ideas."

"Let's hear them," Shrake said.

"If this killer man, if he knows he left blood behind, then he knows the jig's up for him. I would expect that he's either running, or he's holed up somewhere with a lot of guns. Or maybe he makes a run at Virgil out of revenge, or something crazy, but you've got all of that covered. Everybody's looking for him, and we've got guys out in the driveway with guns, and guns in here. Right?"

Virgil nodded. "That's right."

"So you can ignore all that—nothing more you can do there. The question is, what can you do?"

Everybody looked at Virgil, and finally he said, "Bust the rest of them. Okay. I need to make a phone call."

He took his phone out, called directory assistance, got a number for Janice Anderson, the woman who'd given him the school budget, and punched it in. She answered on the third ring, sounding cranky. "Who is this?"

"Virgil Flowers. Something terrible happened at the school tonight. I've got to ask, were you at the meeting?"

"Just a minute, let me put the light on, I can't talk in the dark," she said. A few seconds later she said, "Yes, I was at the meeting. What happened?"

"After the meeting, somebody killed Will Bacon, the janitor. I need to tell you, you've got to keep your head down. Don't tell anyone you talked to me, don't even hint that there's a connection."

"I've kept my mouth shut," she said.

"Good. And it wouldn't be a bad idea for you to go on a shopping trip up to the Twin Cities, maybe stay over for a couple of nights."

"You really think that's necessary?"

"It would be helpful—I wouldn't have to worry about you. I think Randall Kerns is the killer, and he's crazy. We're looking for him, but he's out in the wind somewhere. I'd be a lot happier if you were out of sight."

"Okay. I haven't been to the Cities for a while, I'll go first thing in the morning."

"That would be smart," Virgil said. "Now, was the auditor, Masilla . . . was he at the meeting?"

"No. He's hardly ever there."

"But Hetfield was."

"Oh, sure, he had to be, he's the superintendent, he's, you know . . . he runs things, and with the fire . . . they had their insurance agent there, and all that, figuring out what to do, and whether they'd have to delay the start of school and so on."

"Okay. I'm going after those two, just like we talked about in your backyard. If you will take care—"

"I've got a gun in my nightstand, and I will leave for the Cities as soon as it gets light."

"Good night, Janice."

"Good night, Virgil. You take care, too."

Virgil hung up, and looked at the others: "Here's the plan: Jenkins, Shrake, and I are going up to Winona tomorrow, and we're going to scare the living shit out of a guy."

"I like that plan," Jenkins said. He interlaced his fingers out in front of himself, and cracked all his knuckles.

VIRGIL'S HEAD WAS beginning to hurt again, and they all went off to their various beds, leaving Virgil and Frankie alone in the cabin. Frankie said Virgil was too injured and tired for sex, but that a little bodily warmth never hurt anyone, so they wound up huddled together on an old-fashioned double bed, which was almost large enough for them, Frankie being a small woman.

They'd agreed to meet Jenkins and Shrake at nine-thirty at Ma and Pa's Kettle for pancakes; they'd gone to bed late, and there was little point in killing themselves by getting up too early. Winona was an hour or so away, straight up the river, so if they left a little after ten, they'd catch Fred Masilla, of Masilla, Oder, Decker and Klandorst, Certified Public Accountants, Auditors and Consultants, shortly before lunch.

If he was available.

VIRGIL WAS AWAKENED at eight-thirty by an unexpected stimulus, and he groaned and said, "I thought I was too injured for sex," and

Frankie said, "I wouldn't want to give you a pounding, but this is okay."

Virgil agreed that it was okay, and she went back to what she was doing, and after a minute he picked up his cell phone and called Fred Masilla's office, and when a secretary asked, "Who shall I say is calling?" he hung up.

Frankie asked from under the sheet, "He there?"

"Yup."

"Don't think this should take much longer."

"Nope."

But then it did, because they wound up in the shower, and he wrestled her back to the bed for Dr. Flowers's Female Cure, and then they had to get back in the shower again, and they were still damp when they got to the Kettle, running late.

Jenkins and Shrake were in a booth when they arrived, and Shrake patted the seat next to himself for Frankie, and said to Virgil, "You don't look all that injured anymore."

"I'll tell you what I am," Virgil said, deflecting the insinuation and picking up a menu, "I'm as angry as I've ever been in my life. I never in my life really wanted to kill anyone. That has changed. If I had the money, I'd put a bounty on Kerns."

"Then you should stay away from him, wherever he pops up," Jenkins said. "Leave it to the unbiased professionals."

Shrake said, "Kerns is safe as long as Flowers is carrying a pistol."

Virgil: "Fuck you. No wait: fuck you both."

Shrake said, "No sign of Kerns, anywhere. Crime Scene is here. They're working the school. You gotta go over there, pretty quick."

———

JENKINS AND SHRAKE gave him a rundown of everything that had happened overnight, and when they finished eating, Virgil told Frankie to stay away from the cabin, because Kerns could show up there. She said, "I'm gonna stay away from Trippton—I got hay to put up, and small children to oversee. Besides, I been cured, so I'm going home."

She'd drive Virgil's truck back to the cabin and leave it there, and take her own truck home. Virgil would ride with Jenkins and Shrake until he could get back to the cabin.

Virgil kissed Frankie good-bye in the parking lot, and then he, Jenkins, and Shrake drove over to the high school. The state crime-scene truck was parked at the back door closest to the auditorium, along with a couple of sheriff's cars.

Inside, the crime-scene crew, Beatrice Sawyer and Don Baldwin, were working around the pit where Bacon's body had been found.

"We're getting stuff, but we won't know what it is until we get to a lab," Sawyer said. She was a middle-aged woman who carried a few extra pounds, with carefully coiffed hair that changed color weekly.

"Let me show you the guy's blood," Virgil said.

Sawyer had already been up to Bacon's secret apartment, but had not begun processing it, waiting for Virgil to show up and tell her what had happened. He pointed out the brass from the shooter's gun, and his own brass, and his blood, and the shooter's. The shooter's had already been sampled by Alewort, but he'd carefully left enough for a second sample.

The blood made Sawyer happy: "With your description, we can nail down precisely what happened, all the technical details, right down to who did the shooting and when. Take a little time, but we can do it. We need to get into Kerns's house, get some samples off his bed, but there seems to be some problem with that."

"I'll talk to the sheriff."

VIRGIL TALKED TO PURDY, who said he was working with a judge on the county court, but the judge was reluctant to issue a warrant. "I did my tap dance, and he says he'll give us a warrant, as soon as we can, quote, Give me one single piece of evidence that he was involved."

"We'll get it—I could get it this afternoon," Virgil said. "I've got a guy I can squeeze, I think. If I get it, I'll call you."

WITH THE CRIME-SCENE crew occupied, Virgil, Shrake, and Jenkins dropped Jenkins's Crown Vic at the cabin and headed north on Highway 26 to Winona.

MASILLA, ODER OCCUPIED a restored four-story redbrick warehouse-style building on the corner of Walnut and E. Third, between the Merchants bank on one side, and a car repair place across the street; inside it was glass, exposed wooden beams, and hanging stairways. The interior of the building was blocked by thick glass doors; two receptionists sat at a curving Plexiglas desk out front. Virgil, dressed in jeans, a black sport coat, cowboy boots, and a new pumpkin-colored T-shirt from the band Pup, with a pale white bandage on top of his head, led the way in; Jenkins and Shrake, both in overly expensive gray suits with silvery-gray neckties and sunglasses, moved in at his elbows.

Virgil said to the receptionists, "We're here to see Fred Masilla." He dropped open his BCA identification. "We're with the state Bureau of Criminal Apprehension."

In the silence that followed, Shrake leaned toward them and said, "Apprehension."

One of the receptionists said, "Let me see if Mr. Masilla is in."

"Oh, he's in," Shrake said.

The receptionist made a call, then hung up and said, "Somebody will come down to get you."

A painting hung from the wall on the visitor's side of the reception desk, an impressionistic oil of a dozen or so colorful river barges parked in an upriver pond, surrounded by red and yellow autumn foliage. Shrake put his nose three inches from it, studied it, then turned to Jenkins and asked, "Where do they get this shit?"

"Well, you know, impressionism has become a technique that you learn about in magazines, rather than an exploration of light," Jenkins said. "Slap a little pretty paint around a canvas, sell that sucker. I'd call this late Monet. Very late."

"Yeah. So late he's dead and buried," Shrake said.

One of the receptionists, a thin woman with short black hair and tight eyeglasses, said to Virgil, "I really like Pup."

The other woman, a carefully coiffed blonde with daylight pearls, said, "They somewhat rock, but they're a little too . . . out there . . . for me."

Virgil didn't know what to say, but was saved when an elevator dinged, a door opened, and a woman stepped out and asked, "You're BCA officials?"

Virgil showed her his ID, and they all stepped inside the elevator. When the door closed, Shrake said to Virgil, "You radical rocker, you."

FRED MASILLA WORKED in a corner office that was veneered in walnut on two sides, and had floor-to-ceiling windows on the other two, the windows carefully shaded by razor-thin venetian blinds. His large walnut veneer desk was covered with a sheet of glass, on which there was a neat stack of papers and a ledger book, which he closed when they walked in. The secretary said, "Mr. Flowers and his associates."

Masilla was a tall, thin man, with a passing resemblance to the Grant Wood character in the *American Gothic* painting: old for his age, with a hound-dog face and thin sandy hair, cut short, and steel-rimmed eyeglasses. He was sunburned from the nose down, a weekend boater's burn. He said, "What can I do for you gentlemen?"

Virgil could see fear in his eyes.

"We need to talk to you about your audits of the Buchanan County school system books."

The secretary left on clacking sandals, pulling the door closed behind her.

Virgil said, "We believe that you have been falsifying your audits of the Buchanan County school system finances. We think that you don't know the extent to which your coconspirators have gone off the rails, because you don't go to their after-meetings, when they make their plans. We want you to tell us what they've done. What you've done."

Masilla sat down suddenly, took off his glasses, and said, "Ah, no."

Virgil didn't say anything. He was still standing, but Jenkins and Shrake took side chairs and sat, and so Virgil moved to the chair directly in front of Masilla's desk, and sat.

Masilla finally said, "I should have an attorney."

"That's your absolute right," Virgil said. He turned and looked over his shoulder and said, "Shrake, you wanna recite the chapter and verse?"

Shrake recited the Miranda warning, and when he'd finished, Virgil asked, "Did you understand that?"

Masilla swallowed and said, "Yes. And I want one."

Virgil said, "So I won't ask any more questions, but I'm going to make a speech, that you can repeat when you call your lawyer. And you better get one quick, because I'm also going to make you an offer, but the offer is only going to be open for a short time. Like, two hours. Do you understand?"

A weak "Yes."

Virgil told him about the three murders, and all the blood drained out of Masilla's face. "How I . . . I don't know anything about violence."

"Well, your coconspirators do. If you're convicted along with them, you're going to go to prison . . . well, for you, forever. This kind of murder is going to be thirty years, no questions asked," Virgil said. "What you need to do, and right quick, is come to an agreement to provide evidence in return for leniency and reduced charges."

"But I didn't . . . I . . . I better call my attorney."

"You call. We'll come back"—Virgil looked at his cell phone clock—"in an hour."

"That's not enough time—"

"Fine. Make it ninety minutes. But if we can't reach an agreement, Mr. Masilla . . . you're toast."

Jenkins and Shrake stood up, and Virgil nodded at Masilla: "Ninety minutes."

THE SECRETARY SAW THEM to the elevator, but didn't ride down with them, and inside, Jenkins said, "That worked."

Virgil, "You think?"

Shrake said, "I got a hundred dollars that says it did. But, come to think of it, if I were you, I'd call up our own attorneys and make sure they'll support a deal. I mean, you're sort of out here on your own."

"That's called self-reliance," Virgil said.

"That's called having your head up your butt," Jenkins said.

OUTSIDE ON THE SIDEWALK, they were at loose ends, and Virgil said, "Let's go look around."

"Maybe find a gun store, or something," Shrake suggested.

Jenkins said, "I saw a sign for a museum. . . ."

They were crossing the street toward the auto repair shop, and Virgil saw a man looking up past their heads. He turned and looked, and on the fourth story of the Masilla, Oder building, Fred Masilla had lifted his venetian blinds and opened one of his tall windows. He was standing there, looking out, almost pensively, and Virgil blurted, "Oh, boy, look at this."

Jenkins and Shrake turned and looked up, and Masilla looked down at them. Virgil thought, *Fifty feet, sixty feet? Really wouldn't make any difference if he jumped.*

Shrake was walking back toward the corner and bellowed: "Fred! Hey, Fred! Shut the window! Shut the fuckin' window!"

Masilla looked down at them for another beat, then seemed to sigh, nodded, and shut the window. A moment later, the blinds came down.

Jenkins said, "Good going," and the partners bumped knuckles.

Shrake asked Virgil, "You gonna put me in for a citation? I saved that guy's life."

"Quiet," Virgil said. "I'm listening."

"For what?"

"The gunshot."

They all looked up at the window, but Masilla never came back.

20

THE THREE OF THEM spent some time in a café, eating pecan pie with ice cream, and Virgil called his friend at the attorney general's office and told him that he was about to offer "consideration" to Masilla for any help he could give them.

"He's a fool if he takes it, because we'll repudiate it instantly," the attorney said.

"I will testify in his behalf, if he gives these people up," Virgil said. "I don't have any reason to think he was in on the killings."

"Do what you want, but you could get your ass kicked in court, in any number of directions," the attorney said.

"So you're saying I should do what I want, and it's okay with you?"

After a moment of silence, the attorney said, "No, that's exactly not what I said. I'm advising you not to do this, and if you do, you're on your own. I'll tell everybody I know that I never heard of you."

"Thanks, that's what I needed," Virgil said. "It's okay with you."

He clicked off, and when the attorney called back seven seconds later, he didn't answer. "I think we're good," he said to Jenkins and Shrake.

They spent some time at the public library, which looked like either a courthouse or a post office, but not a library, trying to read magazines, but that was boring, so Virgil went outside and sat on a bus bench and called Frankie and they talked about nothing, and eventually it was time to go back to Masilla, Oder.

MASILLA WAS SITTING in his office chair, in shirtsleeves, and a large, pink-faced, sweaty man in a blue suit sat in a corner chair. When Virgil, Jenkins, and Shrake arrived, there weren't enough chairs, but a secretary quickly wheeled in another one, and they all sat down, and the man in the blue suit said, "I'm Benjamin Rogers, Mr. Masilla's attorney, and Mr. Masilla isn't going to say anything at all until I hear your story, and then we'll decide how to proceed."

Virgil said, "Well, the Buchanan County school board has been stealing a lot of money, could be as much as a million dollars a year, and this has been going on for some time, and Mr. Masilla is in on it."

Masilla blurted, "I am not."

The attorney said, "Shut up, Fred. Just keep your mouth shut." He turned back to Virgil and said, "Mr. Masilla rejects your claim, of course. I would like to hear what you have to support it, just as a matter of curiosity."

"Sure," Virgil said, keeping his tone amiable. "A reporter working for the newspaper down in Trippton was shot to death last week. Upon investigation, we found his notes, along with copies of the school district's financial records. Even if we didn't have the records, we have so many entries into this embezzlement that the whole scheme is coming down. More important than the theft, however, is that three murders have been committed to cover up the thefts. They are part of the whole process of the crime, of course, so everybody involved is going to Stillwater prison for thirty years . . . unless they get some consideration for their testimony."

Masilla cried, "Murders—"

"Shut up, Fred," Rogers said. He turned to Virgil and said, "I can tell you, son—can I call you son?"

Virgil said, "No."

Rogers said, "I'll tell you, son, if, hypothetically, Fred could tell you anything at all about this case, he'd need absolute and total immunity from prosecution, and I'd have to insist on a written arrangement with whatever county attorney you've got covering this case."

"I'm actually working this out of the AG's office." He looked at Masilla, and enlarged: "The state attorney general's office. I've got a name you could call, but I've got to tell you that we have no time. A man was beaten to death last night, and the man we believe is the killer can't be found. We're talking to three different people, and the first person who puts a finger on him gets the consideration. Everybody else hangs."

Masilla groaned, and Rogers glared him into silence, then said to Virgil, "Give me the name of your guy in the AG's office."

Virgil gave him the name, and asked, "You want to call him from here? We could step outside if you want privacy."

"If you wouldn't mind," Rogers said.

Virgil led the way out, and the instant he was in the hallway, pressed the redial number for his friend in the attorney general's office, who answered: "What? I've been trying to call you—"

"Our guy here is ready to pop, but you're going to have to deal with him. You know what we've got, and we don't think this guy knew about the murders. You can shape the deal so that if he lies about that, and we find out otherwise, you can hang him. I gotta tell you, if these folks down in Trippton walk, it's gonna look bad when your guy runs for governor, and you let them get away."

"You motherfucker, Flowers, this is blackmail—"

"Careful, you're impugning my integrity. Tell you what—talk to this guy's attorney, his name is Rogers, he's probably on your other line right now, pretend you know all about it. But, Dave—we got no time. We've got three dead, and a guy running, and we got no time."

"Flowers—"

"I'll buy you a handcrafted boutique beer the next time you see me."

"Fuck you, and your girlfriend, and all her children. . . . Shit, here's Rogers, fuck you again."

He slammed the phone down and Virgil said to Jenkins and Shrake, "Everything's running smooth."

"I got that impression," Shrake said. To Jenkins: "How fast can we get to the Iowa border?"

Virgil sat in Masilla's outer office for nearly an hour, while Jenkins

and Shrake went down to the lobby to talk to the two attractive receptionists. After an hour, he took a call from his friend in the AG's office,
who was calmer, and perhaps even collegial: "Mr. Masilla will cooperate in every way he can, and we have faxed him a letter saying that we
will give strong consideration to leniency should it prove that he inadvertently violated any Minnesota statutes."

"What if he violated them on purpose?"

"Rogers insisted on a wording that makes the intent of the
letter . . . mmm . . . questionable, so that if it goes to court, a court
might reasonably find that we have offered him immunity. Or, a
court could find the other way, and decide we didn't, but there
would be a strong presumption of a leniency."

"Jesus, sometimes I feel like my hands are dirty."

"You owe me a beer, my friend, and, Virgil, if you ever do this
again, I'll put you in jail for contempt of attorney, I swear to God."

Virgil called Shrake and Jenkins, who came up a minute later and
looked happy as they got off the elevator, and Virgil asked, "You got
dates?"

"We do," Jenkins said. "They're golfers, can you believe that?
We're playing golf tomorrow afternoon, unless we have to shoot
somebody. What happened with Masilla?"

"We're about to find out."

ROGERS SAID, "My client is eager to help. We've spoken with the
AG's office, and so we're ready to go ahead. If you don't mind, we'd
like to record this session, just so there's no question afterwards
about what was said."

"It's okay with me," Virgil said. "We'll all have to make some speeches before we start asking questions."

Rogers had a recorder, a small but high-fidelity pocket recorder of the kind used by musicians and lawyers. He made his speech, beginning with, "As you know, we've spoken to the attorney general's office, and as we understand it, we have been given blanket immunity from prosecution as long as Mr. Masilla gives you his frank cooperation."

Virgil identified himself on the tape and replied with, "We have no idea of the details of the agreement you worked out with the attorney general's office, what degree of immunity your client may or may not have been given, so you'll have to decide on a case-by-case basis which questions you will answer or refuse to answer, depending on your understanding."

They argued about that, politely, for a few minutes, and then Virgil turned to Masilla and asked, "Mr. Masilla, have you, in your position as auditor of the Buchanan County school system, noticed any fiscal irregularities—"

Masilla replied with, "I was given only limited access to the school records, but in my examination I noticed what seemed to be some inconsistent reporting of costs. . . ."

That went on for more than an hour. Virgil was able to build a picture that implicated the school superintendent, the finance officer, and all the members of the school board in fiscal irregularities "which I pointed out from time to time, and recommended strong action upon."

Masilla noted the presence of Viking Laughton and Randolph Kerns during some of the meetings with school officials. The discussion was moderated by Rogers, who tried to keep responsibility as fuzzy as possible, while delivering the goods, which was required by the deal.

They were still hard at it when Virgil's phone rang. He glanced at it, intending to let the call go, but saw it was from Buchanan County's Sheriff Purdy. He said, "Gotta take this. Let's recess for one minute."

He answered while he was headed for the hall. Purdy said, "We found Randy Kerns."

"Where is he?"

"Sitting in his truck, off Thunderbolt Road."

"When you say sitting . . ." That sounded bad.

"Looks like he shot himself," Purdy said. "Bullet went through his head and the driver's-side window."

"Ah . . . God."

"You coming down?"

"I'm up in Winona. I'll be down as fast as I can get there. Don't touch anything."

"We knew you'd say that, so we haven't," Purdy said. "I see a couple of gun suicides every year, somewhere in the county. This one is somewhat unusual."

"Why is that?"

"Never seen a guy shoot himself in the eye."

VIRGIL EXCUSED HIMSELF, Jenkins, and Shrake from the meeting: "We will resume soon."

Rogers asked, "When?"

"Don't know. We have another murder related to the first three.

That's four murders," Virgil said. "There's not going to be much judicial mercy here. If I were you, I'd try to tighten up that deal with the AG."

WHEN THEY GOT BACK to Trippton, they went down Thunderbolt Road past the town prostitute's house—she was standing on her porch, looking down the road, and when she saw Virgil's truck coming, pointed him farther on down. There was a turnout where the road bent closest to the Mississippi, a lovers' lane, perhaps, and three sheriff's cars were parked in the dirt circle, along with a couple of unmarked trucks. Purdy was there, talking with Alewort, his crime-scene guy, and they were all facing a narrow overgrown track that apparently led down to the river. Virgil could see the grille of a truck down through the brush, and Beatrice Sawyer, his own crime-scene investigator, looking in the passenger-side window.

Alewort said, "We didn't touch, just called Beatrice in, except that I was worried about blood and bone and brain tissue soaking further into the dirt outside the truck, where it'd be harder to recover, so I thought I'd go ahead and start that process."

"That's fine," Virgil said.

"Yeah, well, it was pretty interesting, is what it was, just like that shot-in-the-eye thing," Alewort said. "There was no blood or bone or brain matter. Not that I could find. Or Beatrice, either. And there should have been, there's plenty of it on the window, around the gunshot hole."

"So what you're saying is," Jenkins offered, "this guy Kerns shot himself through the eye, blowing his brains out, and then drove over here from somewhere else."

"That would be one interpretation," Alewort said.

Virgil, Jenkins, and Shrake walked down the track. Virgil said, "Hey, Bea."

Sawyer said, "What with that Black Hole case, and now your two here, I'm getting pretty goddamned tired of looking at dead bodies."

"So go apply at Target, I hear they're hiring," Virgil said. He wasn't much interested in any complaints, given what had happened to the subjects of her research: he thought of Will Bacon stuffed under the stage.

"You've gotten a little testy since this morning," Sawyer said.

"Yeah, well . . ." He gestured at the truck.

Kerns was sprawled faceup across the passenger-side seat, his legs bent awkwardly backward into the foot well. One eye was a mass of dried blood, and the blood had poured out of the hole and down his face. He looked worse than Bacon had. Something about missing eyes, Virgil thought with a shudder. A small-frame .38 caliber hammerless revolver lay on the seat next to his leg.

While Kerns was on the passenger seat, a bullet hole went out the driver's-side window, and the window was spattered with blood and shards of bone. All of the body tissue had dried: Kerns had been dead for a while.

"When do you think he was shot?"

She shook her head: "Last night? Seems like a good bet."

Virgil turned back to Purdy and said, "We're both thinking the same thing. Somebody shot him. That's no suicide."

Purdy said, "We've got to stop this shit."

Virgil nodded and said, "The guy who shot him was inside the truck, probably in the passenger seat. Kerns was either talking to him or turned his face to him just as the killer pulled the trigger, and that knocked the hole in the window. The killer dragged Kerns into the passenger seat, then ran around to the other side, got in, drove the truck here, and walked away."

"That's what we think," Sawyer said. "Since the killer was in both seats, there'll be DNA. We'll sample everything in sight."

Purdy said, "Kerns lived by himself. We've got a car outside his house, but we haven't been inside it yet."

"Let's go over there, then. . . . But give me a minute." Virgil got a flashlight from his truck and looked through the heavily smoked windows on Kerns's camper-back. Kerns had packed up, ready to run—two big suitcases, a duffel bag, and a half-filled plastic garbage bag lay in the back. The garbage bag interested Virgil.

Virgil said to Sawyer, "Since the back is isolated from the front, where the shooting happened, maybe we could open the back. I want to look in that garbage bag."

"The keys are in the ignition, but I don't want to touch them, because the killer had to use them, at least to turn the engine off," Sawyer said.

"You got a pry bar?" Virgil asked Purdy, looking at the lock on the camper-back doors. "This lock isn't too much."

"Be right back," Alewort said.

He came trotting back a moment later with a crowbar, and after some screwing around in which Alewort tried not to do much damage, Jenkins took the bar from him, jammed it in the crack between the door and the frame, and yanked the door open, breaking the lock loose. "There you go."

Virgil took some vinyl gloves from Sawyer and used them to pick up the end of the garbage bag. The video camera was inside.

"Excellent," he said. But when he pulled it out, the memory card was gone. "Shoot. Okay, guys, the number one thing we're looking for now is the memory card." He hastily corrected himself: "The memory cards, they're CompactFlash cards, two of them. They're red and black, I don't know, maybe an inch and a half square. We find them, we break everything open."

"Could be in his pockets," Alewort suggested.

"We'll look there first," Sawyer said.

Alewort got some tape and taped the door shut, and Virgil said to Purdy, "Let's go look at his house. Maybe the cards are there."

"Not likely. Probably trashed them."

"Gotta look."

VIRGIL GOT KERNS'S ADDRESS from Purdy, but on the way out to the highway, stopped at Wendy McComb's house. She came out and leaned in the truck window and said, "So somebody shot Randy Kerns?"

"That's what we believe," Virgil said. "You hear anybody going past here last night or early this morning?"

"Yes. I already told the sheriff. Last night, late—after midnight—and it sounded heavy, like Randy's truck. I listened for it coming back out, but it never did. Didn't hear anything else, either. No shot, or anything. The thing is, you wouldn't come down here at night unless you were coming back out the same way. The rest of the road just wanders around past nothing."

"I've been down it," Virgil said.

"Sometimes kids go down to the turnout to park, but that's not common," McComb said. "Too dark and spooky down there. The only ones we usually see down there are catfishermen. They'll haul their jon boats down there, in their pickups, and throw them in the river. But that didn't sound so much like a pickup last night—they usually rattle. And it was too late—the catfishermen are usually coming in then, not going out."

"You never saw the truck?"

"Never did. It went past, and that was all."

"You didn't have any visitors at the time?" Virgil asked.

"Nope. Just me. And my gun, of course."

"You keep the gun close, Wendy," Virgil said. "Just in case the killer starts to worry that you might be a witness."

As they drove out to the highway, Jenkins said, "That young lady . . . ?"

Virgil said, "Yeah, she is. Conley, the first guy killed, was one of her clients. He left a message with her. That's why I wound up looking in that tire swing."

Jenkins said, "Good detectin', there, Flowers."

THEY NO LONGER needed a warrant for Kerns's house, since nobody else lived there, and Kerns had been murdered. Virgil was most interested in the garbage—was there any possibility that he'd simply thrown away the memory card from the camera? With Alewort's help, he dug through every wastebasket and garbage sack in the house, as well as the garbage can in back, and found nothing.

"It was always a pretty thin possibility," Shrake said. "It was the one thing that could hang him for sure."

"Didn't get rid of the camera," Virgil said. "You'd think he would have gotten rid of them both at the same time."

"Maybe Bea will find something in his shirt pocket."

But Bea didn't.

IT WAS NEARLY six o'clock before Virgil, Shrake, and Jenkins walked out of Kerns's house for the last time. They stopped to see how the work was going on Kerns's truck, but again, it would all come down to lab work—there was nothing obvious lying about.

"No hope in tracing the pistol—or very damn little," Sawyer told them. "I checked, and it's seventy years old. It's an old military model from World War Two. The shells themselves are probably twenty years old."

"How about the keys?"

"Wiped—or the killer was wearing gloves, or used a hankie or something."

Virgil sighed: "Why can't this be easier?"

They were still talking when his cell phone rang. The BCA duty officer. "A kid name Muddy just called, and said you should call right back. He said you have the number."

21

VIRGIL FOUND the Ruff phone number on his cell phone's "recents" list, punched it up, and Muddy picked up on the first ring. "Dad's over in La Crosse with Dog Butt, and I was sort of out walking around, and guess what? D. Wayne Sharf is back."

"Where?" Virgil asked.

"I don't know exactly what's going on, because I was inside practicing when he got back, but now he and somebody else, a woman, are sneaking in and out of his house. I think they're taking stuff out."

The house had been sealed by the DEA, but "sealed by the DEA" meant that there was some tape on the doors. Everything Sharf owned, aside from a few pounds of methamphetamine, was still inside.

Virgil said, "Okay—Muddy, you stay there at your house. Don't go fooling around with this guy. We've been looking for him, federal agents are looking for him. He could be seriously dangerous."

"I'll tell you, he doesn't seem to have a car with him. He's either sneaking over the hills, or somebody's going to come pick him up. If you go crashing in there, he'll take off in the night, and you won't see him again."

"Right. Tell you what, we'll come up to your house and walk down. It's an old car, not a truck. We'll be there in fifteen minutes."

JENKINS: "WHAT HAPPENED?"

"We gotta get back to your car. You guys are gonna need to get out of those suits, and we gotta do it in a hurry."

They made a flying stop at Johnson's cabin. On the way, Virgil explained the dog situation and the DEA interest in the case, and Sharf's fugitive status. After a quick change of clothes, Virgil got two flashlights from his truck, including the jacklight, and Jenkins got his six-cell Maglite, and then Jenkins drove far too fast north up Highway 26, slowing only when they were a mile south of Orly's Creek. At that point, Virgil and Shrake slumped over in their seats, so only Jenkins was visible at the wheel, and they took the turn on Orly's Creek Road.

"Rough road," Jenkins said, as they bounced past the first trailer, the one Johnson had called the lookout. "Good thing we took a well-sprung car."

"Good thing we're driving a piece of shit, so we don't have to worry about breaking it," Virgil said from the backseat.

As they came to the end of the road, Jenkins said, "I haven't seen a single soul. Hope the guy didn't split."

They made the Ruffs' house in a little over twenty minutes, rather than the fifteen that Virgil had promised. Muddy was sitting on the porch, in the dark; the only light was from the back of the house, through a window onto the porch.

"Virgil," Muddy said.

Virgil introduced everybody and asked, "You see any cars?"

"Nothing. D. Wayne is about as lazy as a man can get, so there's no way that he's going to walk if he can ride. He's still there."

Shrake looked back down the valley and said, "Dark out there. I'm more of a snatch-him-off-the-barstool type."

"I'll take you down," Muddy said. And quickly, to Virgil: "I'll get you there and then I'll come right back here. Promise."

Virgil said, "All right. You just get us close."

INSTEAD OF TAKING the road, they went through the woods. Virgil passed around the insect repellent before they went in—Muddy said, "This stuff still stinks"—and then they followed Muddy along a game trail that paralleled the creek, on the opposite side from the road. The going was slow, with Muddy whispering warnings at two shallow ravines and a fallen tree trunk, and ten minutes after they left Muddy's house, they were behind Sharf's place, looking down the hill.

There were at least two people inside, because they could see the light from at least two flashlights, one on the bottom floor, one in the upstairs bedroom. Virgil sent Muddy back home, and after he disappeared, he, Jenkins, and Shrake began easing down the hill.

They were fifty yards away when somebody came out of the house. Whoever it was had turned off his flashlight before leaving the house, but turned it on briefly, two or three times, as he crossed the bridge to the road. They could see that he was carrying a bundle, which he left by the road. Then he hurried back to the house, and Jenkins, leaning close to Virgil, said, "That looked like a woman."

Shrake: "Yeah. If your Sharf guy is in there, he's the one upstairs."

As THEY CLOSED on Sharf's cabin, they could hear what sounded like a dresser drawer opening and closing, and then a man's voice calling: "Get the TV."

At that moment, a dog started barking. Not a big dog, a small, yappy dog, starting inside, and then, from the sound of it, moving out on the side stoop. They couldn't see it, but it sounded like it was barking right at them, and a woman called, "Wayne! There's some-body out there. Wayne!"

"That's our guy," Virgil said. "Let's go."

Virgil turned on his jacklight, illuminating the entire cabin and a good piece of the woods around it. Jenkins went right, and Shrake went forward, as Virgil shouted, "Police! Police! D. Wayne Sharf— you're under arrest!"

Shrake, who'd run ahead, called, "I've got the front door, watch the side door, Virg—"

A woman screamed, "Don't shoot, don't shoot! We give up."

Jenkins came in from the dark, into the lighted circle, gun out, to the side door, where a Chihuahua was jumping up and down and barking its tiny heart out. Jenkins peeked in the door and shouted, "Come out of there, keep your hands over your head. Come out of there!"

The woman shouted, "I'm coming, I'm coming, don't shoot me. Don't hurt my dog."

The dog was still yapping and the woman appeared at the screen door, hands over her head. She was a large woman, with shoulder-length brown hair, wearing jeans and a long-sleeved man's shirt. Behind her, they heard a POP! and she half-turned and screamed, "Wayne! Wayne! Come out of there."

From the front, Shrake shouted, "Fire! There's a fire!"

Virgil saw the flickering lights of a fire, and the woman bolted out on the porch, stumbled off the side, and fell flat on her face, screaming for her dog. Her hands were empty, and Jenkins grabbed her by the collar of her shirt, and the small dog launched itself at Jenkins's ankle. Jenkins shook it off and the woman screamed, "Don't hurt the dog, don't hurt the dog . . ." and wrenched free and crawled toward the dog, trying to catch it. The dog eluded her and went after Jenkins again.

Jenkins shook it off again and the woman scooped it up as Virgil pushed through the screen door and shouted, "Sharf. Where are you? Sharf?"

From the front of the house, Shrake was yelling, "Get out of there! Virgil, get out of there."

Virgil took one more step, holding his shirt to his nose and mouth against the smoke, and saw that the living room had become a furnace, six-foot-high flames eating through the old knotty-pine walls. Both Shrake and Jenkins were screaming at him, and he backed up, decided that running was better than walking, and ran out of the place.

The woman was shouting, "Get Wayne, help Wayne, get Wayne."

She'd moved to the edge of the yard and was peering in horror at the tiny one-room upper floor, and windows began popping around the house. No sign of D. Wayne Sharf. Shrake ran around to the far side of the house, and a second later, shouted, "Virgil! Virgil! Here!"

Virgil ran that way. The upper floor had a window in it, which was open, and dangling from the window was a thick bright-yellow nylon rope, the kind sold to apartment dwellers as fire escapes.

"He set it on purpose," Shrake yelled.

Jenkins shouted, "Give me some light," and dashed into the woods, to the east of the cabin. Virgil still had his jacklight and lit the place up again, and at the farthest extreme of the light's penetration, saw the back of D. Wayne Sharf rapidly fading into the trees. Virgil ran after Jenkins, hoping to give him enough light to keep up the chase. Jenkins was a fast and nimble runner, and was pulling away from the light when he suddenly broke left, toward the creek, and Virgil pivoted that way. Then Jenkins burst through some trees and fell into the creek, with an impact like that of a breaching whale.

Farther down the road a set of headlights swung off the highway and accelerated toward them, suddenly braked, swerved, and did a three-point turn. Virgil had a clear-enough sight line to see D. Wayne Sharf break from the tree line, run alongside the car for a few steps, yank open the door, and throw himself inside.

The car accelerated away, turned left on the highway, away from Trippton, and was gone.

Shrake had run down to the creek and shouted at Jenkins, "Back-stroke, backstroke!"

Jenkins stood up in knee-deep water and said, "Fuck you," and, "Somebody's got to call the fire department."

Virgil turned to look at Sharf's cabin, which looked like a burn-ing haystack, flames shooting up into the sky. He fished out his phone, but failed to get a signal. They were three hundred yards from the mouth of the valley, and he said, "You guys go collect that woman. I'm going to run down to the highway and see if I can get a signal."

But at that moment a man and a woman ran into the road from the opposite side of the valley, saw the three of them, and yelled, "We called the fire department, they're on the way."

The three of them jogged past the neighbors, and Virgil said, "Call the sheriff, tell them that Virgil Flowers said we have a situa-tion here."

"You sure do," the woman said, and, "You're a police officer?"

"Yes. Tell him we need a couple of cars."

WHEN VIRGIL, Jenkins, and Shrake got back to the cabin, the Chi-huahua was gone, and so was the woman.

"They're on foot, so they've gotta be around here someplace," Shrake said.

Jenkins had taken his wallet out of his pants pocket and was pull-ing out damp pieces of paper, spreading them on a rock next to a weed garden. "Goddamn job, I'm gonna quit. That fuckin' dog bit me twice. I'm putting in for disability leave, or maybe retirement."

"If you do that, you won't be able to beat up people," Shrake said.

Jenkins said, "Oh . . . yeah."

Virgil looked past them, down at the road, where a dozen neighbors had gathered to witness the festivities, and as a lone fire truck turned the corner at the end of the valley, saw Muddy ambling along, looking up at them.

"Talk to the fire guys," Virgil told the other two. Then he stared at Muddy until he was sure Muddy was looking back at him, and tilted his head toward the woods. Muddy nodded, and drifted back up the road where he'd come from.

The fire truck arrived, and another one turned the corner at the end of the valley, and a fireman ran up the hill, and Jenkins and Shrake went to meet him. The cabin was more than fully involved—the fire was actually beginning to slow, from lack of anything more to burn, and smoke, and the stink of burning insulation, suffused the air.

Virgil nodded at Shrake and backed away from the fire into the woods, until he was out of sight of the road, then hurried deeper in. A hundred feet from the cabin, Muddy stepped out of the dark, and Virgil said, "There was a woman with Sharf. When the cabin caught fire, she must've run into the woods. I'd like to find her."

Muddy said, "All right. You think she went deeper into the valley, or out toward the highway?"

Virgil had to think about it for a moment, then said, "If she's like everybody else, she's got a cell phone, and once she can get some damn reception, she'll be calling somebody to come get her. I expect she'd either go higher, or toward the highway. She was a pretty big woman, and didn't look like she was in that good of shape."

"So she probably walked up a ways, to get around the cabin. . . ."

MUDDY KNEW THE TRAILS around the place, took them up a hundred feet or so, behind the cabin, and then along the valley wall. The light wind was in their faces, and after they were clear of the cabin, they were also clear of the smoke. They moved slowly, stopping to listen, and eventually were out of range of the voices around the burning house, but not out of range of the sound of the heavy engines on the fire trucks.

Four hundred yards down the valley, and maybe two hundred from the highway, Muddy stopped so abruptly that Virgil nearly bumped into him. They stood for a moment, then Muddy whispered, "Smell it?"

Virgil closed his eyes and smelled, very faintly, an odor somewhere between roses and violets. Perfume. He whispered, "Yes."

Muddy moved on another twenty or thirty feet, and then stopped again and whispered, "We're close now."

Virgil cleared his throat and said, in a normal speaking voice, "I've got a gun, and I don't want to shoot you, but I can see you, and I'm not sure if you have a gun or not, so if you move suddenly, I'm going to have to use my gun."

Two or three seconds later, the woman said, "Don't shoot me."

"Then come out of there."

She'd been huddled behind a tree, clutching the dog, which yapped once at Virgil and then shut up. Virgil turned on the jacklight, aimed over her head, but still lighting her up: she put up a hand to shade her eyes, and Virgil whispered to Muddy, "Better take off."

The boy slipped away, and Virgil said to the woman, "What's your name?"

"Judy. Burk."

"Let's go down to the road, Judy. We need to talk this over."

VIRGIL WALKED JUDY and the dog down to the road, where an elderly white-haired man named John seemed to be having some kind of seizure. Somebody said something to him as Virgil and Judy came up, and he spun around, saw Virgil, and asked, "Are you the man in charge of this disaster?"

"I'm with the BCA," Virgil said.

"You burned down my house! You owe me for a house!"

Virgil said, "I'm sorry, I didn't burn it down. D. Wayne Sharf did. I was standing outside when he set it on fire."

John spun in a crazed dervish-like circle, making gargling sounds as he did, and when he came out of it, wild-eyed, he said, "He wouldn't have burned it down if you hadn't been there."

Virgil said, "I'm sorry about the house—you said it was your house?"

"Yes, it's my house! It was worth . . ." He hesitated, the better to pump the price, Virgil thought. "At least a hundred and twenty thousand!"

Several people in the crowd laughed, and a tough-looking guy in a T-shirt said, "Shit, John, if I'd known you'd shingled it with gold, I might have come over and stolen some shingles."

There was more laughter, which made the man angrier, and then Shrake came up behind him and patted him on the shoulder and said, "It's not going to be worth anything to you if you have a heart attack and die. You've got to ease up a little."

John pulled himself together, then raised a finger at Virgil, but before he could say what he was going to say, Virgil asked, "Has the DEA been in touch with you, about the drugs?"

The finger stopped in mid-shake. "What drugs?"

"The basement was full of methamphetamine. Probably a half-million dollars' worth. Was that yours? Or was it D. Wayne's?"

John slowed some more. "Well, it wasn't mine. I rented the place."

A voice in the crowd asked, "Do you have to pay income taxes on drugs?"

"If you sell them, you do," Shrake said.

"I don't know about any drugs," John said.

"Why don't you give me your name, address, and phone number," Virgil said. "I'll have the DEA guy get in touch."

John looked around and then said, "Give me your card. I'll call you tomorrow."

RIGHT. Virgil gave him a card, and took his name, and John went away. Virgil, Shrake, and Judy walked up the valley wall to the clearing where the cabin once stood. Jenkins was chatting to one of the firemen, like two guys at a barbecue. A fire hose led up to the site from one of the trucks, but nothing was being sprayed on the fire.

"So . . . couldn't save it?" Virgil asked.

The fireman shook his head: "It was gone before we got here. The problem is, half-burned houses attract people, and they get hurt. Once they're that far gone, better to let them burn. You get a nice clean ash."

"We're all gonna stink," Jenkins said to Virgil. And to Judy, "Nice to see you again. Your dog bit me. Twice."

"He thought you were attacking me."

"I was standing on the porch, I—"

"Okay, okay, okay," Virgil said. "The thing is, Judy, I don't know, it looks like you might have been involved in a bunch of crimes. Theft, arson, harboring a fugitive, breaking the federal seals off the house. I mean, we've got some stuff to talk about."

Judy began to weep, what appeared to be honest tears, and Shrake said, "Hey, Virgil, take it easy. She looks like a pretty nice lady." He turned to Judy and said, "You know, you're entitled to a lawyer, you don't have to tell Virgil a single darn thing."

Virgil said to Jenkins, "Read her rights to her, huh?"

Jenkins did the Miranda, and then Shrake said, in his most kindly voice, "Did you understand that? You don't even have to pay for a lawyer."

Jenkins said, "Jesus, Shrake, you trying to get a date? Let's put the cuffs on her and haul her ass down to the Buchanan County jail, get her processed in, throw the mutt in the pound or whatever they've got down there, and get some sleep."

Judy began to cry again, and Shrake said, "C'mon, I'll walk you down to the road." To Virgil: "Get the car, pick us up."

They started down the hill, and when they were out of earshot, Virgil said, "Makes me feel bad."

"'Cause you're Mr. Softy," Jenkins said. "Let Shrake empty her out, and then, you know . . . whatever."

"Still makes me feel bad."

"Not as bad as I feel. My ankle burns like fire. That dog has jaws like a fuckin' alligator."

"It's a fuckin' Chihuahua," Virgil said. "It's practically a fuckin' hamster."

"I don't care if it's a fuckin' chickadee, it bit me on the fuckin' leg."

"Ah, fuck it," Virgil said.

JENKINS AND VIRGIL walked back up the valley to the Ruff house, and found Muddy inside, tootling on a black electric guitar, a complex version of Creedence's "Lookin' Out My Back Door," on which he was playing two separate guitar parts. "You gonna play in a band?" Virgil asked.

"Maybe. I'm good enough," Muddy said. "But . . . my old man says it's a tough way to make a living, if you're not one in a million."

"Probably right about that," Jenkins said. "On the other hand, you may be. If you are, it'd be a shame to miss out on it."

"Dad says if I get really good at it, the discipline will let me be good at anything."

"I wish my dad had told me that," Jenkins said. "My old man told me to stay away from Lone Star beer. Which he was drinking at the time."

Virgil told Muddy to have his father call. "I need to talk to him about what happened tonight. I have a feeling he might be a little pissed."

"Probably. But it goes away pretty quick. He told me he thought you were a good guy, considering the T-shirt you had on."

Virgil nodded: "Good to know. But tell him to call."

THEY TOOK THE CAR back to the fire scene, where Shrake was waiting with Judy Burk. When they came up, Shrake gave Virgil a wave, so Virgil parked at the side of the road and he and Jenkins got out into the lights of a dozen vehicles.

"Judy is really torn up about all of this—she didn't know what Sharf was up to," Shrake said. "He told her that the landlord had kicked him out and was going to take all of his stuff, and she just came down here with him and another friend to help get his clothes. Then, all of this, and he wound up ditching her and Brutus."

Jenkins flinched: "The dog is named Brutus? Why? Because he stabs people with his teeth?"

Judy backed into Shrake, and Shrake said, "Hey, listen to what I'm telling you. She didn't have anything to do with all this. I think we just give her a ride home—she lives in CarryTown, just on the other side of Trippton—it's an extra two minutes for us."

"How do you know she didn't have anything to do with this?" Virgil asked. "Looked to me like she was involved."

"I wasn't—"

"How did that fire start? Looked like more than a match. Smelled like gasoline. Did D. Wayne carry a gas can in there?"

Her lip trembled and she said, "No, no, he didn't have a gas can."

"A bottle?"

"He had a backpack . . . maybe there was a bottle in it."

"Maybe?"

"I think I saw a bottle," she admitted. "I didn't know what was in it."

"Molotov cocktail," Jenkins said to Virgil. "He went in knowing he was gonna torch the place. Probably afraid that the DEA was going to process the house and come up with about a million of his fingerprints."

"Which they would have," Virgil said. "In fact, I've got to call Gomez and tell him the house went to heaven." He looked back at Judy, pursed his lips. "He might be interested in talking to Judy here."

Judy choked a little, then said, "I'll tell you anything you want."

AFTER A WHILE, they loaded into the car, with Jenkins in the back with Judy and the dog, so he could lean on her, if necessary. Shrake was still friendly from the driver's seat, and Judy told the whole thing: D. Wayne Sharf was a hanger-on, one of life's losers who'd never been allowed to ride with the Seed. They wouldn't even make him an associate member. But Roy Zorn used him to haul ingredients for his meth, and D. Wayne helped him cook it.

The dogs, she said, were D. Wayne's own sideline, which she

didn't much care for, since she was a dog lover herself. At the moment, all of D. Wayne's dogs were in a makeshift pen somewhere in western Buchanan County, she didn't know exactly where. Wherever it was, she said, was where D. Wayne would be.

"The guy who drove us here, his name is Lee, I don't know his last name, he and Wayne are gonna put the dogs in these crates and drive them over to this dog-trading sale. . . . The good ones go down south to hunt, the bad ones and the mutts and the puppies get sold off to these bunchers, they call them."

"I know what bunchers are," Virgil said.

"Yeah, well, they sell them to medical laboratories—"

"I know that," Virgil said.

"In fact," said Jenkins, leaning over her, "you really haven't told us much that we didn't already know."

"I know one thing you don't," she said.

Jenkins: "Yeah? What's that?"

"I know where the dog sale is gonna be, and when. And I know D. Wayne is gonna be there with all his dogs and his flatbed trailer—that's what I know."

Jenkins leaned away from her, taking off the pressure, and said, "Babe—you should have said something earlier."

22

THEY CONTINUED to push and pull on Burk, arguing among themselves, for her benefit, whether they should drop her in jail or take her home, and finally Virgil asked her, "Are you going to find D. Wayne Sharf again and tell him that we'll be waiting for him Saturday?"

"No. I will not. Cross my heart." She pulled the Chihuahua off to one side so she could cross her heart with her index finger.

"If you're lying to us, we won't be talking about jail—we'll be talking about the women's prison up in Shakopee. You stay away from him," Virgil said. "If he calls, tell him you ran away in the woods and had to walk home. Or hitchhike. Yell at him a little."

"You don't have to encourage me," she said. "D. Wayne left me in a burning house and never looked back."

"Remember that, if he calls," Virgil said.

CarryTown turned out to be a cluster of aging mobile homes built in no particular place south of Trippton, around a convenience store called the Cash 'n Carry. Burk pointed out her trailer and Shrake pulled up next to it, and Burk said, "Let me ask you all something, before you blame me for hanging out with D. Wayne."

"Ask," Virgil said.

"When you were eighteen years old, wearing your blue graduation robe, sitting in a folding chair with your funny hat, listening to some old guy telling you about *Oh, The Places You'll Go!*, did you ever think you'd wind up being forty-eight years old and living in a shithole like this one?"

She got out of the car, slammed the door, and walked up to her concrete-block stoop, and Jenkins said, "Well, that sort of pisses on the evening's festivities."

Shrake backed the Crown Vic in a circle, and they drove back to Trippton. On the way, Virgil asked Shrake, "How bad do you feel about punkin' Judy Burk? Bein' the good cop?"

Shrake said, "Oh . . . you know. She was hanging out with a guy who sells crank to kids. She's sort of sad on her own, but she knew what he was doing, and she helped him out. Maybe I'll reincarnate as a termite, but I don't feel that bad."

As they rolled through town, Virgil called Gomez, who said, "Honest to God, do you ever call anyone during business hours? You didn't find another meth mill, did you?"

"No. I just wanted to tell you that D. Wayne Sharf burned that house to the ground," Virgil said. "You won't have to come back for any further processing."

"Great. I assume you grabbed him?"

"No, not exactly," Virgil said. "But—I know where he'll be on Saturday."

"Grab him, then. We'll come and take him off your hands," Gomez said.

JENKINS AND SHRAKE dropped Virgil at Johnson's cabin, and went off to their motel, with plans to play golf in the morning, to make up for the evening's overtime.

Virgil got a good night's sleep, and the next morning took a call from Dave at the attorney general's office. "We've been conferencing on the Buchanan County matter, and I'm going down to Winona this morning, with my assistant, to talk to Masilla. I'm calling you more as a courtesy than anything—happy to have you, but it's not required."

"I'll hang down here," Virgil said. "I got enough information from Masilla to go around and knock on some doors. I'll stay in touch with what I get—you might want to plan to come down here tomorrow or the next day, depending on what breaks."

"Call me when life gets serious," the lawyer said, and hung up.

VIRGIL ATE BREAKFAST, blocking out his day on a yellow pad. When he was done, he called the attorney back: "I'm going to interview a guy name Russell Ross, who runs a wholesale diesel business, then I'm going to see the guy who runs the school's motor pool. His name is Dick Brown. If I'm found floating facedown in the river, he'll be the one to talk to about it."

"If you're found floating in the river, I'll return to my comfortable middle-class home in St. Paul, barricade myself in the TV room, and let somebody else investigate. You take it easy down there."

TriPoint Fuel was named after the river landmark used by the old steamboats, when Trippton had been a refueling stop. Four well-used tank trucks were parked in the dirt lot when Virgil arrived, and another was just leaving. The place looked like an environmental nightmare, Virgil thought: it was backed against the levee and the ground was soaked with oil drippings.

Rusty Ross—his name was on a slightly rusty plaque above the only office door in the building—looked like a golfer, wearing tan slacks and a red golf shirt, with a pencil pushed behind one ear. He wore aviator glasses of the kind that changed shades in sunlight, and that gave his brown eyes a vaguely overcast look.

"What can I do you for?" he asked Virgil, when Virgil stuck his head in the office.

Virgil said, "I'm an investigator for the Bureau of Criminal Apprehension, out of St. Paul. I was wondering if you've been kicking money back to Dick Brown, for buying the school's fuel from you."

Ross's Adam's apple bobbed once before he said, "Well . . . no."

Virgil tried to stay cheerful: "I hope you're telling the truth there, Mr. Ross, because this has become a rather serious matter, involving murder."

Ross pointed at one of the two orange-plastic chairs that faced his desk, and Virgil nodded and took one.

"I have never kicked anything back to Dick Brown—aside from a bottle of Jim Beam I pass out to my customers at Christmas— because I don't have to. As far as the schools are concerned, I'm the only game in town."

"I don't know much about your business," Virgil confessed, "but I know that there are other fuel places around. Up in Winona, over in La Crosse . . ."

"And sayin' that proves you don't know anything about my business," Ross said. "You know what the number one, two, and three costs in this business are?"

"No, I don't," Virgil said.

"It's trucks, drivers, and fuel." Ross leaned forward, over his desk, his face interested and intent. "The stuff we sell, the diesel, is the same price for every wholesaler. That's why the business is so good, if you've already got it—and why nobody else can get into it. To compete with me, somebody would have to buy at least a million dollars' worth of trucks, and then hire a bunch of drivers who are making thirty thousand a year, and then . . . they couldn't sell the fuel for a penny a gallon more than I do. Or say a guy already runs a business up in Winona, and he wants to compete with me. He has to drive the diesel down here, and put that mileage and wear and tear on his trucks to do it, and pay the drivers for their time, and keep a salesman down here. That pushes the cost of every gallon he sells. He can't underbid me, because we pay exactly the same amount for the wholesale diesel. So you see, I'm the only game in town. And that won't change. That means that I don't have to kickback to anyone—they take my diesel, or they find some other fuel. And I already supply the gas to the cut-rate stations in town."

Virgil said, "That sounded like a prepared speech."

"I think about it a lot. I once thought about buying a golf course, but a guy said, 'Rusty, you don't know shit about golf courses. Stick to what you know.' He was right. But: I gotta say, I've heard you were sniffing around that whole school bus situation. I don't want to know what's going on there, because the schools are my biggest single customer, other than the three gas stations I service. I do suspect something's going on. I've heard that their reported costs seemed to be a little out of line."

"Really. You heard that?"

"A big-city guy like you probably doesn't understand this—"

"I was born and raised in Marshall, and I live in Mankato."

"Then maybe you do. In towns like this, you hear everything, sooner or later. Everybody in town knows you've been sniffing around the schools, and a lot of people are beginning to talk about why that might be," Ross said. "A couple of those school board members have been known to spend more money than they really have. And everybody knows how much they have, since we all live in one big pile down here—the bankers, the lawyers, the loan company people, the lady who runs the Edward Jones franchise . . . everybody."

Virgil wiggled once to get comfortable in his chair, and asked, "Let me give you a hypothetical. Hypothetically, if something is going on with the school buses, if somebody's creaming off some money there . . . then Dick Brown must know about it."

Ross leaned back in his office chair and put his heels up on his desk, looked up at the ceiling. "Well, I don't know. The school could just put down one number for fuel costs, and pay me a different one. A different number. Nobody really compares them. I've never had a single person come here and ask how much the schools pay me for fuel. I've kinda wondered about that, too. Shouldn't an auditor be coming by every few years?"

"Did Clancy Conley ever ask?"

"Nope. I knew the man, he used to try to sell me ads, but I told him the same thing I just told you: Why in the hell would I buy an ad, when everybody knows I'm the only guy who delivers fuel oil? Diesel? Anyway, you sayin' that's why he was killed, because of the fuel numbers?"

"Because of all the numbers," Virgil said.

"How much are they stealing?" Ross asked.

"Don't know yet. A lot. They're buying houses in Tucson."

Ross whistled: "You gotta expect a little leakage, but that's more like a mountain stream. No taxes, either."

Virgil asked, "You have records of all your deliveries and the amounts?"

"Going back six years. In case the IRS asks."

"Hang on to them," Virgil said. "Somebody's gonna want to take a look."

Virgil got up to leave, but as he was scuffing out the door, Ross said, "Something occurs to me . . ."

"Yeah?"

"Of course Dick would know. He knows how much I deliver, and how much the buses burn. And sitting where he does, he's gotta know what the schools report on fuel prices. No matter how they do it, he'd know."

ALTHOUGH VIRGIL DIDN'T necessarily have to believe what Ross said, he did—he'd been reasonably convinced by the no-option argument that Ross had made, and also by the fact that he had six years' worth of records. It was likely that Ross gave away more than a few bottles of booze at Christmas, but it probably wouldn't be much more . . . because he didn't have to. He didn't look like a guy who would pay a bill he didn't have to pay.

DICK BROWN was sitting at a greasy-looking desk in the school motor pool, working over some greasy-looking paper. He took one look at Virgil and said, "Ah, shit."

"You knew I was coming," Virgil said.

"I gotta talk to a lawyer. I haven't done anything illegal, I just did what I was told," Brown said.

"You shared in some embezzled money. I think any jury—"

"No, I didn't," Brown said. "Not the way you think. I never took a penny from any of those weasels."

"Then why would you do it?"

"I gotta talk to a lawyer, but I never took a penny."

Virgil looked at him with deep curiosity, working through it. Then, "Dick, what was your salary last year? You might as well tell me, there's a public record."

Brown shrugged. "Seventy thousand."

Virgil nodded, and then laughed. "Seventy thousand. Not too many other seventy-thousand-dollar jobs in Trippton."

"Not for grease monkeys," Brown said. "But it's all right there in the records, all legal and straight-up, voted on by the board. Paid taxes on every nickel of it, too."

Virgil said, "Listen, Dick: if we can't track the money back to you, then you've got a chance to stay out of prison. Not much of a chance, but some. Your chances would be a lot better if you, and your attorney if you have one, had a talk with our attorney—a prosecutor for the attorney general's office. I could work out an appointment for you in Winona this afternoon. Nobody down here would have to know."

They talked around it until Virgil got a phone call from the sheriff's office: "You probably want to get over to Jennifer Houser's house," the dispatcher said. "Sheriff Purdy's on his way there now."

"She's the school board member," Virgil said.

"Is, or was," the dispatcher said. "They think they found blood on her kitchen floor."

Virgil got the address and then rang off and said to Brown, "If I were you, I'd get in your car and drive to Winona as fast as I possibly could, and try to get a deal. They found blood on the floor at Jennifer Houser's house. If she's dead, that'd be the fifth murder. You guys are about to go big-time on the nightly news."

"Look, I got a salary—"

"Tell that to the grand jury," Virgil said. "I've given you an option. Kidnap your lawyer, force him to drive to Winona."

Virgil gave him Dave's name and phone number, and took off

for Houser's place, leaving Brown standing in the garage with his wrench in his hand.

JENNIFER HOUSER LIVED, or had lived, in a plain-vanilla fifties house with a tuck-under garage, three bedrooms—one had been converted to an office devoted to school board business—and no obvious expensive decoration or furniture that would indicate extra money. The best that could be said was that the house was nicely painted, and Houser's best friend, Janet Serna, said that Houser had painted it herself.

"She did it every five years, like clockwork," Serna told Virgil. "The landlord took it off the rent."

"She doesn't own it?"

"She was funny that way—she hardly owned anything. Even leased her car."

ALEWORT, the sheriff's crime-scene guy, was looking at blood on the tan kitchen tile. "It's blood, all right," he'd said, when Virgil showed up. "Can't tell you if it's human blood, and if it is, if it's Jen's blood. But it's blood."

Purdy said, "This is out of control. You gotta do something, Virgil."

"I'm hurrying as fast as I can, Jeff," Virgil said. "I think we'll wrap things up in a day or so."

Purdy said, "Hey—I'll buy Kerns as the killer of Conley and

Zorn and poor old Bacon, but who killed Kerns? And who killed Jen? I mean, maybe it isn't a homicide, but I've got to believe that blood is hers."

"Probably," Virgil said. "Kinda weird, though. It looks like a footprint."

"It does," said Alewort. "I've seen a bloody footprint before, in a training film. They're not uncommon, I'm told."

"They're really uncommon if there's not a puddle of blood to track through," Virgil said. "Look around—where's the puddle?"

"Well, say he caught her in the bathroom, killed her there, cleaned up the blood with toilet paper, flushed it, but missed some . . ."

"How come there aren't any tracks to the kitchen?" Virgil asked.

Alewort considered that for a few seconds then said, "All right, he whacks her in the kitchen, cleans up the blood, hauls her out to his car, doesn't see the one track—"

"The track is pretty big," Virgil said. To Serna: "You saw it as soon as you came in, right?"

"Oh, yeah, right away," she said. "I mean . . . it's pretty obvious."

Serna said that Houser was supposed to come to her house the night before to play canasta. "She never missed. When she didn't call, didn't come by . . . I thought maybe there was some new emergency with the school board, and she was distracted. But we have coffee every morning, and when she didn't come over . . . We both have each other's keys, so I came over, and knocked on the door, and when she didn't answer, I came in and saw the footprint and called the sheriff."

The first cops had noticed that her car was gone, the garage was empty.

"Just like Kerns," Purdy said, "transported in his own vehicle. I've got to get some guys looking down by the river, and out on the back roads, walking distance to town."

"That's an idea," Virgil said, and Purdy went to get a search started.

Virgil sat Serna on a living room couch and asked about Houser: money, boyfriends, or girlfriends—"Well, she's certainly not a lesbian, I would have noticed that, I think"—or anybody she might have been visiting.

Serna said not only did she not have any ideas about that, she'd talked to Houser the morning before, and Houser had been planning to come to the card game, and apparently planned to go about her usual routine.

HOUSER HAD MARRIED YOUNG and had two children right away, back in her twenties, Serna said. Her husband, Vernon, had fallen off a rented houseboat fifteen years earlier and drowned in the Mississippi. He'd left enough money behind to finish raising the children, and to send them to college: they were both now working in the Twin Cities. Vernon Houser's insurance had not been enough to provide a decent lifestyle for Jennifer, and so she'd gone to work for a real-estate dealer, and had been good at it. "She liked being busy, and being in the public eye, and when an open seat came up on the school board, she ran for it, and she won. She was the public watchdog on spending issues."

Houser got a small salary for serving on the school board, Serna said, "but very little, really, for the time she put in. Something like five hundred dollars a month."

"Did she say anything to you about trouble at the schools? About being frightened of anybody?"

"No, nothing like that—although everybody knew that you were sniffing around."

"That's the second time today that somebody said I was sniffing," Virgil said.

"Well, the idea that Jen would take anything from the schools . . . that's simply ridiculous. If you're sniffing, you're sniffing up the wrong tree."

Virgil left Serna sitting on a couch, and did a quick tour of the house, peering in closets, finding clothes, looking in drawers, finding socks and underwear, probing medicine cabinets, finding a high blood pressure prescription, partly used. A desk in the converted bedroom yielded a checkbook, showing a neatly entered balance of one thousand, six hundred and eighty-four dollars.

The hall leading from the short flight of stairs across the upper floor to the office was decorated with two dozen family photos; most prominent was a fleshy man wearing large plastic-rimmed glasses, and, Virgil thought, a bad brown toupee. Vernon? He thought so.

Back in the living room, Virgil asked Serna, "Was Miz Houser close to her children?"

"Oh . . . I guess. They didn't really . . . visit back and forth much. Why?"

"I noticed that most of the family photos were older. Kids were small in all of the pictures."

"Yeah, she wasn't much for photography, I guess. Not sentimental that way, except for that little picture of her with her mom, when she was a toddler."

"Where's that?"

"Right there in the hallway. It's the little black-and-white one," Serna said.

"There aren't any black-and-white ones," Virgil said.

"Yes, it's right there in the center, down from that awful picture of Vernon."

"Show me," Virgil said.

THERE WAS NO PHOTO of Jennifer Houser and her mother. Serna put her fingers to her mouth, puzzled: "Jeez. It's always been right there. Forever. It was the centerpiece."

Virgil relaxed.

There was no murder: Houser was running.

And she'd had to take just one little memento.

23

Vike Laughton called for an emergency meeting of the Buchanan County school board in the back storage room of the newspaper. The remaining four members of the board arrived at intervals of a minute or two, slinking in the back door from the busy parking lot that served both Village Pizza and Quartermain's Bar and BBQ.

Laughton offered beer, but nobody took one, except him. "What happened?" Bob Owens demanded, as Laughton popped the top on a Coors Light. "Why are we here?"

"What do you mean, why are we here?" Jennifer Gedney said. "Randy's dead. Who knows what he left behind? Obviously, we've got to find out—"

Laughton interrupted: "Jen Houser disappeared. The police found blood on her kitchen floor."

That stopped everybody short.

Then, "She's been killed?" Jennifer Gedney put a hand to her mouth. "Oh, my God, what's going on? I heard that Randy was murdered, too. Some people said it looked like suicide, but now everybody's saying it was murder. They say the police know for sure—"

"Where're Henry and Del?" Larry Parsons asked.

"That's what I want to talk about," Laughton said. He took one of the folding chairs he'd set out, flopped his hands in the air and flopped them back down on his thighs, sloshing a little beer on the floor without noticing. "The fact of the matter is, this Flowers guy is breaking things down. The biggest thing we always had going for us is that nobody worried about the school board. We're all upstanding citizens, committed to educating the kids, keeping an eye on things. But once somebody starts looking hard, a police officer or an attorney or a CPA . . . things are going to come bubbling out."

Jennifer Barns: "You're telling us that our goose is cooked?"

Laughton shook his head: "Not quite yet. I think I might be able to skate, unless you all decide to take me down with you. I mean, I have no power over the school budget—"

"You sure took the money, that's all the police would have to know," said Owens.

"Like I said, you all could drag me down. I know that," Laughton said. "Listen: if we hang together, we could still make it. But to do that, we may have to throw Henry and Del overboard. They actually moved the money, they're the ones who always talked with Masilla, they made the deals. They were Randy's boss—Henry hired Randy himself. I think we could argue that it was a three-man arrangement, and we didn't know about it."

"But we knew every step," Barns said. "If we tried to throw them overboard, they'd take us down out of revenge. I mean, that's what I would do, if I was in their shoes."

"They might try, if they had nothing to lose, but they do have something to lose," Laughton said. "They both have families."

The board members looked at each other, and then Parsons said, "Stop beating around the bush. Tell us what you're thinking."

"Very simple," Laughton said. "I'm pretty sure that Flowers is going to tear the house down. He's smarter than he looks, and he's been working everybody. Suppose we went to Henry and Del and said, 'We're not going to make it. If you take the rap, the other six of us . . . well, five of us, if Jen Houser doesn't show up . . . we'll take care of your families. They can go off to live with their folks, and every year they'll get X amount of dollars in the mail.'"

"How big an X?" Gedney asked. She looked unhappy with the prospect.

"We'd have to work that out," Laughton said. "I'm thinking, you know, if each one of us put two hundred thousand dollars into a trust at Vanguard or Fidelity, and if we had to have all five signatures to move money, we could probably get both families twenty thousand a year, and still keep the million. We'd just send them the interest, four percent, and anything over that we'd keep. Then, when this is all blown over, and nobody remembers it . . . we cash the fund out. Take our money back."

They all sat silently for a minute, then Jen 1 said, "You really think . . . I don't know. It seems crazy. Maybe too easy."

Owens said, almost conversationally, "You know, Henry and Del have got to know they'll be the first to go. There's no way we could have done any of this without them knowing. So maybe . . . they might buy it."

"If Henry doesn't stick a gun in his ear," Jennifer Gedney said.

"Which would save us all some money," Laughton said. "Wouldn't have to take care of his family."

The other four turned to look at him, then Owens said, "You went out the door with Randy the other night. I saw you talking."

"Saying good-bye," Laughton said.

They all looked at him some more, then Parsons said, "I'll be goddamned. You killed him."

Laughton started to deny it, but felt the sweat pop out on his forehead, and finally said, "It had to be done. No way he was going to get away—and if he did, he'd have been bleeding us for years. Forever."

Jen Gedney said, "Viking—that's awful. You really killed him?"

Laughton waved his hands at them: "He was a dead man, anyway. He would have wound up shooting it out with some cops, somewhere, probably kill one or two of them. I saw the chance, and I took it. Saved us fifty thousand bucks, each."

They all thought about that for a minute, and Jennifer Gedney made a couple of choking sounds, almost like sobs, but her eyes were dry.

"Let's skip that for the moment," Owens said. "Even if we agreed to throw Henry and Del overboard, they're gonna deny knowing anything about Randy getting killed, or Jennifer Houser—"

"Why'd you kill Jennifer?" Jennifer Gedney demanded. "She was in it with the rest of us, she wasn't going to tell—"

"I didn't," Laughton interrupted. "I don't know what happened to her, but to tell you the truth, she was always a little too smart for her own good. There's no sign that she's dead, except a little smear of blood on her kitchen floor. I think she took off. The way she was acting the other night . . ."

Parsons said, "You're right. She was a little too . . . pleased . . . going out the door. I think she's got something tricky set up."

They sat without speaking for a few more seconds, still digesting it all. Then Barns asked, "If we decide to throw Henry and Del overboard, as we're calling it, how would we do that?"

"We don't do it right now, this minute," Laughton said. "I keep monitoring the investigation. I've got a good source inside the sheriff's office, he'll keep me up on things. Freedom of the press, and so on. Also, he wants to run for sheriff someday . . ."

"Josh Becker," Jennifer Gedney guessed.

"Whatever," Laughton said. "If it looks like it's all going to come down on us, I'll go directly to Flowers and tell him that Clancy Conley suspected Henry and Del and Randy of conspiring to do this. I'll tell Flowers I didn't believe it, because Clancy was a pill head, and all that. How I told him it was nonsense—making myself look naive. Then I say that I've gone to all you board members, and all of you are horrified at the prospect that this may have happened, and that we'd all be willing to testify against Henry and Del if it came to that. Back up any evidence he finds—that Flowers finds—and help reconstruct budgets and amounts, and so on."

"And we'd get immunity from prosecution?" Jen Gedney asked.

"Asking for that would be touchy," Laughton said. "If we're innocent, why would we need it? I could come up with some reasons, but the best reason would be that our individual attorneys insist on it before we testify. Not us. Our attorneys. We'd say we feel that we have to go with their advice, which we're paying them for."

"I wonder if we could get the board attorneys to cover that, charge it off to the schools," Owens wondered.

"Possibly," said the chairwoman. "If we were innocent, it'd be a legitimate expense."

"This idea sounds pretty sketchy, the whole story," Gedney said.

"It is sketchy. And it's getting sketchier by the minute," Laughton said. "If we wait too long, it won't even be an option. You have to remember, though, that if we get charged, the state has to prove us guilty beyond any reasonable doubt. We don't have to create a great story—just a serious doubt."

THEY ARGUED ABOUT IT for a half hour, all the time feeling the prison walls closing down on them. Finally Barns asked, "If it's our only way out, it's worth a try. Should we tell Henry what we're going to do? You know, about supporting the families?"

"Not yet," Laughton said. "Things could change. Let's see what Flowers does next. If anyone hears anything that makes you think we've got to move, we'll talk by phone, instead of trying to meet. Everybody keep your ears open. If Flowers comes to visit anyone— Jen Gedney, I'm thinking of you, since he's already talked to you— let us know."

The meeting broke up, and they left a couple minutes apart. When only Laughton and Jennifer Barns were left in the newspaper office, she asked, "What about Randy? Was it awful?"

"Awful for me," Laughton said. He leaned toward her, talking in a hoarse whisper. "He never saw it coming. One minute he was there, and the next he wasn't. Fast, painless. Not a bad way to go. But I'll remember it forever."

She looked him over for a moment, then said, "You couldn't kill all of us, and get away with it."

"I know. Not that I didn't think about it," Laughton said. "It's just not feasible. I try to stick to that standard—doing what's feasible. If Flowers had any hard evidence against us, he would have moved already. That makes me think we've still got a chance."

"Unless he's focused on catching the killer, and is letting the money thing go until that's done," Barns said.

"I don't think that's likely. That's just not the way cops think," Laughton said. He looked at his watch. "It's been a couple minutes. You better get out of here."

BARNS WALKED ACROSS the parking lot and got into her Subaru, and it occurred to her that Flowers probably would place a premium on finding the killer, rather than the money thing. And Laughton had just confessed to the four board members that he'd killed Kerns. That had to be a chip worth something.

Her phone rang, and she glanced at it: Owens.

"What's up?"

"Vike just confessed to killing Randy."

"I was thinking that exact thought, just now," Barns said. "It's like you pulled it out of my brain."

"If the four of us board members stuck together, we might be able to throw Vike overboard along with Henry and Del," Owens said. "We might claim that Henry and Del directed Randy, and that Vike was in on all of that. We could say that we met and that Jen Houser said she was going to confront Vike about all of this, on our behalf, and then she disappeared—"

"But how do we explain that Vike confessed to us?"

"Well, it's a little weak, but we could say that Jen Houser saw him with Randy, in Randy's truck, just before Randy was killed, and told us about it. Then Jen Houser disappeared, and we all went together and confronted him. He told us he was going to drag us all down if we didn't support him—"

"Okay. Listen, Bob, we need to talk to the others . . . the other board members. I think you've got something there, a kernel of something, but it's not quite right yet. For example, if Vike confessed to us, why didn't we drive right over and tell Flowers?"

"Okay. Okay, we have to work on it. Maybe we don't say he confessed—just that Jen Houser saw them together. Listen, let's call the others and let it cook for a while, see what we come up with. In the meantime, stay the hell away from Vike. He has wigged out. As they used to say many years ago."

"Many," Barns said. "All right. Let's talk. If we can give them all the killers, all wrapped up . . . we might slip through this."

SHE PUT THE SUBARU in gear, drove across the parking lot, and never saw Del Cray in his aging gray Pathfinder, slumped in his seat, eating a slice of mushroom and sausage.

The pizza smelled so good that he hadn't been able to wait until he got back to his house, so he opened the box and pulled a slice free . . . and saw Gedney come out the back of the newspaper office. That was interesting, but not astonishing. Then, a minute later, Owens emerged, looking guilty, checking around, before scurrying over to his car. That was even more interesting.

By the time all four board members had emerged, he was no longer interested: he was frightened. He got on his phone and called Hetfield. "Henry. This is Del. Where are you? Right now?"

"Getting gas at the QuikTrip," Hetfield said. He must have sensed something in Cray's voice. "What happened?"

"Were you invited to a board meeting at Vike Laughton's office?"

Hetfield's voice went cold. "No. You're saying there was one?"

"Yeah. I'm at Village Pizza, you know, across from Vike's back door. Not spying, just getting a pizza. All four of them came sneaking out of there, and they were sneaking—they came out one at a time, a minute or two apart, and took off."

"Sonsofbitches have decided to rat us out," Hetfield said. "They're gonna try to give us up, make a deal, convince Flowers that they didn't know about it."

"I wish you hadn't said that," Cray said. "I was hoping you'd come up with something else. 'Cause that's sorta what I think, too. What're we gonna do?"

24

NEAR THE END of every successful investigation in the history of the world, the suits show up to take the credit. Both Virgil and his boss, Lucas Davenport, were friendly with the governor, who'd helped find a new boat for Virgil, after his first boat had been blown up by a mad bomber. The governor, however, was planning to vacate the office, perhaps to make a run at the vice presidency.

So, one way or another, there'd be a new suit in town.

The current attorney general had already hinted that he was going to run for the governor's office, and between now and then, would not be averse to favorable publicity that portrayed him as a protector of the people, a defender of freedom, but also a sincere, heartfelt, and honest spokesman for the larger and richer special interests.

As it happened, the Buchanan County school district presented a perfect chance to protect the public: it largely voted Republican, so, since the AG was a Democrat, a vigorous prosecution wouldn't piss off anybody critical, and would generally show up the Republicans as the pack of thieving, money-gouging, scheming hyenas that all true-blue Americans knew them to be.

That was the general idea; the actual words would be repackaged into something much softer and much, much more hypocritical.

WHICH WAS WHY DAVE, the assistant AG, slapped Virgil on the back before he slipped into the booth at Ma & Pa's Kettle, then ordered a pitcher of Bloody Marys—"I can't drink bourbon at breakfast"— and began the debriefing. When Virgil outlined what he had, a slender line appeared in Dave's forehead. "What you're telling me is, it's gonna be easy to nail down, but at this very moment, it's not quite nailed down."

"That's about right," Virgil said. "I gotta emphasize, it will be. The whole pack of rats is coming apart. Two of them have run. I assume you got decent stuff from Masilla."

"I did—but you're telling me it's the whole school board, and this Viking guy and Masilla have really only handed over the heads of the superintendent and his money guy. Even that will take a little further nailing, since all those records went up in smoke."

"Not all of them," Virgil said. He slid the folder of Clancy Conley's photos across the table. Dave left the folder closed as the waitress delivered two plates of French toast with link sausage, and the pitcher of Bloody Marys for Dave, and Virgil's Diet Coke. When she was gone, Dave opened the folder, as he sipped the first of his drinks, slowly thumbed through the photos, then said, "My, my."

"I've got some supporting documents for that stuff. They were uncovered by the reporter who got murdered, and he put a bunch of notes in a flash drive file, explaining what it all was . . . and naming a suspect in his own murder."

Virgil dug the flash drive out of his pocket and slid it across to Dave. "I'm gonna want a receipt for that, you know, chain of evidence and so on."

"Who was the reporter's suspect?" Dave asked.

"A guy named Randolph Kerns, who was murdered night before last."

"Ain't that a pisser," Dave said.

"For Randy, anyway. He's the guy who tried to shoot me up at the high school, and frankly, I wasn't all that sad to see him go. I mean, if the bell's gotta toll, might as well be for an asshole."

"Who killed Randy?"

"You got the list—one of the school board members, one of the others," Virgil said. "I've got my eye on the newspaper editor, there. He has a nice sociopathic edge on him."

"Any possible way of getting the killer out in the open? Or do we just start busting people?"

"What I'd do, if I were you, is start taking the school board members aside," Virgil said. "Be a jerk—I know you can do that. One of them will crack. You only need one, with Masilla already on your side, and those photos."

"If we go to court, we like to have things pretty well wrapped up."

"Dave, I've been doing this for quite a while," Virgil said. "You don't want them wrapped up, you want a goddamned gold-plated guarantee, because otherwise you're afraid you'll screw up your conviction stats. Well, by the time you get finished fucking with them all, it oughta be at least silver-plated. Dopey, Sneezy, and Grumpy could get a conviction."

"Unfortunately, Dopey, Sneezy, and Grumpy aren't licensed to practice law in Minnesota," Dave said. "The boss is thinking of handling the prosecution himself."

"Ah, Jesus, why do I even bother to arrest people?"

If the AG had been a lightbulb instead of a lawyer, he would have been about a twenty-watt.

"He'll have good advisers," Dave said. "Like me. But any other little bits and pieces you can find would be welcome."

VIRGIL WALKED HIM through the records, pointing out the prices for fuel as shown in the fake books, and the discrepancies reported by the garage manager and the bus driver. "Dick, the garage guy, thinks he can walk away, because he got a legal salary, though the salary is way out of line. I told him he ought to call you, and come up and see you—"

"He didn't."

"Probably talking to his lawyer. But if you want to give him a little consideration, he's another straw on the camel's back."

"Another log on the fire."

"Another piss into the wind."

Dave frowned at his second Bloody Mary and said, "This tastes kinda strange. Wonder what kind of vodka they use?"

Virgil was impatient: "Dave, you're eating at Ma & Pa's Kettle in Trippton. Pa probably made it himself, out of possum squeezin's."

IN THE END, Dave was satisfied that the investigation warranted a call for legal assistance. "I'll have a couple more guys down here tomorrow, and we'll go see the county attorney about it—courtesy call. You don't have any reason to think that he might . . . mmm . . . have an interest? I mean, this has gone on under his nose for years."

"I don't have any reason to think that," Virgil said.

"Okay," Dave said. "We're good. Now I go make a lot of phone calls, and tomorrow morning, rain, fire, and brimstone on the local Republican hyenas."

"And I'll go talk to Vike Laughton," Virgil said. "As a sociopath, it's possible that he'll rat out all the others."

"Don't get your ass shot," Dave said.

WHEN VIRGIL SHOWED UP at the newspaper office, Laughton was working on a story about the murders of Bacon and Kerns; he had an old-fashioned telephone receiver pinned between his shoulder and his ear, held a finger up to Virgil, telling him to wait, and two minutes later when he hung up, he said, "You know the problem with cell phones? They won't stay between your shoulder and your ear."

"You put them on speakerphone," Virgil said.

"Then, if it's a confidential call, like that one, everybody who wandered in would hear what was said."

"Well, it's not my problem. When do you put the newspaper to sleep, or whatever you call it?"

"'Put it to bed' is the phrase, though in the case of the *Republican-River*, 'put it to sleep' is probably more accurate," Laughton said. "Anyway—tomorrow. Finish around six in the evening, haul it over to the printing plant, pick up the papers in the morning, have them all out by early afternoon. Then start over."

The advertising lady came in and said, "I got the last of it," and went back to her desk, and Virgil looked at Laughton and said, "You have time for a walk up to the Dairy Queen?"

"Always got time for a chocolate dip," Laughton said, heaving himself out of his chair.

The Dairy Queen was at the end of the block, and on the way down, Laughton wanted to know everything about the Kerns and Bacon murders, and was especially curious about Bacon's apartment up in the high school. When Virgil finished telling him about it, Laughton shook his head, his jowls flapping, and said, "Damn. Wish he hadn't been killed, that'd be a hell of a story. The AP would want that one."

"The AP will want the Bacon-Kerns killings, won't they?"

"Yeah, but people get murdered all the time. I mean, they just get popped off like . . . like popcorn. Pop, pop, pop. People don't want to read it, unless it's their next-door neighbor. But a guy living for years, secretly, the high school attic . . . people would read that."

At the Dairy Queen they both got chocolate dip cones—Laughton was correct in his choice—and they sat on a bench outside and Laughton asked, "Was this a social visit?"

"Not entirely. I'll tell you what, Vike, you've been covering the school board for years now, and you had a reporter who dug up some pretty amazing stuff on those guys. So you're saying he didn't tell you about it?"

Laughton bobbed his head. "That's what I'm saying. I don't know why. Maybe because he knew all the board members were my friends, and he just wanted to present me with a whole package. I can only tell you what I believe, Virgil—if there's trouble with the school finances, the school board didn't know anything about it. Neither did I. But I'm not dumb, and I've heard about the questions you've been asking, and about that camera you put up in the rafters at the meeting room. The auditorium. If there's any substance to anything you're chasing, the people who would have to be involved would be Henry Hetfield and Del Cray, the financial officer. And Kerns, I suspect, though I don't know why they would have let him in on it."

"What about Jennifer Houser? The sheriff thinks she might have been killed, but I don't think so. I think she's running, because she knows the shit is about to hit the fan."

Laughton shrugged. "I don't know. She's a nice lady, but . . . who knows? Maybe she was in on it, maybe they needed a board member to tip them in case anybody on the board got curious about spending amounts, or something. You know, sometimes the board just throws everybody out . . . they can do that when they discuss personnel matters . . . and they talk privately. Maybe Henry and the others were worried about that, and brought Jen into it."

"I've got to think about that. I'd like to tell you something off the record here . . . you could probably get some official word on it tomorrow, if you inquire around . . . off the record?"

Laughton nodded. "Sure. Unless I get it from another source."

"The attorney general's office is sending down a really hard-nosed hit team—prosecutors. They're going to start taking the school board apart tomorrow, and then home in on the others. The feeling is, somebody's going to crack."

Laughton shook his head. "I'll be amazed if any of them are involved. But I'll tell you what I'll do, if you want. The board members are my friends. I'll call them, one at a time, and see what they have to say—maybe somebody will tell me that they do know something. Or suspect something. Maybe we could work out some kind of arrangement where the board members tell you everything about Henry and Del and Kerns, instead of getting all frozen up. I mean, if they think you're after them, they're going to be talking to lawyers and you might not get anything at all."

Virgil said, "That's . . . a possibility. I could tell the AG's main guy to talk to you first, see what you've found out."

They both took a moment to lick around the sides of their cones, then Laughton said, "Go ahead and tell him. Tell him to give me a call. I'll do what I can to help."

"Wish that goddamned Kerns hadn't been killed," Virgil said. "I wish I knew the sequence of events when he killed Bacon. I talked to Bacon, on my phone, not ten minutes before he was murdered.

And when I get there, he'd already disappeared—dead. And Kerns tries to shoot me. Which I find pretty goddamned interesting."

"I wouldn't find it so much interesting, as I would freakin' horrifying. Somebody shooting at you? No thanks. I'll stick to keyboards."

Virgil said, "The question I'd like to ask him is, why? Why shoot at me? There was nobody else in the school. He'd already killed Bacon, he could have snuck out the back, nobody the wiser."

"I don't know. Sounds stupid," Laughton said.

"He might not have been the sharpest knife in the dishwasher, Vike, but I believe he had a reason. That camera took two memory cards—you could either run them sequentially, to make a longer recording, or simultaneously, to make a duplicate. We had it set for a duplicate. I suspect that Kerns caught Bacon putting up the ladder to get the camera down, waited to see what he was doing, and then came in and challenged him. And Bacon knew Kerns was probably a killer, because I told him. So I think old Will Bacon pulled out either one or both of those cards, and hid them. Maybe up on top, in the rafters. I think that's why he was beaten to death—Kerns was trying to find out where he put them. The crime-scene people will be done in there by the end of the day, so I can get in. I'm going in there tonight and I'm gonna crawl all over that room. Bacon would have left it somewhere I could find it. And I'm going to."

"Well, good luck with that," Laughton said. "Some of those memory cards are about the size of my dick."

That made Virgil chuckle, and they finished the cones, and Laughton sighed and said, "Glad I decided to stick around my little river town, instead of going up to the Cities. Nothing like peace and quiet, and then four or five murders."

"Yeah, well. Maybe we'll know more tonight. Whatever, there's gonna be a genuine North Dakota goat-fuck tomorrow, when the AG's people hit town. You wouldn't want to miss that."

25

VIRGIL, JENKINS, and Shrake rendezvoused at Johnson Johnson's cabin, decided that shotguns-only would be appropriate, along with body armor. "I'm thinking of inventing the world's first office camo," Jenkins said, as he dug his Kevlar vest out of a duffel bag. "I bet half of all shoot-outs are inside buildings—why would you want the shooter to mistake you for an oak tree? Have to be a dumb shooter. With my camo, you'd look like a file cabinet, or maybe a water cooler."

"The way you dress now, they'd mistake you for a trash can," Shrake said. "I'm not sure a file cabinet would be a big enough change to be worthwhile."

"You're already jealous of my incipient riches," Jenkins said.

"My biggest fear is getting shot in the ass," Virgil said. "He's got to make some kind of move before we can take him. If I've gotta climb that ladder before he tries to jump me, he'll be shooting up at me, not straight at me. And the armor doesn't fit that well around my ass."

"That could be Jenkins's second product," Shrake said. "Ass armor."

"I gotta be honest, I don't think he's gonna fall for anything at all," Jenkins said. "We tried to ambush Kerns, and he never showed up. Now we try to ambush Laughton . . . I'd be surprised if he shows up."

"If he doesn't, he's given up," Virgil said. "If he thinks I'm going to get a recording of the school board meeting, he's either got to show up, or concede the fact that he's going to prison for murder. There has to be something serious on that memory card or Kerns wouldn't have murdered Will Bacon to get it."

"But there isn't a second memory card," Shrake said. "There was only one."

"But there are two slots. Whoever killed Kerns got one card— but can't take the chance that there really is a second one. He can't know that there isn't a second one."

"Maybe. I guess we'll see."

It was just getting dark when they started over to the school in Virgil's truck. On the way, Shrake said that Jenkins's talk of making his fortune with office camo reminded him of a rumor going around BCA headquarters. According to the rumor, a BCA team had been digging out financial information about a defunct investment company in St. Paul. Virgil knew about the criminal part of the investigation, because it had been handled by Lucas Davenport, his boss.

"The question was, did a bunch of other people take out money before the collapse, because they'd been tipped off by the owner that trouble was coming?" Shrake said. "And if so, should that money be reclaimed?"

"That's the kind of shit that puts me asleep," Jenkins said.

"Me, too," Shrake said. "But that's not what the rumor was about. Supposedly this team was looking at all these income tax returns, and somebody decided to take just a wee peek at Davenport's returns."

Virgil said, "Uh-oh. If they did that, and anybody official found out, they'd be fired."

"Probably," Shrake agreed. "But the rumor is, they took a peek, and as close as they can figure it, he's worth something between thirty-five and forty-five million. Can you believe that?"

Virgil thought it over for a few seconds and finally said, "I honestly have no idea. I know he's richer than Jesus Christ and all the Apostles. I know that two weeks ago, when he flew down to El Paso after Del got shot, he wrote a check for the plane he borrowed from the governor. I know he buys what he wants, he has expensive cars . . . but I don't know a number. You could do all that if you had a half-million in the bank."

"It's not a half-million," Shrake said. "He's way, way on the other side of that. The question is, say the guy is worth something like the rumor says he is. What the hell is he doing working for the BCA? Why's he going mano a mano with some psycho fruit in the basement of a torture castle? What the fuck is he doing? He could be living in . . . LA. Or Paris, if he likes cheese."

"If he likes cheese, he could be living in River Falls, Wisconsin," Jenkins said.

"You know what I mean, man."

Virgil said to Shrake, "You know why he does it."

Shrake said, "No, I don't. I really don't. Not if he's got forty million . . ."

Virgil said, "Shrake, you've got a fuckin' shotgun between your knees, you're wearing an armored vest, and there's a chance you're about to shoot it out with a psycho killer in the dark. Why is that?"

Jenkins laughed, and said, "Yeah, why is that, putter boy? How come so many guys, including you, try to get on SWAT squads? Come on, admit it."

Shrake tried to hold out: "It's my job."

"Oh, bullshit," Jenkins said. "You do it because you like it, because you get that feeling in your balls like you're in a falling elevator, and you like it. We all like it. We get all grim and warriored-up about it, but the bottom line is, we like it."

"That's somewhat true," Shrake admitted.

"That's why Davenport does it: it's better than money," Jenkins said.

"You guys bum me out sometimes," Virgil said.

"Getting that feeling in your balls?" Jenkins asked.

"I've had it for about three days now," Virgil said.

"Attaboy."

As THEY CAME UP to the school, Jenkins said, "The question is, is he inside waiting for us, so we get hosed the minute we go through the door, or is he planning to come in after you have a chance to find the memory card?"

"Or is he home eating fried chicken and trying to decide what to watch on TV?" Shrake added.

"I got a key from the crime-scene crew that'll let us in the back door, all the way around by the ball diamond, where he won't be expecting us," Virgil said. "We go around there right quick, and in through the doors. Once we're inside, we'll be even."

"What are the chances he's got night-vision glasses?" Jenkins asked.

"Unlikely—no reason for him to have them. Besides, right inside the door there's a whole bank of switches. I'm going to light up the halls all the way down to the auditorium. Then, inside the auditorium, there's another bank that'll light that place up."

They thought about that for a minute, then Jenkins said, "Most likely hiding inside a classroom. Hard to know exactly where, but probably between the auditorium and the door he thought you'd come through. He'd make sure you're alone, then he'd watch you go in there, and maybe peek to see if you were finding anything . . . and then, boom."

"Or he could already be stashed in the auditorium. There are quite a few places on the stage, or in the projection booth, at the back, that'd give him cover," Virgil said.

"So we go in, with full lights, and we watch for any classroom doors that are cracked open. Then we go into the auditorium in a regular clearance formation, ready to hose him. If he's not there, we wait."

"One of us up high, one low, while Virgil climbs up the ladder and looks for the chip. You know where the ladder is?"

"Still in the auditorium," Virgil said. "The crime-scene guys were processing it, and I told them to leave it."

AT THE SCHOOL, Virgil said, "I haven't seen his truck."

"Probably wouldn't show it," Shrake said. "But he'd want to have it close, in case he had to run—so he's probably not here yet."

"Probably at home, eating chicken," Jenkins said.

Virgil took the truck into the student parking lot, then swung onto the track that took them behind the school by the baseball practice diamond, then across some grass and right up to the back door. They piled out of the truck, jacking shells into their shotguns, and Virgil knelt below the windows in the door, and fitted the key into the door lock.

"Okay," he said, and turned the key and the lock popped. The door was sheathed in thin steel; good against a shotgun, but not against a deer rifle. He pulled the door open, staying behind the door, waited, and then crawled inside, felt for the light switches, turned on five or six of them at once.

The lights flickered down the long hallway—which was empty. Jenkins and Shrake moved inside, and Virgil pulled the door shut. They walked cautiously forward, spread across the hall, their shotgun muzzles at chest height.

Fifty feet in, Shrake said, "Door on the left." Virgil saw the crack between the door and the jamb. He and Shrake kept their weapons pointed at it, while Jenkins kept his tracking down the hall. As they came up to the open door, they moved to the door side of the hall.

As they got to it, Virgil called, "If there's anybody in room 120, you best come out, because we've got three shotguns pointed at it."

There was no response, no sound, no feel of presence. Virgil, closest to the door, moved up and pushed it open with the muzzle of his gun. When it was fully open, he reached around the jamb, felt the light switches and turned them on. A conference room—empty.

They continued down the hall, around a corner, turned on more lights. Moving faster now, with the feeling that the building was empty. They turned the last corner, and Virgil said, "Auditorium is straight ahead, on the left."

They continued, looking for open doors, Shrake now walking backwards, watching their backs, past the burned-out district offices, then into the hallway beyond, to the auditorium door.

Again, with the door and lights: and inside, the auditorium was empty. "No wild geese," Jenkins said.

"Let's get into the act," Virgil said. "If he's coming, he saw my truck pull around the building. Jenkins, you get up in the top row of seats, on the floor. Shrake, get between those curtain rolls at the back of the stage. Anybody hears movement, snap your fingers at me."

JENKINS AND SHRAKE set up; Virgil waited, listening, then went to the ladder, which had been left in a corner, and with a little nervous tickle between his shoulder blades, extended it and then set it against a crossbar in the light rack on the ceiling. He fussed over it a bit, giving Laughton a little more time to show, then climbed the ladder.

A couple of pieces of tape hung down from a crossbar where they'd mounted the camera. He muttered, "Anything?"

Shrake said, in a nearly inaudible grunt, "Nope."

Virgil took a foot off the ladder rung where he was standing, then frowned: a piece of the gaffer's tape seemed to rise above the rest. He climbed back up, pulled the tape off.

"My goodness." The memory card was there, stuck under the tape. Kerns must have challenged Bacon while he was on the ladder, and Bacon had popped the card and hidden it under the tape, for Virgil to find.

Virgil, still talking low, said, "All right, guys, we're not hiding anymore. My good buddy Will Bacon actually did leave the memory card up here, so just point your guns at anything that moves. I'm coming down."

VIRGIL COULD HARDLY BELIEVE the luck—if it was indeed luck, if the card had anything worthwhile on it. Jenkins and Shrake had set up to cover both the stage entrance and the other two corridor entrances, and Virgil rattled down the ladder, and left it standing.

At the bottom, he picked up his own shotgun and said, "Let's get out of here, but let's take it easy. We've got the memory card, we just need to get it somewhere safe."

They backed out the same way they'd come in, leaving the lights to burn. At the back door, next to Virgil's truck, Shrake said, "This would be another obvious spot to ambush you. You had to come out sooner or later."

Virgil looked out the window at the truck: "Jenkins, you go out first, but don't go for the doors: just brace yourself up against the front bumper, ready to fire either direction. Then Shrake comes out, and he posts up to the right, and you take the left side. Then I'll come out around to the left—instead of the driver's side, I should be okay—and I'll pop the door and crawl across to the driver's seat."

THE PROCEDURE WAS FINE, and one minute later they were bouncing back around the high school and out to Main Street, feeling a little foolish about all the guns and armor and entry and exit dramatics.

Shrake, from the backseat, said, "Now, if what you got on that chip is what you think you've got . . ."

"Then we've got it all," Virgil said. "I've got a Mac program that'll run the film. We can load it up as soon as we get back to the cabin."

They were just coming to the turnoff for the cabin when Jenkins said sharply, "Hey, Virgil. Stop! Stop the car!"

Thinking Jenkins had seen something, Virgil yanked the car to the side of the road and asked, "What?"

"We've done everything right so far, but . . . If you really think about it, why would Laughton challenge you in the school? He'd have to creep down all those empty hallways, and if there was a shoot-out, he'd be right there in the middle of town, where everybody could see him coming and going. Same thing about ambushing you at the back door—he doesn't just have to kill you, he has to find the chip, if you've got it. He'd want to get you someplace where he'd have at least a couple of minutes to empty out your pockets. Someplace a little private . . ."

Virgil looked into the darkness up ahead: "Like the cabin."

"Like we thought Kerns would do," Shrake said.

Jenkins said, "Shrake and I found that back way in. What do you say we drive around that way? Just . . . to take a look."

"All right by me," Virgil said.

He waited for a car to pass and then pulled back out on the high-way. A bit more than a quarter-mile farther along, Jenkins pointed at a turnoff and said, "There it is—that's where you go in, there's a little boat launch just over there."

There was a truck in the boat launch parking area, and Virgil said, "Well, I'll be damned. That's Vike's truck. Jenkins, you proba-bly just saved your own life."

"Or yours," Jenkins said.

"No, I always make you go first," Virgil said. "I'm going to block his truck in, and then let's see if we can locate Mr. Laughton back in the weeds."

"This could be a little delicate," Jenkins said. "It's darker than a black cat's ass in a coal mine, when you get back there."

"There's some light around the house," Shrake said. "We know he's got to be close to the house—probably around in front, so he'd have a clear shot at the porch when Virgil crosses it."

VIRGIL CROWDED HIS TRUCK up next to Vike's until the bumpers touched; the nose of Vike's truck was nestled in the riverside brush in front of it, and there was no way out. Virgil killed the truck lights, and they got out with their weapons, patting the armor back in place.

Shrake said quietly, "Sound carries along the track, we could hear you talking on your phone in the cabin when we were a hundred yards out. Then maybe a hundred yards in, give or take twenty or so, there's a low spot that's full of water—you can go in up to your shins in mud. Stay close behind me, off on the right side of the track, and I'll get you past that. You can't see much left or right, but you can see the stars overhead when you're on the track, so watch the stars."

Jenkins: "I'll lead the way in. He's gotta be out front, I think, or maybe where we set up, off to the side, although that'd be taking a chance. There'll be some light when we get close, so don't go waving your arms around, swatting mosquitoes. Just let them bite."

"And don't shoot me in the back," Shrake said.

They started down the track, single file, moving slowly, not so much out of caution as blindness: the black cat/coal mine problem; the strongest sensory input came through their noses, which told them that there were lots of dead carp somewhere close. A hundred yards down the track, Virgil could sense Shrake but not really see him, and then Shrake reached back and pushed him to the right and whispered, "Puddle."

Mosquitoes were bumping off Virgil's face and the exposed part of his neck, and he flipped his shirt collar up and followed, keeping the muzzle of his shotgun pointed up and to the left.

They moved on, almost silently, then saw the light from the cabin, yellow against the gray/blue of the night. Virgil walked into Shrake, who'd bumped into Jenkins. Jenkins whispered, "There's another truck in the driveway. My car, and it looks like a black pickup."

"That's Johnson," Virgil whispered back. "Jesus, I hope he hasn't hurt Johnson."

"Could be a hostage deal," Shrake suggested.

Virgil said, "No. He can't afford a hostage deal. He can't afford anyone be left alive to know he was involved in this . . . so he's either in there with Johnson, or he's outside."

"Okay. Keep an interval . . . ten yards," Jenkins said.

Virgil: "I'm going first. I can see now, and I know the layout better than you guys. No argument. Ten yards, I'm going first."

He led the way in, Jenkins staying almost in the brush on the left side of the track. As he got closer, he had to make a decision: Would Laughton be behind the cabin, or in front? He stopped, and crouched, and let Jenkins and Shrake come up. As he waited, Virgil noticed that he was sweating.

"What do you think?" Virgil asked.

"It occurred to me that you should send a cell phone message to Johnson, is what occurred to me," Jenkins said. "Tell him we're here, that Laughton is here, and to lay low."

Virgil said, "Why didn't I think of that? Wait here for a minute. I'm gonna crawl back behind that bush and send one."

They squatted in the dirt, a few yards apart, and Virgil eased backward, pulled his shirt up over his head, stuck his hands in under the front, with his cell phone, and tapped out a quick message. "Think Vike Laughton's outside the cabin with gun. I'm coming for him. If you okay, not hostage, send me my girlfriend's first name."

Twenty seconds later, he got "Frankie." And then, "I'll break him out."

Virgil tried to type "No!" but he'd only gotten the "N" typed in when a side window on the cabin flew open and Johnson bellowed into the night, "Hey! Vike! You're surrounded! Everybody knows you're out there. Give it up, you fuckin' cocksucker!"

There was a moment of dead silence, then a six-inch flame reached out toward the cabin and blew out a window, and Jenkins and Shrake opened up on the muzzle flash, and were rolling away from their own flashes when there were three fast shots from the same point, or a little left, then a woman started screaming, and Jenkins and Shrake and Virgil opened up on the muzzle flash point, and the woman kept screaming, and Shrake screamed at Jenkins, "He's got cover, go to slugs," and Virgil emptied his shotgun at the point of the incoming muzzle flashes and rolled off behind a tree, and the woman kept screaming, and Virgil wished she'd stop doing that and wondered in a very thin stream of curious thought in the middle of a gunfight if Johnson and Clarice had been getting it on in the cabin. . . .

JENKINS'S FIRST SLUG knocked a hole in the bottom of the boat that Laughton and Barns were using for cover, and also took a piece of Jennifer 1's ass, and she dropped her shotgun and started screaming for help, and Vike said, "Sorry about this, Jen," and he slid backward on his belly down the bank toward the river and then scuttled away in the dark. Incoming slugs were knocking holes in the boat and Jennifer 1 began screaming, "No no no no no . . . I give up give up give up . . ."

Virgil shouted, "Stop, stop, stop . . ."

———

WHEN THE SHOOTING STOPPED, Virgil shouted, "Vike, throw out your gun. There are a whole bunch of us here. All you'll get is killed, if you keep shooting."

A woman's voice: "Vike ran away. I'm shot, I'm hurt bad, I'm dying. Get me help, get me an ambulance, help me . . ."

They took a good two minutes closing in on her, and found her hiding behind Johnson's upturned jon boat. She was bleeding heavily from a wound in the buttocks, and Virgil said to Jenkins, "Get an ambulance."

Jenkins stepped back to call, and Virgil moved around behind the boat and picked up a shotgun and put it out of reach, and asked, "Who are you?"

Before she could answer, a light hit her in the face, and Johnson, standing behind the flashlight, said, "Hey, it's Jennifer Barns, the honorable school board chairwoman or -person."

"Where'd Vike go?" Virgil asked.

"He went down the river . . . down the bank," she groaned.

And Johnson said, suddenly louder, "Hey, hey! That's my boat. Jesus Christ, look what you assholes did to my boat. It's all—"

"Shut up!" Virgil shouted.

Johnson shut up, and Jenkins came back and said, "Ambulance is on the way. They said they know the place, they've been here before."

"I'm dying," Barns screamed. "Get me a doctor. I'm dying . . ."

Jenkins said, "I got a little issue here myself. I might have caught some buckshot."

Virgil: "Aw, shit. How bad? Where're you hit?"

"Right in the calf. Could be gravel or something, but there's some blood."

Shrake said, "Let me look, get up on the porch . . ."

JOHNSON STAYED WITH BARNS, and Virgil and Shrake followed Jenkins up to the porch. Jenkins sat down and pulled up a pant leg. A trickle of blood was flowing from a hole in his calf, but there was no exit wound.

"The red ones down low are where that fuckin' Chihuahua bit me, but that big one—"

"Ah, you're shot. Now we really need that fuckin' ambulance," Virgil said.

"It's not that bad," Jenkins said.

"They're all fuckin' bad," Shrake said. "You know what that's going to do to your downswing? You'll have no fuckin' follow-through for a fuckin' month, and then the season'll almost be over."

Barns screamed, "Where's the ambulance?"

Virgil got on the phone to the sheriff's office, in eight crisp sentences told the duty officer what had happened, told him to get some deputies to the cabin. When he was sure the duty officer understood, Virgil rang off and asked Jenkins, "You got a problem with shock?"

"No, I'm fine, although my leg's beginning to annoy me."

"Could you stay with what's-her-name? And talk to the deputies?"

"Sure. You going after Laughton?"

"Yeah—he's running downriver, but he's got no place to go. Half-mile from here, he'll be hitting the town lights. It's just a matter of flushing him out."

"Take off. I've got it here," Jenkins said.

Barns screamed, "I'm dying, I'm dying, where's the goddamned ambulance?"

She sounded like a blackboard being run through a table saw.

VIRGIL RAN INSIDE for ten seconds, got his jacklight, and then he and Shrake started downriver in a measured jog, shotguns at port arms, Johnson following behind. Virgil called, "Go away, Johnson, we don't want you."

"Fuck you, you shot my boat. I'm coming."

"Go away!"

"Fuck you!"

SO THEY WENT DOWN the track, slowly, until they came to an artificial harbor with a half-dozen barges inside, small lights at the corner of each barge, and three brighter pole lights scattered down the waterfront. The levee was coming in from their right, pinching them against the river, and Johnson climbed up the side of it and walked along the top as they got closer to town, and then Johnson shouted down, "There he is, the fuckin' rat. He's going for the marina."

Virgil searched the waterline up ahead, and though there was some light, and the lights were getting brighter, he didn't see Laughton until the fugitive made a sudden jog down a catwalk that led behind a row of boats, probably five hundred yards ahead.

Virgil, Shrake, and Johnson broke into a trot, and Virgil shouted, "Don't forget, he's got that shotgun." He was almost instantly proven correct when they saw a flash and heard a BOOM from the marina, and Johnson shouted, "He shot someone."

They were running hard now, and thirty seconds or so later they heard a buzzing noise, and Johnson shouted, "He's got a boat. He's running in a boat."

Another half-minute and they were at the marina, which was basically an indentation in the shoreline with a rambling dock that ran alongside it, with a few finger docks attached. They found no bodies, but did find the remnant of a boat's bowline that appeared to have been shot in half.

They could still hear the buzzing from the fleeing boat, and Johnson yelled, "This one, get this one, get the rope, get the line . . ."

He'd jumped into a jon boat with a small engine on the back.

"We need a faster boat," Virgil shouted.

"Can't. They all need keys," Johnson shouted back. "This one's just a rope pull." To prove the point, he yanked on the starter rope and nothing happened. Johnson said something that would have embarrassed the entire state of Minnesota, had the entire state overheard it. He whacked the motor a few times, pulled again, and the outboard sputtered to life. "We're good: get in."

Shrake and Virgil jumped in the boat, and Virgil unwrapped the dock line, and Johnson backed the boat away from the pier and they took off, more or less.

"This is really fuckin' slow," Shrake said. "Can't we get more speed?"

"You could jump overboard," Johnson suggested. "That'd lighten the load." And to Virgil: "Hey, Virgie, put your jacklight on that sucker."

They couldn't see Laughton's boat, and they couldn't hear it any-more, over the buzz of their own small engine, but had an idea of where he was. Virgil turned on the jacklight. Laughton was already a long way out, but the light pinned him, three or four hundred yards ahead, pointed out into the river. He was also in a jon boat, and also had a small engine on the back.

"All right," Johnson shouted. "The chase is on."

Virgil and Shrake were looking at Laughton's back, trying to keep it in sight. Johnson, who was standing in the stern, pulled his Para-Ordnance .45 out of his beltline and fired two shots so quickly they almost blended into one, and almost inspired both Virgil and Shrake to jump over the side.

Virgil screamed, "Johnson, what the fuck are you doing?"

"Chasing him," Johnson shouted back. "Is this a great country, or what?"

26

NOTHING LIKE a slow-speed chase on a pleasant summer night on the Mississippi. They could see a towboat, but it was far upriver, and no immediate danger; far downstream they could see a hint of the lights on the lock and dam, and across the river, on the far bluffs, radio towers sending flashing red light out into the ether. Halfway across, Laughton fired a shot at them, but he was far enough away that they didn't even see the shot hit the water.

"Wonder what the maximum range for shot is?" Virgil asked.

Shrake said, "There's a range I shoot at in Wisconsin, they say four hundred yards to be safe. But everybody says not even buckshot carries much further than three hundred."

Johnson said, "My .45'll carry a lot further than that."

Virgil: "Johnson, I swear to God, if you take that gun out again, I'll throw both of you in the fuckin' river."

———

SHRAKE: "I WONDER if he thinks if he makes it to Wisconsin, we won't be able to follow because we're Minnesota cops?"

"Only if he's got his head up his ass," Virgil said. "Though we probably ought to call the Wisconsin sheriff's office, whichever one it is, and tell them we're coming. Maybe we could get a little help."

Virgil got on the line to Purdy's office, and when the duty officer answered, gave him a quick explanation, and he said he'd call the sheriff across the river: "But don't expect them too quick, this time of night, they'll be coming all the way from Viroqua."

"Call them, and have them call me, and I'll tell them about it," Virgil said. "They're gonna have to take custody, anyway, I can't just haul him back across the river."

Virgil hung up, and Johnson, who was still standing up in the back of the boat and steering with occasional foot nudges on the tiller, said, "You see that tiny gold speck of light straight ahead?"

"Yeah?"

"That's the Schlitz beer sign hanging outside of the Rattlesnake Golf and Country Club. They'd be closed by now, but there might still be somebody around. He could hijack a truck, maybe."

Virgil went back to the phone, and after some fooling around, found a phone number for the club, but nobody answered: it clicked over to the pro shop's answering machine. "No answer."

"How much longer?" Shrake asked.

"At this speed . . . four or five minutes."

"When we see him land, we can't go straight in after him, we've got to unload either downstream or upstream, or he'll take us all out with one shot," Virgil said.

Virgil took a call from the Vernon County sheriff, and explained quickly what was going on. "We're in hot pursuit," he said for the sheriff's recorder. "We've got him pinned in a spotlight. He's coming up to the Rattlesnake golf club. We'll keep you posted on what happens."

"We'll start a car that way, but we don't have a hell of a lot of resources available to come that way, at this very minute."

"You tell your people to be careful—he's armed, and he doesn't have anything to lose."

"I'll tell 'em."

THIRTY SECONDS LATER he took another call, this one from Davenport: "Yeah?"

"You busy?"

"Yeah, as a matter of fact, I've got a couple things going on right now," Virgil said.

"Is that an outboard I hear in the background?"

"As a matter of fact it is, Lucas. I'm chasing a guy with a shotgun across the Mississippi River, because he and a woman ambushed me and Shrake and Jenkins at Johnson Johnson's cabin, and Jenkins took a shotgun pellet in the leg, and the woman was shot in the butt, and they're waiting for an ambulance—that should be there by now—so I'm a little fuckin' busy and I gotta go. Talk to you later."

He clicked off, and Shrake asked, "Think he believed you?"

Virgil's phone chirped, and he pulled it out and looked at the screen. A message from Davenport that said: "OK. Call when you get a minute."

Virgil said, "Yeah, I guess he did."

JOHNSON: "Vike's right at the shoreline."

Virgil said, "You know the golf club, what do you think—upstream or downstream?"

"Down. It'll be faster, and there's a track that runs out to the river," Johnson said. "We can tie up there and we can follow the track right into the clubhouse, even without light."

Johnson started angling south, and a few seconds later Shrake said, "I think he just hit land." In the light shaft from Virgil's jacklight, they saw Laughton scramble up the riverbank.

As they got closer, they could see Laughton's empty boat turning in the river, just offshore. "That's Larry Gale's boat. He's gonna be pissed if it goes over the lock and dam. We oughta try to get it back," Johnson said.

"You get it back," Virgil said. "Shrake and I will go after Vike. I don't want you there with a gun if the Wisconsin cops show up. At this point, we can just tell them you were the boat driver."

Johnson grumbled a bit, but he was worried about the other boat. He put them ashore two hundred yards down from where Laughton had landed, and said, "Just angle in right toward the beer sign. The track is straight as an arrow. Don't get shot, it's a long ride back to the clinic."

SHRAKE AND VIRGIL climbed ten or twelve feet up the bank, found the end of the track. Virgil turned off the spotlight, which was way too bright, and they started following the track toward the clubhouse, staying ten or fifteen yards apart, moving slowly. They came to a circle of trees around a green, and Virgil said, "Find a place to take cover. I'm going to yell at him."

They squatted behind separate tree trunks, and Virgil shouted, "Vike! There's no point! The Wisconsin cops are on the way! There's no way out, we know all about the house in Tucson, you can't go there. Give it up before you get killed—"

Boom!

Laughton, who'd been waiting by the corner of the clubhouse, fired in their direction, and Virgil thought he might have heard buckshot tearing through the trees twenty or thirty yards to his left.

. He heard Shrake move, and move fast, jogging hard to come in at the clubhouse from the back. Virgil went left thirty yards, found another tree, and shouted again. No response this time.

He moved forward: there was an overhead pole light at the clubhouse, in addition to the beer sign, enough light to see by. He moved forward another thirty yards: at this range, if Laughton showed himself, Virgil could reach him with the shotgun. His phone dinged, and he slid down on his side and pulled it out of his pocket: a note from Shrake: "Now what?"

Virgil texted back: "Wait just a bit, and I'll start yelling again."

He never had the chance.

———

Ten seconds later, there was another Boom! but from some distance away. Virgil shouted, "Shrake, don't shoot me, I'm coming in."

He started running toward the clubhouse, and saw Shrake come in out of the dark and peek around the corner. Down toward what appeared to be the entrance road, under another pole light, they could see a yellow corrugated metal shed.

"Must be a maintenance—" Shrake began.

A moment later, Laughton rolled under the light, and then out the exit driveway, away from them, driving a golf cart.

"You gotta be shittin' me," Shrake said.

They both began running after the golf cart, which had two tiny taillights. They saw the lights make a turn to the left, apparently out at the road, and Virgil shouted, "You follow, I'm going to try to cut across and see if I can catch him that way."

Shrake grunted and Virgil broke away, running left as hard as he could, up a fairway distinguishable by starlight. The fairway was lined by trees and, Virgil suspected, a fence to separate it from the road. Before he got to the fence, he saw Laughton coming down the road—Virgil wasn't close enough to stop him, but he hit Laughton in the face with the jacklight and saw him swerve to the far side of the road, blinded, putting a hand up against the light. Laughton passed in front of him, and on down the road, and Virgil kept him pinned in the light, watching for Laughton's shotgun, and chased after him with no hope of catching up.

He went through the tree line, found the fence, clambered over, went down into a ditch and up the other side in time to see Shrake coming, in another golf cart.

Virgil shouted at him, and Shrake slowed just enough to get Virgil onboard, and Shrake said, "Get your gun out, we're faster than he is. We're catching him."

They were running alongside the golf course, which stretched between the river and the road. Virgil could see the taillights on Laughton's vehicle no more than a hundred and fifty yards ahead.

"Shoot one up beside him," Shrake suggested.

The golf cart had a Plexiglas windshield, but Shrake poked it a couple times with the heel of his hand and it folded down, and Virgil aimed unsteadily off to one side of the other golf cart and fired.

They saw the tiny taillights swerve, maybe off the road, because it bumped hard a couple times, and they gained another thirty yards, and Shrake said, "Try that again. See if you can bounce it off the road behind him."

Virgil fired again, and this time the other golf cart swerved hard left and went down into the ditch.

"Got him," Shrake said.

"He's got that shotgun," Virgil said, and they pulled off sideways and got out, and Virgil shouted, "Vike, give it up."

They heard him moving like a bear through the ditch. Virgil pinned him with the light again, as they ran forward, ready to shoot, but Laughton did a somersault over the fairway fence and they ran after him. Shrake said, "I think he lost the gun."

Then came a strangled shriek from the golf course, and silence.

THEY CROSSED the fence and spread apart, moving slowly now, up a mound . . .

The mound was the top of a sand trap. In the brilliant illumination of Virgil's jacklight, they found Laughton spread-eagled in the white sand below. He'd run right off the top of the sand trap, and had fallen in, maybe ten feet straight down, into fine white river sand.

Virgil ran around the trap, keeping the muzzle of the gun out in front of him, and asked, "You alive in there?"

"Heart attack. I'm having a heart attack," Laughton groaned.

"Really?" Virgil asked.

"Oh, God, don't let me suffer. Shoot me."

"Could happen," Virgil said. "You've got two shotguns pointed at your head." He moved quickly around to Shrake and whispered, "Cuff his hands in front of him. We're going to run him back to the boats, evacuate him to the clinic."

Shrake whispered, "Why not just call an ambulance? He's faking, anyway."

Virgil whispered, "Because then he'll be in Minnesota. And what if he's not faking?"

So they climbed down into the trap, and Virgil said, "Think about the shotguns," and he put his aside and helped Laughton roll over. Shrake stepped in with the cuffs, and Laughton groaned again, "It hurts so bad. This is the end."

Shrake ran the cuffs under Laughton's belt, and Virgil got out of the trap and waved the light in a circle. "Johnson! Johnson! Over here!"

Johnson shouted back, and, following the light, arrived a minute later, breathing hard, and asked, "What?"

"We have to evacuate Vike to the clinic. He's having a heart attack. You guys get his body, I'll get his legs."

"Call an ambulance," Laughton said.

"Not enough time. Time is critical," Virgil said.

They picked Laughton up, and Johnson said, "Jesus, wide load, huh?" and they carried him three hundred yards, across two fairways and down the embankment where Johnson had tied up the boats. Laughton bitched every inch of the way: "It's killing me. You're killing me. Oh, God, I'm hurt . . ."

Virgil was almost, but not quite, convinced when they lowered him into the boat. Johnson and Shrake got in the boat with him, and Virgil followed in the second boat, and Virgil called the sheriff's department and asked that an ambulance meet them at the marina.

Again, Virgil thought what a nice night it was, out on the river. The towboat passed in front of them, throwing out a healthy wake, which they rode up and over, and then they rolled on into the marina, where two paramedics were waiting. Shrake rode in the ambulance with them, so he could manage the handcuffs, and also shake Laughton down to make sure he had no more weapons.

Virgil and Johnson tied off the two boats, and Johnson said he'd call their owners with an explanation. "What I want to know is, who's going to pay for my boat?"

"Your boat was a piece of shit," Virgil said. "I do mean was. Right now it wouldn't even make a good petunia planter. Had more holes in it than a fuckin' colander. Looked like some kinda industrial sprinkler head. Looked—"

"Okay, okay," Johnson said. "But somebody's gonna pay."

They walked back down the dark lane to the cabin, and Virgil went inside and washed his face and hands, while Johnson counted holes in his boat. "They picked it up and dragged it over here and used it as a fuckin' armored duck blind," Johnson said. "You were the duck."

AT THE CLINIC, they found that both Jenkins and Jennifer 1 were on their way to Rochester, the nearest surgical hospital. The doc at the clinic told them that Jenkins had a buckshot lodged in his calf, and it might take a little surgery to remove it. Jennifer Barns needed to be cleaned up and repaired, and it would be some time before she'd be sitting up again.

Laughton had probably faked the heart attack, although the doc said, "Sometimes stress can give you chest pains that aren't related directly to the heart. I understand he was under quite a bit of stress lately."

Shrake said, "Not as much as he's gonna be."

Johnson: "Not much of a Viking, was he? More like a, more like a, more like . . ."

"A sissy," Shrake offered.

"Yes," Johnson said. "Like that."

27

VIRGIL CALLED DAVENPORT from the hospital: "We're all back in Minnesota. We might have a little legal whoop-de-do, because we had the guy, and we were gonna hold him for the Wisconsin authorities, but he claimed he was having a heart attack, so we evacuated him to the nearest clinic . . . which was back across the river, here in Minnesota."

"Did he have a heart attack?" Davenport asked.

"They're not sure, but they think not," Virgil said. "At the end of the chase, he fell in a golf course sand trap. I think he was mostly embarrassed." Virgil gave him a succinct summation of the shootout and chase.

"Let the legal guys sort it out. Maybe we'll have to drive him back over, then extradite him. Who cares? I talked to Jenkins, on the way up to the Mayo. He's pissed."

"I hope his leg's not bad."

"It's not. He'll be off his feet for a day or two. Weather says any-time you've got a bullet-like object penetrating into a muscle, it's not something you want to take lightly."

"Especially if it's your heart muscle," Virgil said. "I'll stop and see him on the way home. We got a mountain of paperwork to do, and he can do that sitting down. Right now, I've got to look at a movie."

"You found the chip?"

"Yup. Will Bacon left it where I could find it. Couldn't believe it," Virgil said. "He must've been up on that ladder when Kerns walked in—he knew what was going to happen, and instead of freezing up, he kept thinking."

"Good for him. Goddamnit, makes you proud."

"Yes, it does."

PURDY SHOWED UP at the clinic, and Virgil outlined what had hap-pened, and said he'd be down to the sheriff's office in the morning to make a full statement. Purdy said they'd chain Laughton to his bed: "That boy ain't goin' nowhere. We'll truss him up like an Eas-ter ham."

Virgil, Johnson, and Shrake stopped at Tony's for a six-pack of Leinenkugel's and an everything pizza, then drove back to Johnson's cabin, where Johnson bitched and moaned about the boat until he had a mouthful of pizza, and Virgil fired up his laptop and plugged in the memory card.

The sound was tinny—it'd get better with decent speakers—but the picture was very clear, and about the time Jennifer Barns, she of the butt wound, said, "I think we're in the clear—I talked to the fire chief, and he said there'd be no way to recover the records. I made out like it was a disaster, but told him we'd figure out a way to live through it," they had them.

"As long as that fuckin' Flowers moves along," Kerns said, as they watched.

"Flowers can think anything he wants, but if he doesn't have the records to prove it, we should be fine," Barns said. "Just keep our heads down and our mouths shut."

"Unless they catch Buster," said Jennifer Gedney. "He knew where the money was coming from. I mean, I didn't tell him, but he knew."

Kerns said, "If we have to, we handle Buster the same way we handled Conley. The same way we handle anyone who talks."

"I think we've done enough killing," said Henry Hetfield. "More killing will just get more attention."

"When was the last time you saw something like that?" Shrake asked. "I mean, like, never?"

The camera had been movement- and voice-activated, and at the end of the recording, the camera shook and then a man's voice said, "Bacon. Get down out of there!"

Bacon: "Randy. What's up?"

Kerns: "That's a camera, right? Get down out of there, you asshole. Bring the camera."

Bacon: "I . . . I . . . sure . . . Just a minute, I have to unwrap the tape. The camera belongs to Virgil Flowers, Randy. He's on his way here, he'll be here in the next minute or so. He's gonna be really pissed—"

Kerns: "Get down that fuckin' ladder and bring that fuckin' camera, or I swear to God I'll blow your legs off."

Bacon muttered, almost under his breath, but loud enough to be heard by the recorder: "Hurry, Virgil. Hurry."

What may have been a hand crossed close in front of the lens, and then there was a flash of electronic noise—the card being unplugged—and the video ended.

"Oh, Jesus," Shrake said.

Virgil sat frozen. "I killed that guy."

Johnson said, "No, you didn't. Randy Kerns did. Don't go taking on any extra blame, if you don't have to. You can go crazy doing that."

Virgil said, "I hurried, but I was just too far away. I should have told him to wait for me."

"When you got out of the truck, to go in the school, did you have your gun with you? I mean, before you had to break that window out?" Shrake asked.

"No, I had to go back for the gun."

"Which means that if Bacon had waited for you, and you'd gone right in . . . Kerns would have killed both of you, instead of just killing Bacon. You didn't fuck up, Virgil: you just got crazy unlucky with the timing."

THEY WERE STILL talking it over when headlights flashed in the side yard. Shrake and Virgil got their shotguns, and Johnson unlocked and raised a side window and shouted through the screen, "Who's there?"

A man called back, "Henry Hetfield and Del Cray. We're looking for Agent Flowers."

"What do you want?"

"We have some information we think he needs. About the school board," Hetfield shouted back.

Johnson looked at Virgil, who shrugged. Johnson shouted back, "Too late, dickhead."

"Wait, this is important. We gotta talk."

Virgil shouted back, "Oh, all right. Come on in. But we've got two shotguns and a .45, and at this short distance, they'd take off your heads. You understand that?"

"Please don't shoot us. . . ."

THE NEXT MORNING, Virgil met Dave the lawyer at Ma and Pa's Kettle, gave him some headphones and plugged him into the video of the school board meeting. Dave ate bacon and French toast, and drank Bloody Marys, and watched, fascinated, as it all came out.

"Not gonna wait," he said, when the video ended and he'd pulled off the earphones. "We're gonna bust them all. Now, today."

"We've also got a couple of direct witnesses for you," Virgil said, and he told him about Henry Hetfield and Del Cray from the night before.

"What'd you promise them?"

"Not a goddamn thing," Virgil said. "I've got it on a voice recorder, me not promising them anything. I told them that I'd mention it to the judge, that they'd made a voluntary statement to me. That's all on a flash drive," Virgil said. He slid the flash drive across the table.

"This almost takes the fun out of it," Dave grumbled. "We don't have to negotiate, we don't have to argue with anyone, we don't have to do any real serious lawyer shit. A law student could convict them."

Virgil told him about their hasty export of Vike Laughton from Wisconsin to Minnesota. "Well, that's something," Dave said, brightening a bit. "Those Cheeseheads can get a little testy about such things. Gonna have to look up the precise Latin phrase that means 'Fuck off.'"

THE ROUNDUP STARTED at one o'clock. Dave had spent some time talking to the attorney general, who'd sent down a stack of warrants specifying a list of crimes that included murder, conspiracy to murder, attempted murder (the ambush at the cabin), a variety of charges involving assault on police officers and conspiracy to do the same, embezzlement, and a bunch of other stuff, including, as a garnish, charges of misprision of a felony against everybody. "That'll get them an extra two weeks on top of the thirty years," Dave said with satisfaction. "We'll go for consecutive sentences."

Jennifer Gedney wept. "I don't have any money, I don't have any money. How can you say I took money, when I don't have any money. . . . Is that a TV camera?"

Bob Owens also wept, and kept saying, "Everything I worked for. Everything I worked for. Who'll take care of the kids?"

"You were stealing from the kids, you miserable ratfucker," said Shrake, who was putting on the cuffs. "Excuse me—I mean, you miserable ratfucker, sir."

Larry Parsons shouted at them, ran back through his house, and tried to squeeze out the bedroom window, but a couple of deputies got him by the feet and pulled him back in, so Virgil could arrest him. Shrake had gone with a couple more deputies to serve the arrest warrants on Jennifer Barns, at the hospital in Rochester, who screamed, "You can't do this, I'm wounded. I'll sue everybody. Those criminals shot me last night. I'll sue!"

Vike Laughton hadn't said anything. He'd just waved his free hand at them, from his hospital bed, and turned his face away, the cuff on his other hand rattling against the bedframe. He had a bad case of sand-burn on his face, and especially his nose.

Henry Hetfield and Del Cray were calm enough: they'd known since the night before what was coming, and since Virgil had arrested them and stuck them in the Buchanan County jail, they'd had time to think about it. Both of their houses were raided for evidence. Cray's wife and two children were gone, and so were quite a few things in the house, including the memory foam cover on the king-sized bed. A neighbor said they'd rolled out of their driveway the evening before, towing a large U-Haul trailer behind the newer of the Crays' two trucks.

With a little speed to keep her going, she could be in Canada or Alabama or Montana or Pennsylvania. Dave said they'd look for her.

Jennifer Houser was simply gone.

DAVENPORT CALLED and said, "You still on vacation? Or are you ready to go back to work?"

"I will be on Monday," Virgil said. "I got one more thing to do on Saturday." And, "How's Del?"

"Messed up. He might need another op, there were some bone splinters from his pelvic bone that bounced all over the place."

"Maybe he'll retire."

"His wife wants him to," Davenport said. "We'll see. I can't believe he could get through life without hanging out on the street, talking to assholes."

"It's like a curse," Virgil said.

"Listen, do what you're gonna do on Saturday, but don't get hurt, and don't get anybody else hurt. Then on Monday, a kind of peculiar thing has come up out in Windom. . . . "

28

SATURDAY MORNING DAWNED bright but humid; there'd been just enough rain overnight to create a few muddy spots outside the cabin door. The river was looking as dark as it usually did, snaking along toward New Orleans, but the sun was coming up orange over the rain clouds, which were drifting across to Wisconsin.

Virgil was up at seven, and at seven-thirty, met Johnson Johnson at Shanker's for breakfast, which they shared with four couples and a bald old man who'd be following them over to Dillard's farm. The farm was twenty-odd miles directly west, as the crow flies. If the crow was driving a 4Runner, the distance was around thirty-six miles, right on the border of Buchanan and Fillmore counties.

Noting that as they worked out a route on a paper map, Johnson said, "Two of the worst presidents in the history of the United States, Buchanan and Fillmore."

Virgil said, "I didn't know you read history, Johnson."

Johnson said, "Well, that was in the 'local information' in the old Buchanan County Yellow Pages. But, you know, I'm not a complete ignoramus."

"I told somebody that, recently, but she disagreed, and eventually talked me around."

"Thanks, old buddy," Johnson said. He yawned, stretched, and said, "I probably lost five pounds this past couple of weeks, running around with you. Maybe I ought to write a diet book: *The Virgil Flowers Weight-Loss Plan.* Start by leaving your gun in the truck. . . ."

Virgil leaned across the table and asked, in a near-whisper, "When you said a posse was coming with us, you meant four couples in four trucks, and one old guy with a missing tooth?"

"Maybe somebody else will show up," Johnson said. His eyes slid sideways, and Virgil detected a likely prevarication.

"You lying motherfucker, Johnson, what have you done?"

"Not a fuckin' thing," he said. "I'm completely innocent."

"Your mom told me that you were a difficult baby," Virgil said. "You haven't been innocent since you were a half hour old."

"Fuck you. And Mom," Johnson said. "She always liked Mercury better."

THE WORD WAS that the dog roundup was scheduled to start at eight o'clock, when bunchers from Iowa, Wisconsin, and Minnesota would open for business at Dillard's farm, which also held occasional farm equipment auctions. Johnson had learned that to prevent disputes, no dogs would be sold even a minute before nine o'clock, although the dogs would be available for survey before then. Dillard was expecting upwards of three hundred dogs. A few would be sold as hunting dogs, most as lab dogs, and "trash" would be handled by Dillard.

"That's what he called them," Johnson Johnson said. "Trash. Is that anything to call a dog? They're man's best friend. And when he said 'handling them,' you know what he's gonna do? He's gonna shoot them, is what I think."

A little after eight, they were in their trucks. Virgil was alone in his, because Johnson wanted to take his own truck in case he had to haul some dogs back, and Virgil, with any luck, would have D. Wayne Sharf handcuffed to the steel ring in the backseat of the 4Runner. The little caravan stretched out over a half-mile, with Virgil in the lead.

The drive was pleasant enough, rolling along the back highways, none of them straight, listening to country music on satellite radio. They were still in the Driftless Area, with heavily wooded hills overhanging small farms and narrow farm fields that twisted up the hillsides, the small farmhouses neat and usually white, with gardens and fruit trees and older cars parked in side yards.

They arrived at Dillard's farm at eight forty-five. There were three larger trucks and a dozen pickups, some with trailers, already parked in a field that stretched along the gravel road, between the road and a dry creek a hundred yards downslope. Except for the barking of several hundred dogs, it might have been the beginning of some low-rent hippie music festival.

A few pickups and SUVs were parked on the shoulder of the road. Virgil pulled off behind them, and his caravan pulled off with him. He'd already asked them not to get out of their trucks until he'd spotted D. Wayne Sharf, just in case Sharf should recognize any of them. They'd all agreed, with a little bitching from the Bald Old Man with One Tooth, who, Virgil had been told, was looking for a stolen dachshund named Dixie.

Virgil had asked Johnson, "Is he sure it was stolen? Maybe it was eaten by coyotes."

"Coyotes don't eat dachshunds," Johnson said. "Dachshunds were bred to go down badger tunnels and drag the badgers out by their ass. A good-sized dachshund could weigh thirty pounds and has jaws like a crocodile. Old Dixie would straight-out fuck up a coyote."

"Didn't know that," Virgil said.

WHEN VIRGIL HAD PARKED, he looked over the trucks parked in the field. D. Wayne Sharf's wasn't there, unless Sharf had changed vehicles, which was possible. Virgil knew what he looked like, and so climbed out of his 4Runner, wandered over to the driveway and down to the sales field. Fifteen or twenty guys were standing beside their vehicles, drinking from Big Gulp cups or steel coffee cups, and talking with each other, country-looking guys in jeans and boots and long-sleeved shirts.

Most of the trucks and trailers were small, but three larger trucks, pulling larger trailers, showed stacks of empty cages with hard floors and wire sides: they were the bunchers, Virgil guessed. A red-faced older man in jeans, a rodeo belt, and cowboy boots and hat was talking to the men by the bunchers' trucks. He had a sheaf of papers in his hands, and Virgil thought he was probably Dillard, the farm owner.

Virgil wandered down the line of trucks, looking at the men and peering through windows. He didn't find Sharf, but he got a bad impression about the handling of the dogs: a lot of the pens had three or four animals stuffed inside, so they could hardly move. He saw one dog he thought was either sick or dead.

He'd just finished his initial survey when a couple more trucks arrived, both pulling trailers. One trailer was covered, but the other was open, stacked with wooden and fiberglass pens full of dogs, like chickens being hauled away for slaughter. The truck with the open trailer, an aging red GMC, rolled down the line of early arrivals and wedged itself into an opening in the line. It was not D. Wayne Sharf's truck, but it was D. Wayne Sharf who got out of the passenger side.

The driver was a young, thin man, who might've been Roy Zorn's younger brother: same red hair and freckles, a nose that somebody had pushed out of line, aviator sunglasses. Sharf was dressed like everybody else, with cowboy boots, got out and yawned and walked down the side of the trailer, looking up at the dogs. The freckled guy joined him, and pointed at something at the top of the pile of cages: they were talking about unloading.

Virgil ambled toward them; he didn't want to startle Sharf. He'd closed the gap to twenty yards when he noticed that his caravan was rolling down the driveway into the parking area. Actually, he thought, they were blocking the driveway. Johnson got out of the lead truck, and Virgil saw that he was talking on a cell phone—but he wasn't talking to Virgil.

Whatever . . .

Virgil started walking toward Sharf again, when somebody asked, "What the heck is this?"

Virgil looked where he was looking—and saw another caravan of cars, probably thirty or forty of them, rolling over the hill. He looked toward Johnson, and Johnson was looking at them, too, and still talking on the cell phone.

Now everybody was looking, and the caravan pulled to the side of the road, further blocking exit from the farm field.

Somebody nearby said, "They aren't here to sell dogs."

"Hey, those are TV trucks."

Two white trucks with television call signs swerved off the road, and cameramen got out, already hoisting cameras to their shoulders.

Somebody else started shouting, "Hey, Arnie? Arnie Dillard? You better come look at this."

Virgil knew that Dillard's first name was Arnie, but he wasn't sure that Arnie could fix whatever was about to happen. People, lots of them, probably eighty or ninety, were climbing out of the cars and trucks. Most of them were empty-handed, but right in the middle of the caravan, twelve or fifteen women got out of five or six SUVs. They were dressed identically, in black jeans, black shirts, and black bicycle or motorcycle helmets, some with face plates. Some wore knee pads or football shoulder pads. Most of them carried aluminum baseball bats; two or three carried iron bars that looked like spears.

Another voice, close by: "Oh, shit."

Virgil turned and asked, "What?"

"It's the Auntie Vivians."

"Who's that?"

"The Minnesota Women's Anti-Vivisection League. I'm gettin' the fuck outa here." And the guy started running. He turned back just long enough to blurt, "Save yourself."

VIRGIL WASN'T SURE what movie it was, but he remembered a scene in which a medieval Scottish army attacked an English army, the Scots sweeping down a long grassy hillside with swords, axes, hammers, spears, and apparently whatever else they had in their barns. This was sort of like that. The people got out of the trucks and looked back and forth, calling to each other, spreading out, and some of them were shouting down the hill to where Virgil and the dog sellers were. The women in the helmets moved to the front of the long line, a wedge of them, and then one of them screamed, and then all of them screamed, and suddenly the line broke and the whole crowd charged down the hill, led by the women with aluminum baseball bats.

Virgil thought of running out in front of the wedge with his arms raised, and his ID in his hand, but only for a split second: somebody would hit him with a baseball bat, and that would be that. He also thought about pulling his pistol and firing a shot in the air, but his pistol, as usual, was locked in the truck's gun safe.

In the end, he ran around behind the truck he was standing next to, then down the line of trucks to where he'd seen D. Wayne Sharf a few seconds before the charge. Truck engines were coming alive when he ran around the nose of a Ford Super Duty pulling a twenty-foot trailer stacked with animal crates, just in time to see D. Wayne jump in the passenger seat of the truck he'd come in.

Virgil ran up and yanked open the door and said, "D. Wayne, you're under arrest—"

That was as far as he got before D. Wayne hit him on the forehead with a half-empty two-liter plastic bottle of Dr. Pepper. Virgil went down, and D. Wayne slammed the door and Virgil rolled away, staggered to his feet, and jumped on the fender over the trailer's double wheels, and held on to two of the stacked crates. Inside one of the crates, a half-dozen small dogs were rolling around on the hard plastic crate floor as the truck driver wheeled around the end of the line of trucks; in the other crate, a big yellow dog with floppy ears looked out at him with interest.

About then, the driver found out that there was no place to go. He went anyway, bouncing over what had been a fairly decent alfalfa field, trying to stay away from the crowd that was spreading out over the pasture.

The dog sellers looked like a tough bunch, and there were certainly a few guns in the various vehicles, but they were outnumbered four or five to one, and as Virgil clung to the dog crate, he saw a woman run alongside a fleeing truck and spear the back tire with one of the long iron rods.

The tire blew, and the back of the truck sagged; farther down the field, the driver of one of the trucks had been pulled out into the alfalfa, and part of the crowd swarmed over his trailer, unloading the dog crates onto the ground, opening the doors and freeing the dogs, which ran in excited circles, howling and barking.

One truck driver tried to break through the fence, but the fence hadn't been made in Hollywood. He dragged a few fence posts loose, but the fence didn't break and the truck wound up nose-down in the border ditch, where it was swarmed by attackers.

Virgil thought about jumping off the trailer, fearing that it would roll on him, but the driver made a turn and then a woman in a motorcycle helmet was running alongside, and she speared one of the front truck wheels, and Virgil heard it go out with a POOF-WOP-WOP, and then she got the back one POOF-WOP-WOP-WOP, and the truck began to stall out and parts of the crowd began running toward it.

Virgil jumped off the fender and ran to the passenger-side door, but got there a few seconds late: a woman with an aluminum baseball bat knocked out the window, then took a swing at Virgil, who shouted, "I'm a cop, I'm a cop," and she hesitated and asked, "Virgil?" and he shouted, "Yes," and she ran away.

Behind the broken glass, D. Wayne Sharf was peering out at them, and Virgil shouted, "You're under arrest. Open the fuckin' door."

"Fuck you," Sharf shouted back. He turned toward the driver and looked like he might try to crawl over him, but Virgil reached through the shattered window and got him by the shirt collar and dragged him all the way back to the window and shouted, "Open the fuckin' door or I'll drag you right through the broken glass."

Sharf twisted and turned and couldn't get free, then cut himself on the window, and on the next pass, got blood on his hand and finally screamed, "Okay. Okay."

Virgil heard a woman shouting, "That's Virgil, that's Virgil," and the truck was rocking as the attackers crawled over it, breaking every piece of glass they could find, breaking out headlights and taillights and knocking off mirrors, while others began unloading the dog crates and freeing the dogs.

There were a half-dozen dog brawls going on around the pasture, the dogs howling and barking with excitement, gathering in crowds to prance across the alfalfa, and stopping to mark various lumps and humps and truck tires.

Then D. Wayne popped the door locks and Virgil had him out of the truck and on the ground, and he rolled the other man on his back, dragged him fifteen or twenty feet to a perimeter fence post, and cuffed him and said, "You're in a whole lot of trouble. Don't make it worse by breaking out of these cuffs and trying to run."

"I didn't do anything," D. Wayne whined. The woman with the aluminum bat ran up and asked, "You got him?"

"Yeah, this is the guy who stole all the dogs in Trippton. He's going to try to get out of these cuffs. I've got to try to stop this mess." Virgil waved at the field, where two pickups now lay on their sides, and a bunch of large men were standing in a circle, facing a crowd of attackers, and one of the men appeared to be holding a shotgun. Virgil said to the woman, "So if he tries to escape, use the bat and break his legs. Not his head, just his legs. Okay?"

"I can do that," she said. She waved the bat at D. Wayne, who shrank back into the fence.

Virgil started running down toward the man with the gun, just about the time the man pointed the shotgun up in the air and fired a shot. BOOM! Twelve-gauge.

In the sudden silence after the gunshot, Virgil was shouting, "Stop! Stop! Everybody stop!"

One of the women in the crowd shouted, "That's one! Two more shots and we put ropes around your necks. Somebody get the ropes."

One of the men in the circle broke out, running across the pasture, and nobody chased him, but the crowd pressed the circle tighter, and the two TV cameramen, who turned out to be camerawomen, were riding on the shoulders of two men, getting the cameras up in the air, and then Virgil got there, shouting, "State police. State police. Put the gun down, put the gun down."

The man with the gun, who had the muzzle still pointing in the air, shouted back, "They're gonna lynch us—"

Virgil shouted, "No, no, no . . . Move that way." He pointed toward the far end of the field, and then, "Everybody else, everybody else, go that way." He pointed the other way. "Take care of the dogs, take care of the dogs, the dogs are freaking out."

Most of the dogs seemed pretty happy: there were now dozens of them, even hundreds, of every color and size, racing around the field, in celebration.

That got the dog rescuers looking away from the circle, and the two groups pulled apart, and when the circle of men, including the guy with the shotgun, were moving down the field, Virgil shouted to them, "Listen! Listen! We don't want anybody to get killed. You've all got insurance on your trucks, you can get them fixed, these people . . . just let them go."

One of the men, white-faced, scared but angry, said, "If you're a cop, go arrest them."

Everybody stopped and looked at him, and Virgil looked back down the field, where dozens of people were either freeing dogs or beating the hell out of the trucks. One of the big trucks, the buncher truck, went over on its side, and the other was rocking.

He turned back to the group and said, "Tell me what to do. Huh? What the hell am I supposed to do? You guys stay here. Sooner or later, you'll get back to your trucks. Some of those people, you saw it yourself, weren't afraid of your gun. They're willing to be martyrs, if you're willing to go to prison for murder. And, tell the truth, I'd hate to think of what they'd do to you guys if you shot one of them. So calm down and stay here, and I'll try to get everybody I can out of here alive."

VIRGIL JOGGED AWAY from them. People were still beating up the trucks, but four of them had brought down a roll of fencing and a dozen tall stakes, and were setting up an impromptu pen in the center of the field. Virgil had to walk close to them, so he swerved over and asked, "Who are you guys?"

"Buchanan County Humane Society. We're all legal here, we're just seizing distressed and stolen dogs, the ones we can get inside the fence."

"God bless you," Virgil said.

VIRGIL CONTINUED WALKING toward the last of the trucks that were still being unloaded. As the attackers finished the unloading process, they'd unhitch the trailers and turn both the trucks and trailers over on their sides. Virtually everybody was now wearing bandannas over their faces, and the TV camerawomen and a couple of Big Hairs were interviewing the raiders.

Johnson Johnson, who would have been unmistakable for his tattooed arms even if he hadn't been wearing a black bandanna, came jogging up and said, "I hope you're not pissed."

"Get away from me, fuckhead."

Johnson veered away.

The yellow dog, the same one that Virgil had seen in the crate, came loping up and sniffed his knee, and then fell in beside him. Virgil said, "Go away. Shoo."

The dog looked up at him and stuck its tongue out, and hung next to his knee as Virgil got into the heart of the crowd and shouted, "Hey! Everybody! You've made the point. These dogs are gonna die out here if they run off and hide and we don't find them. So start herding them up to the Humane Society pen while we've still got them here."

That got the crowd interested in something besides wrecking the trucks, although one more truck went over onto its side, and then ten or twelve people cooperated in rolling it over onto its roof. The roof flattened a bit, and oil and other fluids began dripping out from under the upside-down hood.

"Did you just have to do that one more?" Virgil asked. "Did you just have to do that?"

"Yeah, we did," said a man behind a red cowboy mask.

Virgil asked, "Winky? Did you get your dogs back?"

Winky said, "Yup. I owe you big, Virgil. Carol wants to have you over for dinner."

A WOMAN'S SMALL HAND slipped into Virgil's back pocket, and Virgil turned and found Daisy Jones smiling up at him. "Virgil Flowers. My, my, my. Did you organize this shindig all by your little ol' self?"

"I would arrest everybody here, including you, if I could," Virgil said.

Virgil and Jones had known each other for years: she was a smart, good-looking if slightly tattered TV reporter from the Twin Cities. She gave the yellow dog a scratch on the forehead and, "Nice dog you got there."

"Not mine," Virgil said.

"Have you arrested anybody?" she asked.

"Yes, I have," Virgil said. "I've arrested D. Wayne Sharf, on a variety of state and federal charges. He is now handcuffed to that fence over there."

"Guarded by the lady with the baseball bat?"

"Yes. Somebody had to guard him, while I tried to stop the shooting," Virgil said.

"That was very brave of you, Virgil. It makes me feel all funny inside."

"Daisy, a machine screw makes you feel all funny inside."

"That's rude."

"Yes. It is. I apologize. Now. For your TV station, if you want it, you can say I arrested D. Wayne Sharf. You can say that many of the dogs here were stolen, and that the actions of the crowd were illegal, but sorting it out here, by myself, with no help, was simply impractical. I will be turning this investigation over to the Buchanan

County attorney's office for possible criminal prosecutions. That's all I got."

She leaned closer, so that he could smell the Chanel: "Could you tell me, is there any one person here who'd be best to interview?"

Virgil pointed out Johnson, who was still wearing the stupid mask: "That's the ringleader."

"Ooo. He has big muscles."

"He's a simple country boy, Daisy. Go easy on him."

A SHERIFF'S CAR rolled up on the road, and a single deputy got out. Virgil walked across the field toward him, the yellow dog right at his knee, and the deputy came to meet him and said, "Virgil. Uh, what's up?"

Virgil turned and looked at the field. The dognapper crowd and the bunchers were in a bunch at one end, and were a tough-looking, mmm . . . bunch. The raiders were at the other end, trying to herd loose dogs across the alfalfa. Scattered among them were a dozen overturned trucks and trailers, and a few more still on their wheels. Even those on their wheels had been pounded like brass ashtrays, and none of them showed glass or rearview mirrors.

"Well . . . what can I say?" Virgil waved a hand at the field.

"What are we going to do?"

"I've got a federal prisoner I've got to haul back to Trippton," Virgil said. "As for these people . . . I think, well, hell, go ahead and arrest them."

"What?"

"They busted up all these trucks." He pointed to the circle of men at the far end of the field. "Arrest them, too. A lot of the dogs are stolen."

The deputy looked up and down the field and then said, "I would estimate—don't hold me to this exactly—if I arrested these people, the sheriff would lose the next election by about ninety to ten."

"Do what you think is right," Virgil said. "I'm going back to town."

The deputy looked at the yellow dog and said, "That's a great dog. Wish I had one like that."

"Not mine," Virgil said. "You ought to see if you could herd him back to the pen. If nobody claims him, maybe you could adopt him."

The deputy stepped toward the dog, which shied away and moved closer to Virgil. "I'll let you handle it," the deputy said. "But I think he's your dog."

VIRGIL GOT D. Wayne Sharf in the backseat of the 4Runner, thanked the woman with the aluminum bat, who said, "Maybe I should break his legs anyway," and Virgil said, "No, that's okay," and cuffed Sharf to the ringbolt in the floor. Sharf said, "I'm gonna sue your ass for—"

"Shut up, or I'll turn you over to the Auntie Vivians," Virgil said.

The woman with the bat told Sharf, "You really wouldn't want that."

Virgil walked around to the driver's side, tagged by the yellow dog. Virgil looked at the dog, and the dog looked at Virgil. The dog had golden eyes, and it looked past Virgil into the empty passenger side of the truck.

Virgil said, "All right," and waved his hand, and the dog hopped up onto the driver's seat, then crossed to the passenger seat and sat down. Virgil said to the dog, "With my lifestyle, I can't have a dog."

The dog nodded, and looked out through the windshield, ready to roll.

D. Wayne said from the backseat, "When I get you—"

"Shut the fuck up." And to the dog, "Really. I can't. I'll give you a lift back to Trippton."

The dog nodded again and smiled a dog smile.

Virgil said, "Really."

29

JOHNSON JOHNSON did the entire TV interview wearing his mask, which didn't keep anyone in Buchanan County from knowing who he was. He got a death threat from one of the local dog-stealing morons, and being a moron, the moron hadn't thought that his cell phone number would pop up on Johnson's phone.

Johnson being Johnson, he traced the number, using an Internet service, recognized both the name and the attitude that went with it, jumped in his truck, drove to the guy's usual bar, and dragged him outside. After a humiliating confrontation in the parking lot, the other guy drove away in his truck, while the other bar patrons laughed at him and even threw a couple of rocks at his truck. Dog-nappers were not popular people in Trippton.

JOHNSON DID NOT FARE so well with Clarice, who thought that he'd been entirely too friendly with Daisy Jones. "And right on camera. You had your hand on her ass, Johnson, I could see where your arm was going, I saw the way her eyes got wide. You had to give her cheek a squeeze, didn't you? You think my girlfriends didn't see that? How can I hold up my head?"

Virgil said, "Give it to him, Clarice, he deserves every bit of it."

"Shut up, Mr. Big-Time Cop," Clarice said, poking Virgil in the chest with her index finger, hard enough that it hurt. "Who did he go out there with? Who told this Daisy person who to talk to?"

She wound down after a while, but Johnson was worried, and told Virgil, "I might have to propose again just to get right with her. Seems like a lot of trouble over a friendly gesture."

"By 'friendly gesture,' you mean squeezing Daisy's ass while you were on the air."

"That's an uninflected way of looking at it," Johnson said. "I assumed you were more sophisticated than that."

JOHNSON HAD a lot more to say about his shot-up jon boat. Virgil found an identical jon boat online for $565, and pointed out that Johnson had already gotten eighteen years' use out of the old one, but Johnson sensed a chance to step up. It took several dozen calls over the next month, but he eventually convinced a claims clerk with the state government that the only similar and available jon boat was a $1,149 model from Bass Pro Shops. By late autumn, he'd launched it on the Mississippi.

ON THE DAY of the dog raid, Virgil delivered D. Wayne Sharf to the Buchanan County jail, where he was held on a federal warrant. The feds left him there for two days, then a marshal showed up and hauled him away to Chicago. Nobody in Trippton ever saw him again, and Virgil heard later that he'd been convicted of something, but never heard what happened after that.

THE ATTORNEY GENERAL at first denied knowledge of the dog raid, but when it became apparent that the pro-dog people outnumbered the anti-dog people by about 99.5 percent to 0.5 percent, he quickly shouldered his way into a number of TV interviews in which he implied that the dog raid was part and parcel of his investigation into the Buchanan County school board murders and embezzlement.

That whole circus was good for several consecutive days of coverage. The governor's race was a long way off, however, so the AG slow-walked the prosecution, squeezing as much juice out of it as he could. Since the school board members were accused of multiple murder-ones, he could hold them in jail as long as he wished, without bail, as long as the defense attorneys didn't file for a speedy trial.

The defense attorneys weren't filing for speedy trials because they were all going to Mass on Sundays to pray for some kind of intervening information or event that would give their clients at least a chance for a reduced sentence. That didn't work out.

In the end, after six months of meticulous and media-saturated investigation, in which it was determined that the defendants had embezzled very close to eight million dollars from the Buchanan County schools, they were all convicted of murder and a variety of subsidiary crimes involving murder (conspiracy to murder, attempted murder, etc.) and embezzlement. They all received thirty-year terms, with no chance of parole.

Viking Laughton tried to argue that he was a humble newspaper reporter with no knowledge of the crimes, which made the rest of the defendants so angry that they ratted him out on the Kerns murder, and he went down on all counts.

Masilla, the auditor, ratted them all out, and since there was no evidence that he knew of the planned murders, and since his deal eliminated the possibility of charging him with felony murder (murders in the process of committing another felony, the embezzlement), he was convicted only of the various money crimes, and given ten years. Minnesota being a socialist state that allows prisoners to set up businesses inside the prison (they get to keep relatively little of what they earn, much of it going to the state or to a victims' fund), Masilla was able to create an accounting business for the many convicts who had money or dope hidden on the outside. His reputation for probity quickly spread, and within a year or so he had a clientele that stretched from the Attica Correctional Facility in New York to Folsom State Prison in California.

"You know what we didn't get?" the assistant attorney general, Dave, asked Virgil. "Those bonds for the new school stadium. I know of the dealers on those, and I suspect the board and the dealers would have split up a cool three mil on that deal alone. The way they worked it, they'd have front-ended the payout. . . ."

He went on for a while, but Virgil dozed off; bond amortization discussions did that to him.

BUSTER GEDNEY GOT as far as Biloxi, Mississippi, where he rented a mobile home and got a half-time job as a welder and machinist working for a farm implement dealer, under the name Jefferson Jones. He could hardly make it on that money, so he began manufacturing three-shot burst kits for .223s, and sound suppressors. His first really good customer was a meth cooker who brought a DEA undercover agent to Buster's first sales meeting.

Buster delivered the equipment, right on schedule, and was arrested right on schedule, along with the meth cooker, and when his fingerprints delivered an immediate hit, was extradited to Minnesota to stand trial on the murder and embezzlement charges. He was so pathetic, blubbering on the witness stand, that the jury acquitted him of the most serious charges, and he drew a five-year sentence for misprision of a felony.

JENNIFER HOUSER, of Puerto Vallarta, Mexico, bought a J/27 sailboat and hired a very attractive instructor to teach her how to sail. His instruction was comprehensive, and she's still sailing. "And now I know why they call it the cockpit," she told a similarly aged lady from New York. She also began taking piano lessons, and has that photo of her mother in a silver frame on top of the baby grand. Her Spanish, which had been quite good already, got even better, and she was often mistaken for a native. BCA follow-up investigators came to believe that she'd been murdered by Kerns and dropped in the river, though Virgil insisted that she was on the run.

AFTER DELIVERING D. Wayne Sharf to the county jail, Virgil took the yellow dog to the Buchanan County Humane Society. He had a little trouble getting the dog out of the truck, because the dog was large and didn't want to get out. Virgil thought that the dog might even recognize the look of the Humane Society building, even though it had never been there, according to the young lady behind the counter.

"I've been here for four years," she said, "and I would have remembered him. Nope, never been here."

Virgil gave her a little history on the dog, who kept crowding closer and closer to his knee, and looking up at him with stricken eyes, and then the girl said, "Look, you gotta do what you gotta do, but that dog is your soul mate. You can tell by the way he's already bonded to you. If you leave him with us, there's probably a thirty percent chance he'll eventually be put down."

"Aw, man, I thought you guys place them all—"

"Impossible. We've always got a lot more dogs than we have people to adopt them, and he's a big dog, and he's probably four or five years old," she said. "People usually want a younger dog."

Back outside, Virgil said to the dog, "Get in the fuckin' truck."

The dog jumped into the truck, settled into the passenger seat, and hung its tongue out.

"I'm calling you That Fuckin' Fido," Virgil said, as he got in the driver's seat.

The dog didn't say anything, but he might have nodded, figuring he could change his name later, when they'd gotten the hell away from the Humane Society.

VIRGIL WAS SCHEDULED to go home that night, but Johnson Johnson asked him to stop by Shanker's for a Diet Coke, and when Virgil walked in, he found a hundred dog lovers crowded into the place, and they all sang "For He's a Jolly Good Fellow," in his honor, backed by the band Dog Butt Plus Muddy, and Johnson hugged him three or four times, and Winky Butterfield gave him a gilded trophy with a dog on top of it and a blank plate under the dog.

"We didn't have time to get it engraved with your name, but Johnson's going to get it done, and he'll send it to you," Butterfield said. Virgil was intensely embarrassed, but agreed to have a beer or two, and eat some of the wedding-style cake, and a couple of attractive dog lovers asked him to dance, and he did, and then he danced some more, and when Johnson finally poured him into bed, back at the cabin, it was one o'clock in the morning.

"Don't worry about a thing. I told Frankie what happened, and I did NOT mention your groupies," Johnson said. "Lucky for you that you talked me out of being an alcoholic, or we'd both be drunk in a ditch somewhere."

———

Virgil left town the next morning with a yellow dog and a hang-over, and Virgil found that the dog was an attentive listener who panted in all the right spots. He stopped at a bookstore in Rochester and bought a book on how to care for dogs, and how much to feed them, and then stopped at a store and bought a dog food bowl, a sack of kibble, and two pounds of ground round, and fed the dog, and walked it around until it pooped, got back in the truck and said to the dog, "I really can't have a dog."

The dog just nodded and hung its tongue out.

At home in Mankato, Virgil unhooked the boat and did a bit of cleanup, then went inside and cleaned up himself. Frankie was at home: "We figured you'd call about now," she said. "The last of the hay just went in the barn."

"I was hoping you'd hold off until I got there," he lied. "Are you in any shape to receive visitors?"

"I suppose," she said. "I'm all hot and sweaty, and I was thinking of going out to the creek."

"I will be there in fifteen minutes," Virgil said.

When Virgil got to the farm, Frankie's youngest son, Sam, was working on the front porch with some two-by-two boards, a saw, and a hammer and nails. He was making stilts, Virgil realized, on his way to a Gold Arrow Point for his Cub Scouts Wolf Badge.

Virgil got out of the truck and Sam called, "You bring me any-thing?"

"Yeah, myself," Virgil said.

"Big deal," Sam said. Though he was only a second-grader, he said, "I can't get these fuckin' foot supports to hold. The nails keep pulling out, and when I use bigger nails, the wood splits."

"You need to drill holes, and use screws and Gorilla glue," Virgil said. "And don't say 'fuck' or I'll tell your mother, and she'll kick your young ass."

He walked around the truck and popped the passenger door, and the yellow dog jumped out and looked around. Sam, on the porch, stood up and gawked. "All right! We got us a dog?"

The dog loped up on the porch and gave Sam a sniff and a lick, and Sam shouted into the house: "Ma! Ma!"

"What!"

"We got us a dog!"

"What?"

"We got us a dog!"

He opened the door and ran into the house with the dog a step behind him, leaving Virgil in the driveway by himself.

From inside the house: "We got us a dog!"

"What?"

"We got us a dog," Virgil said.